The Asgardian Exchange

The Rise of The Jotuns

MARK E. BRYAN

This story is a work of fiction. Any resemblance in the names, places, or characters to reality is purely coincidental.

DEDICATION

For Shaun, whose love, strength, and encouragement helped me reach for the stars.

Mark E. Bryan

The Asgardian Exchange: The Rise of The Jotuns

Edited by Thomas Jacobs

CONTENTS

CHAPTER 1:
AN UNFORTUNATE DUMPING OF SNOW

The ravens arrived unnoticed with the third snowstorm right before Thanksgiving. The residents of Wreathen, Delaware were too preoccupied with making preparations to survive the storm to notice the gray specks that were swooping and winging about their town. They were more concerned with the flaky white snow that was piling up around them faster than the line at the coffee shop on a Monday morning. Living near the coast, the inhabitants knew how to bundle-up against the cold and frost, but the snowfall accumulation this year had been more than the past five years put together.

The school buses had been outfitted with wheel chains after the first storm but were rendered useless after the second wave of flurries made it impossible to tell a bank of bushes from a regular bank of snow. Poor Mrs. Schott nearly crashed into her own house, having mistaken it for her garage; although to be fair, she probably would have done the same even if there were no snow.

The residents of Wreathen were definitely divided between those who loved the snow, as it allowed for sledding and snowmen, and those who despised the wintery weather, as they wished for nothing more than to never have to pry open their ice-encrusted mailbox ever again. But after the second storm, even those who loved winter began to tire of its drudgery. And soon, most could agree that they were all looking forward to the red, circled date on their calendars that marked the first day of spring.

So it was no wonder than no one noticed as the ravens watched them scurry about. Alighting on the tinsel-covered lampposts, the two birds would cock their heads and observe each passersby. They would bob or shake their heads, as if inspecting each person they watched and passing judgement, before moving onto the next post. After several days of flying about Main Street, they began zipping their way through the rest of the small downtown. They crisscrossed around the elementary and middle school playgrounds, circled the big-box store U-Buy, and then flapped their way to the outlying farmhouses. Each day the ravens would find a new spot in town to sit and watch. There were several times they would caw or cackle as someone walked under their gaze, but that seemed more of a commentary than any real item of note.

By December 9th, the two birds had covered the entire town except for one final neighborhood. It was a tiny street, really, with a cul-de-sac at the end that held four homes. On this particular day, the ravens' squawking drew only the attention of howling dogs as they alighted on a snow-covered fencepost beside a small blue house with a red door and black shutters. The birds nodded to themselves as a petite girl with long blond hair and gangly legs shouldered her way through the red door.

"Ack!" Amanda West cried, skidding on an ice patch that had hardened over the old planks of their front porch, and flapping her arms while tumbling down the steps.

A chorus of cackling laughter rang through the morning air as Amanda caught herself on the railing, barely avoiding landing bottom first on the ice-cold pavement. Two ravens, their black and gray feathers tipped with white, sat watching as she pulled herself up. They looked like two elderly gentlemen rocking on the banister of the fencepost that divided the Wests' yard from their neighbor's.

"Nice swan dive, Amanda. I'd give it a 9.5 for form, but a deduction for the landing." Jack Isen was standing at the end of his driveway, trying to speak between large fits of laughter. Wearing his standard denim on denim, her friend stood like a blue jean post in the snow with a mane of curly dark hair.

Behind him was Jack's latest take on holiday decorations. Santa was riding a rocket ship that flashed and beeped the notes of a song popular on the radio. Every year Amanda's mother would shake her head as she watched her neighbors get more and more adventurous with their spin on holiday traditions. Amanda would never tell her, but she had secretly been helping the Isens plan their decorations each year since she was five.

"What do you know of good form? You were the one who skated into the side of the ice rink last week." Amanda tried to wave the birds away, but they blinked and ignored her. Amanda picked her way across the sidewalk toward Jack. Thanks to the snow, the sides of every driveway along the street were flanked by mounds that were taller than she was. Amanda thought it made the cul-de-sac look like a valley of white death.

"I blame that on the Zamboni."

Amanda paused as she heard some kind of lilting notes filter through her scarf that was wrapped around her head. She saw an old woman was making her way down the street, salting the sidewalk, and humming to herself. Amanda grimaced as a gust of snow caught her in the face. "How are you not freezing?"

Jack, who was only wearing a light denim jacket, spread his arms wide. "This doesn't bother me at all. I am immune to the cold!"

Amanda groaned. "Well, I'm always cold. I wish I could live in a place where I never saw ice or snow again. I also wish we could live somewhere where Ms. Biggs wasn't our neighbor."

Ms. Madge Biggs was the Wreathen Middle School vice principal, and unfortunately for Amanda – her neighbor. Citing a historical lack of demonstrating disciplinary skills, the Sussex County School Board decided to promote Mr. Carmack to principal over Ms. Biggs. As vice principal of the smaller school, she was also responsible for substituting for any of the teachers that were out for longer than a week. So, thanks to her lack of promotion and an unfortunate allergic reaction that Amanda's history teacher had just recovered from, Ms. Biggs had been performing both her duties as vice principal and substitute history teacher since the beginning of the year. To say she had been unpleasant as a teacher and frustrated by what she referred to as the "Carmack Coup," would be a jarring understatement for Amanda and her classmates. As such, she also happened to be a sore subject around the West family home due to the sudden influx of detention slips Amanda was bringing home with her on almost a weekly basis.

Every time Ms. Biggs found Amanda or anyone of her classmates in violation of even the slightest infraction, she sent them to detention. There was the time Amanda had used a pen instead of a No. 2 pencil, which earned her two detentions. Then there was the time she raised her hand to answer a question and, when called upon, hadn't spoken loudly enough, which meant detention for three Wednesdays in a row. The list went on. This last time Amanda found herself in trouble was for being a minute late to lunch because Ms. Biggs had sent her to the gym teacher with a note right as the second period bell had rung. Since the cafeteria and the gymnasium were on opposite sides of school, Amanda had to cross two different sets of stairs, make it through the lunch crowd in the corridors, listen to Mr. Zucker read the note aloud and dictate his reply, and then make it all the way back in under ten minutes. Needless to say, her efforts had been in vain. For her late arrival, Amanda was rewarded with a pink slip and a puddle of sweat running down her back. Her parents knew of the infractions, of course, but were too preoccupied with the store to listen to her side of the story. It stung that her parents didn't take her side. She had never before gotten even a warning before Ms. Biggs started teaching her class.

Jack waved his hands. "Hey, no, ixnay on saying that name. We get a day free from her, so let's not jinx it. Mr. Donaldson coming back might be the best Christmas present ever. Did you remember to get your permission slip signed?"

Amanda patted her satchel. "I grabbed it from the counter last night after promising both mom and dad that there would be no more detention slips in my future. I am not sure mom believed me, though, or forgave me for the last one. My oatmeal was lukewarm again this morning. You know she always undercooks my oatmeal when she's really mad at me. She also gave me a ten minute lecture on bus behavior. Thanks, Ms. Biggs." Amanda turned and frowned at the house to her right; it had always reminded her of an evil pilgrim's hat.

The West family had moved to Wreathen ten years ago, when Keith and Liz got their management jobs with U-Buy. Amanda had only been three at the time. The town itself was pretty much a pass-through – it was known only for the big-box store where vacationers would stop on their way to the Delaware beaches to buy sunscreen or umbrellas, and the old textile mill that closed years ago.

Of all the neighborhoods from which to choose, the Wests moved to the cul-de-sac at the end of Rivers End Road. The cul-de-sac held four houses: the Wests', the Isens', the Whybans', and Ms. Biggs'. The first two on the right side of the circle, owned by the Whybans and the Isens, were identical, with yellow siding, white trim, and brick chimneys where ivy liked to grow during the spring. Then there was the West's home. It was a bit run down when they moved in, but they soon hired a crew to spruce up the siding and give the door a new red coat of paint. Lastly was Ms. Biggs' house, which had a black pointed roof and a brown railing that went around all four white sides.

"Put all of that out of your mind. We can deal with that later. Today we get to go to the Museum of Natural History in D.C.! We are just a short bus ride away from getting to see -- wait for it -- dinosaurs! They are the best distraction ever from Ms. Biggs, detention slips, and lukewarm oatmeal-making parents. We also don't even have to go to school because they got us one of those charter buses!" Jack bounced his shoulders up and down. Jack was obsessed with anything dinosaur related; he even subscribed to several magazines to have on hand to read when Ms. Prian was taking her nap during their daily pop quiz.

Rolling her eyes, Amanda rubbed her hands up and down on her shoulders. Amanda almost lost her footing as she started rocking forward on her toes to try and keep warm; her thermal leggings, boots, and thick green overcoat were apparently indefensible against the cold. "You're right. Although, not about the dinosaurs. I am going to sit in front of the Hope Diamond for as long as they let me. *That* is something to look forward to."

"You do your thing, and I will do mine." Jack gave Amanda a dopey grin as a long black and red bus turned on their street, looking slightly ominous against the blinding white snow. Coming to a sluggish stop beside the old magnolia tree between their houses, the bus driver waved them over. Amanda followed Jack to the center of the circle, slipped several times, and paused at the slick-looking black treads that led up to the bus. She had fallen one too many times up the bus steps to take these in one bound, as Jack was doing.

She carefully placed one foot ahead of the other, and held onto the railing for dear life. Feeling quite proud when she reached the top, having only slid twice, Amanda almost missed Laurie snicker at her from the front seat.

"W-what are you doing here?" Amanda's surprise made her half shout the end of her question.

In Amanda's opinion, being an eighth-grader sucked, and not just for the usual reasons. There was Ms. Biggs, of course. But the other reason was something even worse. No, it had nothing to do with all the homework, pop quizzes, or very boring lectures on ancient civilizations. It was Laurie Gellar.

Laurie Gellar had moved to Wreathen over the summer. Her previous school had been unwilling to overlook her issues with spelling and math, even though she had won the junior wrestling division for the state, so she had been held back twice, making her at least double the size of anyone in their grade. Whether it was thanks to her larger stature or wrestling prowess, Laurie had become the most popular girl in school by the end of September. Amanda tried to be nice to Laurie, but for some unknown reason Laurie had decided Amanda was her number one enemy.

Laurie smiled, revealing shiny braces wrapped in dark red bands to match her tracksuit. "Did you miss me, West?"

"You're not supposed to be here today. You're supposed to be taking a make-up test." Amanda's voice rose even higher, causing the other students on the bus to pivot their attention to her.

Laurie smiled at Amanda's dismay. "Well, I guess I'm not – if it's any of your business. My parents convinced Ms. Biggs to let me take that stupid test another day so I wouldn't miss out on today's trip. We just couldn't let you go and have all this fun by yourself. Could we girls?" Susan and Nicole quickly nodded from the seat behind Laurie, sporting new matching red tracksuits.

"Look, Laurie, just leave me alone today."

"Now why would I do that? You could get lost in the museum or trapped in one of the tombs. I would feel just awful if something like that happened. I'll keep a close eye on you to keep you safe." Laurie punched the back of her seat and laughed.

Jack waved to her from the back of the bus and mouthed "Come on!"

Amanda ducked her head as she tried to skirt past the group of girls. Without warning, although she should have anticipated it, a foot shot out, sending Amanda and her bag flying. Amanda screamed like a strangled flamingo, and she went down hard onto the wet floor, the contents of her bag scattering about. The front of the bus erupted into laughter. Amanda pushed herself up from the floor with a wet leaf clinging to her hair.

Jack charged down the aisle. "I saw that, Laurie. That was *no bueno!*"

"You saw what, Isen? All I saw was West here trip and fall. Right, everyone?" Laurie got up from her seat and cracked her knuckles as she looked to see if anyone else wanted to contradict her.

5

"Why can't you just leave Amanda alone and stop being such a dumb ape?" Jack reached down to help Amanda and the bus instantly quieted as if someone had turned off the TV.

Laurie towered over both Amanda and Jack with red hair that was pulled into a messy ponytail and looked like the frayed end of a pompom. "Who are you calling an ape?"

"I thought I came across your picture near the ape section of the dictionary yesterday. You mean that wasn't you?" Someone bit back a laugh and the tension in the bus changed its focus from Amanda to Jack.

"What is going on here, Miss Gellar? Miss West? Mr. Isen?" Laurie jumped as a shrill voice chirped from the steps of the bus. Amanda and Jack looked at each other and groaned. Jack helped Amanda to her feet while they scurried to refill Amanda's soggy satchel.

Ms. Biggs was brushing the snow off the shoulders of her gray and black striped faux fox fur jacket and looked to her three students for a response. Standing with her head tilted slightly to avoid her brown, permed hair touching the ceiling of the bus she began to play with one of the strings of her pearl necklace. "Am I missing something or are you waiting for an engraved invitation? No? Then take your seats – immediately."

Laurie dove into her seat as Jack helped Amanda limp back to theirs. Ms. Biggs looked around the bus as she pulled off her gloves one finger at a time. "Unfortunately, Mr. Donaldson will not be able to take you to the Smithsonian today. He has fallen ill, with some *other* kind of allergic reaction, and as such, I have been tasked to be your chaperone." The eighth-graders shifted uneasily, and Jack looked longingly at the emergency exit at the back of the bus.

"You all know my rules. There will be no shouting or loud music. Anything bordering on improper student behavior will earn you a week's worth of detention and a call from me to your parents. Are we clear?" Ms. Biggs looked pointedly at Amanda. "Take out your permission slips and have them ready as I come down the aisle to collect them." Ms. Biggs opened her large purse with the pearl chain and pulled out a clipboard.

Amanda reached into her bag and rummaged through to the bottom to find the paper her mom had signed. The bag was cluttered with a reading light, wet notebooks, pens, and lint, but there was no note. Amanda's stomach dropped and her skin felt clammy. She looked up and then down to the floor where she had fallen, frantically noting Ms. Biggs had already made it halfway down the aisle. There was no note.

Amanda pushed her bangs out of her face and stared into her bag. Where had it gone? She remembered picking it up and putting it in her bag. Just then, she saw Laurie and her crew pop their heads up over their seats to look back at her. Laurie slowly waved a wet and tattered piece of paper that bore her mother's signature and, with a sneer, tossed the permission slip out the window, where it plummeted into the snow.

Amanda turned to Jack and whispered frantically, "Laurie stole my slip!"

Jack had been flipping through *Bones Across America*. "So, get it back."

"I can't. She threw it outside. It's gone!"

"Oh, man. Ms. Biggs isn't going to let you go on the trip without one! No, wait. First she's going to give you detention and *then* not let you go on the trip!"

"My parents will *kill* me!" Amanda couldn't believe her luck. First, her Laurie-and-Ms. Biggs-free day had been ruined, and now she was probably going to get another detention! Amanda tentatively leaned into the aisle. "Ah, excuse me, Ms. Biggs?"

"Wait your turn, Miss West," Ms. Biggs said crossly. Holding Billy's note by the only corner that didn't have teeth marks, she marked a check onto her list.

Amanda sat back in her seat and closed her eyes. She had to do something! She wished there was a way she could explain to Ms. Biggs what had happened. Jack nudged her in the ribs and Amanda looked up to see Ms. Biggs standing at their seat, looking annoyed as usual.

"Is there a problem, Miss West?" Ms. Biggs looked over her clipboard at Amanda as her eyes narrowed.

"It's my permission slip. It's gone. Laurie…"

"No permission slip, no trip, no excuse." Ms. Biggs raised her eyebrows and smiled as if someone had given her an early Christmas present. Folding the clipboard under her arm, she pointed to the front of the bus. "Exit the bus immediately."

"But," Amanda pointed to the snowbank that held her note.

"No excuses!" Ms. Biggs grabbed Amanda by the jacket and marched her to the front of the bus, and then down the steps. Once outside the bus, "Inform your parents they will be hearing from me for wasting my time. I will also be forced to tell the district manager of U-Buy, Mr. Burr, how your parents, his employees, couldn't be bothered to make sure their daughter was prepared for the day. They are a sponsor of our trip after all." With that, Ms. Biggs got back on the bus and barked at the bus driver that they were ready to leave.

Amanda walked numbly back to her driveway, but then her anger began to boil within her chest. She couldn't let Ms. Biggs tell Mr. Burr. Not after she promised her mom and dad that she was done getting into trouble at school. Amanda felt her skin tingle again as if a porcupine had been rolled across her entire body. The bus's tires squelched as they pivoted and began to turn in the snow. Amanda clenched her fists as she felt another wave of anger hit her. There was a burst of light, accompanied by the sound of jingling bells, and the back tires of the bus began to spin out of control as if they were being held in place. Amanda turned in surprise.

Ms. Biggs threw open the bus doors and glared at Amanda. Amanda held up her hands. Ms. Biggs grumbled as she stalked to the back of the bus, and began to push. Without warning, there was another flash of light and the bus suddenly lurched forward. As if in slow motion, Ms. Biggs looked up in horror while she flailed about before falling face first into the dirty snow in the street. Amanda couldn't help but laugh before wondering where that strange light had come from. She hoped it would come back again.

The snow blower from the Wests' freshly cleared driveway shuddered and green arcs of light shot across the machine as it launched itself forward, mowed through the snow of Amanda's yard, making a beeline straight into the magnolia tree. The snow blower crumpled upon impact, but its collision caused the tree to rain down the snow it was holding on its branches on top of Ms. Biggs and the bus. Amanda couldn't help herself from laughing, the entire bus joining her as they crammed into the back seats to see what was going on. Ms. Biggs coughed and gagged from the snow. Frantically trying to brush the snow from her coat, Ms. Biggs looked like a disheveled raccoon trying to empty a garbage can.

"You will pay for this, Miss West! Consider yourself suspended until further notice. I don't know how you did it, but I know this was your doing!" Ms. Biggs screeched as she staggered her way back onto the bus. Amanda could see the rest of the students on the bus trying not to laugh at Ms. Biggs as the bus shot forward, trailing snow and debris down the street. The ravens from the fencepost flew behind the bus, laughing the entire way.

.

CHAPTER 2:
AN UNWANTED DAY OFF

Amanda's elation at what happened to Ms. Biggs lasted only until she realized she had to go back inside her house and face her parents. She hoped her mom had cooled off from her earlier rant, but that dream was dashed as soon as she opened the door and heard her mother yelling at the weatherman. Amanda cringed and tiptoed into the living room to listen to her parents' conversation. She thought for a moment about running upstairs and hiding in her room, perhaps indefinitely, but only a ninja had a chance to make it up the stairs without one of the boards creaking. She paused to listen again, hoping to find a good moment to announce her presence.

Liz West wasn't an overly tall woman, and her cardigan bulged at the buttons a bit, as she had taken to eating Christmas chocolates to help ease her stress. Marching toward the refrigerator, and sucking in her stomach to fit between the counter and the chair, Liz snatched the clipboard off of the refrigerator door. Pulling a pen from her hair, she crossed off a few lines. "Is it too much to ask that that Neanderthalic weatherman give us some kind of hope? Look at this. Our quota for the fourth quarter will be completely ruined by this 'act of God,' as he calls it. People don't spend money when there is a blizzard outside. All they do is stand around and eat the free samples to avoid going back outside. The least that man could do is tell us there could be a hint of warmth coming our way, but instead he just stands there looking like an ape who has been asked to count to two."

Keith West would have been a domineering man if he were the type that wore business suits. Instead, he was simply a tall man with broad shoulders. He had blond hair that was peppered with gray, and mostly wore blue button-down shirts and khakis. Unlike his wife, Keith wore his weight at his waist, and his pants with an elastic waistband. He also didn't entirely believe the weather was to blame for their problems at U-Buy. Amanda had heard him comment that, in his opinion, the merchandising choices had been lackluster this year. "Let's not get too upset just yet. We could have a…sale."

"A sale?" Liz asked incredulously? "You mean another sale on top of the one we already have going on? Sales make us look desperate and lazy!"

Keith hid behind his newspaper and pulled at his right eyebrow. Before

9

the holidays Keith's brows had been bushy, but after having to convince Liz to have a fall and then holiday sale, his right eyebrow now sported a gap the size of his pinky. Pulling two more gray sprouts from his highly diminished brow, Keith rolled the hairs between his thumb and forefinger before casting them to the linoleum floor.

"It's only the beginning of December, Liz – remember? We still have plenty of time to make up our losses. Who knows, maybe they'll stock up on food instead of toys. Speaking of which, don't forget we need to talk with the produce manager today. The oranges are looking a bit too ripe again. Perhaps we can pair them with some of the other merchandise that isn't moving."

Liz punched a few buttons on her phone, huffed impatiently, and arched a full eyebrow. "The incompetence of that man. Is it too much to expect for him to get fresh produce in December? The way the school keeps pestering us about buying oranges from Florida, you would think they would at least be easy to have on hand. Yesterday's batch looked they were fished out of the garbage.

The news anchor broke in on her parents' conversation. "*Authorities are still looking into the cases of three more children that have vanished, this time from the Baltimore area. The police implore anyone who has information on their whereabouts to contact local authorities. In other news, there is a national recall for anyone who purchased a bag of 'Salty Ice.' The salt has been linked to an allergic reaction in some adults, due to the addition of a new ingredient. The salt was sent out during the rash of winter storms over Thanksgiving. They urge anyone who might have purchased a bag of 'Salty Ice', to return it to your local store for a full refund.*"

"Well, that's just great news for us." There was a soft buzzing from Liz's phone on the green laminate counter. She snapped her fingers twice at Keith as she picked up the phone, and then pointed to turn the volume of the TV down. Sitting down she shook took a breath before answering. "Hello, this is Liz from U-Buy."

Amanda bit the side of her cheek. She knew she should go in and just tell her parents and get it over with, but her feet didn't want to move. Taking a deep breath, Amanda tried to come up with a way to present what had happened that might not get her grounded until her eighteenth birthday. She decided it was now or never. If she waited any longer, or one of them saw her before she came into the small gray kitchen on her own steam, it would be worse off for her.

Liz was finishing up her call as Amanda stepped into the kitchen. "Uh, Mom. Dad. Hi." Keith looked up from his readings and Liz pivoted on the barstool she had sat down on at the counter. "Look, something happened. It is NOT my fault. You see I had my permission slip and then…" Amanda stopped mid-sentence at her mother's withering expression of rage as she tapped her phone on the counter three times.

"What on earth were you thinking? You got…" Amanda's mother started and then paused as if needing to take in sufficient air to continue. This was quickly followed by a word she made sound almost as bad as the phrase paid time off – "Suspended!"

"What?" Amanda's father dropped the paper and twisted the hairs on his right eyebrow.

"That was Mr. Burr. He just got a very disturbing call from Ms. Biggs. She informed him that Amanda hadn't bothered to take her permission slip for the class trip – the one that *we* were sponsoring, mind you – and then proceeded to cause the bus to spin out and crash our snow blower into the magnolia tree, which dropped a ton of snow onto Ms. Biggs. He has decided that we should take the day off and bring in someone from the district to help us in our time of crisis! Did I miss anything, Amanda?"

"Well, I didn't know anything about Mr. Burr, but the rest of it happened. But it wasn't my fault," Amanda quickly added. Their kitchen was only big enough for the peninsula counter Keith and Liz were at and the side counter that had their sink, dishwasher and refrigerator. Amanda wished there was a bit more space between her and her parents.

"Not your fault? That's something we keep hearing from you. Like the latest detention due to your tardiness, which Mr. Burr also heard about? Can you imagine what he must be thinking? First, our numbers are down because of this weather, and now this! We could lose the store!" Liz put a hand over her eyes as she reached for the shelf under the counter and slid a box of chocolate-covered almonds into her lap.

"I don't think anyone is going to fire you because I got in trouble, Mom."

Liz glared at her daughter. "Well, thank heavens you see it that way. I am sure the rest of this town will feel exactly the same as our daughter, who has seemingly made it her mission in life to see how much trouble she can get into in one semester." Stuffing three chocolates into her mouth, "So what are you going to do about this?"

"Me?" Amanda looked indignantly at her mother, but then shrank back when Keith cleared his throat. "It's not my fault…"

"Not your fault? Whose fault is it then?" Liz pursed her lips.

"It's just Ms. Biggs, she…" Amanda stopped talking as her mother slammed the clipboard onto the counter, chipping off the corner.

"Not another word, Amanda Elizabeth West. I am tired of your excuses. She has been a huge supporter of our store and a personal friend of Mr. Burr for many years. I think it is time you grew up a bit and took a look at your own behavior. Mr. Burr said Ms. Biggs called you a hoodlum, Amanda. A hoodlum!" Liz shook her head, taking several breaths to try and steady herself. "I don't understand what has happened to you."

"I'm telling you it wasn't my fault! Why don't you ever take my side? I don't know what happened. Laurie tripped me on the bus and stole my note, then the thing with the bus and Ms. Biggs…there was this…then I came to tell you…" Amanda shrugged in exasperation.

"Don't you blame us for this mess. Is this some kind of teenage identity crisis?" Amanda's mother's voice was reaching its full zenith.

"No, Mom, it's nothing like that." Amanda bit the side of her cheek and brushed the hair from her face.

"Then please explain it to us so we can try to understand and fix this. I can only imagine what everyone will say about us. They will probably boycott the store." Liz put a hand over her eyes. "Clearly a simple lecture will not suffice this time. Your father and I have worked too hard to let you mess up your life by becoming some kind of miscreant. Maybe we should send you to that reform school for wayward girls Ms. Biggs, suggested. Do you have nothing you want to add, Keith?"

Keith stood at the counter, his face shadowed and his arms crossed. Clearing his throat he suggested, "I think it would be best, dear, if Amanda went to her room for the time being."

Amanda had opened her mouth to try to defend herself once more, but at her father's words she simply nodded and numbly made her way through the living room and up the stairs. As Amanda changed from school clothes into sweatpants and a long-sleeved shirt, she began to cry. Today had started with such hope, and was now in shambles. Lying on her bed, Amanda hung her head over the side, stared up at the ceiling, and let the tears slide to the floor. Not wanting to hear her parents yelling, Amanda wrapped her pillow around her head and tried to turn her focus on to what actually had happened with Ms. Biggs. She had never seen anything like it before. Where had that green light come from? She doubted her parents would believe her if she tried to blame the strange flashing light if they wouldn't even believe her about Ms. Biggs.

After a while there was a soft knock on her door, and Amanda swung herself upright as she tried to wipe the tears from her face. Her father opened the door slowly, and then shut it behind him. Crossing the woven area rug, he sat on the old trunk they had given to her when she went to her first summer camp. He cleared his throat awkwardly for a moment and clasped his hands between his knees.

"Amanda, your mother and I feel you are going through something right now. What that is – we quite frankly do not know."

"Dad, I…" Amanda stopped as her father held up a hand.

"Your behavior has been erratic lately, and a complete surprise to us." As he spoke he stared at the rug, purposefully not looking at Amanda and keeping his words measured. "We are wondering if this has something to do with Jack – if he hasn't started to put certain ideas in your head about ways young ladies are supposed to act – ways we don't agree with."

"None of this was Jack's fault, Dad. There was this flash and then…" Amanda stopped as Keith banged his knees with his fists, his anger breaking through.

"Enough! No more lies, Amanda. No more stories. Your mother and I are done with your excuses. You are grounded until you can either tell us the truth, or you serve out your punishment with Ms. Biggs. Starting tomorrow you are grounded. There will be no more hanging around with Jack, or any of your other friends, and you will apologize to Ms. Biggs for all the trouble you've caused." Clearing his throat as he regained his composure, Keith stood to leave. "We love you Amanda, but this behavior will not be tolerated."

"But that's not fair, Dad!"

"That is enough, young lady," Keith bellowed. "I said it before, and I meant it – take some responsibility."

For the rest of the day Amanda sat in her room, refusing to come down – even for dinner. At eight o'clock, Amanda heard her parents fussing with their coats. Her mother was insisting Keith wear the long coat to look more presentable at the Winter Festival. Amanda groaned and put her head in her hands. The Winter Festival was one of the best parties of the whole year! When there was snow, the Festival Committee would make dozens of blank snowmen for the entire town to decorate. Last year she and Jack had made an "Under the Sea" themed snowman that won an honorable mention ribbon.

Tiptoeing to the edge of the stairs, Amanda called down to her parents. "Mom…Dad…" There was a pause in the activity below. "Can I please go to the festival?"

Liz's head appeared around the banister, followed by the rest of her, as she walked to the bottom of the stairs. "Have you had a change to your story, young lady?" Amanda didn't respond. Liz pressed her lips together so hard they looked like a thin line. "If I were you, Amanda, I would seriously consider thinking less about the festival and more about your family. Thank goodness we will be at the sponsor tent tonight. Maybe Mr. Burr will see it as a sign of the good we are trying to do to make up for your stunt today."

Amanda rubbed the back of her leg with her foot. "But Mom…"

Keith stepped behind his wife. "Amanda, your mother and I are going out. I think we could all do with some time apart."

With that, her parents turned and left. Amanda slunk down the steps to the bay window in their living room to watch her parents walk down the street. The town park was only a few blocks away, and Amanda could see the soft lights above the trees that separated her from the festivities. She could picture the bell players by the Chocolate Hut, and the kids lined up to get a steaming mug of hot coco. The frozen lake was probably full of ice skaters doing figure eights around the island. Some of the more rambunctious children would be building forts and having snowball fights. Not being able to go felt like she had awakened on Christmas morning to find a lump of coal in her stocking.

"This is totally unfair."

"Life's unfair," someone called from outside. Amanda jumped as something splattered against the windowpane. A giant snowball was sliding down the glass. Amanda tried to peer through the slush to see where it had come from, but the street was empty except for the snow that was drifting from snowbank to snowbank.

"Boo!" Jack jumped out from behind one of the shrubs that lined the front of Amanda's porch. He was wearing a floppy hat tied under his chin, his usual denim jacket and jeans, and big black galoshes. He motioned Amanda toward the door.

"Jack, what are you doing?" Amanda shuffled to the entryway. Jack drew a lopsided smiley face in the condensation from his breath on the windowpanes beside the red door.

Amanda opened the door and hid behind it, letting the cold air swirl past her feet. "Why aren't you at the festival?"

Jack looked at Amanda quizzically. "We said we'd go together. Remember? I saw your parents leave without you, so I came to see where you were. Judging by your lack of winter wear, I'd say you need to get a move on. Go put on a snowsuit or something and let's scoot. I want to get there before the line for the Chocolate Hut gets too long." Jack rubbed his mittens together and grinned.

Amanda's face fell. "I can't go. My parents grounded me." She left off the part about being banned from seeing him.

"What? Aw, nuts." Jack kicked at a pile of snow and missed. "Was it because of what happened with that weird light and the snow blower?"

"Wait, you saw the light too?" Amanda opened the door wider, curling her toes underneath her feet.

"Well, yeah, I mean it was kind of hard to miss. It was like something out of an alien movie." Jack made an explosive motion with his gloved hands.

Amanda felt silly for even considering it, but maybe it *had* been aliens. She also couldn't blame Jack for not saying anything, when she hadn't said a word about it either. "At least now I know I am not crazy."

"You aren't an alien, are you? I mean it would be OK if you were. I could be the alien's cool sidekick." Jack was trying to make Amanda laugh, and he succeeded as he hopped up and down excitedly.

Amanda exhaled through her nose. "Sorry to disappoint, but I'm not an alien. If I was, why would I live in Wreathen?"

Jack shrugged. "The food?"

Amanda rolled her eyes. "Regardless, there is no festival in my future tonight."

"Eh." Jack waved a hand and feigned disinterest. "Festival, shmestival. Why go there when we can have our own here?" Jack's eyes sparkled mischievously and his voice had taken on the quality of a car salesman trying to make a deal.

"I'm not supposed to go out. I bet they're having me watched." Amanda was only half joking.

Jack looked around. "You see someone I don't? The neighborhood is dead. Who's going to know? Go put on your snow gear and meet me on the front lawn!" Without explaining himself further, Jack dashed down the front steps.

Amanda rolled her eyes again. This was probably not going to end well, but her parents were going to be gone for hours – so what could it hurt? Besides, Jack was the only one in Wreathen who believed she was telling the truth about anything. Forbidden or not, she wasn't going to let her parents keep them apart.

CHAPTER 3:
JOTUNS IN THE SNOW

"So, now what?" Amanda asked through chattering teeth. She was standing with Jack in a snowbank up to her shins. The cold was starting to creep through her boots and her knee-length thermal socks.

"Now we are going to build the best Winter Festival snowman ever! It will be better than anything this stinking town has ever seen. None of that silly elf stuff." Jack took it as a personal insult that his snowmen had yet to win first place. He still couldn't watch wrestling after his Hulk Hogan snowman didn't even get an honorable mention. "It can't be just any old snowman, of course. I've got it! A snowman spider! It goes great with both Halloween and Christmas. Think of it, people could build one snowman spider and it can be their décor for months!"

Amanda was laughing and groaning, and when Jack made a show for applause for his idea, Amanda waved him off and asked, "What do we do first?"

Jack began listing ingredients, and they split up to find their items. Amanda felt some of her bad mood recede as she raced to the woods behind her house. When she made it to the first clump of trees, she found a clearing with what she needed – several branches and an assortment of pinecones of various sizes.

Fumbling to gather as much as she could, Amanda's boot hit something in the snow and she snapped forward. Dropping her findings, her hands made it a foot down into the snow before the compacted knoll stopped her fall. Amanda winced as she pulled her hands free. Inspecting the side of her right hand, she found her glove was sliced open. A small red cut stung from being exposed to the cold air.

Jack called from the side of the house, "Amanda? What are you doing back there? Taking a nap?"

"I'm fine. I'll be right there." Grabbing as many branches and pinecones as she could carry, Amanda pulled her right foot up to clear the next hill of snow and then made a dash for it in the shallower areas.

Jack was taking up residence on a smooth patch of snow by the fence that separated Amanda's yard from Ms. Biggs'. It was snowing so heavily that it looked like a white curtain hung from the clouds above. Jack was waiting with his pile of appropriated items, which consisted of icicle lights, Santa's beard, two red ornaments, and tinsel.

"Hey, are you OK?" Jack took a hold of Amanda's wrist and inspected her torn glove.

Amanda froze as Jack touched her exposed skin. She swallowed hard. "Yeah, just snagged it on a toy or something under the snow. It's more annoying than anything."

Jack looked up at Amanda, but kept his head bent down. "You want to go inside and get another pair of gloves? I know how you and cold don't like to mix."

Pulling her arm free, Amanda took a deep breath and tucked her hand under her other arm to warm it up for a minute. "No. I definitely don't want to be inside. I will probably be inside for the rest of winter once my mom and dad get back from the festival. I might as well enjoy the freedom while I can."

"Alright. Then let's start with the body."

They began to shovel the snow with their hands – first into one large mound, and then a smaller one. When they finished, the body stood about waist high on Amanda, and the head was up to her knees. Sniffling from the cold, Amanda could smell the tang of the snow mingled with the dampness of her scarf.

"Awesome! Now for the legs." Jack picked up two sticks and walked around to one of the sides. Snapping off the smaller twigs until they were almost smooth, Jack jabbed the larger of the two into the snow, so the branch angled up and away from the body. The stick dipped slightly when Jack released it, but it held. Taking the other stick and placing it in the snow so the tops formed a point, Jack pointed to Amanda's pile. "Toss me a pinecone."

"One pinecone coming up." Amanda picked up a prickly cone and lobbed it into the air.

The pinecone went wide, but Jack dove into a snow mound and caught it before it disappeared. Dusting himself off, he gently placed the cone onto the snow so it faced out like a little foot. "And that's how you build a spider leg."

Amanda picked up two more sticks, and a pinecone, and made a leg opposite Jack's. Jack continued on his side, and after a few minutes their spider had eight legs of woodsy debris. Amanda wiped her nose, now freely running from the cold.

"The Gellars don't have anything on this. Do you remember the stupid elf snowman they made last year? How much more basic can you get?" Jack walked over to his pile of mismatched decorations. "Although if you can manage a little bit more of that green light, I'm sure we could make their creation this year look like that pile of snow you dumped on Ms. Biggs."

"Jack!" Amanda yelled while tossing some snow at her friend, missing him by a foot.

"Whoa! Whoa! I give! Don't turn me into a Jack-sicle." Jack laughed. Amanda joined begrudgingly. Picking up the ornaments and icicle lights, Jack walked to the front of the spider and began to embed the icicles one at a time into a goofy smile. Amanda took the ornaments from Jack and gently pushed two red eyes into the snowman spider's head.

The spider mischievously leered at them now, mirroring Jack's earlier expression. "I think this has to be the best darn snowman spider ever – don't you?"

Amanda nodded. "It's certainly unique."

Taking a free hand, Jack caught a snowflake and held it toward Amanda. "Just as pretty and unique as the both of you."

Amanda blushed and blew the snowflake from Jack's hand. She had never heard Jack talk that way before. It was the first time anyone had spoken to her like that, in fact. Not knowing how to respond, she stood there and watched the flake float lazily to join its brothers and sisters on the ground.

"I don't know about that. I –" Amanda began, but was interrupted as a pair of headlights rounded the corner of their street. Amanda and Jack ducked instinctively behind their snowspider. They both knew who the black sedan belonged to.

"Amanda!" Jack was tugging at her sleeve, "You've got to make a run for it!"

"Are you kidding? I can't leave you here!" Amanda popped her head above the snowman spider to see Ms. Biggs' car sliding, and then stopping as the engine sputtered out. "Besides, I can't make it back to my house without her seeing me."

"Your parents, though... just go! I will distract Ms. Biggs." Jack gave Amanda one of his smiles and then leapt up from behind the snowspider.

Ms. Biggs was still fighting to get out of her car. As if on cue, the wind howled down the street, blowing snow into the air. The haze of snow was just the cover Amanda needed. Seizing her opportunity, Amanda dashed across the yard. She hated herself for allowing Jack to take all the blame for their fun, but he was right about her parents. Glancing behind her, she saw Jack had somehow made his way around so that Ms. Biggs, who had finally made it out of her car, had her back to Amanda. Throwing all caution aside, Amanda dashed up her icy steps and into her house.

The inside of her house was almost tropical compared to the weather outside. Amanda would have enjoyed the warmth if she hadn't been so worried about Jack. Her living room window was too conspicuous for Amanda to look through – it faced the exact spot she had been a few seconds before. She carefully tiptoed up the stairs instead. Trying to avoid leaving any puddles of snow as evidence, Amanda took off her gloves, wiped the steps, and made it to the window in her room just in time to see her parents walking over to Ms. Biggs and Jack.

"Oh, no! What are they doing back so soon?" Ms. Biggs was clearly in a tizzy, pointing wildly at the snowman spider. Amanda raised her hand to the window and placed her fingertips against the glass. With a gasp, she jerked her hand back and stared. Steam rose from each finger, but it wasn't heat that caused her to pull away. It was the intense cold she felt. Even lightly resting her fingers on the glass felt as if she'd thrust her hand into an ice bath. Sharp needles of pain jabbed into her fingertips, and smoke rose from her hand like dry ice when it is exposed to water.

Thunder shook the house, followed by an eerie wail as a shower of blue snowflakes sped toward the ground. The flakes fell like sick falling stars and were bright, bright blue. Something deep inside Amanda shuddered at the sight, and a fear for Jack and her parents rose sharply in her stomach.

Where each snowflake landed, the snow began to writhe as if a nest of snakes had suddenly burrowed up from below, sending tendrils of whatever had been awakened throughout the yards of the entire neighborhood. Amanda stepped back from the window as fingers of ice began to creep along the divided panes. Within seconds she could no longer see Jack, her parents, or Ms. Biggs.

Amanda panicked. Was this part of the weird light from earlier? She ran from her room, slipping on the stairs and banging her elbow into the wall as she made her way to the front door. She didn't know what it was, but she knew she needed to get everyone away from whatever was in the snow. She tried to turn the knob, but the door wouldn't open. Amanda twisted and pulled on the doorknob, but it wouldn't budge. The intense cold had frozen the door's hinges.

"Jack!" Amanda called, pounding on the door and then ran to the bay window. More creeping frost grew like prison bars across the glass. Through her obscured view, Amanda could just make out Ms. Biggs trying to stay upright, her arms waving like two windmills. When another gust of wind hit them, Ms. Biggs reached up to keep her hat from blowing off but instinctively grabbed Jack's arm to steady herself. As if sensing the movement, something blue and wriggly erupted from beneath Amanda's parents' feet, sending them into the street and knocking them unconscious. One of the blue creatures hit Ms. Biggs in the chest, the other got Jack in the back of the neck, and a third vanished into the snowman spider. A blast of wind coursed through the neighborhood with the force of a runaway train, shattering Amanda's front door, spitting pieces of wood onto the carpet, and knocking Ms. Biggs and Jack into the snow. The rushing air hit Amanda in the face. She began to cough as her breath was sucked from her chest by the piercing cold.

Amanda struggled back to the entryway and clung to the railing as she fought her way down the porch steps. The wind pushed against her as if willing her to stay away. Amanda fell to the sidewalk, landing face down and skinning the palms of her hands and side of her face. She cried out and looked up toward Jack and Ms. Biggs. Cold blue light now radiated from Jack and Ms. Biggs, both frozen and unmoving, as a sour sound echoed in her ears. Amanda couldn't see her parents and was about to run to them when the light that slid over Ms. Biggs and Jack like an oily cocoon began evaporating into shards of blue that fell to the ground.

Trying to catch her breath, Amanda pushed herself up and made her way over to the fence where Jack and Ms. Biggs had been propelled. "Jack? Ms. Biggs?"

Neither moved, but something in the snow stirred and the snowspider began to twitch. The once jolly spider grew, its form changing, until it was as tall as Amanda's house and looked like a giant gorilla-like caveman. Jagged armor made from sheets of ice formed on the giant's forearms as it leaned forward, smashing through the fence as it rested its knuckles in the snow. Tusks grew from the sides of the giant's head and curled upward. Amanda moved to try to cover Jack as the caveman opened its mouth, roaring into the night.

More tendrils of snow began to make their way toward them, and the light that had fallen into the snow from Jack and Ms. Biggs generated three more swirling nests. Scratching sounds started coming from the snow, and the ground beside Amanda suddenly shifted. She screamed as a tiny blue creature with horns leapt at her with snapping teeth. The creature sported three fingers on each hand, with sharp claws that raked at Amanda as she shuffled backward. The giant's face swung down toward Amanda, its fangs protruding over its lips. It reached out a muscular hand covered in white fur. The devil-like creature leapt at her again, and Amanda raised her hands in defense.

"Get away from me!" Amanda felt her skin tingle as she yelled. A flare of green light burst from her hands and evaporated both the creature and the giant. For a moment, the night seemed to pause. Amanda examined her shaking hands. She felt sure the light had come from her now, just as it must have earlier, but what did it mean?

There was a strange sucking sound, and the snow stirred under Amanda. A dozen more horned creatures jumped from the snow and latched onto her legs. Before she had time to react, the horned fiends embedded their sharp claws into her boots and were transformed into a manacle of ice. Amanda tried to pull her feet free but was yanked backward as something scuttled up her back. Amanda tried shaking her hands again, praying for more green light, but it was too late. As more of the creatures piled on top of her, she felt freezing spots blossom and harden around her torso and arms until she was completely encased in a bodysuit of ice.

A slow, murmuring hiss rose from the ground and with an explosion of snow Ms. Biggs was suddenly thrown into the air. Amanda tried to scream, but her jaw had gone numb. She watched helplessly as Ms. Biggs' eyes turned blue and her skin slowly turned a pale blue like the top layer of ice on a frozen lake. The light from the haloed streetlamps illuminated newly angular features as her body began to grow to twice its original size. Her round cheeks were replaced with hard, sharp planes and her nose and mouth became a flat, square line that looked like the end of a chisel.

The slick patches of ice on the sidewalk around Amanda began to dance and flow toward Ms. Biggs, overlapping one another until her overcoat had been transformed into a plated chainmail that flowed seamlessly into the snow. Ms. Biggs took a slow breath that rattled in her throat.

"Favoured!"

Amanda forced her lips to move. "Ms. Biggs? Wh-what happened?" Ms. Biggs' transformation terrified Amanda. The woman she had been before had been completely replaced by something otherworldly and menacing. She felt her chest constrict in a sob as she looked toward Jack and saw that his once pale complexion now resembled that of whatever it was that had possessed Ms. Biggs' body.

The new creature inside of Ms. Biggs didn't respond for a moment, but instead smiled, which was especially unsettling because its mouth opened to a chasm of darkness. "I smell you, Favoured, and your magick too." The creature spoke with a strange accent, and its words ended with a sound somewhere between a groan and a hiss.

"P-please. I don't know what is happening. I need to help Jack and my parents." Amanda was cut off as the monster suddenly darted toward her – like a shark skimming the surface of the water. It grabbed Amanda's hand and pulled her free from her confinement, shattering the ice.

Hoisting Amanda into the air, the ice-clad monster inspected the cut along the side of Amanda's hand. It pulled away suddenly and dropped Amanda into the snow. "You reek of it – of them. Why are you here and not with your brethren?"

Amanda reeled. "I don't know what you are talking about. Please, we have to help Jack. Look at him!"

"I care not for mortals, Favoured. I felt your magick through my Jotuns, and I smell it on you like the noxious odor of spring. I came to eliminate the foolish one who prevented my Jotuns from doing their work. Did the Prelate send you? Answer quickly or I will make you suffer in ways that would make Hel herself turn you away from her gates." The dark creature raised a hand and a host of blue flakes rained from the sky, finding their way to various snowmen and embankments. Within seconds more of the enormous cavemen had formed, beating their chests and breaking off tree branches for clubs as a swarm of blue devils spread throughout the cul-de-sac.

Amanda sobbed, "Ms. Biggs... or... whoever you are... please, I..." Her body felt like it was shutting down. The cold was surging into her muscles, sapping any strength or concentration she tried to maintain.

"Ms. Biggs no longer resides in this body, mortal. I am Bergelmir, Lord of the Frost Jotuns." Bergelmir whirled about as something struck him from behind. "Who dares?"

"Ms. Biggs, I think you've gotten knocked in the head. Who comes up with a name like Bergelmir? Let's go inside, figure out how to turn your face back into something that looks remotely normal, and leave Amanda alone." Jack was standing in the divot that had been left by the snowspider's transformation. He had hurled one of the jagged pieces of the fence at Bergelmir and held another like a spear.

"Jack!" Amanda cried out in relief.

"You dare to tell me what to do? How is your soul not mine by my imp's touch? Your skin betrays that you have been tainted, and yet you still stand." Bergelmir paused and then leered as he raised a hand toward Jack. Looking back at Amanda, "Since you refuse to tell me what I wish to know, let us see if this loosens your tongue."

Amanda felt the coldness of the night air coalesce. A beam of blue energy crackled and spun toward Jack from Bergelmir's outstretched hand. Jack leapt toward Bergelmir and hurled the fence post with all his might as the beam connected with his chest. There was the sound of a tree branch snapping and Jack vanished. Bergelmir batted the missile from the air, sending it into Ms. Biggs' car, revealing the prone forms of Amanda's parents.

"Jack! No!" Amanda sobbed. "You monster. You killed him!"

Bergelmir snapped and Amanda's parents were lifted from the ground and came to hang between Amanda and Bergelmir. "Wait! No!"

"This will be your final chance. Clearly you care for these mortals. Are they your family? Tell me what brought you to Midgard, away from your protectors, and perhaps these mortals will live to see tomorrow's dawn. Deny me, and they will feed my Jotuns." The cavemen shuffled forward, hunched over and walking on their knuckles, until they formed a semicircle around Amanda and Bergelmir.

"Ms. Biggs, I mean Bergelmir – PLEASE STOP THIS!" Burning green light like liquid fire flared around Amanda. She tried to force it to attack Bergelmir, but it vanished before it could reach him. The sound of a raven broke through the night and Amanda looked up to see two dark gray outlines fade into the clouds above.

Bergelmir had pulled his cloak in front of him at Amanda's outburst. When she collapsed, he moved forward but stopped at the sound of the cawing birds. "Ravens," Bergelmir started and then stopped. "Jotuns, gather this Favoured and the two mortals! We must be away from here at once!"

"No!" Amanda screamed and flung herself toward her mom and dad. There was another blinding flash of green light and Amanda's parents vanished.

Bergelmir held up a fist. "Hold, Jotuns! Favoured you are, and yet your favouring is unknown to me. Its magick is not like the others I have experienced. It is a favouring of... magick alone."

Before Amanda could react, Bergelmir's eyes widened and he roared as he sent a swirling blast of ice toward her, gathering anything it touched as it rushed forward.

The sound of a raven's call reverberated around Amanda. A kaleidoscope of rainbow-colored light blossomed in an arc that intercepted Bergelmir's attack, stopping it only feet from where Amanda lay. A figure stepped through the blazing light and the light was refracted into the night as the arc's glow bounced off shiny white armor. Small feathers protruded up the back of the warrior's arm until they reached a glowing gauntlet that steamed from having blocked the blast that Bergelmir aimed at Amanda. Amanda's eyes were trying to readjust when several more arcs of light formed in the air beside her new protector, blinding her again.

The armored woman who appeared first looked to Amanda. "Fear not, child. No harm will come to you tonight." As two boys, a girl, and a woman in golden armor stepped from their own shimmering portals, the woman in white armor turned back toward Bergelmir, her red hair bright against the dark night. "You should not be here, Jotun. How have you found your way to Midgard after being barred from setting foot on its soil?"

"The Allfather is not as all-powerful as he would like to believe, Valkyrie. You should not have come, Prelate. You are not my match in this realm or any other."

"I fear no Jotun, and the Favoured are under my protection. I will always answer the call to defend them." The Prelate's fists drew apart and a golden glow surrounded her and Amanda.

Bergelmir pointed a finger to Amanda. "You would do well to tremble in her presence. I came to Midgard for other purposes, but she will be mine!" The Jotun fired three needles of ice and the giants converged.

"Lady Freyja, Sean, Connor – attend to the Jotuns! Cassie – protect the girl!" The ice projectiles melted as they came into contact with the field around Amanda and the Prelate.

The woman in gold armor flung back a cloak of black feathers and launched herself toward the nearest giant. Drawing a dark blade from her back, she began to hack away at the giant's forearm. Large chunks of ice flew to the ground with each swipe of her blade. The golden armor looped about her limbs in concentric circles, allowing the warrior woman to move freely. She landed with her legs bent, both hands holding her weapon, and she spun to find another target.

One of the two boys raised his fists, which looked like they were made of stone, and drove them into the ground. When his hands met the earth, a shockwave blasted toward two of the giants. While they were off balance, the other boy pulled a double-sided hammer from his belt. A jolt of blue electricity traveled up his hand and into the hammer, causing it to sizzle and snap. Swinging the hammer twice, he hurled it like an electric comet and shattered the legs of both giants. A second later, the hammer flew through the air into his hand. The boy twirled the hammer between his fingers as he crouched – ready to strike again.

"Hello." Amanda jumped as a girl with dark skin and a head full of black and pink curls landed beside her. Both the girl and the boys were wearing sky blue and gold bodysuits with golden discs on their shoulders that resembled balls of flames that had been stamped flat. "Nice to make your acquaintance. I'm Cassie."

"I… I'm Amanda." Amanda jumped again as the woman in white leapt toward Bergelmir, her fists flashing as she began to attack. "My parents… my friend, Jack. You've got to help them."

"We'll have you sorted in a moment." Cassie pushed Amanda aside and thrust out a hand. "Melt in pain, you buggers!"

Amanda turned to see a hill of the blue imps writhe suddenly and slowly dissolve into puddles. Two more giants loomed above Amanda and Cassie, holding uprooted trees for clubs. "Hey, Sis. Got yourself in another spot of trouble, have you?" The boy with rock-hands dashed forward and knocked the giant closest to Amanda off its feet.

"I could have handled it, Connor!" Cassie yelled.

"Imps are one thing. You know these Jotun giants don't feel anything except hunger. They're like bears waking up from hibernating," the other boy shouted. He threw his hammer through the shoulder of the last giant bearing down on the girls, sending the tree it was holding crashing down on top of Connor.

Amanda jumped up, afraid the boy had been crushed to death, but Cassie held her back. A fist tore through the tree and Connor pulled himself out. "Don't worry about Connor. It's pretty much impossible to hurt him, which he likes to remind us of constantly. I mean, I am no slouch, to be sure. You saw what I did to those imps." Cassie smiled at Amanda. "Hey, look there. The Prelate is about to take down Bergelmir!"

Amanda watched as yellow light encased the woman in white armor's fists as she hammered Bergelmir with lightning-fast fury. Bergelmir spun as a blow caught him on the shoulder and then his side. The Prelate brought her fists up to her sides and the yellow light crackled around her in waves. The light illuminated layered etching along the white metal that looked like wings. The bands around her wrists pulsed with each wave of surging light. "You will tell us how you broke through the barrier, Frost Jotun, and why you have invaded Midgard," ordered the Prelate.

Bergelmir fired several more blasts that missed the attacking warriors.

"Foolish Valkyrie, you are as narrow sighted as ever. Do you think you, a goddess, and a few mortal children can stop me?" Bergelmir bellowed to the giants, and they shifted to protect him as Lady Freyja and the Prelate began to attack them from all sides.

Freyja swung her cape in an arc and sliced through the armored leg of one of the giants. She then plunged her sword hilt-deep into the giant's furry side. Before she could remove the blade, Bergelmir sent a flurry of ice missiles toward the goddess. Lady Freyja jumped with both hands extended and sliced through the attack with the sharp talons at the end of her armored fingers. "Bah! You cannot win, Jotun! I am not just any goddess. I am the goddess of battle, and your head will hang in my hall as a trophy!" Retrieving her sword, Lady Freyja launched herself at Bergelmir. She began to swing her blade with greater ferocity, putting Bergelmir even more on the defensive. "It seems time has weakened you, frozen one, whereas it has made my blade only sharper!"

"I must agree with Lady Freyja, Bergelmir. Your advance is less than impressive. Perhaps your host is not as acquiescent to your presence as you had hoped. Or is it that my lord's spells are not as ineffectual as you claim?" The Prelate swung a fist toward Bergelmir. The yellow light from her gauntlets missed, and the Frost Jotun grabbed her arm.

"You think me weak?" Bergelmir's flat mouth widened in its grotesque smile. A surge of cold shook the Prelate's body. "Your epitaph shall be, 'She who underestimated the Lord of the Frost Jotuns, and paid with her life!'"

The Prelate's body violently jerked as ice began to creep along her arms, up to her neck, and across her cheeks. Jumping from behind a downed tree, Connor raised his clasped hands above his head, and then brought them down with all his might on Bergelmir's forearms. His hands looked like dark granite, and the impact sounded as if a boulder was cracking in two. The Jotun roared and pulled back at the unexpected attack, releasing the Prelate.

Freyja darted in while Bergelmir was distracted, but the Jotun snapped his fingers and the warrior flew into a swarm of imps. "Fools! I am winter's might! My strength lies in the magicks at my command. Watch as it tears you asunder." Flinging his hands out, deadly lances of magick tore through the night. Lady Freyja and the others cried out as they began to fall one by one under the attack.

The Prelate raised a fist to the sky. "We will never allow ourselves to fall at your hands when we have the protection of Asgard! I claim this child for Odin and for Asgard." Thunder clapped and lighting flashed, breaking up the clouds around them. A halo of golden fire encircled Amanda and the rest of her defenders.

Bergelmir roared and threw back his head. For a moment he stood and flexed his fingers. His magick still whirled about, but it could not penetrate the fiery protection that now enveloped them. Narrowing his eyes, he waved and the Jotun giants and imps began to crumble into shards of ice. "This is not over, warrior maid. Your spells may protect you for now, but it will not save you from the avalanche that shall descend upon you and your Favoured. The claiming magick's protection can only be enacted with a new Favoured, and she will be the last!" Before the Prelate could respond, Bergelmir slumped forward and a pale Ms. Biggs fell into the snow. The five defenders relaxed their stances and turned to the girl who cowered behind them.

CHAPTER 4:
GOLDEN GLOBES

"We should be out there finding the Frost Jotun, and defeating him once and for all! By the stars, why did the Prelate hesitate?"

Sean looked up from where he was crouched in the West's entryway. He was waving a rock the size of a skipping stone that glowed every time he passed it over the broken door. Acting like a magnet, the stone was attracting little bits of wood to fit back into the door's paneling, like a puzzle putting itself together. "Beggin' your pardon, Lady Freyja, ma'am, but that wasn't our objective. Both the Prelate and the Queen agreed we needed to get to the Favoured and bring her to Asgard safely. Besides, it isn't like the Prelate just stood by and let him waltz down the street. He up and vanished. I'm also pretty sure if the Prelate hadn't claimed Amanda when she did, we would have been in some serious trouble. That Bergelmir is feistier than a raccoon during camping season."

"All battles present opportunities that must be taken, and we are missing ours now. Bergelmir may have had the upper hand for a moment, but once the girl was claimed we should have descended on the Jotun. I say we leave her behind the claiming line and scout the area to see whether Bergelmir still remains. He may have jumped into another mortal his imps tainted." Freyja stalked around Amanda's living room, stopping every few steps to drop a stone similar to the one Sean held into a vase or behind a picture frame. Her cloak of feathers rustled as she slid around the couch.

"You think? He may not have made it to Niflheim, but why would he hang around here on Midgard?" Sean looked over to Amanda, who was sitting on the sofa. Once Bergelmir vanished, the Prelate and Sean had helped Amanda inside. She had been on the verge of a meltdown, so the Prelate had used a simple spell to calm Amanda down. Since then, she hadn't said a word, and only half seemed to be listening to them. "Besides, we can't leave Amanda here alone in the state she's in."

"I do not know why Bergelmir would stay on Midgard, but I sense his departure was not as final as you and the Prelate assume it to be. We waste time securing this mortal's home, and in doing so we lose our advantage." Freyja paused her pacing to look at Amanda. "And for a Favoured to be so overcome by shock… it makes me wonder if this evening was all for nothing."

"By order of Lord Odin, Lady Freyja, our first charge is the safety of all mortals. We were able to save a mortal from Bergelmir tonight. There is victory in that. She faced down a fierce foe, and the ravens told us she lost her friend and her parents in doing so. I think that shows remarkable stamina considering most mortals will never know but a shadow of what lies outside their realm. I seem to remember a time when you were beside yourself after facing Bergelmir as well." The Prelate came down the stairs, her gauntlets emanating a warm, golden light that scoured the walls, windows, and ceilings like a searchlight, leaving an almost invisible film on anything it touched.

Lady Freyja dismissed the Prelate's words. "That was different. The Jotun trickster had entombed my brother in the heart of a mountain in Hel. I traveled the wastelands of that wretched realm for months to rescue him, only to be attacked by Bergelmir just as Freyr was about to be consumed by a Hel bee swarm. I was justifiably tired after I turned the swarm toward Bergelmir."

"I believe the words you used at the time were, 'in shock.'"

"No kidding?" Sean laughed, and then quickly focused back to his task when Lady Freyja glared at him.

Amanda half turned as the Prelate made it to the bottom of the stairs. Her brain felt calm, even though there were strangers in strange armor in her home. For a moment she focused on their words. The two women spoke with an accent that almost sounded British; their vowels were elongated and slower, as if the words were mixed with something more ancient sounding. The boy, however, spoke with a Texan drawl.

The goddess turned and her golden armor reflected the light from a fire that glowed in the Wests' fireplace. "Regardless, she is now safe within this dwelling. Would it not be more prudent to figure out how the Lord of the Frost Jotuns came to Midgard, or, better yet, to defeat him? The Jotun could have taken residence in any number of mortals within this hamlet. Are we not concerned for their well-being? If not, then perhaps we should address the other disconcerting questions we are left with when we look at the events of this evening as a whole."

"Meaning what?" Sean paused over a large chunk of wood as it wobbled on the floor.

"Hugin and Munin have always been able to find the Favoured, but the Allfather made no mention that they were out scouting. How did they know to look for her? They also should not have known about her before you were alerted, Prelate. Could the ravens have been fooled into thinking there was another Favoured and brought us here to leave our realm open to an attack?"

"You really think someone could conjure up a spell that could fool two birds that hang out with Lord Odin on a daily basis to make us come to

Midgard?" Sean ducked his head when Lady Freyja glared at him again.

The Prelate came to stand between Amanda and the fireplace. Extending her hands, the dark marks on the Prelate's gauntlets flashed. "The runes confirm it. She has a favouring, Lady Freyja. The ravens saw her use magick – Asgardian magick. She is one of us. I do not know how the ravens knew before I did, but their magick and connection to the realms, the Allfather, and the Favoured have always been a mystery. Somehow, this girl is a Favoured."

Freyja made an exasperated noise. "Fine, so the ravens' message was true. That does not answer how and why the Jotuns were here on Midgard. The ravens summoned us to the Bifrost a scant few moments after Bergelmir appeared, but according to their accounting, there were other Jotun imps and giants already present that focused on Amanda only after she attacked two of their fold. That means she was not their primary target. Even Bergelmir said so. They had other purposes on Midgard tonight, and possibly have continued to further those aims while we delay here."

The Prelate nodded her head in agreement. "I do not deny that to be true. That is something we will focus on upon our return. Connor and Cassie should have made it to Queen Frigga with our message of the skirmish, and she will no doubt gather our warriors to be at the ready to scout the realm for traces of Bergelmir. Furthermore, I have no doubt Heimdall has put even more concentration into observing all he can in this realm since we left. If there remains a Jotun nearby or a mortal in jeopardy, he will send word, and the Queen will dispatch us back to Midgard to find them. I would think it best to be cautious and return with a host of warriors if Bergelmir is still about, as you suppose. He was weakened tonight, but even still he nearly bested our combined might."

"Speak of your own might and not of mine own strength. We should at least lay a trap for Bergelmir should he return." Freyja's black eyes narrowed as something occurred to her. "Or perhaps the trap has been sprung on us already. This evening could be nothing more than a ruse to bring this Favoured into our city, thinking she is our ally when really they plan to use her to strike at us while we are unsuspecting."

Sean tapped the stone in his hand. Its light had dimmed to barely a whisper of a glow. "That's a stretch. I'll admit it's a bit squirrely how everything went down tonight. However, from what Hugin and Munin said, Amanda is either one heck of an actress, or she really didn't know what to make of Bergelmir."

"We have given Amanda time to collect herself, and have secured the mortals' home from future attacks or magicks. Let us waken the girl from her stupor. I sense she is even now finding her way free from the spell I placed on her. She may provide us the answers you seek, Lady Freyja."

The Prelate raised a hand and sent a wave of sparkling light over Amanda.

The words and actions the others had spoken around her finally made some sense. Shifting from side to side, Amanda could feel her mind beginning to find its way out of the haze. There was a word, or a name, that was tugging at the edges of her mind.

"Bergelmir!" Amanda sat up with a shout, flinging her hands forward. There was a burst of green light and the mantle crumbled.

"You see? She calls for her master!" Freyja crossed the room and cupped Amanda's chin. The cat-like claws of her armored gloves pricked the sides of Amanda's face, causing the scratches from the sidewalk to sting. "Tell us child, where is the Jotun lord?"

"What are you talking about?" Amanda jerked her head away and scooted back into the pillows of the sofa. "Get away from me!"

"Lady Freyja – please. Give the child some space. She calls for no one but that which tormented her tonight." The other woman pushed Freyja back. "Steady, Amanda. Take deep breaths. I bespelled you to recover while we made your home secure. You must forgive Lady Freyja. Her temperament befits her warrior caste, but not for comforting those in distress or waiting to ask questions when the time is appropriate. Until your thoughts fully settle, perhaps we should start with some introductions. My name is Tess and I am the Prelate of Asgard. This is Sean Chord, a Favoured like you. He is the Favoured of Prince Thor. And this is the Goddess of War and Love, Lady Freyja."

"Asgard? As in the Norse gods?" Amanda vaguely remembered the different deities from when she studied how the days of the week got their names.

"The one and the same."

Amanda must have made a face because Sean laughed. "Now before you go calling the funny farm on us, just remember everything you saw tonight and try to tell me that you don't think there might be something to what she's sayin'. I know it's a big pill to swallow but it's real, just as real as you and me. By the way, you never did give us your name. Cassie said it was Amanda. Do you have a last name?"

"I… I'm Amanda. Amanda West."

"Howdy." Sean waved. Amanda just stared at him. He was tall and muscular with sandy blond hair and shocking blue eyes.

Brushing back her hair, Amanda leaned over her pillow. How could Norse gods be real? How could any of this be real? "What happened tonight? And what are you doing to my door?" Amanda pointed to the glowing stone Sean was holding.

"They're rune stones. The Prelate and Lady Freyja are putting them around the house to keep it safe, but this one here is a fixing rune. The Prelate has a ton of them that we use for different things like fixing doors when they get blown up. I burned two out putting your neighborhood back together.

Wish it could help that lady Bergelmir possessed with what she's going to go through when she wakes up." Sean looked out to the silent street.

"A fixing rune?" Amanda parroted. She wasn't sure what a rune was, but she had never seen anything fixed like that before.

"Sean, please. Let us not entangle Amanda's mind in magickal remedies when we have more important things to discuss." The Prelate's tone became more measured as she spoke next, "Tonight's events are due to what and who you are, Amanda. You are part of a great lineage, a favoured mortal that links your realm to the realm of the gods." Prelate Tess tapped several black figures that ringed the gold bands around her wrists. They flashed at her touch. Holding out a hand, three golden rolls of parchment-thin light appeared along the walls, opening like tapestries being unfurled from a long winter. Her voice grew deep and the room dimmed. "If you have heard of Asgard, then perhaps you have heard that what you call Earth is but one of nine realms." At her words, eight orbs appeared, with another in the center. The Prelate pointed to each of the orbs as she spoke. "Asgard is the realm of the gods. It sits amongst the clouds and looks down on all other realms. Vanaheim is a realm of sea and forests. Alfheim is the realm of the fair and light, while Svartalfheim is a realm of fell darkness and rocky caverns. Jotunheim, Muspelheim, and Niflheim are of mountains, fire, and ice, respectively. Hel is for the dead. And lastly, Midgard is where we are now, for the mortals." The last orb, Midgard, was the one that hung in the center.

"Long ago the other realms were all but destroyed in a battle called Ragnarok. The fire demon, Surtur, and those who joined him in his treachery, cast a spell that engulfed the realms. The spell took anyone it touched and transformed them into Surtur's army of living dead before consuming them completely. The realms fought, but alas were no match for the fell magick that had been unleashed. In our last moments, the Norn, the fates of Asgard, gave us a way to save ourselves from annihilation. The price was an exchange."

The banners rippled and began to show a swirl of people, and then warriors dressed like Freyja and the Prelate in shining armor, fighting monsters so grotesque that it made Amanda's nightmares seem like fairy tales. Skeletal creatures engulfed in flames rose from a wave of oil and ash that washed through the land, and sucked the life out of the warriors who fought it, only to become like their attackers. Giant, winged bats with three heads snatched the warriors from the ground and cast them into chasms of fire that fueled the dark spell as it continued its invasion. The scenes shifted to different lands made of rocky caverns, beautiful gardens, and deep seas that raged in battles of galactic proportion. Eventually, the fiery army completely overwhelmed the warriors that were defending their homes. The images faded and, as one, all three banners showed the Prelate standing in a circle with other warrior women as a blazing sun burst forth and came into

Amanda's living room. The ball of golden flames spun once and began casting off tiny stars, two of which landed on Sean and Amanda.

"The Norn gave us the Spell of Favouring. The spell required a sacrifice, however. It required the lives of my sisters, the Valkyrie, who were the defenders of the Nine Realms. The Valkyrie were the fist of Asgard's army, and feared by any who dared to disrupt the peace we fought for. We had magick over life and death, and it was that magick the spell needed to fuel its purpose. And so, my sisters willingly gave up their lives, but the spell required one of us to stay amongst the living to act as the focus of the spell. The Norn told us that the one remaining would still lose their magick, but they would bear the gauntlets that would wield a power to defend the Favoured to come. It was decided that I should carry that honor. Once the spell was cast, it stopped the fires of Ragnarok and brought about a rebirth to the realms. It also bound the lives of certain mortals of Midgard to the gods of Asgard. Once every hundred years the spell must be renewed in order to prevent Ragnarok's return. During a period of nine years, mortals are chosen to be favoured with the magick of the gods. Whether it is by their nature, by their deeds, or by their affinity to the elements, they are chosen to be our champions and protectors by being given a small amount of the gods' magick by the Spell of Favouring. The Spell of Favouring grants magick to the mortals chosen, and for a time the gods teach their Favoured and do battle with them. While the realms have been rebuilt and now thrive again, there are still those that hunger for power and destruction, and they must be stopped. That is the role of the gods except during the time the Spell of Favouring is enacted. When the spell so chooses, however, it takes the remaining might from the gods to renew itself and keep Ragnarok's flames at bay. During this time the rest of the Nine Realms rely on the Favoured to defend them. Once the spell is complete, the magick of the gods is restored to them until the spell must again be refueled in a hundred years' time. The mortals who exchanged their lives to defend the realms can choose what their fate shall be once the spell takes back the magick of the gods. Some stay on Asgard, some return to Midgard."

"These gauntlets not only channel the remaining magick of my sisters, but also are used to find, train, teach, protect, and lead the Favoured when they are chosen. Even though it was the ravens who found you, it is these gauntlets that tell me you are one of us – that you have Asgardian magick." The gauntlets around the Prelate's wrists flashed as she held them up.

"So, you're saying that I have… magick?" Amanda looked around the room at the others as they nodded.

Sean paused his work on the door and held up his hand. It crackled with blue energy as the smell of ozone filled the room. "You're a Favoured, just like me. Just like Cassie and Connor you met tonight as well. We all have a bit of our benefactors' magick. I get my powers from Prince Thor. He's the god of thunder, so I can charge things with electricity and do a few other storm-related magickal tricks. I think the spell chose me because I used to love watching storms with my dad back in Texas. Cassie is Lady Freyja here's Favoured." Lady Freyja scowled at Sean's words and paced around the room. "As Cassie tells it, she could always kind of tell what people were feeling before her Favouring. Now, since Lady Freyja is a goddess of love and war, Cassie can turn any emotion her enemies feel into a weapon."

Amanda reached out to tap a piece of the golden parchment that rolled onto her foot. It shimmered as she ran her finger over its surface. "Bergelmir said something about me being a Favoured. He said he felt my magick through his imps. Who is my benefactor? Who does my magick come from?"

Freyja moved to the window to stare at something outside. Her golden armor and the way she prowled about made her look like a cat ready to pounce. "If your favouring is from whom we suspect, then I say we are all the more foolish for not sending you straight to the Gruneling."

Amanda's stomach felt like it was full of lead as she heard both the condemnation and accusation in Lady Freyja's words. "What do you mean? What's wrong with my... favour... um favouringly?"

"Favouring," Sean corrected with a smile. "It's like this, Amanda. After a millennium of having only fifty Favoured, you now make fifty-one. And the one who we think is your benefactor was one of the traitors who turned against Asgard and helped cause its destruction during Ragnarok." Sean tapped the side of his leg with nervous energy.

"Why do you think my magick comes from them?" Amanda watched as they exchanged looks.

The dying coals illuminated the Prelate's armor, showing the tracery that wound over the smooth surfaces. "Because of what the ravens Hugin and Munin told us, and what we witnessed when you awoke. The spell usually begins to act upon mortals at a very young age, causing a variety of strange events to occur. Sean called up an electrical storm that caused his entire town to lose power. Others have caused unusual crops to grow or fish to suddenly appear to save a sinking ship. Usually we are alerted to a Favoured's presence by my gauntlets and have the ravens find them around the age of nine. If I am not mistaken, you are four years older than that, and first found your magick today. Somehow the ravens knew before we did and found you, and from what they witnessed, there is but one goddess from whom you could gain such a favouring – a favouring of spells and magick."

Freyja frowned and made an exasperated sound. "I am going to inspect the claiming line, to see whether I can find a trace of Bergelmir. Perhaps there can still be some good to come from this evening's adventures. If you continue with this one, do not say you were not warned when she turns on us like her benefactor."

The goddess banged her fist to her chest and strode out the nearly completed door into the cold. Amanda watched the goddess pace around her front yard and then down the street. "Why does she talk about me like I'm a bomb about to explode? I didn't ask for any of this."

"Lady Freyja doesn't trust mortals in general, but in your case it's a bit more than that because of your benefactor and what your favouring could bring." The last piece of the wood popped into place and the red door slammed shut as Sean spoke. He ruffled the hair on his head and then rubbed the back of his neck.

Prelate Tess nodded gravely. "We believe that your benefactor is Sigyn. She is the wife of Loki, and an enchantress. The magick you performed today were spells that have no link to any of the other gods. Sigyn could create spells and wield magick to rival Lord Odin, and as Sean stated she also aided Surtur and Loki during Ragnarok. I do not see your connection to her yet, but Lady Freyja is concerned of what it could be."

"Oh. So... Sigyn? I get my magick from her?"

Sean and Prelate Tess nodded. Amanda repeated the name again in her head. It sounded like the words sea and gin put together. Amanda took a moment to process Sean and the Prelate's words. She was linked to a goddess that caused destruction and harm to all of the Nine Realms. Maybe the spell meant to choose Ms. Biggs but got her instead. "H-how do we tell? How can we know for sure?"

Prelate Tess pulled a golden disc from a bag at her side. "This is the symbol of Asgard reborn; a golden flame that can never be extinguished. We wear this medallion as a reminder of from whence we came and how everything was almost lost. If you will accept your new fate, then place it upon your shoulder and repeat these words: 'On the Wings of Asgard.' The spell inside will tell us who your benefactor is."

Amanda took the disc. The metal was warm to the touch. "Are you sure about this?" Amanda suddenly remembered Jack and her parents. "My friend... my parents... they were killed tonight because of me. Why would you still want me? I mean, all the things you just said about my benefactor make it sound like Lady Freyja might be right."

The Prelate paused as a thought occurred to her, and then stretched her fingers out toward the street. Amanda looked to Sean for an explanation, but he just held up his hands for Amanda to wait. A soft chorus of whispers entered the room and coalesced around the Prelate. The Prelate relaxed her stance and shook her head. "There has been no death here tonight."

Amanda's heart quickened. "Are you sure? I saw Bergelmir attack Jack and then my parents vanished. I... I thought maybe Bergelmir did it, but maybe it was me."

"I may not control death, but I am still a Valkyrie. I can still sense death's presence, and there was no death of a mortal in this neighborhood. The ravens told us of the attack, but I did not think to look for their deathmarks earlier as I assumed as you did that they were no longer amongst the living. If they were not killed here, Bergelmir must have spirited your friend away. Your parents though, may have been sent elsewhere by your magicks. We will search for them and bring them home."

At these words, Amanda sobbed in relief. She closed her eyes and clasped the disc in both hands. "Thank you."

Sean came and laid a hand on Amanda's shoulder. "Bergelmir is the one who did all of this tonight. We don't know how or why he came to Midgard, but we will find out, and find a way to make sure your friend and parents are OK. You'll get your people back. I swear on my dad's Ford F-350. You were chosen for a reason, and we need all the help we can get. It's not just the Jotuns we have to worry about. We monitor the realms for all kind of trouble. Sometimes it's a pack of sea serpents that have gotten through from Vanaheim; sometimes it's woodland sprites from Alfheim. You can never tell. There's the Bifrost to guard, missions to the other realms, and patrolling Asgard's defenses. Once you get up to speed, I'm sure you'll see how useful you can be. Things won't always seem this bad."

The Prelate's eyes flashed, and she looked battle ready. "Well spoken, Favoured of Thor. We have many mysteries to solve from this evening, but we will do it together."

"Then I am coming to Asgard to help. No matter what anyone thinks of my benefactor, I am going to save Jack and my parents."

Standing, Amanda placed the disc on her shoulder. A wind rushed through the room, and the same sad-yet-happy notes Amanda had heard earlier that morning echoed in her ears. Taking a deep breath, Amanda repeated the Prelate's words: "On the Wings of Asgard."

As she spoke, the room filled with a blinding light, transforming her clothes into the same uniform Sean wore. Blue pants and combat boots replaced her snow pants and snowshoes. A fitted tunic with a gold chest piece wrapped her torso. A layered belt was the final piece that appeared to complete her new uniform. She flexed her hands as golden gloves appeared. It felt hard like armor, but soft and flexible.

A flaming symbol appeared in front of Amanda and she breathed out its meaning without knowing how she knew what it meant, "Sigyn."

"Aye. You are her Favoured. Welcome." The Prelate touched her fist to her chest and Sean mimicked her.

Before Amanda could respond, the door flew open and Lady Freyja darted in, knocking Sean and the coatrack to the floor. She made a face when she saw Amanda's transformation. "We have little time left, Prelate. The claiming line is fading faster than normal. I cannot see the Jotun, but I can feel his magick attacking our protection. I also found these." Freyja held out her hand, which held two brown mice. Amanda recoiled.

"Why do you turn away child? Do you not recognize your own kin? I would know this spell in any realm. Sigyn's magick is no doubt your own, as it is your own magick that turned these two mortals into these pitiful creatures. It is something your benefactor has done on numerous occasions. I wouldn't try to transform them again until you know your magick better. You wouldn't want to do them more harm."

"You're saying those are my parents?" Amanda looked at Freyja for some sign that this was all an elaborate joke, but the goddess's face held no mirth. Amanda's mouth quivered as she reached out to take the two mice. One squeaked in such a way she could almost imagine it was yelling at her for what she had done. Tears streaked Amanda's face as she pressed them to her cheek. "Thank you, Lady Freyja."

Lady Freyja sniffed. The Prelate saluted the goddess. "It seems the Norn are helping us to fulfill our promise already, thanks to you, Lady Freyja."

Sean jumped as the sound of bells invaded Amanda's living room, followed by a flash of light as the fiery ring around the house vanished. "Time to go, y'all." Sean scooped up Amanda's parents and put them in the pouch that hung from his waist. "I'll take your parents with me, Amanda."

Prelate Tess moved to the center of the room and raised her fists upwards as a sound like a runaway train shook the walls. Freyja and Sean took positions beside Amanda. "Say your farewell, Favoured of Asgard, for tonight we journey to the Golden Realm." As Prelate Tess brought both hands down, the air was disturbed by her movement and shimmered with brilliant colors. An oval shaped portal opened in the middle of Amanda's living room and, one by one, they walked into the light.

***

Opening his eyes through yet another mortal, Bergelmir shuddered at the feeling of his magick being reduced to being contained within the pudgy shell he now wore. It had taken more magick than he had expected to transform his last host and battle the wretched Asgardians, so now he was forced to retain the mortal's form. Fuming with rage, Bergelmir fumbled with the sheets the mortal boy had been sleeping under a moment before. One of his imps chittered at him and pointed to the window at the end of the bedroom as Bergelmir freed himself. Stalking toward the gray light from outside, Bergelmir began to weave dark spells and sent his magick toward the mortal girl's house. The claiming line shuddered. Bergelmir continued his assault, even as Freyja came out into the yard. He muttered spells that would have sent the goddess to an icy grave, but they bounced off the protections set about by the mortal girl's claiming. The goddess must have sensed the attacks, for she darted back inside. A few moments later the house was lit from inside with a blinding flash and Bergelmir knew it was too late.

Turning, Bergelmir banished the imp as he uttered a two-syllable word. "Myrkr!" As the imp's form crumbled, a vortex of black magick formed before him.

A voice drifted from the void. "The news must be great for you to risk such communication. Speak quickly."

If Bergelmir's voice was ice, this voice was pure bone and shadow. If there were other mortals in the house, Bergelmir was sure they would have nightmares from the sound. "The Prelate found my Jotuns on Midgard."

"And you as well, I surmise. Did she discover the reason or how you broke the Allfather's spell?"

Bergelmir struck the wall beside him. "She was preoccupied with other matters."

"Then there is no reason for us to risk her doing so now by this communication."

"That is not all. There has been another Favoured claimed."

The blackened air rippled as the voice emanated forth. "We should not rush to conclusions, Jotun lord."

"Her favouring is of magick. It is not based in the elements or anything else we have seen from the Favoured before. Only those who returned after the fire of Surtur will know what this means. If we are to believe the words of the spell, then not even the Norn can escape their own web. Her appearance was foretold." Bergelmir growled in the back of his throat.

The dark swirl began to fade and the voice spoke again: "My power wains, but soon I shall be free to join you. Engage our contacts in the Golden Realm. Have them begin the summons so we may take advantage of the distraction this Favoured will bring. Perhaps she shall mature into a weapon, but for now our plan still holds."

Their first meeting happened centuries ago, but still the dark power and the promise of revenge made Bergelmir clench his fists with anticipation. "I will relay your message, and will continue to further our plan here on Midgard. My troops will stand at the ready to smash the Asgardians when we deem the time to be right." Gnashing his teeth, Bergelmir looked to the stars and the house trembled at his rage. With that, the Jotun and dark vortex vanished, leaving nothing but the unconscious form of Billy Bunson lying on the floor of his bedroom. An imp wriggled through a crack in the window frame, and jumped onto Billy. The imp drew a mark in the air, and Billy vanished.

CHAPTER 5:
RAINBOW BAGGAGE

Light and color mixed together around Amanda as she rocketed toward a blinding light. A wash of green passed over her hand, staining the skin slightly as it curled around her fingers. Her arms were pressed to her sides due to the speed at which they traveled, but she could swivel her head to see Prelate Tess ahead of her with Sean and Lady Freyja on either side. Images collided together around them, making it feel as if they were flying through a giant kaleidoscope. Amanda thought she saw her school and then the Eiffel Tower, and then as if someone flipped a switch everything went dark.

Blinking to try and adjust to the sudden change, Amanda felt something solid form under her feet. Tiny pinpricks of light began to flicker into existence in the distance and then rushed toward her. Amanda gasped as she realized she was seeing stars. They ranged in size from no bigger than a baseball, to one that was as large as Wreathen Middle School's gymnasium. Light began to fill in the darkness around them, and Amanda could see they were standing on a giant stone disc with nothing between them and empty space but a golden railing. Above them was a canopy of arches that looked like a white, curvy trellis. Where the arches met, illuminated lamps rotated like balloons hovering on the ceiling. Amanda's knees wobbled and she felt the familiar sensation of falling.

"Careful there, rainbow travel takes some getting used to." Sean quickly reached out and caught Amanda's arm. After righting her he patted some glittering dust from her shoulders.

"That was incredible." Amanda brushed her tousled hair from her face.

"Most efficient way to get around. It can be a bit draining on us Favoured, though." Sean nodded to the railing. "The first time I did it by myself I nearly fell off into space. We'll show you how to summon a portal to travel by yourself after you've mastered a bit of your magick."

Amanda turned to follow Sean as he turned away from the sea of stars, "Whoa."

Up three massive steps, the dark horizon of space was broken by a celestial metropolis. Everything inside the city was tinted a pale shade of yellow by concentric rings of translucent gold that formed a perfect sphere around the tiered levels of Asgard. A trio of warriors in golden armor like Lady Freyja's soared around on the backs of winged horses, and then through the realm's shields toward them.

"Welcome to the Golden Realm of Asgard. This is the Bifrost, the bridge that connects our realm to all others." Prelate Tess pointed just ahead of them to a jeweled gate that opened onto a wide road. It spanned at least a dozen football fields in length from where they stood over empty space to the city. The bridge shifted colors and flashed merrily, as if it was made of electric rainbows. The gate itself was framed by an arch of white marble that ended in two towers on each side. Sean moved to the side of the platform as another portal opened. The travelers who emerged wore green tunics woven from blades of grass. "Takes your breath away, doesn't it?"

A giant tree towered over the uppermost parts of Asgard with long, leafy bowers and a trunk that gleamed with an iridescent light. Clouds gathered around its middle and the underside of the lower branches. It swayed and seemed to reach out to welcome Amanda. "It's beautiful. What is that tree?"

"The World Tree, Yggdrasil. Every creature and realm is connected to each other by its roots, and from it comes the three Great Stars that provide us light." The Prelate scanned the steps in front of them while Amanda continued to take it all in.

Beyond the golden sphere around Asgard, hazy mountains rose to the east, with the tip of the tallest peak piercing a large crescent-shaped cloud. There were huts on stilts that stood on the plains leading up to the cliffs, and Amanda could just make out a crystal palace that looked like pleated folds of diamonds that merged seamlessly into the mountainside. Rolling hills of green and a forest of white-bark trees with golden leaves sparkled to the west.

The Prelate looked to Freyja, who was pacing unhappily behind Amanda, "Where is Cassie? She should be here by now. She was to report here after notifying the Queen about Bergelmir. There are matters that need to be dealt with, including finding Amanda's friend, along with our own account to be given to Keeper Fulla and Queen Frigga."

Before Amanda could ask what a Keeper was, she spotted a streak of sky blue and gold barrel through the gate, nearly knocking over two guards. Sliding to a stop at the top of the steps, Cassie leaned over, panting, "Sorry I'm late! There was a traffic jam by the Mead Hall. I bumped into an Aesir, who dumped a pitcher of water from Mimir's well onto a bear carrying sulfur sand, which blew up like an inflatable raft – but much stickier. It took two rune stones to get my feet out."

Freyja clenched her jaw. "Cassandra Pritchett, did you stop for a meal? Your orders were to be quick and not tarry. Time is of the essence. We need to see if we can return in time to defeat Bergelmir before he returns to Niflheim."

The girl hopped down each step and bound over to the group. She stopped in front of the angry goddess and gave an awkward curtsy. "I know, I know, but you know how hungry I get after I use my magick. Plus, that Aesir stepped in front of me. And again, please don't call me Cassandra. It's Cassie."

"Maybe another week of cleaning the Rimstock stables will help you to remember to quicken your pace and not be so concerned with food." Freyja folded her cloak over her arm and undid a pin from her hair, allowing it to fall into a long ebony ponytail.

Cassie swallowed hard and her eyes fluttered with embarrassment as she shook her head vigorously. "No need for that, Lady Freyja. I will not be late again, I promise. How you doing, Amanda? Feel like you landed somewhere west of Oz?"

"Something like that." Amanda felt awkward as everyone stared at her for a moment. "Uh, Sean, how are my parents doing?"

"Your parents? You mean they're here?" Cassie looked around the platform.

"They're doing just fine. Here." Sean opened the pouch he had put Keith and Liz in and pulled them out. Amanda gently lifted her parents and examined them. The mice looked identical except one seemed to have a tuft of hair that suspiciously reminded Amanda of her mother's bun.

"Aw. How cute!" Cassie put a hand to her head, "Whoa!"

"What?" Amanda shielded her parents protectively against her chest.

"That mouse with the barmy hair is not happy. Actually, not happy would be a giant step up from what it is feeling."

"That must be mom! You can tell what she's feeling? What about my dad? Are they OK?" Amanda brought her parents closer to Cassie.

"May I?" Cassie held out her hand. "If I can touch them, I can get a clearer picture."

Amanda moved to place her parents in Cassie's hand when one of the mice, the one who looked most disapprovingly at Amanda, nipped at her finger. "Ow! Um, maybe later? Sorry, Mom."

Prelate Tess cleared her throat, pulling the girls' attention back. "Cassie, I was hoping you would be Amanda's roommate and help her adjust to living here in Asgard. It seems fitting since your current roommate has asked to be moved."

"It was just a misunderstanding." Cassie dug the toe of her boot into the stone platform.

A commotion coming from the Bifrost prevented the Prelate from replying. "Prelate Tess! Prelate Tess!" A gruff voice called from a stocky ball of yellow fur that was lumbering toward them.

Waving at them was a three-fingered hand wrapped in thick leather straps. Coming to a stop in front of the Prelate, the diminutive creature and Amanda eyed each other warily for a moment. The furry stump scowled, and then smiled with large white teeth as he turned to address Prelate Tess. "Prelate Tess, I've brought ye the latest reports from the frontlines."

Cassie leaned over toward Amanda and whispered, "That's a Dwarf. Not quite what you were expecting I bet."

Amanda raised an eyebrow. "How did you know that's what I was wondering? Did you... sense it?"

Cassie smiled and shook her head. "No need. It's what we all go through when we first get here."

Tess saluted the Dwarf. "My thanks, Thram. How do our efforts go in Svartalfheim?"

As the Dwarf handed a scroll to the Prelate, Amanda continued to study him. The Dwarf's height was what one would expect, only coming up to Amanda's shoulders. He was clad in bulky armor made of carved stone, which glinted faintly with tiny chips that bore runes. His yellow coloring came from the short fur that covered every part of his body except for the mop of brown hair. Amanda thought he looked like an overgrown armadillo.

Thram whipped his head around and caught Amanda staring. "Keep your eyes to yourself, lass." Spinning back to the Prelate, "The latest reports are that the gods are locked in a skirmish with some errant trolls. The craggy lot has holed up in a cavern under Nidavellir."

"Can Tyr and Tiki not simply collapse the cavern and crush the bottom dwellers?" Freyja looked only slightly less disgusted when she spoke to Thram than she did when she addressed Amanda.

Thram ground his flat teeth at the goddess's words. "They took out several of the bridges and supports that hold our kingdom aloft. If they collapse the cave, it could destroy the homes of many of my people. Lord Tyr and Lord Tiki are managing what they can, but my lord is requesting any other aid you can send. We care more about the safety of others, and discovering how the trolls made it this close to the surface, than winning a hollow victory. Something you would know a bit about Lady Freyja."

"Watch your words, you misaligned ball of fur." Freyja sharpened the tips of her gauntlets as she spoke without looking at Thram.

Prelate Tess handed the scroll back to Thram. "Sean – I want you to find Cassie's brother, take a dozen triads of Einherjar with you, and see if you can aid our brethren. Lord Odin is settling a dispute amongst the Vanir and will want the gods to have returned when he is finished; especially with the appearance of Bergelmir. Thram, you may return to Svartalfheim and tell the gods and your lord we shall send support to help defeat their enemy." Thram bowed deeply and took off toward the bridge, but not before glaring at Amanda and Lady Freyja.

"Well, you got off easy. The first time I met Thram, he had me on my back and questioned me for twenty minutes before he thought I wasn't a threat. Sorry to rainbow and run, but I'm sure I will see you around for training. Welcome to Asgard!" Sean waved and ran off after Thram.

"And we should be on our way as well," added Prelate Tess as she led them up the steps.

"Is there a war going on?" Amanda asked. She hadn't been able to follow much of what was being said, but she picked up on the word "skirmish." Amanda's stomach lurched as she remembered when she heard the word for the first time. Jack had been helping her with her homework on the Revolutionary War, and that word came up a lot when they talked about the battles.

"Tis nothing to be concerned over. The gods teach their Favoured when they can, but the Nine Realms also require much of their attention. Currently they are dealing with several incursions that merit their might, but will return once the situations are dealt with." A skiff led by two goats carrying a load of cauldrons skidded past them. Cassie had to jump out of the way to avoid being run over.

"What about Sigyn?" The other travelers around them paused as the group approached the gate to the Bifrost. Everyone was peering around one another to see who the new mortal girl was. "Is she with them as well?"

"Your benefactor is where she has been kept since the time of rebirth – her prison." Freyja gave Amanda a sly smile.

Amanda felt her face color and looked away from the goddess. "You never said she was still in prison." Amanda looked to the Prelate.

Freyja laughed. "What did you expect? That we would let the traitor who aided Surtur by creating the spell that almost wiped out all of existence run free?"

Amanda swallowed hard. "So that's why you were worried about my favouring."

Cassie made a sound somewhere between a squeak and a hiccup. She had just finished yelling at the drivers who had nearly turned her into a blue stain on the street. "So, it's true then? Amanda's the Favoured of Sigyn? I mean Hugin and Munin said so, but I never thought it could be true."

Prelate Tess clasped her hands behind her back. The light from above made her red hair look like fiery waves as it fell down her back. "Aye, Cassie."

Cassie looked impressed. "Well isn't that the bee's knees? That is, if you don't turn out like she did."

Freyja moved behind Amanda. Taking a swipe at a small star passing by, the goddess's talons ripped the orb into pieces. "That is the first sensible thing you have said, Cassandra. Enchantresses are a dangerous bunch."

"Well, let us see if that is so," said a soft voice from a corner hidden behind the gate as they arrived. Stepping from the shadows was the most beautiful man Amanda had ever seen. He wore long white robes that swaddled his body and covered most of his golden armor. "If you are going to question the girl's motives, perhaps you should allow me to see if she is worthy of passing onto the Bifrost."

Prelate Tess extended a hand, "Amanda, I am pleased to introduce you to Heimdall, Gatekeeper of the Rainbow Bridge."

"Welcome to the crossroads, Amanda West. I have been watching you since the Allfather's ravens told us of your presence. You have been on quite the journey to come to us, but all who desire to enter Asgard's golden realm must pass through here, and by me, first. Those with pure intentions I let pass, those with fell hearts will be challenged, and those that try to hide from me will be discovered; for I can see and hear almost anything in all of the Nine Realms." The curved horn that hung from a slender chain around Heimdall's shoulders swung forward as he placed a hand on the crystalline and golden gate.

"Is there... do you give them... me some kind of a test?" Amanda felt everyone watching her as she spoke.

"I can discern intent by simply observing my subject for a moment. The answers I seek lie on the surface of their skin and in the twitch of their eyes." The golden disc of flames on Heimdall's shoulder shimmered as a star flew past them.

Amanda swallowed, stood up straight, and tried not to fidget. "What do you see when you look at me?"

When Heimdall spoke again his eyes flashed blue, then red, then green. "I see nothing but concern for your family and friend. You have a fire within you that is most admirably ready to fight those who have wronged you. Fair maiden, I deem you worthy to carry on to the Golden Realm."

"Way to go, Amanda!" Cassie patted Amanda on the back.

Freyja crossed her arms and scowled. "Just because Heimdall approves of her does not mean she will not betray us in the future."

"Lady Freyja, that is quite enough. She is one of us and shall be treated as such. I expect you to train her as you have trained all the other Favoured before her," countered the Prelate as she and the goddess squared off.

"As Prelate, your roles are to teach and guard our realm. Lord Odin shall most certainly not concur with this breach of our safety."

Stepping forward, her gauntlets flashing, the Prelate suddenly seemed to tower over Lady Freyja even though she was a good head shorter than the goddess. "Lord Odin decreed at the time of rebirth, that as our fates are tied to the mortals we shall find and watch over all the Favoured, and until either the Spell of Favouring ends, or I perish, that is what we shall do. While the gods are away, you and I must remain with the Favoured to continue their training – all of them. Oh, by the Eye, what now?" Prelate Tess turned toward the bridge as another commotion could be heard.

Hurrying toward them was a portly woman wearing a yellow and black dress with an apron tied at her waist. As she passed people on the bridge, they pulled away and covered their faces with a look of disgust. When she passed Heimdall, he took a step back, blinked, and wrinkled his nose. "Keeper Fulla, by your odiferous smell...do you carry frost lilies?"

"My apologies, Heimdall, but I had to deliver a supply of them to Eir's Manor. There has been an outbreak of alfblot, and the flowers were needed for a remedy should anyone become infected." The woman had dark brown hair with threads of gray, and was only slightly taller than the Prelate. Her dress ended above her ankles to reveal worn leather boots that were spattered with dark spots. The way she spoke gave Amanda a sense that she was constantly nervous about something. Her eyes darted around the group, pausing at Amanda. Turning, she wrung her hands with worry, "Prelate, I am so glad you have returned."

"And with our newest Favoured," the Prelate indicated Amanda. "Amanda, this is Keeper Fulla; she assists us in our daily tasks."

"Stars above." Fulla looked at Amanda oddly; something she was starting to assume she would have to get used to for a while. "So, it is really true what you said in your message? I just received word from the Queen."

"Aye, Fulla, there was an attack by Bergelmir."

Fulla gave a small squeak and clutched her apron. "So, the Frost Jotuns have begun to stir. This will upset the order around here indeed. I should set out some extra rune stones, prep the vindsvolla, and then..."

Prelate Tess laid a hand on the agitated woman's shoulder. "Peace, Keeper Fulla. All we know is that Bergelmir found a way to break the wards to enter Midgard. Let us not rush to panic." The Prelate turned to Heimdall. "Did you observe our battle or anything of use afterward? Did you see Bergelmir, or where the Jotun disappeared to?"

Heimdall slowly nodded as a band of warriors passed them, but then shook his head. "Apologies Prelate, I did watch as you set off to do battle, but could not keep track of the frozen trickster. His minions I could perceive quite clearly, but Bergelmir himself was only a shadow. It may have to do with his possession of the mortal. After you claimed Amanda, there was no sign I could find that would point to where Bergelmir has gone. There has been a deepening of some kind of concealment around Niflheim and parts of the realm are now completely shielded from my sight. I will of course continue to try until I can break the veil surrounding it."

Prelate Tess frowned. "That means that our foe's strength has grown considerably. We will put the Favoured to the task to understand what our enemy is up to while the gods are away. I will gather a handful of the Favoured and have them meet us at Valaskjalf. We must begin to investigate how Bergelmir made his way into Midgard immediately. Gatekeeper, one more question. Our newest Favoured lost a friend tonight during Bergelmir's attack. I would ask that in your searches of the realms for you to look for the boy as well. I will have Amanda send his description after she is settled."

"Of... course, Prelate." Heimdall's eyes fluttered.

Fulla's concern turned now to Heimdall. "Are you unwell, Heimdall? Maybe the strain of trying to pierce the shielding spell that surrounds Niflheim is too much for you to undertake alone."

Heimdall snorted, "I am fine. I now have a headache from my sensitivity to the frost lilies you carry. My sight has never failed and will not do so now. It will require time, but I shall peel the layers back to find our enemy. It is more than you could ever hope to do, Keeper."

Fulla tugged at her apron, "I am sorry. I meant no disrespect. Prelate Tess, perhaps we should make our way to Queen Frigga. She will be anxious to hear your tale firsthand, and it will allow me to take the frost lilies away from Heimdall."

"And I will be glad to give her my *full* account and begin a full investigation into tonight's events and for our prey." Lady Freyja attempted to pass through the arch, but Heimdall held up a hand. For a moment Amanda thought Lady Freyja would draw her sword and strike him, but then he bowed, motioned for her to continue, and turned his gaze back to the others. Lady Freyja's angular face tightened as she briskly strode past Heimdall. Calling over her shoulder, "Cassandra, do try not to break Amanda before our time in the Einherjarium – I would like to see if she is worthy of the trust the Prelate has placed within her."

"Shouldn't we all go together?" Fulla looked torn between the Prelate and Lady Freyja.

"We will leave in a moment, but we have one small task for you first. We could also use your help with Amanda's parents. They were bespelled by Amanda and are now trapped in the form of the mice that she carries. Perhaps your magicks could help return them to their normal state, or at least keep them comfortable, as Amanda learns how to do so on her own." Keeper Fulla looked taken aback but held out her hand to Amanda.

"I'll see you soon, Mom and Dad." Surprisingly, Amanda's parents didn't seem to object, and went to Fulla without even a glance back at Amanda.

Prelate Tess turned to Cassie who was staring dreamily at Heimdall. "Cassie, I would like for you to escort Amanda to the Favoured's Stave."

The girl straightened and then gave an awkward curtsey. "No worries, your Prelateshipness. I got this."

"Thank you, Cassie. I will check on you soon, Amanda, and I trust you will be in good hands with Cassie until then. I would recommend you try and get some rest, as your training will begin tomorrow. I am glad to have found you, and I am sure the Norn have great plans for you."

The women moved along the bridge quickly, leaving Amanda and Cassie alone for a moment. "Boy, you sure seemed to have ruffled Lady Freyja's feathers. It would make sense though since your benefactor is Sigyn. Lady Freyja once asked her for a spell, and let's just say it didn't end well – she was turned into a butterfly. But don't worry, she calms down after she gets to know you – unless you're me. She's never been nice to me. She's peeved her Favoured isn't better at fighting. As if it is my fault the Spell of Favouring decided to give me magick over emotions instead of making me a warrior like her. Not that I am not great in other ways, but I think she's given up on me."

"Something tells me you and I are in the same boat." Considering the flashing magick beneath her, the bridge felt surprisingly still under Amanda's feet as they began to cross over it.

CHAPTER 6:
AN ALFBLOT BATH

Within the golden shields, the streets of Asgard were abuzz with the life and sounds of a celestial city. Horses whinnied from above as they flew from towers toward the fields off to the west; oxen and Aesir pulled carts of golden apples across cobbled roads of smooth stone and glass, and there was still that odd sprinkling of soft musical notes like the ones Amanda had heard when she had put on the medallion. Gentle breezes blew tufts of clouds about some of the upper echelons of the city, like a continually shifting fog bank. People dressed in long robes and ornate armor walked on roads that looped around and on top of one another, creating overlooks that held sparkling ponds and colorful flowerbeds. There were strange beings with blue skin and fins instead of hair that walked alongside men and women that looked like they were made of pure light. Goats and birds and bees and other creatures she had no names for worked alongside the people in the robes. Buildings and towers made of a lighter stone trimmed in gold sloped up and away from the heart of the city on tiered levels, giving the city the look of a giant stadium. Oval windows made of colored glass faced upward on each of the roofs toward the light of three giant stars that circled in and out of the clouds.

As Cassie led them, she would wave to a group they were passing or stop to point something out, giving Amanda even more names and places to try and remember. For starters, the triangular hall in the mountains was Valhalla, where only Prelate Tess was allowed to go as the last of the Valkyrie. Lord Freyr had a grove named Barri and Lady Freyja had a hall named Folkvangr. It turned out that each of the gods had their own hall, tower, or grove – and sometimes all three. Amanda quickly discovered the city was built on a spiraling grid system, so as they walked down one of the main thoroughfares they repeatedly crossed over and under several of the same streets. It became quite confusing, but Cassie helped by giving landmarks to look for. For example, there was a giant statue of Thor wrestling a wild boar by the Mead Hall where they ate. You could always find the Einherjarium, where they would train with Lady Freyja, by listening for the sounds of swords and spears clashing. In addition to the landmarks, there were also tall spires of white and gold brick that stood at directional points that all led to a glass palace at the heart of the city, Valaskjalf. The mirrored dome encased Lord Odin's throne room and was one of the few places where the Favoured were forbidden to enter without permission.

Cassie's excitement followed them like a perfume, which made Amanda wonder if she wasn't inadvertently drawing more attention to themselves because the deeper they made their way into the city the more people began to stop and even follow them. Cassie waved to a group of the blue men and women with fins who were staring at them. "I forgot having a new mortal on Asgard is like having a visiting royal. The Vanir over there are bursting with curiosity."

Amanda turned, "Who?"

"Sorry! I totally forgot how overwhelming all of this could be at first. Here." Cassie stopped by a wooden post that had a carved set of circles that represented the Nine Realms. "So you said Prelate Tess gave you a bit of a rundown of the realms back on Midgard, right? Well, in terms of the races of the Nine Realms, we have those that are from Asgard, which, besides the gods, there are the ones in the robes you'll see. They are the Aesir. They're like the gods' cousins, but with very little magick. The Aesir help by using rune stones and other magickal items, or they train to become the Einherjar, who guard the city."

As Amanda listened, she saw several Aesir pass them. She noted that the hoods of their white cloaks were embroidered in a complex pattern of symbols similar to the ones on the Prelate's gauntlets. "OK, so gods and Aesir. Prelate Tess said Hel is where people go when they die."

Cassie nodded, "Yup. It is also the name of the goddess of death. Also, there are other places for the dead, but let's save that for later. From there, you have to kind of think of the realms in terms of opposites attract. You have realms of ice and ocean versus fire and rock. So Niflheim, where the Frost Jotuns are, is opposite Muspelheim, where the Fire Jotuns used to live – there haven't been any of those since Ragnarok. Vanaheim, which is mostly seas, beaches, and forests, are where the Vanir live. The Vanir can be like those folks over there with fins, look like warrior surfers, or look like they belong with Robinhood in Sherwood Forest. Opposite from Vanaheim is the mountain realm of Jotunheim where the Rock Jotuns live."

"Wait, Frost Jotuns like Bergelmir are from Niflheim, and then there are Fire Jotuns from Muspelheium. But Rock Jotuns are from Jotunheim?"

"Yeah, I am not so sure they thought the whole naming thing through back when the realms were formed. It's a bit tricky because Jotun means giant, and they aren't always big. They aren't always ugly either, but most of the time they are both. Although, technically speaking, some of the gods are Jotuns, too."

"OK... I think I'll have to figure that out later. So then... those were Vanir who live on Vana...White?"

"Close! Vanaheim. So, that's six realms and six races. The other three are pretty simple. Midgard, which is at the very center of the circle, is Earth. Alfheim and Svartalfheim would be on either side of Midgard. Alfheim is where the Light Elves live, and is probably the most beautiful place in all of the realms. That leaves the realm of the Dwarves and Fell Elves – Svartalfheim. Again, not many of the Fell Elves running around. Svartalfheim is filled with caves and dark wastelands. That's about as simple as I can make it. I mean, we're leaving out a ton of other creatures, but does that help?"

Amanda and Cassie began to walk again passing through a row of planters filled with trees that spiraled upwards with sharp leaves. "Ish."

Cassie smiled encouragingly. "You'll learn it all in no time. Trust me, you'll have to. Otherwise Mimir will dowse you until you do."

Amanda gave a half smile back. "I'll take your word for it. Did you know what the Vanir were feeling because of your favouring? Sean said you could do something with emotions… turn them into a weapon or something."

"The empathic part is out of my hands. I just know things. I can also accidentally give people my emotions too. The other part is a bit more complicated. Since Lady Freyja is part love and part war, my favouring allows me to take what people feel and use it as a weapon against them. But they have to have feelings in the first place, and I have to be worked up. Each of the Favoured gets only a small fraction of their benefactor's magick and it's different each time. I guess the Spell of Favouring just knows what magicks we would work best with, and even then the knowing of how to use your magick can be tricky. Once you start to get the hang of it, though, it feels like a new part of you has come to life that you never knew existed." They crossed over a bridge that had a small cluster of Dwarves huddled around an anvil. The Dwarves paused as they passed, hiding whatever it was they were working on.

Amanda got the sense that dwarves liked their privacy. "Well, so far all I can do is cause things to break and turn people into mice."

"That's not that bad! It could be fun to find a way to make Lady Freyja's chariot break when she is showing off during training. Oh, and maybe you could learn to turn someone into a puppy! I miss puppies!" Cassie grabbed two red apples from a stall and passed one to Amanda after she dropped a few coins into the merchant's hand.

"Aren't there dogs on Asgard?"

"Sure, but they're about the size of a pony. I miss small, wriggling puppies. My stepmum had a litter every year that she would groom into show dogs. They were so soft and warm. The dogs around here are bred for battle. Nothing soft about them." Noticing Amanda had devoured her apple down to the core, Cassie paid the merchant again, but this time handed Amanda a pewter mug. "Here, have some mead. The stuff is like a frothy apple drink, and good for you too like a kombucha. It also fills you up like you ate a big dinner. Anyway, I'm certain they will get your magick straightened out. It will be interesting to see how you develop, what with your benefactor and all that."

Amanda hoped it was as easy as Cassie made it sound. She wanted to get to work on finding a way to find Jack, help her parents, and pay Bergelmir back as soon as possible. Something occurred to Amanda, "Are all the gods like Lady Freyja?" Several Aesir women passed them, carrying baskets of food.

"Not at all." Cassie emphasized each word. She twirled a few strands of her hair. "Most are actually quite decent. You met Heimdall. He is a god, even though he isn't technically a god of any one thing. The ones that are gods of battle or war are a bit harsher, but even they have a sense of humor. Lady Freyja is just… special. I am still waiting to see the goddess of love side of her. I think she keeps that part hidden away, or has it permanently suppressed."

"What about the Favoured? Are they like their benefactors, and what kind of powers do they have?"

"Most are nice. We all have some connection to our benefactors, but it doesn't mean our personalities match. Again, reference Lady Freyja and myself. There are a couple though that I could do without. It's a bit like primary school here with them. You've got the ones who have to be the best, be teacher's pet, or rack up the most trophies. Then there are some who need a bit more discipline, or motivation. They end up doing more chores than the rest of us. No one from our group has ever really gotten into too much trouble except for one kid who took some rune stones he shouldn't have. He had his magick taken away for a bit, but it was all sorted out eventually. They can't really expel us, but they can make it pretty miserable. We can leave if we want to, but our magick would be bound until the Spell of Favouring was done with. Honestly, I don't think any one of us would give up our magick or the chance to fight off a pack of trolls because we have to train a bit harder. I know I wouldn't want to go back to tests and football over this. Can you imagine how boring it would be?"

"The favouring bit, though, is probably the most interesting part. The spell just takes an aspect of each of us and magnifies it with the god's specific magick. Some of the Favoured can become super strong, cast an unbreakable barrier, control animals, or even turn into water. Lord Mimir's Favoured is like a human encyclopedia. He can tell you the spelling and definition of any word – from any realm. It's not much help in a fight, but he can help with peace talks between warring Elf factions." When they got past Valaskjalf, they started winding their way along a stone street that sloped gently upward. Pretty soon the crowd following them had grown so large and boisterous that it began to drown out Cassie's monologue.

Cassie suddenly turned to their followers. "Oy! A girl has to have some room to breathe. I'll bring Amanda around when she is good and settled, and you can all say hello. Until then, let us have some peace!"

"Thank you." Amanda felt some small relief as the crowd disbanded. She had never liked being the center of attention.

"No worries. Now, where was I? Oh yes! The other Favoured. So, like I was saying, Connor, my brother you met back on Midgard, and I are from London."

"He was the boy with rocks on his hands."

"Hands and brains depending the day, but that's him. He gets his strength from the rocks and stones of the earth, and can transform his skin into a stone that is so hard that he is pretty much indestructible. His benefactor is Lady Freyja's brother, Lord Freyr, so we were claimed together like a brother-sister combo. Lord Freyr's powers are over... well let's just say making things stronger... or more fruitful. You'll read about it later. So, Connor and I, we're the only ones from England. There's a boy from Scotland and a girl from Ireland, though. You and Sean are from America, and pretty much everyone else is from all over Midgard."

Cassie stopped as they crested the hill they had been climbing for the past few minutes. On the other side of the hill sat a group of buildings that made a squared-off U-shape. The small buildings looked like stacked triangular huts, and were connected by glass hallways. Pointed spires and cantilevered beams supported roofs thatched with golden feathers, and at the center of the plaza stood an elongated hall with a ribbon of clerestory windows featuring the glass oculi that the other buildings in Asgard displayed.

"So here is our stop – the Stave of the Favoured. It's like a dormitory but *way* better, and it's co-ed too. Most of the Favoured should be about, as it is still a couple hours before lights out. We're a bit offset from time on Midgard, you see. I'll introduce you to a few before we head into our room. You'll meet the others during our lessons and training."

Amanda glanced nervously at the valley below. Milling about were teenage boys and girls who all wore the blue and gold leather uniforms. Some also sported cloaks that billowed to their sides as they walked. Cassie read Amanda's emotions and gave her a slight sympathetic smile. "Don't worry so much; once they get to know you, they probably won't worry you'll betray us."

"Is that supposed to make me feel better?" Amanda was worried what the others would think because of her connection to Sigyn. She bit the side of her cheek.

"We all had to go through this, so they'll understand. Just be yourself and I know you'll fit in just fine. OK?" Cassie rested a hand on Amanda's shoulder, but then turned her head sharply toward the Favoured as they began to gather around a boy and a girl with close-cropped hair.

Amanda watched as Cassie's face became taut. "Something wrong?"

Cassie took a breath. "Just felt a strong sense of worry – then excitement. It's hard to tell from this far away, but it has something to do with Lena and Lev and… a puddle. See the twins there? They're brother and sister, like Connor and me, except we aren't complete toads. Also, technically, Connor is my stepbrother. We were born the same year, and were both adopted by our stepmum. He is a few months older than me. Anyway, what are the Zukovs up to now?"

Following Cassie down the hill, Amanda could see the other Favoured pointing excitedly at some kind of dark stain on the ground beside a boulder. One of the boys hopped on top of the large rock and watched them as they made their way down. Amanda tried to ignore his stare as they came toward the bottom of the hill. She wanted to make a good impression, so she smiled and tried to ignore the butterflies in her stomach. As they approached the group, Amanda could see Lena was holding her hand over the dark liquid.

"I told you to stand back, Dominique." Lev was standing in between the group and his sister. Up close, Amanda could see his white-blond hair was cropped short, just like his sister's. Both Lena and Lev were lean, and tall enough to look down on the other Favoured. Lev's voice was softer than Amanda expected, and his tone held equal parts boredom and irritation.

"We just want to see it, Lev. We've never seen real alfblot before – only what Mimir has shown us." A girl with black hair and light brown skin was peering over Lev's extended arms. She started to shake and quickly grew a foot taller.

"Fine. If you wish to be infected, then by all means get as close as you wish." Lev dropped his arms and rolled his eyes. "It's not like I care if you end up in Eir's Manor. Nor, apparently, does Keeper Fulla, since she couldn't be bothered to deal with this on her own."

"It can't hurt me." Another boy suddenly became transparent and stepped through Dominique. "I can't be touched. Besides, what's it going to do? Jump off the ground?"

Dominique stepped back and nearly tripped over a group of girls behind her. "Don't do that, Carlos. You know how that bothers me."

Amanda felt a wave of heat and everyone jumped. "Be quiet, you idiots." Lena turned her attention from the puddle to the group. She spoke more harshly than her brother, but had the same look of disdain and superiority as Lev did when he spoke to the others.

Cassie cleared her throat loudly, "Right – now that you are all properly distracted. Lev, everyone, this is Amanda. She's our newest Favoured."

The group that had been crowding around Lena looked up and then shifted forward hesitantly. The boy on the boulder hopped down, using a shepherd's crook to balance as he landed on one foot. Amanda looked up, swallowed, and then extended her hand. "Hi, I'm Amanda West."

The boy had dark brown eyes, and towered above the others in a blue cloak with a cowl that gave him a monk-like appearance. Amanda held her breath and felt her cheeks warm as she stood with her hand out. Cassie stepped up beside Amanda, "Amanda this is Mykola Patera from the Ukraine. Unfortunately, he can't shake your hand because of his favouring. His favouring causes anything magickal or with magick he touches to lose its power. It comes back, but it feels like you have the flu magnified by a thousand. He also had to take a vow of silence when he started training with his benefactor, Forseti, the god of truth and justice. Something about knowing too much can hurt you, but he does say 'hello.'"

Amanda lowered her hand, feeling a bit like she had just asked a priest to perform a séance, but Mykola tapped the ground with his staff and she looked up to see him smiling broadly. She returned the smile. In short order Cassie introduced Amanda to the Favoured gathered around Lena and Lev. Just as Cassie said, the Favoured were from all over. Dominique, Favoured by Sif who was the goddess of the fields, was from France, and Carlos, Favoured by Balder who was the god of light, was from Mexico. There was also Lara, Favoured by Skadi the goddess of winter, from Switzerland, and Rani, Favoured by Idunn the goddess of youth, from India.

When they made their way to Lena and Lev, Lev sighed deeply before quickly shaking Amanda's hand. Lena cocked an eyebrow at Cassie. The two stared at each other for a moment until Cassie lowered her eyes.

"I told you I was sorry, Lena. Leave it be. Amanda, this is Lena. Her benefactor is Sol, the goddess of the sun, and her brother's is Mani, the moon god. They are from Russia."

"Nice to meet you." Amanda held out her hand, but Lena didn't move.

"I heard you were going to get us a new Favoured." Lena sniffed and flicked her fingers toward Amanda. "Is this her?"

Amanda looked bewildered. "Uh, yes. I am Amanda. Favoured of Sigyn." The group began murmuring behind her.

"I didn't ask you. Tell me, Cassie, does she like to run at the mouth as much as you do?"

Amanda dropped her hand. "Excuse me?" Amanda looked to Cassie, but she was keeping her eyes down.

Lena smirked and turned her attention to Amanda. "Cassie and I were roommates. That is, until she decided to insult me. Since you are new here, you might not know any better, but I would stay away from this one. Also, stay out of our way."

Cassie clenched her fists and found her voice. "You know what? I thought we were bonding, so forgive me for speaking my mind. I stand beside what I said. The ballet, to me, is boring. You didn't have to try to burn a hole through my chest because you disagree. Now why don't you stop trying to make me pop off and tell us what's going on with this alfblot. Decided to add custodian to your résumé?"

Lena raised her hand and clenched it into a fist. Behind her, her brother jumped back as the dark patch that looked like spilled motor oil flared and vanished in a cloud of smoke. "Keeper Fulla instructed us to find a dozen or so alfblot sites and remove them. She knew we would be able to handle the fell liquid. It requires real magick, which is probably why she came to my brother and me rather than someone who requires *feelings* to get their magick to work. As Lady Freyja has taught us, feelings are nothing but a weakness and a distraction."

Cassie looked to the ground again, and Amanda could almost feel the embarrassment pour off her. Whether it was from her months of torment by Laurie, or because of losing her parents and Jack, Amanda snapped. "I don't know what you're so proud of – you can set things on fire. All we would need is a match to do the same thing. Sounds to me like they gave you the simplest favouring they could find."

Lena sucked in a breath and put a finger to Amanda's chest. A tiny green spark flared from where Lena touched Amanda, and the ground beneath their feet suddenly shifted as a geyser of alfblot spewed forth, showering Lena, Lev, Cassie, and Amanda. Lena screeched, but recovered quickly. Flicking her fingers about, Lena quickly began to vaporize the alfblot before it could rain down on her and her brother. The alfblot quickly coated the ground and Amanda fell backward as she tried to get away. As she fell, there was a burst of her magick from her hands. A howling wind blew through the alfblot, splashing more of the fell stuff directly into Lena and Lev's faces.

"You clumsy fool!" Lev cried out angrily and tried to wipe away the murky water as it slid down his cheeks.

"Sorry! How do we make it stop?" As if at Amanda's words, the alfblot lessened and then stilled.

Lena raised her hands and the dark liquid evaporated from her clothing. She then waved a hand over her brother, cleaning him in the same manner. In unison, the twins pivoted to regard Amanda with icy expressions. Cassie had managed to stand, and offered Amanda a hand after shaking the sludge from her glove. Once both girls were standing, they tried to wipe the alfblot from their uniforms.

"Care to lend us a hand?" Cassie's hand was stuck to her leg as the alfblot she had been trying to wipe away trapped it in place when it began to congeal.

"An Aesir child knows how to be rid of the fell stuff. Bother one of them with your incompetence." Lev turned and pushed his way through the crowd, vanishing into a dark cloud the moment he was outside the circle.

Instead of marching off with her brother, Lena took a moment and stepped in closer to Amanda, holding her finger an inch from her chest. "I'll only say this once again, Amanda. Stay away from my brother and me. Asgard already has enough useless Favoured that besmirch our reputation, and you clearly are in the same category as they are. Our first priority is to this realm, and to show the Prelate that we can defend it – by whatever means necessary. If you get in our way, or do anything like that again, you will find out what happens to something that feels the full heat of the Midgardian sun." She pulled her hand away and there was a black mark where the leather had been melted.

"Hey, now, Lena – I thought that was our thing." Cassie pushed an arm in between Lena and Amanda. Lena glared at Cassie and stormed off after her brother.

Amanda rubbed the warm spot on her chest and winced as the alfblot began to sting. "Great. Just what I needed."

"Don't pay them any attention. I thought maybe Lena would forgive me for making that crack about ballet, but apparently not. They are just stuck up snobs who think they are better than the rest of us. I almost told her to get stuffed, but with my magick and all she might have turned into some kind of evil teddy bear. Anyway, thanks for standing up for me. How about for now we focus on getting the alfblot off."

"What is alfblot anyway?" The oily patches that still clung to Amanda began to smell like rotten eggs and form a gooey consistency.

"It's worse than the cough syrup and castor oil mum used to make us take when we got the sniffles. It's Fell Elf magick; those were the ones from the darkest parts of Svartalfheim. It can corrupt Asgardians, Aesir, and Favoured if they come in contact with it for too long. Fell Elves and their servants used to use it to drain Asgardians of their magick and change them to be their slaves or worse."

Amanda began to pull on the dark spots on her clothes, but it only seemed to spread and hold on tighter. "How do you get it off?"

"Mykola, could you help us out, please?" Cassie looked up to Mykola and he removed his white gloves, which were embroidered with the symbol of Asgard. "Hold still. He can't touch our skin, but if he touches the alfblot he should be able to neutralize it."

With a careful tap, each coagulated patch of alfblot began to sizzle and fade until the dark spots that covered Amanda and Cassie disappeared. Taking his staff in both hands, he dipped the tip of the crook into the puddle at their feet and the alfblot vanished. When he was done, he quickly pulled his gloves back onto his hands.

Amanda smiled at him in relief. "Thank you. Do you think we have to worry about being infected by it?"

Mykola shook his head, and then pointed up the hill toward the city. He began gesturing and Cassie translated. "Mykola says he doesn't think we have anything to worry about. That was a small batch of alfblot, nothing too strong. Let's get you changed and to the Manor to be checked out, though. After that we can take you to meet the other Favoured and get you tucked in to our room." Cassie took a deep breath and registered Amanda's anxiety.

"Don't worry, Amanda, you just need to learn the ropes around here and we'll get you all sorted out. You'll see."

CHAPTER 7:
A DAY OF HALLS, WATER, AND SPEARS

Amanda's eyes flew open. She sat up quickly, crying out as her head knocked the wooden slats of the bunk bed above her. "Ow!"

"Well that is one way to start the day. Is that something you do every morning?" Cassie was sitting in a chair across their room.

Rubbing her head, Amanda grunted. "No. I just… forgot where I was." Her hand continued down to rub her eyes, and then her cheeks as she struggled to wake up. Her dream lingered in her mind, but she couldn't remember what it was about. There had been something about Jack, though. He had been in pain, and no matter how much she tried she couldn't help him.

"Not surprising there. Yesterday you were back on Midgard in your bed. Today, you are living in the lap of luxury." Cassie's smiled as she waved around the room.

Amanda grinned back at her. The room looked different in the morning light. Last night they had made it back from the Manor, which turned out to be a cluster of stone towers that housed the healing beds of Asgard, right as the three stars above dipped below the horizon. The corridors leading to their rooms were illuminated by torches lit with miniature crystal stars, and the room itself glowed faintly from the golden symbols carved into the stone walls. The room had seemed cozy and safe. Cassie had used a rune stone to turn Amanda's uniform into a fluffy pair of pajamas, and then Amanda crawled into the lower bunk bed and drifted off to sleep.

With light pouring in through the colored glass windows, Amanda could see what Cassie meant. The room was austere to the point of feeling as if someone had made off with the furniture. Amanda could tell they took the less is more approach. There was a dresser, two X-shaped chairs with an embroidered seat, and the bunk bed the girls shared. Beyond that, there were a few banners with ferocious scenes of battles, and an arched wooden opening that led to the bathroom with its single marble sink and shower. It still felt safe, but it definitely didn't feel cozy or luxurious.

"But, hey, we get magick. So, there are some tradeoffs." Cassie smiled again and traced one of the symbols on the wall.

A second later, there was a knock on the door. Cassie picked up a rune stone, closed her eyes, and her clothes swirled into the gold and blue uniform. Tapping her toe to straighten her boot, she opened the door. A tray floated in the doorway, with two large steins, some fruit, and two steaming bowls.

"We also have room service," Cassie clucked her tongue and handed Amanda her breakfast.

Amanda took a deep breath, smelling earthy spices and a touch of garlic wafting from her bowl. She took a bite, and gave a small moan. It had to be the most delicious stew she had ever tasted, and she instantly felt awake and ready for the day. Amanda paused mid-bite to savor her food, while Cassie, she noticed, was quickly devouring her food. A horn blew, and Cassie crammed four more bites into her mouth.

"We have to get going otherwise we will be late. Hold up," Cassie picked up a rune stone on the tray and tossed it into the only other item that adorned the walls — a small metal basin that stood under one of the windows.

The rune sparkled, and the Prelate's face appeared. "Amanda. I hope you have rested after your trials yesterday. I was informed by Keeper Fulla that you were involved in an incident with alfblot. Thank the Allfather, the Aesir at the Manor say you are well. However, I would like to give you the morning to make sure you are settled. Cassie will attend to her chores and shall come to take you to your first lesson with Lord Mimir in about an hour. If you need anything else, please ask Keeper Fulla or one of the Aesir. Cassie, please show Amanda how to dress. On the Wings of Asgard." The Prelate's face vanished.

"How did she know about the alfblot? Do you think Lena and Lev told her?" Amanda ducked as she stood to avoid hitting her head again. The stone floor was surprisingly warm under her bare feet.

"I am sure they told her something, but she probably also read the reports from the healing beds. She wasn't mad, so I am betting Lena and Lev just told her how great they were and that they tried to save you." Cassie rolled her eyes as she finished two apple slices. "Ok, I have to run or else I will have to do laps. Take this," Cassie handed the rune stone she used a few moments ago to Amanda. "Just close your eyes and picture the uniform and it will change whatever you are wearing into our leathers. Since you have a bit of time, head around the Stave to get familiar with it. Probably best to not venture too far for the time being. The Hall of Tapestries can be quite fun once you figure it out!" With a conniving grin, Cassie dashed out the door.

Amanda stared as the door swung shut, the metal strapping and decorative studs glinted in the morning light. Setting her bowl on her bed, Amanda closed her eyes and took a deep breath. She sorted her thoughts from all that she had learned yesterday and felt a small bit of doubt creep into her mind. Another sharp blast from a horn broke her moment of quiet. There was no doubt this was real.

After a scalding shower and a brisk brushing of her hair, Amanda held the rune stone Cassie gave her in her hand and closed her eyes. She pictured the leather uniform and heard a rustling sigh. Opening her eyes, Amanda smiled at the blue and gold leather clothing that she now wore. Amanda dropped the stone on the dresser and hefted the hooped door-pull.

The corridor was dancing with light, and a sweet tinkle of notes floated down toward Amanda. Following the sound, she found the common area that connected her room to three others. A glass ceiling and walls opened to a pure blue sky above and the rolling green valley around the Stave. The ornate furniture centered around a stone basin with a crackling ball of fire suspended in the air. The sound Amanda heard earlier seemed to be coming from the flames, so she leaned in closer to inspect them.

"Favoured, you might not want to get too close." Keeper Fulla was closing the door to one of the rooms behind Amanda. The Keeper shifted a woven basket to her hip. "The speaking fires can give you a nasty burn if you do not know how to use them properly."

Amanda felt her face color and she bit the side of her cheek. "Sorry. I was just trying to see if I could... do you hear...? Never mind." The Keeper looked perplexed as Amanda stumbled on her words. "I was just trying to learn my way around the Stave."

"The Prelate told me she gave you a reprieve from chores. You seem alright for one who came into contact with alfblot. Well then, follow me." Pivoting, the Keeper walked briskly from the common area.

Amanda nearly banged her knee into the sofa as she tried to catch up. After a few minutes, Keeper Fulla stopped at a pair of wooden double doors. Amanda wheezed as she looked up at the massive arched wood panels. A starburst of golden spokes made their way down to wind around curved handles.

Keeper Fulla snapped her fingers and the doors parted where the golden rods intertwined. "This is the Hall of Tapestries, and the entrance to Queen Frigga's hall, Fensalir. Where you reside with the other Favoured is called Gimle. It was the first new building built on Asgard after Ragnarok. Most Favoured come here frequently when they first arrive as the tapestries will answer almost any question you ask of it." Keeper Fulla looked down her nose at Amanda as she shifted the basket under arm. "You will find it quite empty until you come back to train your magick. I would start your exploration here until you begin your lessons." Keeper Fulla made a sharp turn and was off down another corridor before Amanda could respond.

Amanda was about to call out to thank the Keeper when the musical notes she had heard walking through Asgard and in the corridor softly drew her attention. Stepping through the open doors, Amanda saw three tapestries on either side of the larger corridor. The thick banners hung from the windows just under the roof down to the floor. She approached the one closest to the hallway's entrance. Examining the lush weaving, she could see the tapestry was made from brightly colored red and gold threads. The bottom tassels brushed the stone floor as it gently moved, even though the air was still. Reaching out a hand, Amanda ran her fingers over the soft fibers. The notes echoing about her rang louder and the fibers began to shift and swirl until Amanda was staring at a woman holding her hands high. The woman was beautiful, with dark hair gathered into a long ponytail like Lady Freyja's. She wore a billowing white robe with a high golden collar.

Above the woman Amanda read the rune aloud, "Sigyn."

The tapestries began to wave about as if suddenly agitated by Amanda's words. Amanda watched as the scenes on each tapestry mirrored one another. They started with a vision of Sigyn, then fire that turned the tapestries a sickly green, then a desolate landscape filled with nothing but rock and a sky filled with ash, and finally a starry night that shone on a twisting tower in a lonely plain. She felt as if the scenes should mean something, but she had no idea what.

"Amanda?" Amanda jumped as Cassie rounded the corner. "You found it! What did you ask it?" Cassie turned and inspected the tapestry, but it had returned to its blank red state.

"I didn't ask it anything. It just… I don't know what it did."

"Well, later I will show you how to work them properly. It's quite fun to watch when you ask it to tell you a funny story about Keeper Fulla. Now, come on. Chores were cut short because of another outbreak of alfblot the Prelate needed to deal with. We're all heading to lessons, so I came to find you." Cassie took Amanda by the arm, "You might want to bring a towel."

"Why?" Amanda asked.

"You'll see."

***

A quick trip into the city, and Amanda and Cassie were settled in with the other Favoured before a well near Lord Odin's palace. Golden hoops showered water down into a foot-high stone circle. Some of the Favoured Amanda hadn't met the day before had come over to say hello before finding their seats. Lena and Lev didn't even look in Amanda's direction. They sat down on a bench on the opposite side from where Amanda and Cassie sat. Amanda tried to not let it bother her, but she kept looking back to the twins to see if she could try to wave hello.

Cassie jerked her head in their direction. "What boiled troll droppings those two are. Don't give them another thought. They think they are so far above the rest of us, but just the other day Lev almost turned himself into a dragon by touching Andvari's gold. Anyway, so Lord Mimir is our teacher on all things pertaining to the realms, their inhabitants, customs and histories. He can be a bit testy, like a cross between my crotchety Uncle Fergus and Albert Einstein. He likes to hear himself speak and does not like being interrupted during one of his stories." Amanda must have made a face because Cassie just patted her on the arm. "Just try not to stare."

With that, Cassie put a finger to her lips as a great rush of water poured down from the golden hoops and splattered the first three rows of Favoured. Having been through this before, the Favoured held up rune stones or used their magick to keep themselves dry. Amanda looked at Cassie with wide eyes, but Cassie quickly motioned to turn back to face Mimir – who turned out to be a giant head made of water.

"Welcome, Favoured. We will resume our lesson regarding the spirit creatures that serve the Non – the Fyglja. That is spelled F-Y-G-L-J-A and is pronounced fig-lee-ya. These creatures are only found in the Norn's Forest. They serve the Norn, the goddesses of fate. Please see the following display to understand what they look like. Do not scream. It upsets me." Mimir's head vanished, replaced by a vision of something that looked like a scaly leopard with wings. It slithered about and hissed. The Favoured quickly scrambled to take notes, while Amanda tried to process what she was seeing.

"You warn me he can be cranky, but you don't mention he is just a head made of water?" Amanda whispered to Cassie, who frantically waved for her to be quiet, but it was too late.

A geyser of water blasted Cassie and Amanda, nearly knocking them out of their seats. Lord Mimir frowned at them furiously, "Favoured. There is no speaking while I am speaking. Unless you have a question, and then it must wait until I have finished giving the lesson. The knowledge I pass on to you is a tradition that all Favoured have gladly accepted. In fact, many say it has saved their lives during their time on Asgard. I would suggest you conduct yourselves properly and give me my due attention. Is that understood?" Amanda and Cassie nodded emphatically while they tried to wring out their hair.

For the rest of the lesson, Lord Mimir called various Favoured forward to answer his questions regarding the ghostly spirits of the Norn's Forest. When the Favoured answered correctly, they were given a nod and dismissed. If they answered incorrectly, Lord Mimir would hurl a literal mouthful of water at them until they got it right. When the lesson was finished, half the Favoured were soaked through their tunics.

A couple hours later, Amanda and the Favoured were gathered in the Einherjarium for their daily training with Lady Freyja. The Einherjarium reminded Amanda of the Coliseum of Rome. It was a grand stadium with tiered levels that stepped up from the field where the Favoured sparred with the Einherjar. The soil was enchanted by the roots of Yggdrasil to transform into any realm or battle Lady Freyja desired, and could summon creatures as well.

"You must be prepared for the dangers of war in any realm you find yourself!" Lady Freyja cried as she thrust a spear into Amanda's hand.

At the goddess's command, the ground shifted. Boiling tar pits and scalding geysers formed around them. Two creatures erupted from the burning sand. They looked like rotten watermelons with bat-like wings. The creatures bobbed in the air and shrieked as they closed in on Amanda.

"Watch out, Amanda! Those are Svartalfheim gnats! They can breathe fire!" Cassie ducked as a pair of gnats rounded on her.

Amanda tried jabbing at the gnats, but they just hissed, spit flames, and flew away. Gripping the spear, Amanda dashed about wildly, swinging the spear to try and skewer one of her opponents. Lady Freyja stood off to the side of the field, looking at Amanda with smug disdain. Amanda tried to ignore the goddess, but unfortunately, she was proving to be no better at wielding a spear than she had been at playing dodgeball in gym class back on Earth… Midgard. Gripping the spear with her gloved hands, Amanda charged the closest gnat. As she ran, the heavy tip of the spear kept dropping. During another flailing attempt to attack, the sharp point of the spear dug into the ground, catapulting Amanda into the air toward a bubbling pit of Svartalfheim tar. Agnarr, one of the Einherjar charged to stay with the Favoured during their lessons, barely managed to catch her before she plummeted into the boiling depths of the black pool. It wouldn't have killed her, Cassie told her later, but she definitely would have been hurting afterwards.

After training, the Favoured hurried to the Mead Hall where they scarfed down lunch. Cassie introduced Amanda to Andhrimnir, the chef for all of Asgard and the maker of the mead. The man had actually bowed when he met Amanda. He looked like a young Santa Claus with red hair. As soon as they finished eating, Cassie and Mykola escorted Amanda back to Fensalir for her first official lesson in magick.

Inside Fensalir, the walls were covered with miniature rainbows of refracted light reflecting off the hundreds of mirrors of various shapes and sizes that filled its walls. Some mirrors were small enough to fit into the palm of Amanda's hand, and others went to the ceiling. Four statues of giant bears reached upward to support the thatched ceiling above. Beside each of the statues stood an Aesir wearing a deep blue robe with a high collar. They looked older than anyone else Amanda had seen on Asgard. They were all either bald or had white hair, and their faces held deep wrinkles.

"Welcome, Favoured, to today's lesson." The Prelate greeted them from a small raised platform of stone. "Today will be unique, as I have brought the Aesir spellmages to guide you through your trials, challenges, and tasks. I shall be administering our newest Favoured's first test to her personally. When I summon your mirror, you are to accomplish the challenge as noted by the runes on each mirror. Remember, Queen Frigga herself made these mirrors so that you can practice your magick without fear of harming others or yourself. What is shown to you within the glass is but a vision."

The Prelate raised her fists. Her gauntlets' magick ignited and raced about the room, lifting mirrors from the walls and bringing them to Amanda and the others. The Favoured were standing in rows, each beside a set of ornate metal posts. The mirrors flew silently toward the posts and hovered in place as intricate metal strappings unlaced to wrap around the mirrors' frames.

Amanda fidgeted a few feet away from Cassie and Mykola. She turned as a small mirror with a bronze frame and small patches of rust settled beside her. She watched as Cassie touched the top of her mirror, igniting blue runes. One of the Aesir spellmages with a bundle of white hair braided with golden bands stepped beside Mykola. Bending his head, Mykola listened to the mage's soft words and then held up his hand. With a twisting finger, a band of blue magick coalesced around Mykola's palm. Turning, Mykola carefully undid his gloves and pushed his hands into the glass.

"We have to make special exceptions for all the Favoured from time to time." The Prelate's clear voice startled Amanda. "Mykola's favouring presents some unique challenges, but, as you can see, we have found ways to allow him the use of his magick. The mirrors have survived for a hundred years, but Mykola was the first Favoured we were truly concerned might break one." The Prelate gave Amanda a warm smile.

"So, what about my magick? Do you think it could hurt the mirrors? I mean, I did break my mantle."

"I have no doubt it will be unique. Beyond that, I believe we shall manage. Now then, has anyone told you where our magick comes from?" Amanda shook her head. The Prelate raised her hand and the gauntlet's magick touched the glass surface of her mirror. As before in her living room, when the Prelate spoke, images formed on the mirror's surface for Amanda to see.

"Before time, there was nothing but frost, fire, and the great chasm Ginnungagap. It is within that deep void, where the creeping frost and unquenchable fire met, that the spark of life and magick was born. We are uncertain which came first, but we do know that from the Ginnungagap came the first giants, gods, and magick. And since they come from the same place, they are bound to one another. With their emergence came a wild upheaval that shook loose the Nine Realms and the other first creatures. Our oldest arcane lore and accounts from the first gods tell us that the magick infused all it touched. It connects us, just as Yggdrasil does. Some react differently to it, inheriting different magickal aspects just as some mortals are born with red hair and others golden. Most mortals cannot perceive magick or use it. Truly, only those blessed by the gods' favouring can wield true magick." The figures in the mirror danced with light as the magick from the great chasm touched them. Amanda watched as the gods came together and, lifting their hands high, took hold of the magick in the air to raise a city in the highest realm.

"And now you know a bit more about where your magick comes from. Typically, we have the Favoured's benefactor here to help explain how to use their magick, but in your case that cannot happen. I have written the Allfather to see if he might grant us some way to speak to the goddess, as only he knows her location. Until then, we will use all the knowledge of the spellmages of Asgard to help you to focus your magick. Even Queen Frigga has said she would be willing to teach you."

Amanda felt a bit awkward. She had hoped she would be able to blend in with the others, but she wasn't sure that would be possible if she needed to have the Queen to help her with her magick. "So, what do I do?"

"For your first test, let us see what happens naturally." With a gentle tap, the Prelate summoned the runes from the mirror. "All you have to do is capture the knud. It is a special butterfly from Alfheim that moves so slowly that some say it seems to stand still until it senses food. Then it moves like a gentle breeze."

"Ok, that shouldn't be too hard, I guess." Unsure of what to do, Amanda remembered that the others had summoned their magick with simple words or practiced motions. Trying to mimic them, she focused on the mirror, thinking of a net, and pointed to one of the beautiful bird-sized creatures.

"Capture the knud!" Amanda felt her magick rise within her, but it fizzled into nothing more than a few bubbles that fell from her finger. Amanda bit the side of her cheek and tried again. This time her magick flashed, but the mirror only bounced twice as a torrent of magickal motes cascaded off of the frame, causing her to sneeze. Amanda looked to the Prelate, her forehead creased with embarrassment.

The Prelate let out a good-humored chuckle. "That is better than most. How about we see if the spellmages can give you some guidance?" The Prelate beckoned to one of the Aesir.

The spellmage came toward Amanda. He had two identical marks on the right side of his face that looked like interlocking concentric circles. As he walked, he held out his hands and blue magick flashed. A book appeared in his hands.

"Your magick is a bit different than your fellow Favoured." The man's voice was soft but crisp, and his face maintained a stoic expression as he spoke. "We who call forth magick, rather than tap into one of the elements or other forces, must channel it. We must use spells or spellwords that are infused with power to ignite the magick we possess. Spellwords and incantations are the easiest form to connect to our power, but once you have mastered the enchantment it should flow from you with a simple thought. Once you inherit your benefactor's full might, you might even be able to create your own spells. This spellword," the spellmage flipped to a page that had a beautifully drawn image of a word scribbled in black marks, "is a spell to trap those you are after for a time. The particulars we can go over later, but for now simply read the word written in our runic language."

Amanda squinted. The scratchy figures were similar to the ones on the

Prelate's gauntlets. She wasn't completely sure what they said, but a word popped into her mind as she traced the markings with her fingers. "*Ensricle.*"

Green magick flared around Amanda and the mirror in front of them began to reflect the green light. Amanda felt a smile form on her face as she watched her magick travel into the mirror. For a moment, it circled the knud, and then it raced back out of the mirror – bringing the knud with it. Amanda gasped as the giant butterfly fluttered its wings twice and then gently made its way out the giant stone doors to the green valley surrounding the Stave.

The spellmage and the Prelate exchanged a glance. "Well," the spellmage began and then stopped. He took a moment to adjust his collar. "That has never happened before."

"Indeed." The Prelate held out her hand and the mirror left the stand. Another flew to replace it a moment later. The Prelate indicated for the spellmage to continue. "But then again, magick always brings surprises with it. I am curious to see what happens next."

CHAPTER 8:
PARTIES AND SOUL-SUCKING MONSTERS

After several days of the same routine, the other Favoured were sent off to the other realms to gather what scraps of information they could find on Bergelmir, or to retrieve items needed to aid the realm or the gods. Cassie and Mykola were assigned to work with Lena and Lev to find the source of the alfblot, as a dozen more sites had been reported around the realm. Summoning alfblot was strictly forbidden on Asgard, and so the Queen and the Prelate wanted to find who was creating the fell stuff and why.

Amanda, however, was sent to the Halls of Learning to tackle the runes. The runes were the scratchy characters that formed the basic language of anything Asgardian, and what every tablet, scroll, or tome that she had to read was written in. Amanda was surprised to find that she had a natural proficiency for the runic language. The words and markings were suddenly as easy to read as if she had been studying them for years. The Aesir caretakers were delighted and soon had Amanda reading about the history of Asgard, the gods, and what appeared to be a long list of wars between the Light and Fell Elves. As the lights from the stars began to dim, the Aesir loaded Amanda up with several large leather-bound books and sent her back to the Stave to finish her reading.

Several hours later, the sky was dark, and Amanda's eyes were starting to glaze over. She was reading about how the Frost Jotun giant and the imp were the two most prevalent types of Frost Jotuns, but apparently not the only ones Bergelmir could control. The imps were actually more dangerous than the giants due to the destruction they could cause when they gathered *en masse*. After Ragnarok, Bergelmir had been imprisoned, and the Frost Jotuns were so weak that Lord Odin was able to put a spell around Midgard to keep all mortals safe. Jotuns could control any mortal they touched. Bergelmir had escaped from his prison right as the Spell of Favouring began to find the last round of Favoured.

Amanda had reread the same story twice to commit it to memory, and was beginning to wonder when Cassie would be back. Her stomach rumbled. Getting up from her bed, Amanda went to the spot Cassie had touched on her first day to call for a tray of food. She bent down, tucking her hair behind her ear to read the rune. It was a simple one that read, "Sustenance." Amanda had just finished tracing the symbol when the door to her room flew open.

"Hey girl! Ak!" Cassie had been walking in when a flying tray smacked her in the back of the head, dumping steaming mugs of black tea, several pieces of chicken, and leafy greens down her back.

"Shoot!" Amanda rushed to help Cassie.

"Hot, hot, hot, pthhhb, hot!" Cassie yelled while spitting lettuce from her face.

"Sorry! I was just getting hungry. I didn't know it would do that."

Cassie started laughing. "No worries. It's actually not the first time. How was your day?"

Amanda helped Cassie up. "After almost drowning with Lord Mimir and getting near-fried with Lady Freyja yesterday… reading runes is pretty safe. Although, I do think I have read about more wars than there have been in the entire history of… Midgard."

"Yeah, the elves don't play well together. Or, they didn't before Ragnarok." Cassie was wiping her face as she went to their shared bathroom. "Sounds like you picked up the runes pretty quickly. It took Connor a week before he knew the rune for Asgard. He would be so ticked to know you are already reading about the wars. That was his favorite part."

"Reading them just kind of happened. This morning, I had no idea what any of these runes meant," she indicated the runes on the walls, "but now I can read them all. Remembering them, though, and everything else… that's going to take some time. How about you? What did you do today?"

"Mostly tried not to tell Lena to take a bath in the alfblot we had to clean up. She would *not* stop talking about you." Cassie came back into their room and picked up the rune stone they used to change into their uniforms. She closed her eyes, and the uniform swirled into a pair of lounge pants and a baggy t-shirt.

"What about me?" Amanda had figured out how to use the rune stone to change into a pair of jeans and a pale yellow sweater. She hadn't even thought about what she was going to need to bring with her when she left her home, but it seemed Asgard would be providing what she hadn't remembered.

"Just about Sigyn and all of that Ragnarok stuff. She's spouting this theory about how the alfblot appeared when you did. She kept mentioning it any time we were around the Prelate or Keeper Fulla until Mykola actually threatened to take his gloves off and turn his favouring on her if she didn't shut her mouth. That boy doesn't get worked up over anything, but he is defensive of you for certain. I mean, I get it, this much alfblot means someone is either working with a Fell Elf or there is a Fell Elf running loose on Asgard."

"So Lena is saying I… serve Fell Elves?"

"In her own snotty way. Regardless of the fact that I don't think there isn't any truth to what she is saying, there is the fact that there really haven't been any Fell Elf sightings since we became Favoured. I am also fairly certain the Prelate or Queen Frigga would know if there was a Fell Elf on Asgard." Cassie sighed and waved her hands to clear the air as if banishing Lena's presence. "Anyway. Mykola has your back. Now then, let's try this again." Cassie called for another tray.

When it arrived, they ate in silence, Amanda on her bed and Cassie in one of the chairs opposite her. Amanda didn't think Cassie meant anything by what she had said about Mykola, but it made Amanda feel a bit funny. "So, um... do you think Mykola likes me?"

Cassie shrugged as she noisily chewed on her salad. "Maybe. Oh," Cassie exclaimed. "No! Mykola and I are strictly friends. I was just telling you that about him so you would know he has your back."

Amanda let out a sigh. Having her roommate know what she was feeling might come in handy at times when she wasn't sure how to ask an awkward question. "Well, he is cute."

The girls laughed, and Cassie called for another tray of food. When it arrived, she passed Amanda another plate. Amanda examined the room as Cassie climbed up into her bunk. The runes in the room were for all sorts of different purposes. Some were for cleaning, others were to send messages.

Amanda suddenly let out a big laugh. Cassie rolled over and looked down at her. Amanda got up and pointed to a rune beside the window. "Do you know what this says?"

Cassie squinted and propped herself up on her elbows. "Sure, it says bear."

Amanda smiled. She traced the rune with the tip of her finger. "Looks like you might need to go back and work on your runes too." As Amanda's finger left the stone, a white, fluffy rug appeared in the middle of the room.

"Stop it! You mean I have been living with these bare stone floors, which can get a bit cold when it snows mind you, when I could have had a rug all along?" Cassie's eyes quickly swept the rest of the room. "What else have I missed out on?"

"Well, I don't see a rune in here for a puppy, so at least not that."

Cassie sighed and was quiet for a minute. "I think a pet would probably help us adjust a bit better. We get to work with some pretty fantastic creatures, like the talking bears of Jotunheim or the dancing fish from Vanaheim, but it's not the same. We do get to ride the vindsvolla, though. I did ask my stepmum for a pony once. The vindsvolla are kind of pony-like."

The vindsvolla were the majestic, winged horses that could be seen flying about the city, ranging in colors from white to gold to midnight blue. On her first morning after arriving, Amanda had seen no fewer than twenty rocketing back and forth, going in and out of the golden shields around them and flying off toward the Bifrost. She learned from some of her reading that the vindsvolla are blessed by Heimdall to traverse freely in the Nine Realms, and are some of the fastest creatures alive. They can traverse from realm to realm in a few hours when needed.

Amanda had not ridden one yet, and she swallowed hard thinking about what it would be like to fall off in the middle of the nether regions of space between the realms. She sat back down in the leather chair Cassie had occupied. It smelled slightly of lavender and black tea. "Are they hard to ride? None of the Einherjar use saddles. It seems like there should at least be a seatbelt or something."

"It was pretty simple for Connor and me. Some of the other Favoured didn't take to it quite as well. The vindsvolla are trained to keep their riders safe under almost any situation, and they take pride in not letting you slip off. I remember the first time I saw them. Connor and I had just gotten here with the Prelate. I think I was about to pass out from rainbow travel. I am also pretty sure I was going to change my mind and go back, and then I saw a vindsvolla that looked like it was made of gold fly right up to the Prelate and land. The Einherjar warrior jumped off to give a report to the Prelate, and the vindsvolla swung its head toward me. We stared at each other for a minute and then it nuzzled my head as if telling me I would be ok." Cassie stretched a bit and took a bite from a piece of roasted chicken. "Having a pet or something like the vindsvolla would have made it seem a bit more normal and helped us adjust is all I am saying."

Amanda finished her bite and thought for a minute. "I can see that. I know I got here later than the rest of you, but it still is a lot to take in. What was it like for you for that first week?"

"Honestly, it is a bit of a blur. We were so young. Listen to me. I say that like it wasn't just four years ago, but it was. It feels like I have lived three years for each year I have been here. I remember Connor and I agreeing to come, and feeling like we made the right decision, but we were so young that anything this wild probably would have been right up our alley. I think that is why the spell finds us when it does because we can still accept something like all of this and not let it mess us up. I had Connor, so that helped, but it was still a lot. There were a lot of us who had nightmares, but the Aesir, Keeper Fulla, and the Prelate were all there for us. It's a bit different now, though. They expect us to be a bit more responsible."

"Do you ever miss it? Earth... or Midgard?" Amanda took a sip from her stein and then pushed her bangs back behind her ear.

Cassie cocked her head as she finished her mouthful of chicken. "Not too much. I miss my stepmum, but everything else seems like it is part of another life. I have been back a couple times. I even saw my stepmum once, but just from a distance. She looked happy and I didn't want to mess with the rune stones that keep her safe by trying to say hello. I also had to nip off to stop a few root trolls from burrowing into a nearby field and creating a spore cloud that would have killed off all the crops of England." Cassie looked out through the window. She twisted a few strands of her hair, and went quiet. After a minute she perked back up. "Well, then. This has been a bit of a dreary conversation. How about something a bit livelier to talk about?"

Amanda scrunched her face. "Sorry."

Waving her hands, Cassie laughed. She pulled herself up so her back was against the wall with her legs crossed in front of her. "Not at all! What else shall we talk about? Oh! I know! The parties!"

"What parties," Amanda asked. "Like a Christmas party?"

Cassie's eyes got wide and she stuck her tongue between her teeth when she smiled. "Even better. There are four major holidays on Asgard. We celebrate Lord Odin and Queen Frigga's birthdays, but the best parties are Winternights and Jul. Winternights is the best because they tell all these old stories to celebrate the past. Lord Odin conjures this huge tent out toward Mount Valhalla and we go spend a week celebrating all the old battles and warriors. Sounds a bit lame until you see how they do it. It starts with something small, like a sparkler, and then builds with a thousand more little lights that start to form an image. Pretty soon the entire sky is filled with moving lights like the biggest movie screen ever. As it gets going, the gods sometimes join in and reenact the battle. Each battle ends with the most brilliant fireworks you have ever seen. Sometimes the fireworks rain down candy or flowers. And then – there's the food. There are puddings and pies, jams and pastries, mountains of sweets, and the best duck, pheasant and steak you have ever tasted. And even if you don't like any of that stuff, there are also thousands of sculptures made of ice or clouds or water that are frozen in place to look like Lord Odin's eight-legged horse, Sleipnir. Finally there is the hunt. We get to chase Sleipnir through the city, and if you catch him you win a rune stone that is supposed to tell you your future. None of us has ever won it yet, though. Jul is even crazier because right before we get two weeks of snow. They give us a time off from our chores and lessons to sled about the city behind the snow bears that live at the top of Mount Valhalla. Then there is a party that lasts seven full days."

Amanda slid her tray from her lap as she stood. "That sounds incredible. Although, I don't think I am ready for more snow after what happened the night I was claimed. Snow and I never really got along to begin with, and now probably even less. I think I want to keep all things cold as far away as possible. Are you finished?" Amanda held her hand out for Cassie's plate.

"Yes, thanks." Cassie wiped her mouth while Amanda placed their dishes out in the hallway. "Well, we will see when Jul gets here if you change your mind. I would like to say that is the only time to be ready for snow, but we *are* in the middle of space with a bunch of clouds that roll around the realm, so storms pop up all the time. Some bring snow and others bring rain. Mostly we track with the seasons of Midgard, but it can vary. It can also change if

Lord Odin or Queen Frigga gets in a mood. Their magick can set off some pretty wicked storms." Cassie yawned and stretched.

Amanda shut the door behind her and crossed her arms. "Cassie?"

Cassie yawned again before answering. "Hm? Yeah? Sorry, I am a bit knackered."

"What does your magick... what does your magick feel like? What you just said, about Lord Odin and Queen Frigga's magick creating storms... that's what it feels like when I try to use my magick." Amanda felt her cheeks redden as if she had just showed up to lessons with Mimir in her underwear. She wasn't sure why she felt awkward asking the question. For some reason it felt like asking about something deeply personal.

Cassie sensed Amanda's emotions. "We should make a pact now that we are roommates and while you get caught up on all things Nine Realmy. No question is too weird. Trust me, when you get to the love lives of the gods, you will want to be able to ask them freely of me and not Lord Mimir – trust me." She paused and scratched her head. "I've never really thought about it, but I guess it feels like I can sense something like a string between me and who or whatever I want to control. Back on Midgard I was starting to play the violin, and it's kind of like what it feels like when you draw the bow across the strings to make a certain sound. My magick allows me to pull the string a certain way to make people do what I want."

"That sounds... calm compared to what my magick feels like." Amanda held up her hand and repeated one of the spells she had tried the other day in Fensalir. A flash of green light lit the room. "That spell is supposed to make as much light as a Vanir glow-wyrm. You know, the good kind that looks like a nightlight, not the kind that can eat a shark. My magick feels wild, like a million tsunamis are about to break free from me if I am not careful – but only when I try the simple spells. The bigger ones that the spellmages and Prelate Tess say I shouldn't be able to do are easier. When I cast those spells, it feels like I can control almost anything, do anything."

"And you probably can and will. Don't feel rushed, Amanda. You got here later than we did, but you are here now and soon you will be able to make as much or as little glow-wyrm light as you want. Have a little patience, OK? In the meantime, I am going to make sure you know as much as I do. What did the Aesir send you back with to read for tonight?"

Amanda smiled. It felt good to have confided in Cassie. She got up and rustled through some of the scrolls and stone tablets beside her bed. Two were rolled up, so she removed their bindings.

Amanda held up the few sheets of parchment that were covered with deep purple drawings and large red runes. "They wanted me to brush up on the Fell Elves and something called the Disir. Do you know what those are?"

Cassie looked like she had eaten something that disagreed with her, but she nodded. "With all this alfblot running around, it makes sense for you to study them. Chances are that is what is summoning the alfblot. But just know it won't be pleasant. The Disir caused us all to not sleep for about a week when we covered them. Especially when Lord Mimir showed us some of what they did during our lessons."

Amanda put the scrolls down. "Are they that bad? I mean, I've met Bergelmir. What could be worse than that?"

"Let's just say if you wanted any sleep at all tonight, you might want to find something else. The Disir are corrupted by fell magick. Long ago the Fell Elves struck a bargain with some foolish Aesir. In exchange for allowing the dark ones to use a portion of the magick of their long life, they were granted certain spells that gave them power and made them almost unstoppable – but at a cost. Once they used the spells, their souls became tainted and forever changed. They became dependent on alfblot for their power. Their need for it became a craving that destroyed their sanity. Since then, the Fell Elves have been able to make Disir out of anyone they touch. But the really bad ones are the ones who *want* to become a Disir. Those ones want all that power for different reasons, but they always cause a ton of destruction. The worst part is that the Disir are rejected from Hel and from Valhalla. That means they go to a nether region – forever. The last ones who took the power from the Fell Elves destroyed half the realm in their berserker rampage. It took all of the gods to stop them."

Amanda made a face. "That sounds awful. Why would anyone want to become a Disir if that is what happens to them?"

Cassie licked her lips. "They wanted Asgard, and they almost had it too. They thought they could avoid going insane, but they killed anyone they came into contact with – even the Aesir children. If the gods hadn't stopped them, they would have taken Asgard, and then maybe all the Nine Realms. That would have meant the Fell Elves would have also controlled everything too. The Disir are bound to the Fell Elves who create them for eternity."

Amanda looked down at the drawings she held. The outline of the monsters seemed to suddenly shift and move. The room darkened, and Amanda felt like each one of the corners of the room suddenly writhed with shadowy tendrils.

"Perhaps you are right," Amanda stuffed the scrolls under her bed. She sat for a moment, feeling a cold sweat make her clothes cling to her back. "So, what about…" Amanda stopped as she heard Cassie softly snore. She gave a quiet laugh and shook her head. Apparently, Cassie could go from terrified to asleep in less than a minute.

Amanda lay down on her bed. Her eyes traced the ornate wood joinery that supported Cassie, and the linen bed covers that draped down. She took a deep breath and closed her eyes, hoping her dreams wouldn't involve anything to do with the Disir.

CHAPTER 9:
PROJECTILE CAULDRONS

Jack sucked in the sides of his cheeks and bit his tongue, trying to keep himself from screaming. His body shivered uncontrollably as he spun slowly, suspended a few feet above the mouth of a giant skull that looked like a cross between an alligator and a serpent. Bergelmir stood off to his side, casting a spell that sent waves of tiny crab-like ice minions to scour Jack's body and soul. They pinched, jabbed, and then dove through Jack as they searched for their master's answers. With a snarl of disgust, Bergelmir ended the spell, and Jack fell into the mouth of the skull, the teeth curling together above him. He panted through his nose and glared angrily at Bergelmir. He wished he had more fence posts to throw at the Jotun.

When he had first woken up, it had taken Jack a moment to piece together what had happened. The last thing he could clearly remember from Wreathen was fighting with Ms. Biggs. Now, he found himself in an iron cage in a frozen castle. The throne room around him was made of black ice and deadly icicles that swirled down from above. The walls held only windows that looked out over a frozen wasteland, and mirrors that glowed with blue light from etchings along the curved face. Then the imps and Bergelmir appeared, and he knew he wasn't on Earth anymore. He couldn't tell how long it had been, but the Jotun lord visited him often, trying new spells that apparently kept failing to gather the information that Bergelmir desired.

"How do you resist me, mortal?" Bergelmir snapped, and Jack found himself back in his pen, facing the skull he had been in a moment before.

"What's the matter, Bergy? Not up for the challenge? I keep telling you — these aren't the drones you are looking for." Jack mustered as much of a laugh as he could. Truth be told, the more Bergelmir cast his spells on Jack, the less he felt like himself. It was as if the Jotun lord was wearing away at something within him.

"Such misguided petulance. It is irksome amongst your kind, but I have come to find that it is meant more of a show of bravado than actual bravery. You prolong your own suffering. I will find the spell that protects you from my control. No magicks can withstand mine own in my own realm. I am the supreme word in Niflheim. I will break you and then you will join my ranks."

"What makes you think I would ever join you? Don't get me wrong, the rock biscuits you have been serving me are to die for — literally — but that isn't enough to keep me here. You'd be better off letting me go before Amanda finds a way to come rescue me from this

Disney castle reject.”

“I would welcome her to my realm at any time. All Asgardians and their Favoured know better than to challenge the Lord of the Frost Jotuns in his own realm. Their presence would waken the sleeping Jotun giants that surround us here in Utgard, and they would be torn apart within moments. Besides, your friend will not be coming for you. She has forgotten you.”

“Amanda wouldn’t do that,” Jack snarled, surprising himself.

Bergelmir’s mouth widened, his smile churning Jack’s insides. “Oh, but she has. By now she must know you are here, and yet she has made no attempt to enter my realm to find you. You do not know the mortal Favoured as I do. They quickly become enamored with their new magicks, just as the race that birthed them. Their only care is for their own machinations. Even now the entire realm is busy with its celebrations instead of having concern for you.”

Bergelmir held out a hand and the mirror in front of Jack showed a city with clouds and snow lit with thousands of floating lanterns. The people in the city were flying down the streets behind giant shaggy bears that pulled sleighs that looked suspiciously like they belonged to Santa Claus. The vision blurred. When it cleared, Jack could see Amanda laughing, holding onto a girl with dark curls, and racing through the streets. “Clearly, they and your friend no longer even think of you.”

“Amanda isn’t like that. As soon as she can, she will find me, and we’ll be back home.”

“What makes you think you would be welcome anywhere but here in your current condition?” Bergelmir pointed to Jack’s reflection in one of the mirrors inset into the thick layer of folded ice that encased the walls.

Jack didn’t need to look to know what Bergelmir meant. Trying not to give the Jotun the satisfaction, he looked instead to his hands, which were still the color of a ripe blueberry. Their hue bothered him, but it was the other changes he felt within himself that had him really worried. Since arriving here, he found he shivered not from cold but from nervous energy – a fact he hadn’t let on to Bergelmir. Being in this cold place seemed to give him energy and power.

Jack put as much force into his words as he could. “She’s my friend. She will come for me.”

“Enough, mortal. I am done with your tiresome prattling. Let us see if you care for others as much as you say your mortal friend cares for you.” Bergelmir snapped his fingers, and imps appeared through a dark mirror beside Jack. The little minions were carrying something covered in a sackcloth bag. Bergelmir moved to one side as the imps deposited the bag and its contents into the mouth of the giant skull. Watching Jack, Bergelmir pulled the cloth away to reveal an unconscious Billy Bunson.

Jack’s heart stalled and he tried to punch his way through the bars around him. “What are you doing with Billy? Let him go!”

“Give me what I want. Tell me what spell it is that protects you! Deny me and everyone you know will share this mortal’s fate.” Bergelmir began to weave dark magick around Billy. Billy’s body suddenly began to writhe as he shrank and changed until he became a

squirming imp with spikes along its arms. Jack banged on his bars in defeat, and then hung his head. Bergelmir took hold of the imp and held it in front of Jack. "This is the fate that waits for all mortals and those that resist me."

"No. Please. Change him back." Jack kept his head turned. He couldn't bear to look at the imp, knowing it had once been Billy.

"Your mortal friend is now and will be forever more a servant of the Frost Jotuns. There is no spell to return him to his former state. Once a mortal is touched by a Jotun, they are ours to control. It is why Midgard was barred from us by the wretched Asgardian Lord. Thanks to a new spell an acquaintance has brought us, we can now make you into one of us. With each new imp and giant my power grows. Soon, we shall have an army that will raze Asgard and the Nine Realms." Bergelmir flung the imp through one of the open windows into the howling winds outside.

Jack suddenly looked up and his eyes burned blue. "Fine. I will join you Bergelmir, but first you must release me. Once you release me from this prison, we shall get you the answers you seek. I am your greatest ally and will help you defeat all of your enemies."

Jack didn't know what made him say the words, but they tumbled out as he found himself filled with cold fire. To Jack's surprise Bergelmir looked bewildered and made as if to disband the bars around him. Somehow, something inside of Jack was making Bergelmir consider doing what he had said. Jack didn't have time to analyze it. Bergelmir was starting to shake free from his influence. Gripping the bars, Jack pressed his face toward Bergelmir. Throwing as much power into his voice as he could, "That's it, Bergy. Don't stop now. You want to release me. You know it will help give you what you are looking for."

Bergelmir shook for a minute as he fought with himself. With a roar, the Jotun lord flung an arm toward Jack. Jack's head snapped back as a band of ice materialized over his mouth. Bergelmir breathed heavily and the light in the room vanished, replaced by a cold burning glow from the mirrors. "You dare try to bespell me?" Bergelmir's roar shook loose a few of the ice-encrusted stalactites from above. "I am the nightmare that freezes Asgardians and mortals in their beds! I am the chill that brings death and suffering to all who seek to break me. You are nothing!"

Blue and black magick erupted from the mirrors and lanced through Jack. His body contorted as pain seared through his brain. The magick coursed through Jack in a way that felt like a spinning razor had been set loose inside until he felt something break. The fire he had felt inside just moments before vanished and he began to shiver uncontrollably.

Bergelmir surged forward, smashing the bars of the cage. Grabbing Jack by the neck, he lifted him until his feet dangled above the floor. "That is but a fraction of what is in store for you and your friends. However, you have finally proven your worth. You shall not die — today. With your words, you have given me something no other mortal could. You have delivered unto me, a way to devour both Asgard and Midgard with one strike."

Jack struggled in Bergelmir's grip to speak, "I... will... never."

"Silence." Bergelmir's words stopped Jack from speaking further. "You will obey me." Jack's face went slack as he whispered his reply. "I will obey."

"Now our work can begin in earnest," Bergelmir snapped his fingers, and he and Jack vanished.

***

After a month on Asgard, Amanda's brain felt like her stomach after Thanksgiving – dangerously full and close to going on strike. If she had to read one more story about one of the gods enchanting someone or going off on an adventure to save a realm she thought her head would explode. That is, if her body didn't give out first. She had never been so physically exhausted in her entire life. Between running around Asgard for lessons and training with Lady Freyja, it felt as if she was taking a never-ending gym class that involved fire-breathing gnats and sword-wielding goblins.

The Festival of Jul had been just as magickal as Cassie had said. The Favoured were given rune stones to tuck into their cloaks to keep them warm, so Amanda hadn't minded the snow as much as she thought she would have. It did make her miss Jack and home a bit, but it was offset by a week of having no chores, no lessons with Mimir, and no new bruises from training with Lady Freyja.

However, once the week was over, they resumed their schedule and Lady Freyja seemed to redouble her efforts to break Amanda. If it weren't for Cassie and Mykola's help, Amanda was sure she wouldn't have made it. At night, Cassie would quiz Amanda on her reading for the day. Mykola would spar with Amanda in their free time between lessons and whenever he and Cassie weren't off with Lena and Lev. He never made a sound, or got frustrated when Amanda would inevitably trip over her own feet, but would use his staff to help guide Amanda through the various fighting techniques she needed to learn. Even with their help, there were still many nights Amanda was up in the common area of the Stave by herself reading, carefully practicing with her magick, or stacking pillows to punch.

It was exhausting, but whenever she visited her parents, it gave her a renewed determination to find a way to help them and turn Bergelmir into a puddle. Unfortunately, Keeper Fulla had had no luck reversing Amanda's original spell. She wasn't sure if they knew who she was, but the one she thought was her mom would bite her from time to time. Amanda liked to imagine it was her way of yelling at her to hurry up and turn them back into humans.

Amanda felt awful the longer they stayed as mice, especially because she still wasn't anywhere closer to helping them. Her magick was still like a runaway roller coaster. The spellmages were perplexed by her mastery of the more powerful and arcane spells, when she lacked the ability to create a bubble or a single flame on the end of her finger. During her last session, she had learned how to conjure a mirror image of herself, hold back a pack of Hel wolves, and turn sea serpents into tadpoles. They had all clapped and praised her, but when she received her next mirror assignment, she had tried to change a flower's color and caused all of the Favoured's hair to turn the same shade of a ripe red apple instead. Then there was the time she was using a spell to make a pile of feathers float and had evaporated them. Worse was when her magick decided to not work at all, which was mainly whenever she tried to cast a spell to help her parents. The spell she used to transform her parents should have been simple to reverse, but all her attempts had failed so far. The Prelate assured her that with time she would be able to master her favouring, and so she pushed on in her studies.

Amanda hoped today would be a day when her magick would behave exactly as she wanted it to. Heimdall and the Favoured's latest reports indicated new activity from Niflheim, so the Prelate wanted the Favoured to be prepared should the Jotuns attack. Today they would all be facing Frost Jotuns within the mirrors – and Queen Frigga would be joining them to observe Amanda's progress.

Amanda nervously chewed the side of her cheek. She was standing next to Cassie and Mykola in one of the two lines with the other Favoured, waiting for the Queen to arrive. The Prelate had reminded them numerous times how to behave in the Queen's presence. While it was something the other Favoured had heard before, it was a whole new set of protocols for Amanda. The Queen was to be addressed with the utmost respect, and her commands obeyed without hesitation. Her powers were not solely limited to manipulating the atmosphere around them on a molecular level – she was in fact the leader of the spellmages and very adept at most forms of magick. Amanda was nervous, but also hopeful that with the Queen's abilities, she might finally be able to fully control her own magick.

Amanda's stomach growled. Today's training with Lady Freyja had been to wade through the marshes of Vanaheim to track kelp lizards. She wanted to impress the Queen since this was their first official meeting, so she had skipped lunch to clean her uniform of roots and soggy leaves. Amanda rubbed her stomach as the doors swung open.

A whirling mixture of gray and black of clouds rushed forward to the dais in the center of the room. There was a change of pressure in the air, and the Favoured tensed as their ears popped. There was another shift in pressure and the clouds coalesced into the form of the Queen of Asgard. As the clouds parted, Queen Frigga smiled down at them.

"Hello, Favoured." The Queen's warm smile lifted her rosy cheeks.

Queen Frigga looked only slightly older than the Prelate, but her eyes gave away her many years of life and experience. She wore flowing cloaks that shifted in color from white to gray to black, and her dark hair was held up by a diadem of glittering black diamonds. The Queen had a regal elegance, but Amanda could tell she was every bit as much a warrior as Lady Freyja.

"We are honored by your presence, Milady." The Prelate brought her fist to her chest, and the rest of the Favoured followed suit.

Queen Frigga gave a small gesture of dismissal. "Such formalities, Prelate Tess. Please, be about your business." She stepped off the circular disc and began to move around the room.

"As you wish, Milady. Favoured, please step up to you posts," Prelate Tess called out and the Favoured began to find their way to their stands.

As Amanda made her way to her spot, she kept the Queen in the periphery of her vision. The Queen moved about the room with ease, nodding to some of the Favoured and asking questions of the others. At the Prelate's command, the mirrors began to descend. An oval mirror rimmed in black wood floated toward Amanda, settling in between the posts as the Prelate's magick ignited the spell within the looking glass.

"Are you ready, Amanda?"

Amanda jumped. She had not seen one of the spellmages come up beside her. "Yes, Girnka."

"Good. Before we begin, I would like to observe the warding spell we were practicing last time." Girnka was a petite man with a long, braided beard that touched the floor. Girnka held up his hands and a miniature model of Asgard materialized. It looked identical to the realm just outside, complete with drifting clouds.

Amanda hesitated for a moment. The last time she cast the spell, it had caused the mirror she had been using to spit stinging sparks that nearly set Girnka's robes on fire. To try it in the physical world seemed reckless, but she trusted the spellmage. He always spoke to her like her dad had when he had taught Amanda to ride a bike.

With great care, Amanda splayed her fingers on either side of the model. *"Forggia."*

Magick crackled between Amanda's taut fingers and a green bubble slowly began to form under and around the tiny city. Amanda felt something shift behind her, and she quickly glanced to see the Queen and Prelate Tess watching her. Amanda tried to give them a confident smile, but then she felt her magick begin to pour from her hands. She turned in horror just as the spell broke and the cascading magick remnants darted toward the Queen's diadem. The jeweled crown began to suddenly squawk as it transformed into tiny black swans.

Amanda scrambled to try to regain control of her magick, but the Queen calmly waved her hand and her crown turned back to its natural state. "I see you are still having trouble, Amanda." Amanda opened her mouth to apologize, but the Queen held up her hand. "Girnka, what are your thoughts?"

Girnka bowed and began to stroke his beard. "Your majesty, I believe the problem to be one of mental capability. She can understand the complexities of how the spell is to function, but she has a block on what she believes she is capable of."

"Interesting. Is that the case, Amanda?"

"Your majesty, I am so sorry about that. I don't know if that is the case or not. Maybe?" Amanda felt her cheeks redden as she heard Lena and Lev snicker at her from their stands. The twins had already completed their test and were watching her.

"Why do you doubt yourself? I have heard of your triumphs in using spells that even the spellmages have struggled with. Do you not want to succeed?" Queen Frigga circled Amanda.

"No, Milady. I want to do this. I can do this," Amanda said vehemently.

"Then please do so." The Queen indicated her mirror.

Amanda nodded, and turned. The glass surface spun with shifting bands of light until it settled on an empty valley of snow-covered hills. Blue lightning flared and a comet sped through the sky, trailing ice and rock in its wake. Amanda spotted a castle made of two pointed towers. Arched ramparts and buttresses circled the acropolis, which was embedded into jagged cliffs. A figure in white robes was running through the snow.

Runes appeared at the top of the frame. Amanda touched the letters as she read their meaning, "Defeat your foe. Save the Aesir." Amanda tensed as a Jotun giant rose, revealing itself as one of the snow-covered hills. The Frost Jotun giant had skulls hanging from the braces on its forearms, and they swung about madly as it began to swipe at the Aesir. Amanda's face grew tight, and she raised her hands as she prepared to cast one of the spells she knew she could control. "*Fieryr.*"

Magick lanced from her fingers and bells echoed in her ears. The mirror shook. Amanda smiled fiercely as a green wave of fire snaked toward the monster. Just as the flames were about to engulf the Jotun, the giant dug its fist into the snow and pulled a boulder of ice from the ground. With a ferocious roar, the Frost Jotun smashed the boulder into the oncoming fire, stopping the spell and sending a hurricane of snow into the air. Another Jotun giant rose from the disturbed snow, and the two Jotuns began to stalk toward the Aesir. Amanda gritted her teeth and tried again to hurl fire, but nothing happened.

Frustrated, Amanda looked at her clenched fists. "Come on! You can do this!" Amanda yelped as her magick flared around her body. The ground suddenly rumbled under Amanda's feet. Two cauldrons dropped from the sky above the Jotuns in her mirror and knocked them unconscious.

Cassie was in the middle of yelling at her mirror. As the ground tremored again, she grabbed the posts for support and looked about. "What was that?"

The Zukovs and other Favoured were also making a commotion. The spellmages gathered together around Amanda and were inspecting both her and the mirror. Keeper Fulla had been standing in the doorway watching, but now came trotting toward them. Prelate Tess cast her hands about, sending the magick from her gauntlets to inspect Fensalir.

Queen Frigga held up her hands. "Silence!" The room quieted instantly. "Amanda. What spell did you cast?"

"I don't know. I tried to melt the Frost Jotuns, but then cauldrons fell out of the sky." The ground trembled a third time.

"Prelate Tess, look!" Lev pointed to his mirror.

"What is it, Favoured of Sol?" Keeper Fulla careened over to the boy. She examined the mirror and held up a hand. With a whispered word, she touched the mirror's frame. "By the Allfather! It's been bespelled, Prelate. The Queen's spell has been altered. Look!" Keeper Fulla pivoted the stand that held the mirror.

The mirror showed a valley similar to the one in Amanda's, except there were several dark fortresses that ringed a valley. Beyond the valley was a dark green mist. Frost Jotun giants and imps were scurrying about trying to avoid a maelstrom of raining cauldrons. As they watched, giant iron tubs bashed a pair of giants into chunks of ice. More cauldrons fell and flattened a swath of imps.

Queen Frigga held up a hand and magick flared around Amanda. The spellmages also began to scry with their magick. Every mirror in the hall flashed and snowy scenes of Frost Jotuns being bombarded with cauldrons shone in each mirror. "How is this possible? Amanda has taken control of every mirror in the hall."

The floor shook again, and a distant mirror shot one of the cauldrons from its frame through the thatched roof above them. A shower of feathers rained down. They all looked up in surprise for several seconds. Amanda's magick flashed again and a cauldron tore through the mirror in front of Lena, Lev, and Keeper Fulla, knocking them to the ground. The rocketing metal tub crashed into one of the bears supporting the room and tore its arms off. The stone appendages shattered as they hit the floor, and the roof groaned as it lost one of its supports. The Queen spun in a circle, casting a protection shield as the mirrors began to launch volleys of cauldrons into the hall. The walls began to shake and creak, dislodging several mirrors.

The Prelate jumped from the floor up to the armless bear's head. She braced the roof, and the building stilled. "Mykola! We have need of your touch!"

Mykola nodded and pulled the gloves from his hands. Instead of running toward the mirrors, Mykola pivoted and took a hold of Amanda's arms. Instantly the barrage of mirrors stopped. Amanda fell to her knees when Mykola released her. She felt as if all of her energy had been sucked from her, leaving her feeling like a dried husk.

"Blimey, Amanda." Cassie crouched down to help support her friend. "How in the Nine Realms did you manage to do that?"

The doors to the hall burst open as Agnarr and two other Einherjar came running through. They skidded to a stop, stunned at the destruction. Agnarr banged his fist to his chest with one hand while he held his spear ready with the other. "Prelate, is all well here?"

"No!" Keeper Fulla was struggling to her feet and surveying the damage around her. "Apprehend her!" Fulla pointed a wavering finger at Amanda.

The Prelate stopped the Aesir warriors with a motion. "All is well, Agnarr. We have had worse happen with our Favoured, Keeper Fulla. Although none have used cauldrons before. Keeper Fulla, would you please?"

The Keeper scowled at Amanda, but she pushed her sleeves up and spun her hands toward the broken pieces of the bear's arms. The stone fragments flew back to where they had been as the Prelate leapt to the floor. Once the statue was mended, the Keeper began to move about the room, cleaning up any damage that she found.

Queen Frigga held out a hand to help Amanda from the floor. "It seems we still have some work to do, but were successful in your test. Do not give up, Amanda. I feel we will discover the cause of your distress with your favouring soon enough. Agnarr, you may return to your posts. All is well within my hall."

Agnarr lowered his weapon slightly but was still tense. "The Allfather be praised. However, we have more to discuss. There has been a Frost Jotun attack on Midgard again. Bergelmir has possessed an entire town of Midgardians."

CHAPTER 10:
THE MISSING GATEKEEPER

After the debacle in Fensalir, Amanda and the others were escorted back to their rooms while the Prelate left with Agnarr to gather more information about Bergelmir's attack. They waited throughout the evening for the Einherjar or an Aesir to return with news, but no one came. In the morning she woke from dreams about being sent back to Midgard and living with her parents as mice for the rest of her life.

Just after she and Cassie finished dressing, Keeper Fulla knocked on their door. Without making eye contact with Amanda, Fulla tersely told Cassie to report to the Bifrost to join the others on a mission to Midgard to fight the Jotuns with Prelate Tess and Queen Frigga. Cassie had looked at Amanda with concern as she left. Amanda sat quietly with her head down, wondering if her nightmare was about to come true. Surprisingly, the Keeper had only told Amanda that they would be working together while the other Favoured were away. Amanda felt relieved, but also slightly hurt. She knew she needed better control of her powers and didn't have as much combat training as the others, but she had started to feel like part of the Favoured. Now she was being left behind. It made her wonder if the Prelate was actually more afraid of what she could do to the others than any amount of help she might be able to offer.

These feelings were only magnified over the next two weeks as Amanda dealt with a very overbearing Keeper Fulla. It wasn't so much the chores that she had to perform, although counting each and every shipment from Alfheim or Svartalfheim wasn't going to be on her top ten list of favorite Asgardian things to do; it was the way the Keeper treated her every time she made the slightest mistake.

When Amanda hadn't known that the Dwarf tools were counted in threes since they could replicate themselves, the Keeper had given her a look, sighed heavily, and shaken her head as if she were saddled with an inadequate servant that she had no choice but to put up with. Then there was the time Amanda mistook a package of enchanted roots that were supposed to go to some sick vindsvolla to help settle their stomachs for another package of roots from Idunn's orchard of youth-restoring apples. The result was a bunch of vindsvolla that had to regrow their wings. Keeper Fulla had been so irritated that she made Amanda sit outside the shipping house for the rest of the day and count rune stones.

Keeper Fulla had been testily wary of Amanda when she first arrived to be sure – she hated change and was suspicious of Amanda because of her benefactor. But since the events in Fensalir, Amanda felt that the Keeper seemed to think that she was the cause of *all* of their current woes. As the days progressed, the Keeper's attitude worsened, and there had been several tense moments when Amanda had almost lost her cool. It didn't help that Amanda was also feeling angry that she wasn't on Midgard fighting Bergelmir. She should be with the others if for no other reason than to try and look for Jack.

If all of that wasn't bad enough, Keeper Fulla would also sit and critique Amanda at her studies in the Halls of Learning or with Mimir. She would barely finish toweling off before the Keeper would point a finger at her and wave it back and forth as she explained the necessity for accuracy – even when they were discussing Dwarf vowels. It was wearing on Amanda, and each night she would go to bed hoping to hear some news about Jack or her friends, but also hoping the others would return so she could get away from Keeper Fulla. Her magick had returned much sooner than expected after Mykola's touch, yet the Keeper would not allow Amanda to use it in case she might break something else.

Tension within the city rose every day that the Prelate and the Favoured were abroad, which was magnified by the increasing reports of alfblot around the city. After their daily labors and lessons, Keeper Fulla made them take their dinner at the Stave so she could hear reports from the Einherjar and track the alfblot sightings. As they sat in the comfy leather chairs, the Keeper would conjure a map in the flames above the stone basin by Amanda's room. For every location reported, she would mark it in the flames, and then make another mark if the alfblot had caused any illness. Over a dozen Asgardian citizens had become ill due to exposure. The new alfblot was much stronger, and some of the cases were so severe that the ones infected died or went into a berserker rage and attacked anyone around them. The Einherjar subdued those that became berserk and sent them to Eir's Manor to try and rid them of the contamination. Keeper Fulla was now certain there was a Disir on Asgard.

The morning that marked the third week with everyone still abroad in Midgard, the Keeper met Amanda with dire news – Heimdall had gone missing. The Einherjar reported that the Gatekeeper had gone to the Mead Hall, but never returned. Without Heimdall or Queen Frigga to scan the realm, they were even more open to an attack. Keeper Fulla had ordered extra Einherjar to the Bifrost while she and Amanda began to search the realm for Heimdall. Keeper Fulla was certain the alfblot and the disappearance of the guardian of the Bifrost were linked. Using rune stones the two of them began to move sector by sector, scanning the city and its inhabitants for fell magick and the missing Gatekeeper. To be as efficient as possible, the Keeper enlisted the use of Prince Thor's goats and chariot to carry them through the streets.

"Are you sure there isn't another way to go about doing this?" Amanda cowered in the back of the chariot, holding her hair tight to her head with one hand and pressing a bowl of water to her chest with the other. Thor's goats bleated as they whipped around a corner and dodged a group of Aesir. Every time their hooves hit the stone streets, sparks of lightning shot up and threatened to set her hair on fire.

"Prince Thor's goats are the fastest creatures on Asgard next to the winged vindsvolla the Einherjar ride. They can help us cover more of the city in minutes than we could in an entire day. On Tanngrisnir! On Tanngjostr!" Fulla's apron whipped behind her as she pulled at the reins.

They were racing along the streets of Asgard, past the cardinal spires that marked the directions of the city. The elevated echelons of Asgard were mainly comprised of broad roadways and curved battlements holding giant vessels of white crystals. Magick flowed from the crystals to the crackling bands of the city's shields. In between each of the scalloped battlements, sloping walkways arched upward to where heavily armored Einherjar stood guard.

Clouds floated in the streets they flew through, and the goats dove through them like dolphins playing in the waves, making Amanda regret her rather large portion of oatmeal that morning. Each time the goats dashed forward, the water in the bowl would rush toward the rim and spill into her lap.

"Favoured of Sigyn, please focus and hold my bowl steady." The tiny form of Lord Mimir's face tried to speak through the rumbling clamor of the chariot. "It is bad enough I have to speak over those cacophonous behemoths."

"Sorry, Lord Mimir. I was trying not to fall out."

A small splash of water hit Amanda in the face. "That is a poor excuse. My knowledge is an invaluable asset that you and Keeper Fulla have been neglecting. If you had brought me into your search sooner, we would have apprehended the one responsible for the crime of summoning alfblot *before* they abducted Heimdall. My waters give me access to knowledge across this entire city. With my waters to help your rune stones, I can guide you to where I sense the most potent alfblot."

Fulla glared at Amanda, and Amanda gritted her teeth. Yesterday, after searching the city for four hours, she had been forced to read twenty-pages aloud to Lord Mimir and Keeper Fulla regarding the Fell Elves. That was when Amanda asked if Lord Mimir knew anything that could help them find

Heimdall. Mimir had been irate with Keeper Fulla for not reporting the Gatekeeper's disappearance to him, and insisted he accompany them on their search today. Keeper Fulla had looked like she wanted to send Amanda to the Gruneling.

Lord Mimir was waiting for the goats to finish bleating before he continued. "Odiferous beasts. Now then, let us return to the tale of the Fell Elves. Before Ragnarok the Fell Elves, or the dark ones as they are sometimes called, were the epitome of immorality and villainy. They were mischievous, deviously spiteful, and craved to lord over all the Nine Realms. Amongst their other powers, they were most gifted in changeling magick. With a touch they could transform almost any creature into their servant. They were so well practiced in their black arts that they even once managed to turn Prince Thor into a Fell Elf, and then set him loose upon Alfheim. This was after they poisoned the Elivagar Rivers with alfblot. That was a time of many travesties. Those rivers were damaged for almost two centuries. Turn here, Keeper Fulla."

"What about Prince Thor?" Amanda yelped as the chariot bounced to another street below.

"Prince Thor was fine. All he had to do was spend some time in Hel to clear his head. The healers from Eir's Manor, and Eir herself, took Gleipnir, the binding that keeps Fenrir in Hel, and trapped Prince Thor in the same manner for two weeks until the spell abated. Lord Odin took it as a personal matter to deal with punishing the Fell Elves responsible, though of course it was uncertain who had actually done the deed. The Lord of the Fell Elves had already been trapped in the Gruneling. That was the start of a war that decimated the Fell Elf race. Mind you, no one started a war because of the damage to my rivers. Keep left, Keeper Fulla."

Fulla snapped the reins and the goats leapt across a gap to the next level below. Amanda screamed as she gripped the bowl and the wheel well beside her. "So, there aren't that many Fell Elves left?"

Mimir's face lifted from the water and faced Amanda. "That is correct. However, the last known Fell Elves were captured right before the current incarnation of the Spell of Favouring began. There are no known remaining Fell Elves in the Nine Realms except in the Gruneling."

"That is what we have assumed all along. But how would the one responsible have learned the fell magicks or become a Disir if all the Fell Elves cannot be reached? Perhaps a Fell Elf has escaped. Per the rune stones I brought, and Lord Mimir's guidance, we now know there was a powerful convergence of fell magick near the oldest parts of the city. Once we reach that sector, hopefully we will find Heimdall, and perhaps learn more of who is responsible and how they learned to summon alfblot." Fulla looked back to the stones floating within the bowl. They danced about, pointing in the direction they were travelling.

Mimir disdainfully used his waters to push the rune stones to the side. "None can escape the Gruneling. None has, nor will they ever – especially now. Like my well, it was moved after Ragnarok to serve a greater purpose. It sits beneath Yggdrasil's roots. Draupnir, Lord Odin's ring, is now sent there every night to drain the might of the prisoners through the Tree of Life's roots that encircle the prison. This, along with the residual power from the Allfather, is how our realm's defenses are powered when Lord Odin is away from Asgard, and how we ensure that none of the prisoners can use their magick to escape." Mimir vanished and a rippling image of Yggdrasil appeared. The image spun until a black door, laced with chains, appeared. It was surrounded by a corps of Einherjar and a tangled mass of giant roots. "None of the dark ones imprisoned would have a speck of magick to use to escape after being imprisoned for so long."

Amanda closed her eyes a moment as the chariot careened to one side of the road. "Uh… Lord Mimir, didn't I read that Bergelmir actually escaped the prison holding him after Ragnarok?"

"That is –" Mimir paused as he realized he had misspoken. "You are correct, Favoured of Sigyn. I must be suffering from a lack of connection to my full waters. The Jotun trickster is the only being ever to escape the Gruneling. We assume he was somehow able to create Jotuns inside of the prison that gave him enough power to escape. Now that I reflect on it, I may have a theory that is tangential to today's search. Perhaps by using a spell similar to the ones the Fell Elves used to change their prey into more of their race, Bergelmir was able to change someone or something in the prison to create more of his Jotuns to gain enough power to escape the Gruneling. Fascinating. Perhaps the magick drained from the prisoners is not as hollowing as we believed. Stop here, Keeper Fulla. We are close."

Keeper Fulla pulled the goats to a stop and Amanda breathed a huge sigh of relief. "Fascinating? I fail to see what would be of interest in this theory of yours, but do you now concede that a Fell Elf could be loose and teaching an Asgardian their spells."

"I suppose it could be possible. However, it is still highly improbable they did so on their own or that we would not have known about it. It is more likely that the one responsible was able to contact the Fell Elves in the Gruneling. Unlike Bergelmir whose power comes from amassing more Jotuns, the Fell Elves' power only comes from one thing – alfblot. They must consume the energies that alfblot steals in order to gain more power, and I can guarantee you that any loyal Einherjar would not allow alfblot to come within a league of the prison. Therefore, if a Fell Elf has been able to teach someone how to summon alfblot and make them a Disir, it would mean the traitor must be one of the Einherjar. Now if you will excuse me, I must return to my well for a bit to regain my strength. Alert me at once if you find the Gatekeeper or need further assistance. I am sure my help has been of great value today. You are welcome. As I will be leaving, this water will now be of no more use to you. Please dispose of it." With that, Mimir's visage collapsed.

Keeper Fulla grunted. "Bless the Allfather for the silence." Fulla pulled rune stones from her apron and began casting them about into the air where they spun as they searched for any sign of fell magick or Heimdall. She made to follow them, but noticed Amanda was still shaking in the chariot. "Please hurry, we need to move quickly. Take the runes from the waters and use them to help me search."

Amanda felt the trembling in her extremities from their harrowing trip begin to abate. Carefully she stood. Prince Thor's goats bleated as they found a patch of grass to nibble on. Taking the runes, she left the bowl in the chariot. "Coming, Keeper Fulla."

Fulla made an irritated noise. "As soon as you have recovered, I believe I have found something."

Amanda followed Keeper Fulla as she ducked down an alley that led to steep steps. The steps twisted around, taking them lower and lower. As they descended the final step, they entered an old plaza that held several small statues. Above the top of the buildings, Amanda could see the gate of the Bifrost rise in the distance. Dark clouds gathered at their feet, making the air damp with moisture. Keeper Fulla pointed to two trails of dark liquid. Alfblot was scattered about the street as if someone had been carrying two large buckets of it that were too heavy for them to carry. There were also signs of a struggle. Some of the statues had been knocked over, and one of the nearby buildings sported a hole the size of a giant's fist.

"We are close! The one summoning the alfblot must have attacked Heimdall here. The Gatekeeper was known to traverse these roads as he made his way to and from the Bifrost."

Amanda kept her distance as the Keeper circled the plaza. Her skin felt itchy, and something in the air around the plaza felt wrong. "I still don't understand why someone would summon alfblot, or become a Disir."

"The spells grant each Disir something different. Those who use the spells to gain power have done so for different reasons. If what Mimir stated is true, perhaps one of the Einherjar is tired of being given orders or used as a pawn. The gods send them out first in any conflict. Look. The runes sense the presence of the one using fell magick, and this alfblot is freshest. Here." The Keeper handed Amanda several more rune stones. "Throw these at any you encounter, for they surely will be the one we seek. They require no magick other than the strength of your arm, so do not worry yourself with your favouring. We must not stop looking until we find Heimdall, and we cannot let our foe escape now that we are so close. Whatever led us to them today may not do so again. You take the path toward the Bifrost. I shall follow this other toward Yggdrasil. Take care to use the other stones to destroy any alfblot you find. The potency I sense within it makes it more dangerous than any we have encountered before."

Amanda inspected the rune stones. Their markings were ancient bindings that Amanda recognized from some of her readings. Her stomach was jittery with nerves. She had read more on the Disir, and she was glad she had waited to read it during the day. The stories all told of monsters with enough power that they could rip their enemies apart. Amanda wanted to ask if they should call for back-up if there was a Disir nearby, but decided to put on a brave face. "I won't let you down, Keeper Fulla."

The Keeper gave Amanda a worried nod and left through an arched opening. Amanda took one of the original rune stones and held it up. Red light emanated from the rune and the alfblot began to swirl and gather in the air, turning to mist before it was sucked into the stone. After the plaza was cleared, Amanda kept the rune stone high, following the trail toward the Bifrost, and allowed the magic of the stone to cleanse the path before her.

As she walked, Amanda noticed several strange things about the area she passed. Black moss had overrun most of the buildings, and had even begun to crumble some of the foundations. The streets were filled with broken carts, pots, and debris, and the air was stale and still. The rest of the Asgard was pristine and vibrant with life, but here, everything seemed to be decaying.

She was trying not to sneeze when a piece of parchment blew onto her leg. She bent to pick it up. The sheet showed a list of items, with some crossed off. It looked like a potion of some kind, but for what Amanda couldn't tell. The items listed had been smudged a bit so the runes were hard to read; the only one that was clear was the word "apple." She tucked the parchment into her cloak to look at it later. At that moment something echoed from the street in front of her.

Amanda couldn't see beyond the bend in the road in front of her, but she could make out muffled, scratching sounds. Her heart began to beat loudly in her chest. Amanda slowed her steps and backed up against a stone wall along the road. As she crept forward, the rune stone she had been holding flew from her fingers toward a patch of alfblot under the porch of an abandoned building. The chittering noises went silent. Building up her courage, Amanda ran around the corner, but found the street empty. Up ahead, something was bundled in a sackcloth bag on a cart. Under the cart, a purple and black circle of magick swirled, casting the entire street in surreal swirls of eerie light. The rune stones finished cleaning the alfblot from the house and flew toward the dark magick. The hair on Amanda's arms stood on end and she fought back another sneeze as a bolt of magick from the vortex obliterated the stones.

Amanda cautiously approached the cart, keeping a wary eye out for whatever had been making the scratching noises a few moments before. When she was a few feet from the vortex, she noticed the bowl she had left in the chariot was beside the cart, empty. She made her way around to the bowl, but when she bent down to touch it a jolt of purple magick shocked her. She stared at her fingers, which had gone numb, and then clamped her hands over her ears as a screeching hiss echoed through the street. Alfblot began to bubble up from the bowl.

Amanda stepped away to avoid the fell liquid, bumping hard into the cart's handle. A moan came from the lump inside the bundle.

"Heimdall? Is that you?"

Amanda's heart began to race even faster. She wasn't sure what the vortex was, but she knew it was keeping her from Heimdall. Knowing the Keeper would probably be furious with her, she decided to try to use her magick. Stepping back, Amanda recalled a spell one of the spellmages had tried to teach her that could swap one thing for another. Amanda looked about quickly and saw a barrel lying amongst a row of broken planters.

"*Transityr!*" Amanda's magick flashed. The barrel vanished. There was another blaze of light and a pile of wood logs appeared. She had been trying to swap Heimdall and the barrel, but once again her magick hadn't worked.

Amanda chewed the side of her cheek. Lifting her hands, she opened her mouth to cast another spell. Before she could speak, a dozen Frost Jotun imps sprang up from the vortex. They paused when they saw her. The imps closest to her leapt toward her, while the others began to attach themselves to the cart's wheels. Reacting instinctively, Amanda rolled her arms forward and sent green fire to melt the imps.

More imps began to climb out of what Amanda could only guess was their version of a portal and rush at her. While she focused on obliterating her new attackers, the ones attached to the cart began to pull it down into the portal. Remembering the runes the Keeper had given her, she threw them at the cart. The runes ignited and the imps froze, along with the cart that was now halfway submerged into the portal. Amanda frantically tried to think of a way to get to Heimdall again. She wasn't sure how long the rune stones' magick would hold as more imps appeared. She turned as she heard someone running toward her.

"Move!" Lena yelled. Splaying her fingers, the girl sent beams of sun fire toward the frozen Jotuns, but it wasn't fast enough. The rune stones crumbled, and the imps began to swarm toward them.

Lev was right behind his sister. He was holding his hands in front of him, muttering. Amanda jumped as a dozen Fire Jotun beasts, which looked like a cross between a lion and a giant salamander, rose from the ground and galloped toward the imps. One passed right through her, but the Frost Jotun imps couldn't tell they were illusions. The imps retreated, allowing more time for Lena to attack. Amanda joined her, and the fiends were quickly defeated. Mykola came racing down another street, unlacing his gloves as he ran. Amanda cried out to be careful as black magick lanced toward him. Mykola slowed, but held up a hand, his favouring dissipating the magick. When he reached the circle, he placed both hands into the vortex, and the circle of magick vanished.

Amanda dashed over to her friend. He held up a hand to keep her back, indicating that he was alright, and then pointed toward the sack on the cart. Amanda nodded in understanding. She jumped onto the wooden boards and wrestled the bag open to find an unconscious Heimdall holding an enormous purple egg. Heimdall's eyes were coated in alfblot, as were the chains that bound him.

Amanda dug into her cloak's pocket and found the last rune stone for cleaning alfblot. She raised the stone and activated it. Heimdall suddenly began to writhe as the chains tightened. Amanda dropped the rune stone quickly, and the chains stilled.

Lena and Lev jumped up beside Amanda. Lena pushed Amanda out of the way. "Useless. Leave it to me. I shall cleanse the alfblot from his bindings."

Amanda held up her hands to stop Lena. "Wait! I think the chains are bespelled to hurt Heimdall if the alfblot is removed." Unbidden, magick coursed from Amanda's hands into Lena, blowing both girls and Lev backward.

Lena was thrown onto the rails of the cart. She let out a strangled cry and clutched the side of her face. Lev also cried out and rolled away from Mykola, who had held up his unprotected hands to catch Lev instinctively.

At Mykola's touch, Lev's illusions vanished. Amanda watched as magick swirled around Lev and then flew to his sister. Lena cried out again. Lev glared at Mykola and looked as if he were about to strike him, but ran to Lena instead. "Sister!" Lev stopped when he saw her face.

Lena had her back to Amanda, so when she turned around Amanda gasped. The entire right side of Lena's face and neck, as well as her right hand, were covered in silver runes. "You! You will pay for this!" Lena raised her hand, but nothing happened. The markings on her faced burned brighter as Lena tried again to use her magick. Lena looked from her hand to Amanda. "What did you do to me?" Lena's eyes went wide and she leapt at Amanda, grabbing her by the neck.

"S-stop! I-It wasn't my f-fault. I-I didn't do anything." Amanda tried to free herself, but Lena had her up against the cart.

"Lena! Let go! Now!" Cassie's voice came from somewhere behind Amanda.

Lena's arms dropped to her sides, and Amanda fell. Gasping for breath, someone took Amanda by her shoulders and helped her to stand. Amanda turned to find Sean standing beside her.

"Thank you." Her voice was gravelly as she spoke.

"Seems you have gotten yourself into something of a hornet's nest while I was gone." Sean smiled, but his eyes looked tired.

Lena had regained control of herself and pulled her cowl over the side of her face. "You will all pay for this. Especially you, Amanda. I don't know what spell you used, but once I get my magick back you will be sorry. You are the real danger to our realm." She grabbed her brother and they quickly left.

Sean whistled. "She is about one fry short of a happy meal."

Amanda shook her head. She was still a bit dazed. "I didn't mean to. I don't even know what I did."

"You just embarrassed her is all. The Manor will have her fixed up in no time." Cassie waved to a triad of Einherjar and a very worried looking Keeper Fulla. "Good news is we got here in time. Or should I say, you got here in time."

"I was just lucky I took this path and found Heimdall. How did you find me, and what are you doing here, Sean?"

"Why, I am hurt, Amanda. Here I thought you would be happy to see me." Sean smiled again. This time his eyes were bright and it made Amanda chew the inside of her cheek. "I went to Midgard to find the Prelate and the others to give them a warning from something we discovered in Nidavellir. A pack of trolls we captured told us of a plot they heard from some Frost Jotuns to snatch Heimdall and Draupnir." As he moved to help the Einherjar, Amanda could see Sean's uniform was covered in scratches and smudges of dirt as if he had just burrowed his way up from an ant hill.

Cassie's clothing was also a bit disheveled, but slightly cleaner. "Bergelmir vanished with half the town almost as soon as we got there, but the Jotuns he left behind kept multiplying all on their own. It took us weeks to defeat all of them. Once that was done, it took us some time to get the people we rescued put back together. Half were still possessed in ways no one has seen before. The others were dealing with the sickness that comes from being possessed. We were still trying to figure it all out when Sean arrived. The Keeper's message had been blocked by the Jotuns, so we didn't know what was happening here until then. The Prelate sent the five of us to help. Based on what we heard when we arrived, we found the chariot and then we split up to find you and Keeper Fulla."

They all paused as the Einherjar lifted Heimdall and began to carry him off. One of the Einherjar handed Keeper Fulla the egg. "How is Heimdall, Keeper Fulla?" Amanda asked.

"He is alive. It is clear he has been poisoned by alfblot, but we do not know the extent of his condition beyond that. We should be able to reverse the alfblot's affects, but the Aesir at the manor will have to use the older and slower remedies. The previous tonics all contain frost lilies, which are deadly to Heimdall."

Keeper Fulla handed the egg to Cassie as she began to clean up the remaining alfblot and the bowl that had held Mimir's waters. With a snap the bowl vanished. "For now, we will have to continue our search for the one summoning the alfblot. The path I followed led only to the nest of the vindsvolla, where they must have obtained that egg. I hope it is unharmed. If the imps managed to touch it, then it will be a dulhda that will be able to pass into our realms as freely as the other vindsvolla do."

Amanda could finally take a minute to inspect the egg. It was the size of a basketball, and she could now see that its color came from miniscule feathers that covered the entire surface except for the very top. At that moment, a rainbow portal blazed to life and the Prelate and Connor came charging through.

The Prelate saluted them, and they all returned the gesture. "Someone tell me what in the name of the Allfather happened here today. Where are Lena and Lev?"

"I think they went off to the Manor. Lena had some kind of bad reaction to a spell and Lev bumped into Mykola. You ask me, Lena could use a vacation." Cassie smiled and took the Keeper by the arm. "Amanda, why don't you tell the Prelate what happened? I want to talk to Keeper Fulla about the vindsvolla egg."

Cassie pulled the Keeper off to the side of the cart. Amanda looked confused but turned to the Prelate. The warrior woman crossed her arms and looked down at Amanda expectantly. Suddenly Amanda felt her anger at being left behind pounding in her chest.

She began to retell how the day had started with searching for Heimdall and the points Lord Mimir made as they were travelling. She told the Prelate about the alfblot trail and how she had found Heimdall above a portal of some kind. As she spoke, she became even angrier. "So, you see, I can be of some use even when I am left behind because of some accident I had no control over."

The Prelate's sharp ears picked up the tone in Amanda's voice. Her words were soft when she spoke. "Aye, you were. If you had not been here, surely Heimdall would have been taken from our realm. Do you think you were kept here on Asgard because I did not want you with us in Midgard because of what occurred in Fensalir?"

"Well, didn't you?" Amanda huffed and crossed her arms. She looked away from the Prelate.

"Not at all. I knew we could be facing Bergelmir, and I wanted to keep you safe from him. If you had been there, the Jotun most certainly would have tried to kidnap you as he did on the night of your claiming. I was also concerned, and rightfully so, of what might happen should we encounter your friend Jack."

Amanda swallowed and she could feel her anger leaving her. It never occurred to her that the Prelate could have been trying to protect her. "I could still be helpful in other ways, but I guess that makes sense. But what do you mean about encountering Jack? Was he there?"

The Prelate nodded and tapped two runes on her gauntlets. Golden light began to replay a vicious fight between some Einherjar and what looked like a giant Jotun imp. Amanda's eyes widened when she realized it was Jack that was fighting the Aesir warriors – and that he was winning.

"What happened to him?" Amanda looked up as the Prelate ended the broadcasted vision of her friend.

"He has fallen under Bergelmir's control. The Jotun lord used him to infiltrate the town and begin to capture its residents. It was how it went unnoticed by Heimdall until it was almost too late."

"But will he be OK? Can we change him back?"

"That all depends. Spells can take a while to completely change those they are cast upon. If we can rescue him soon, we should be able to save him. Now more than ever, we must find out how the alfblot and the Jotuns are linked. From what I heard in your tale, the one serving the Fell Elves has enough power now to cast a syirce. Those are the portals the dark ones used to enter our realm during our wars with them."

The Prelate summoned the others to circle around her. "Sean, send word to our allies in the other realms and see if they can aid us in finding a cure for Heimdall. Report back to me once you have done so. I will prepare a schedule for the Favoured to guard Draupnir for you to distribute. Since what we heard from the trolls proved to be true, we must assume that the ring's safety is in jeopardy. I will consult with Queen Frigga about the troubling news of the syirce, and see if she can use Lord Odin's throne, Hlidskjalf, to see if there are more in our realm. Since it was summoned on Asgard that means that the one responsible is not only in league with the Fell Elves, but also with Bergelmir, since it was his imps who tried to abduct Heimdall. I will take Lord Mimir's words as a warning and have the Einherjar given the Test of the Disir."

"Prelate Tess? Do you think I could look after the vindsvolla egg? I've just been talking to the Keeper about it and telling her how much I miss having a pet. Perhaps we can make sure it will not turn into a dulhda." Cassie had made her way to Connor to give him a hug.

"Very well. Just be certain to keep it safe. Know that this is no ordinary Midgardian pet. It may also be the focus of the traitor, so be on guard. While a dulhda is one of our enemies' most desired assets to use against us, the egg could be just as valuable to them. The shell puts off a powerful charm that can be used to sway the mind of anyone the egg bearer so desires. When I can, I will come and teach you how to properly care for the egg. Now then, we must be off to our duties."

The Prelate brought her fist to her chest and took off for the palace as the Favoured mirrored her gesture in response.

CHAPTER 11:
RED COMBAT

"Again!" Lady Freyja's yell rang across the Einherjarium.

Amanda shifted her weight and felt a twinge in her side from a bruise that was forming from the last sparring round. Coming toward her was a replica of an Einherjar warrior that Freyja had conjured to spar with the Favoured, complete with eagle armor and a war hammer as big as Amanda. Unlike the clean-cut warriors, these figures bore no faces under their visors.

Sean was standing beside Amanda giving pointers. "Keep your guard up, Amanda. Remember to look for openings. You've got to know your enemy the second you come up to them. It takes practice, but everyone has a way they communicate their intent; you just got to know what to look for. When my dad took me deer hunting near Corpus Christi, he told me to watch for the one moment in between breaths. That's the moment to move in for the kill. He also told me to never turn your back on a cow because they like to nip at your backside when you aren't looking."

The red figure swung its mace at Amanda, so she dove to the right while also avoiding a burst of steam from a vent hole in the ground. The landscape of their training session today was the swirling mud plains of Muspelheim, which included jutting spikes of something that could have been trees millennia ago. Whatever they were, they were now blackened and petrified from being sprayed by hissing geysers that sent boiling, liquefied soil into the air every few minutes. Amanda heard the hammer strike the soil and turned around quickly. The Einherjar replica was struggling to pull its weapon free, so she crossed her arms and tried the double-hit combo she had been practicing for the last hour. Misjudging the soft dirt underfoot though, she stepped forward too fast and her boot sunk into the soil up to her calf.

"Ow, ow, ow!" Yanking her foot free, Amanda patted the steaming dirt from her leg.

"You're trying too hard, Amanda. The movements are quick, but fluid. You were stepping like you were trying to line dance with an angry cow."

"I don't get it. I'm doing what you showed me, it just feels... awkward." Sweeping her bangs from her face, and wiping her forehead to keep the sweat from getting in her eyes, Amanda raised her fists as her sparring partner finally freed its weapon and came at her again.

"I don't know why you are wasting your time with her, Sean. Didn't my sister tell you what happened the other night while she was guarding Draupnir?" Lev called from across the field, expertly jumping up and over the warrior in front of him.

"It was pathetic. She nearly fell into a syirce because she was scared by Ratatosk coming down Yggdrasil." Lena glared at Amanda.

After the entire host of Einherjar passed the Test of the Disir, Agnarr and the other warriors had been called away to search for and guard over a half dozen new syirces that were discovered. Mykola's touch was the fastest remedy to close the portals, but it took him days to recover after each time he used his magick to close one, so it would be a while before the Aesir warriors were free to train with them once more.

Lena was trying to summon enough heat to melt the sand in front of her drone, but nothing was happening. Three nights ago was the first time in two weeks anyone had seen Lena or Lev when they showed up to guard Draupnir with Amanda, Cassie, and Mykola. Amanda had awkwardly tried to ask if they were ok, she was relieved to see Lena's face bore no trace of the silver runes, but the twins kept silently to themselves except. Their only response was to glare at Amanda and turn their backs toward her. They heard the following day from Keeper Fulla that it had taken her and the Aesir hours to remove the runes on Lena's face, but that hadn't helped to bring her or her brother's magick back. They originally thought the runes were a binding spell preventing Lena from using her magick, but when they were gone and nothing happened, they surmised it had to be a combination of Amanda and Lena's magicks along with Mykola's touch that was preventing the twins from regaining their powers. Normally the effects of Mykola's touch wore off within a week, but after a week went by they brought in spellmages to help Keeper Fulla. What they discovered was somehow their favourings had been bound in such a complex way, they weren't sure if they would every fully recover until the Spell of Favouring brought them their benefactor's full magicks.

Amanda had felt awful, even though she knew she hadn't meant to hurt anyone, and she and Mykola tried to apologize to Lena and Lev again when the twins showed up to guard Draupnir. The twins' words back to them were brief and cold. They refused Amanda and Mykola's apology ignoring them only after promising to make them pay.

Amanda was trying to be sensitive, but today, she had finally had enough. "I didn't get scared. I got surprised. I mean who expects to see a squirrel as tall as a Saint Bernard? I read about Ratatosk, of course, but seriously. Besides, I was looking for you two when it was time to leave. You wandered off without telling us where you were going."

Lena shrugged a shoulder and turned back to her drone. "Perhaps you are simply inheriting another of your benefactor's traits – insanity. Maybe we should take your favouring away, just as you took ours, in case you are the one summoning the syirces."

Amanda eyes became slits as she tried to glare at the twins but her mouth betrayed her as she fought back a yawn. It was no longer alfblot that was causing distress around the city, it was the syirces that were now the main source of concern, and the threat of an invasion to steal Lord Odin's ring. This meant double combat lessons and round the clock shifts of guarding Draupnir. So, between lessons, training, and guarding Draupnir at the Gruneling every night, Amanda felt like she was constantly running around half-asleep and completely exhausted. The only sleep she had been getting was the last few hours before breakfast after they returned Draupnir to Lord Odin's palace, and it was plagued with dreams of monsters and Jotuns. Her dreams, however, paled in comparison to the cause of her nightmares – the Gruneling.

After Sean distributed the schedule of guard duty, all of the Favoured gathered at Valaskjalf. The Prelate brought Draupnir forth from the palace on a golden stand. They marched for half an hour through a corridor in Yggdrasil, and then along a dry and decaying flatland filled with rocks and dried bushes until they came to a door the size of Amanda's house. The Prelate placed the ring over a door and touched a rune on the stand. The hair on the back of Amanda's neck had stood on end as a low moan shook the enormous wood beams of the door. The chains had rattled and screeched as they stretched, reaching up toward the golden stand as magick began to seep upward into the ring. But it wasn't the sounds, disturbing as they were, that bothered Amanda. It was the sense that behind the door something was... wrong. It was like the feeling Amanda got when she stared into the woods behind her house late at night, like there was someone there – just watching and waiting for her to go to sleep so they could come for her. After that they were dismissed until it was their time to guard the ring. At the end of their shift, they took the ring and the stand back to the Prelate at Valaskjalf. Amanda and her friends had been the unlucky ones to draw the night shift, so every night afterward they guarded the ring from the darkest hours of night until sunrise.

Sean sent a jolt of electricity at the twins. "Give it a rest, Lena. That squirrel could bite either one of you in half if it mistook you for an acorn. So, make like a fly and buzz off."

Amanda bit the side of her cheek as she smiled her thanks to Sean. Her hands crackled with magick. "Maybe they can make like a bug and get zapped."

"Don't do anything to get yourself into any trouble right now. They're just trying to rile you because they are upset." Sean checked Amanda's stance and adjusted the position of her feet. "Next time make sure you plant before you go after your target. You don't want to give Lady Freyja anything to go in on you for today. She's normally like a mad cat but today she's like a queen bee with no honey."

"And how is that different from every other day? Whatever I or Cassie do is never good enough." Ducking to avoid a swing from the drone, Amanda found that her new positioning helped her keep her balance better. "And those two... I get they are probably worried about their magick, but shouldn't we be focused on working together to help Heimdall and stop the syirces? Maybe if they were a bit nicer we could all work together to help them too."

Sean circled around Amanda. "They'll adjust or they won't. Their magick will come back or it won't. No one ever promised us this was going to be easy. However, this is really the first time being a Favoured has been hard for them. Before this, and I would eat a crow before I would say it to their faces, they were two of the best. When we first got here, we all bumbled around a bit to be sure, but not those two. They were laser focused, like they knew this was coming and they had prepared for it. Now they have to start all over. Probably just makes them even more jealous of you. It's probably just the Norn's way of slapping them with a fish."

"Slapped with a fish? Is that some kind of torture technique?"

"Ha! No, but it should be. Just an expression from back home – although my dad did whack me with a catfish once. Think of it as a rude wake-up call. When you act out or take things for granted, something's going to come back to you and make you pay."

Lady Freyja passed by Amanda and glared at her as Amanda cross-stepped when she should have shuffled back. Sean was right about Lady Freyja, so Amanda tried to ignore her looks of disappointment. The goddess, who was never what anyone would call pleasant, had been laying into the Favoured for anything she could. Amanda wondered if the goddess of war was actually feeling stressed from the syirces and threats of invasion. She pictured Lady Freyja sitting in her hall having a fit as another report of a syirce came in, and then jumping out the window.

Amanda bit back a smile at the thought, and then considered Sean's words. "Why would you think they are jealous of me? I can barely manage to stay standing up with all this mud, let alone do the attack exercise we are supposed to be working on today."

"It's not what you *can* do; it's what you *might* be able to do that has them all riled up. You are the first of your kind. No one knows what you can accomplish. You could be better and bigger than any Favoured has ever been. The Zukovs pride themselves on being the best and doing things no one else can. To them, being the best defenders of the realm is the only thing that matters. They don't like the thought of being shown up by someone who has been here for just two months. Add that to the fact that now that their favouring is on the fritz, and it's no wonder they are acting out the way they are."

"Can we please get some pillows or something for the ground? My backside is going to be sore for a week if these training sessions keep up like this!" Cassie was wiping a splatter of mud from her hair. An unseen geyser had knocked her backward, which her drone had taken as a victory, so it had frozen while awaiting Lady Freyja's next command. Cassie sensed she had interrupted something. "What's with you two?"

Amanda tried to smile sympathetically as she dodged an attack. "Sean thinks Lena and Lev are jealous of me being here because of how great I'm turning out, which is hilarious since I never know if I am going to actually cast the right spell or blow up Fensalir. What does it matter what I could do if I never learn how to control my magick? It's almost enough to make me miss Ms. Biggs."

Cassie made a face like she had just eaten a rotten lemon. "Ok, well let's not start talking crazy. This will all get sorted out as soon as Lord Odin comes back. And don't get too down on yourself about the Zukovs. Those Zukovs are such nasty... ogre boogers. I want to feel sorry for them, but they've never really been nice to anyone. You would think that now they have to deal with something hard, they might be a bit more sensitive, but nope! They came through the stave when I was taking care of the vindsvolla egg yesterday. Lev had the nerve to ask why we even needed the vindsvolla when the Prelate is the last of the Valkyrie. I didn't know what to say... me! Thank goodness the Prelate wasn't about. It's bad enough she has to wear those gauntlets as a daily reminder of what she lost, so how heartless do you have to be say something like that when she could be just around the corner?"

Amanda held up her hands in defeat to her drone, and it paused in mid punch. She watched Lena and Lev for a moment. They acted as if everything was normal, but every now and then she caught them trying to use their magick, and could see a small bit of fear in their eyes as little to nothing happened. "Heartless or not, I wish I knew how to use my magick to undo whatever it is that we did. I'm still not able to help my parents, and now Jack is some kind of zombie-Jotun-attack-imp. I mean he would probably love it if he weren't being used to hurt people. I feel like I am just coasting and not actually improving, or being of any use."

"Your constant whining is certainly of no help." Lady Freyja walked up behind Cassie and pushed her Favoured back to her drone.

"That's it," Amanda began, but Sean laid a hand on her shoulder.

Lady Freyja turned and raised any eyebrow, but Amanda closed her mouth. The goddess gave her a smirk, and raised her hands. New drones appeared so that now each of the Favoured faced two opponents instead of just one. "Less talking! More action! Must I remind you all that Bergelmir is still out there? The syirces are appearing at an even greater rate, and one of our main lines of defense lies in a coma in Eir's Manor. You must work harder than ever before if you are to be ready for what is to come! A pack of gravel snails from Jotunheim could do better. Perhaps you need a little encouragement? If one of you can best your opponent before Cassandra, I will give you a reprieve for the rest of the lesson. However, should Cassandra best her drone first, you shall all run laps around Mimir's well until I say otherwise. And Cassandra, should you fall first, *you* shall run laps until the gods return."

With a few determined grunts, a deep scowl from Amanda, and a groan of dread from Cassie, everyone repositioned themselves as the red battalion began to advance on the group again. This time, when the first battle drone brought down its fist, Amanda kept her right forearm up to block the attack. The leather suits they wore did a pretty good job of absorbing most impact, but the force of the drone's swing slammed into Amanda's defensive block, sending a sharp jolt to her elbow. "Ow!"

"Keep going, Amanda. Next time turn the momentum of the attack against your attacker. The best way to steal someone's thunder is to take it for yourself." Sean circled around behind the drone as he watched.

The next drone struck, and Amanda held her guard up, but instead of trying to stop the attack she let it slide down her forearm. The glancing blow made the dummy tip forward with its own momentum and for a moment the drone looked like it was doing one-footed jumping jacks. Taking advantage of her off-balance foe, Amanda grabbed the red warrior by its armor and threw it down onto the ground. The other faceless Einherjar replica dove toward Amanda, but she spun just in time so that the drone was blasted with a geyser and flew into the stands outside of the arena. Amanda felt a thrill of excitement at her victory and looked up to Sean.

"I did it!" Amanda clapped. Sean smirked and tilted his head. Amanda looked back down at the drone, which had pushed itself up off the ground. Sweeping its leg in an arc, the drone knocked Amanda's feet out from under her, and she found herself on her back sinking half an inch into the heated mud.

Sean's head appeared from above. "Never turn your back on an opponent. Remember?" He extended a hand.

"Way to go, Amanda!" yelled Cassie, which was followed by a grunt. Amanda turned to see her friend sprawled under a charred limb that had fallen on her. Her two opponents had backed her into one of the burnt pillars, and the impact had caused the loose branch to fall.

"Hold!" Lady Freyja called, holding up a fist. The dummies in front of the other Favoured froze with fists raised. "It seems you all have Cassandra to thank for the rest of the afternoon's freedom."

"Come on – those drones were cheating, and Amanda bested her drone first," Cassie groaned while she tried to free herself.

"She's right, Lady Freyja. I technically bested my drones before Cassie was hit, and Cassie was taken out by the branch, not the drone." Amanda helped her friend from the Einherjarium floor.

"Excuses are a pitiful defense. As I see it, Cassandra has failed yet again." Lady Freyja crossed her arms. "Cassandra, you are to complete a hundred cycles around Mimir's well and then report back to me to see if I am satisfied."

Cassie blinked several times and then slumped her shoulders. Amanda had had enough. "That's not fair and you know it. You're pushing us too hard!"

"You think this is hard?" The goddess of war turned and addressed the rest of the Favoured. "We are under attack! The one summoning the syirces has provided openings into our realm they could use at any moment. If that were to happen, you would be captured and tortured. Perhaps that is what it would take to make you work harder at your training. When we find ourselves faced with another Ragnarok, the fires will claim the weak and leave the strong. It would certainly rid us of those who do not belong on Asgard." As she spoke the last part, Lady Freyja locked eyes with Amanda.

"She didn't mean anything by it, Lady Freyja. They are just tired is all," Sean said, trying to placate the goddess.

Ignoring Sean, Lady Freyja pointed at Amanda. "Take a look, Favoured. Here is your downfall, the weakness in your defense and strength. We should have allowed the Jotuns to take you. You could not save your mortal friend, and your family is still trapped by the first of your many failed spells. Sigyn was the same. Her spells were like poisonous snakes. They fed on the despair they created. Lord Odin locking her in the Green Askr was more kindness than she deserves. I hope you and she will rot in there together. Your friend's fate is probably a blessing. He will never know what a failure you are, and will find peace once Bergelmir has no more use for him."

Amanda's chest constricted, and she felt her skin prickle as tiny filaments of heat erupted all over her body. Freyja's words sent anger coursing through Amanda as she thought about everything she had endured for the past two months for her friend and her parents. A spell popped into Amanda's mind, and she threw her hands at the goddess. Freyja's eyes widened as a green flash of lighting struck the ground, sending a storm of sand and obsidian shards flying. The first piece of twisted rock cut through Freyja's armored sleeve and punctured the stone wall that separated the stands from the field. Reacting with lightning speed, Lady Freyja drew her sword and began deflecting the rest of the stones with her dark blade which made small metallic chimes as it redirected each shard. The last piece of rock zinged through the air and embedded itself in the dirt next to Cassie's foot.

"Bloody burgers," Cassie murmured while the rest of the Favoured stared at Amanda.

"Amanda! Are you OK?" Sean had taken a defensive stance when the deflected rocks had come his way. He tentatively stood and lowered his hammer. Stepping beside Amanda he held out a hand which she gripped for support. Amanda swallowed and nodded but leaned onto him to keep from dropping to her knees.

A flash of light suddenly lit the field as the Prelate charged through a glowing portal. She took in the scene for a second and then turned to the war goddess, who was inspecting her wound. "What has transpired here, Lady Freyja?"

"'Tis but a scratch. The Favoured of Sigyn's aim still leaves much to be desired, just as it does in our archery lessons." Lady Freyja sheathed her blade. Surprisingly, the goddess's temper had cooled. "In truth, I am glad that she is finally showing some promise. It took a bit of goading, but I think she has learned the lesson for the day."

"Wha... what lesson could possibly be worth what you said to me?" Amanda was still trying to catch her breath while her heart was doing jumping jacks in her chest.

"Yes, what lesson did you hope to teach by having her use her magick against you?" The Prelate had crossed to Amanda and was examining the girl with her gauntlet's magick. The golden light felt warm as it glided over her skin.

Freyja met the Prelate's eyes and held them. "Anger is an insidious creature. Most emotions are. Fear, once created, can sustain itself and grow until you become immobilized, unable to take the next step. Jealousy can addle your brain and make you lose focus. And anger — it can cause you to lose control. Magick, all magick, requires that these emotions be contained. You asked me to teach her as I would any of the other Favoured, and with each of them I have found a way to instill this lesson into their training. I attempted to teach Cassandra to control her fear when I threatened not to let her eat for a week. It was a wasted effort, but today with Amanda... I believe I was successful." Lady Freyja smiled and Amanda swore she thought she heard the goddess purr with laughter.

A startled cry came from behind Amanda and they all turned to see Lev trying to help his sister. Both twins were bleeding from cuts on their cheeks, but Lena was shaking and flickering as if she were fading in and out of existence. "Help us! I think she has done something to my sister again!" Lev was frantically digging for something in his cloak. He cried out again as he found a hole torn through the fabric.

Amanda and the others gasped as the Prelate leapt over to the twins. Pressing two fingers to Lena's forehead, the Prelate whispered a few words and Lena's body began to stop its convulsions. As Lena's trauma was mended, Lev began to calm down as well. The Prelate spoke a few words to the twins, who nodded before calling a rainbow portal and leaving.

Lady Freyja cleared her throat. "What has the Favoured of Sigyn wrought now? Is it finally time to send her to the Gruneling?"

"That is enough, Lady Freyja. With their favouring already disrupted, being exposed to that much magick had another unintentional effect on Lena and Lev.

Lady Freyja's smile vanished, as did her jovial mood. "You coddle her like a mewling kitten. Your words were that she is to be a warrior, were they not? Warriors need to be disciplined even when their actions have unforeseen outcomes."

For a minute Amanda thought the two warrior women might actually start fighting each other, but the Prelate simply drew up her arm and several runes on her gauntlets flashed. "We will discuss this later. Queen Frigga was searching for the alfblot and syirce sources and found some interesting things near the Forest of Fates. She has requested we investigate since the Einherjar are busy guarding the syirces."

"Then let us not tarry here a moment longer. Favoured, you are dismissed." Raising her arms, Lady Freyja drew open a portal and she and the Prelate vanished as the field around them reverted to the original dark color of the enchanted soil.

Amanda could finally stand without Sean's support, although her vision was still slightly blurry. The spell had left her feeling like she was running on empty. "I've decided. I prefer Ms. Biggs, the possessed version, over Lady Freyja."

Connor and Mykola came up behind Amanda. Connor was holding one of the obsidian shards. "Remind me to never get you riled up, Amanda. That was one heck of a spell. It felt almost like my favouring, using the earth and stones around you to give you strength, but I've never been able to hurl rocks at anyone."

"It only works in Muspelheim, and I am not sure I would want to do that again. I just saw red and then…" Amanda took the stone from Connor.

"You blew up." Cassie looked longingly at the divot where Amanda had poured her magick. "Wish I had been the one to do that… to that… to that pig-faced goddess. Maybe then she would think I am worthy of her instead of the loathing I feel every time she looks at me"

Amanda patted her chest as her breathing was finally returning to normal. "It doesn't feel as good as you make it sound, but… what do you think happened to Lena when… well, after I attacked Lady Freyja?"

"You heard the Prelate. It was just an accident." Connor was stretching as he spoke. "It might be a good spell to have on hand to get the Zukovs out of our hair permanently if you can recreate it."

"Great, another accident." Amanda crossed her arms. "This is what I was talking about earlier. I can't keep letting things like this happen. I need to find out how to fully control my magick like Sigyn, but not end up like her."

Amanda remembered something Lady Freyja said, "And I think I know where I can find the person to teach me."

Cassie jumped as the thought passed from Amanda to her. "Amanda... you can't. I mean, no one but Lord Odin knows where that is."

"Then we will find it together. We need to find Sigyn's prison – we need to find the Green Askr."

CHAPTER 12:
THE TRAP OF LORD ODIN

Once the idea was planted in Amanda's head, it was hard for her to not think about ways to try and find Sigyn's prison. Over the next week, anytime Amanda was alone in the Halls of Learning she would poke around to find whatever scraps of knowledge there were about Sigyn, where she was being kept, or what happened to those imprisoned after Ragnarok. It took her three days to find any mention of Sigyn buried in a pile of scrolls on the Great Rebirth of the realms. The scroll was written by Lord Mimir,

"With regards to those domiciles that have been relocated per Lord Odin's request, they are as follows:

1- Lord Mimir's Well – For reasons that I be closer to assist Lord Odin.

2- Utgard – Since the traitorous Loki was a co-conspirator in Ragnarok, his castle shall be fully removed from Asgard and cast into Niflheim.

3- Loki's wife shall be imprisoned in the Green Askr. Lord Odin has chosen not to share this tower's whereabouts with me, which I supremely objected to. I even cited the several occasions Lord Odin's memory was erased, but it was not taken into account. He has also forbidden anyone to look for the tower, and those that do shall be most severely punished.

The list continued, but Amanda wasn't concerned about the rest because this confirmed Lady Freyja's words. Excitedly she had copied the note down and ran back to the Stave to find the others. The others had begrudgingly come around to the idea, even though Sean was apprehensive to flagrantly break a rule set by Lord Odin. When Amanda was done reading the note, they all looked at her quizzically. None of them knew what the word askr meant. It had surprisingly been Lord Mimir to the rescue again. He had been instructing them on the different atmospheres of the realms and said Hel was full of green askr, which was an enchanted ash. The entire group had looked up and at each other in surprise, and spent that evening finding out all they could about the ash in Hel. Disappointingly, it turned out magickal ash is about exciting as one would think. It can be used in any number of spells, came from certain fire magicks, or made from burning magickal items. They opted not to find out why there was so much of it in Hel, but it did seem as if it pointed to Sigyn's prison residing in the realm of the dead.

The next piece of information came a few days later from a scroll in which an Elf noted a particularly troublesome spell they needed help stopping. The scroll was part of a peace treaty that was signed after Ragnarok between some Aesir and the Light Elves. The scroll mentioned the Light Elves' request for help from Sigyn to deal with a spell that she had originally written for Aesir children to play with, but which was being used to turn the Light Elves' food into bubbles. The request was denied by Lord Odin for the reason that, "the goddess is out of touch with all, and at times even the land itself, until the stars and askr find their alignment." This complicated the puzzle because there were no stars in Hel. Determined not to let her frustration get the better of her, Amanda kept digging.

Unfortunately, after another week, the only other mentions of Sigyn that she found were another list and a poem from Lord Odin. The second list was of favoured, Aesir, and other creatures caught snooping around looking for Sigyn's whereabouts. At the end of the list it gave the reasons those apprehended had for looking for the goddess, and how long it took them to get as close as they did. The fastest person on the list was an Aesir who spent five years searching. The list didn't say what he uncovered in that five years, but it was enough so that when he was caught he was given a choice of the Gruneling or banishment. It also mentioned a new spell that was enacted to trap anyone else who would be foolish enough to attempt to find Sigyn in the future. The only specifics given about the trap was that those captured by it were immediately sent to the Gruneling. The others almost forced Amanda to abandon her search when they heard about the trap, but she convinced them that she was sure they could find Sigyn and not get caught. She had even researched several spells that could counter most entrapments, and had been able to perform them without anything going haywire. This left the poem as the last piece to explore and, to Amanda, felt like their best way to piece together all the information they had gathered so far to lead them in the right direction.

"Where the stars align, and the ash becomes solid – there shall you find the lady you seek. Where no wind blows, and the maze of green traps only your feet – there shall you find the lady you seek." Amanda was pacing the common area of the Stave closest to her and Cassie's room.

"Amanda... please... stop." Connor was laying down on one of the leather sofas with an arm flung over his face. "I have an hour until I have to go guard Draupnir with Sean, I just got back from hiking almost all the way up to Valhalla to get some bloody speck of dirt to help Heimdall get back onto his feet now that he is awake, and I have a headache the size of Lev's ego. There is quite literally a list of people who have found Sigyn but it took them years. I know you want to help your parents and friend, but can we not hear about the tower or that poem for just a few minutes?"

"But it has to mean something! Maybe I can find the tower faster than they could."

"Maybe you can, Amanda, but it might still take some time." Cassie was brushing the vindsvolla egg while sitting cross-legged on the floor.

Amanda folded her arms as she continued to pace about. "It's been three months, Cassie! Three months of Jack being with Bergelmir and my parents being mice. I can't let them stay like that any longer. You know what happens to people under enchantments. The longer you are under them, the harder it is to break free from them."

Cassie patted the egg, which shook slightly. "I get it, but Lord Odin hid the tower. That means it's not going to be easy to find. You have to give yourself a break."

Amanda collapsed into a chair beside Connor. "I know... it's just... how can I really focus on anything else when they are counting on me? I just wish I could figure out what the poem means. Maybe if I knew why he wrote it, I could figure it out."

"Ha. Good luck with that." Connor pulled himself up. Cassie gave him a look. "All I am saying is the Allfather is a man with a plan. And a plan within a plan. And a plan within a plan within a plan."

Cassie stopped him. "We get it, Connor."

"Well sorry for pointing out the obvious. How about a game of rune wars to take your mind off of towers and ash, Amanda?" Connor slid a small square table with nine circles carved into it over. "You owe me a rematch."

Amanda put her face in her hand as she leaned over. Connor and Sean had been teaching her the game over the past few weeks. It was a combination of chess and checkers but using rune stones that were carved with the name of the gods or other creatures. Amanda turned out to be a natural, and hadn't lost a game yet. She shook her head, "Not right now."

Cassie stretched and put the egg into a sling she had fashioned from some Elf hair she requested from Keeper Fulla. "What else is bothering you, Amanda?"

Amanda let out a deep breath. "What do you think will happen when I meet Sigyn? I need her help, but what if I have to become like her in order to save Jack and my parents?"

"No way could that happen." Sean came into the common room and dropped down beside Connor. "We wouldn't let it. We protect each other, Amanda. We all have something in common with our benefactors, but that's it. It's not like I all of a sudden started wanting to grow my hair out and tell bad jokes when I met Prince Thor."

"But that's just it. What do I have in common with someone who would almost destroy the Nine Realms? Lena said," Amanda started.

Cassie jumped to her feet. "Not this, not again!" Her irritation suddenly permeated the whole room, and the fire in the basin jumped two feet higher. "You need to stop letting what those slimy, short-haired, puss-faces say get to you. I thought we were finally past all of that nonsense. You have been here for three months, and are doing amazingly well considering, and have shown no signs of becoming a realm-destroying-baddie. You can't go around being so worried all the time."

Amanda stood up and walked over to Cassie. "You're right. I'm sorry. I just can't help but think about the worst possible scenarios. I am just trying to be careful, and don't get mad, but especially because of what happened to Lena and Lev I have to be."

"Well, I get it, but still. It's ok to say what makes you afraid, but once you say it, let it go. Have a bit of faith in yourself."

Connor looked to Sean. "Well, that was awkwardly emotional."

"Connor, do you really want to tick me off right now? You know I could make you run around and kiss every Dwarf you see," Cassie exclaimed.

There was a sound of crackling flames, and they all looked to the basin. The Prelate's voice rang out with each snap of the fire. "Favoured of Lord Freyr and of Prince Thor, report to Valaskjalf to prepare to take Draupnir to the Gruneling."

The boys slumped their shoulders. Sean rubbed the back of his neck. "So much for a break. I sure do hope Heimdall is back to full steam soon. That stuff we got from the base of Valhalla should help him recover from the last of the alfblot poisoning, but it's still going to take some time. What are you two going to do before your shift?"

"Get some stew from the Mead Hall and wait for Mykola. He should be back soon from dealing with the latest syirces the Queen found near Yggdrasil. We need to set the vindsvolla egg in the window by the banners to get some starlight before we leave tonight, Amanda." Cassie looked to Amanda, but she didn't respond.

"The banners... the banners!" Amanda turned and left the common area. The others scrambled to follow her.

"Amanda! What about the banners?" Cassie called after her as they made their way down the hallway toward the center of the Stave.

"I didn't even think to ask them. They showed me Sigyn being imprisoned when I first came to Asgard, but I never asked them anything more about her." Amanda swerved around an Aesir carrying folded linens. She stopped when she was in the Hall of Tapestries. The banners swayed as they entered the room.

"I doubt they will know more than anyone else, Amanda." Sean pointed to one of the banners. "They know less than what even Lord Mimir knows, I'm betting, and the scroll you found said Lord Odin didn't tell Lord Mimir where the tower was."

"But somehow they knew something. Someone must have told them. How else would they have showed her being imprisoned?" The others looked to each one another, but no one could deny it did make sense. Amanda turned to the nearest tapestry. Its bottom edges curled up toward her as she spoke. "Show me where Sigyn is. Show me the Green Askr."

The tapestries swirled for a minute, but then stopped. The figure of Lord Odin suddenly appeared in each banner around the room. The Allfather did not look pleased. The Lord of Asgard's visage was then replaced by scenes of star-filled skies. Amanda turned and inspected each of the six tapestries.

Sean was standing at the entrance to the hall, checking to make sure no one was coming. "You see? Nothing. We shouldn't be doing this right now anyway. Someone could walk by, and I don't think it would do us any good for people to know what we are looking for. Keeper Fulla would probably lose it, especially with all the syirces that just appeared around Yggdrasil."

"Pipe down, Sean. We all know you like rule-breaking as much as you like sour mead, but we all agreed we need to help Amanda find Sigyn." Sean crossed his arms as Cassie spoke. "What do you think the stars mean, Amanda?"

Amanda put a finger to her chin as she thought. She knew she was close, she could feel it. "The poem and the note from the treaty talked about stars." Amanda pointed to the six tapestries. Each starry sky was practically identical except for nine stars that were in various stages of alignment. "Maybe they are trying to tell us how to find Sigyn by using the stars' positioning."

"Or maybe this is the trap the other scroll mentioned." Sean cleared his throat loudly as a group of Favoured walked by. "What if these tapestries tell Lord Odin what we are looking for?"

Amanda refused to let Sean's worrying stop her. "If that's the case, I hope he is listening and could maybe finally give us an answer that can help us. But here," Amanda took her index finger and traced a rune in the air. It was an older spell she had found that would cling to anything bespelled to trap or capture them. Her magick ignited the air and drifted to the fibers of the tapestry. The spell clung to the banner and then fell to the floor and vanished. "What do you know? I think that means it's safe."

"*That* is the spell that is supposed to tell us there is no trap set by Lord Odin?" Sean asked in disbelief.

"Well… yes." Amanda looked sheepishly at her friends. "I practiced it the other day in the mirrors when Girnka wasn't looking, and it worked just fine on finding a hidden spell in my challenge. If it finds something it sticks to it and glows like its gone radioactive."

"OK. So, no glow means we are… safe." Connor was normally the one to charge into any kind of a challenge, but even he seemed a bit uncertain Amanda had proven anything. "Let's say you are right, Amanda. What does this even mean? It's just a bunch of stars."

"Both notes said the stars need to align. Look. That one on the end is the only one that has the stars in perfect alignment." Amanda walked over to the tapestry closest to the doors into Fensalir. Amanda took a hold of the banner and inspected it from all sides. It seemed the same as all the others except for the binding. There was something etched into the golden fibers that formed the border of the tapestry. "Look! There are runes! They are small, and almost completely invisible. They say that to find what you seek, you must understand the reason why."

"The reason why? The reason is because we need help." Cassie held out a hand and lightly touched the banner. "You know, I never noticed it, but these guys almost have feelings. They want to help us, but they aren't able to fully express what it is they want to say."

"What are you saying, Sis?" Connor touched the tapestry. "It feels pretty normal to me."

Cassie shook her head. "It's not how they feel, it's what they feel. It feels like they are being held back, which is probably what Lord Odin is having them do. Maybe I can help push them."

"Cassie, wait. You are talking about taking on a spell by Lord Odin." Sean cautioned, looking to Connor for support.

Connor shook his head. "That's true, Cassie."

"Boys. You all act so brave, saying how you will protect us, but really you are just scared. I got this. Answer Amanda's question!" Cassie's voice rebounded about the room as her magick snapped back and forth between the banners. Cassie suddenly screamed.

Lord Odin appeared again in the tapestries and magick shot from the banners into Cassie. Connor banged his fists together and his skin shimmered as it turned grey. Stepping in front of his sister, Connor took the brunt of the attack. The magick rebounded from Connor and back into the banners. The bottom hem of the tapestries began to smoke and sizzle.

"Amanda! Do something!" Connor was being driven to his knees.

Amanda waved her hand. "*Forggia!*" A golden bubble encased the group, and the redirected magick ignited the banners into columns of fire. A maelstrom of magick and lightning swept from the burning tapestries, coalescing into the form of an attacking raven whose fiery wings filled the entire hall. The raven dove toward Amanda's shield, spewing magick from its beak. Amanda's arms began to shake, but her shield held. The raven beat its wings twice before launching another attack. After the third volley, a crack appeared in Amanda's defenses.

Sean held up his hammer and sent a blast of lightning to intercept the next attack, barely diverting it before it hit them. Thunder shook the hall as the two elements collided. The sound of glass shattering could be heard through the thick wooden doors of Fensalir. The raven folded its wings inward and a portal opened. They could see dry earth and Yggdrasil's roots as the portal began to draw anything nearby into it. Amanda fell, dropping her spell as she was suddenly sucked forward.

Sean rammed his hammer into the ground as an anchor. His cloak battered about him. "Remind me to tell you I told you so later! We have to find a way to stop this!"

"Connor, how is Cassie doing? Can she command that thing to go away?" Amanda shouted as she grabbed Sean to keep from sliding toward the portal.

Connor planted his feet and was holding Cassie as he crouched near the floor. "She's ok, but I don't think she can help us."

Cassie's eyes were wide and she was breathing heavily. "Answer... it."

Amanda suddenly understood. "This is all a test!"

Sean was sliding toward the portal, his hammer gouging the floor as they slid inch by inch. "Well, hurry up!"

Amanda raised her hands to the raven. "I am looking for Sigyn to help my friends and my family." The raven beat its wings and the force drawing them forward intensified. Amanda bit the side of her cheek. That was the reason she had been giving all along, but was it the real reason? Sure, she came to Asgard to help her parents and Jack, but there had been something else. "I want to make Bergelmir pay. I want to find out why I am Sigyn's Favoured! That whatever is in her isn't in me."

There was a whisper of magick and the raven vanished. The inferno around them was extinguished, and the banners reappeared as if they had never been touched by fire. The entire room suddenly became just as it was when they first entered. The doors into Fensalir opened and the group turned as a mirror floated toward them. The frame of the mirror was twisted gray wood that held a reflective surface the size of the vindsvolla egg. Amanda reached up to take the mirror.

Cassie moaned as she pushed herself into a seated position. "What happened?"

"Easy." Sean bent down to help Cassie up.

"You ok, Sis?" Connor's skin was returning to normal as he stood.

"I think so. It was weird. It felt like my mind was being invaded by the magick in the tapestries. It didn't hurt, but just felt overwhelming." She brushed her hair back a bit and took a deep breath to help clear her head. "So, did it work?"

They all looked to Amanda. Amanda felt embarrassed at her words. She had thought her intentions to find Sigyn were a bit more honorable, but what she said to the raven made it sound like she was just out for revenge. She didn't want to look at anyone to see what their reaction was to her words, so she studied the mirror.

Sean put a hand on Amanda's shoulder. "What you said was your truth, and I for one couldn't agree with you more." Amanda looked up to Sean and her lower lip trembled. There was a clamoring noise from down the hall. "How about we figure all this out somewhere else? It may look brand new in here, but somebody had to have heard all of that."

The group dashed out of the Hall of Tapestries and back to their common area. Cassie quickly grabbed the egg and pretended to teach Amanda how to care for it, while Connor and Sean threw some runes onto the rune war board. Keeper Fulla came bustling through, sweating and wheezing as she ran. She inspected each of them as she passed, but didn't stop. A minute later they heard her anxiously scouring the hall they had just come from. When the Keeper's worried voice died down and moved further into the Stave, they relaxed.

Amanda held up the mirror for the others to see. The image in the pane of glass was of a rolling hill. The grass moved slowly as a silent stream of wind made the taller reeds sway back and forth. A vindsvolla flew through the air and then vanished. There was one rune at the top of the mirror.

"Ash." Amanda spoke quietly.

"That's it?" Sean frowned. "We risked a trip to the Gruneling for that?"

The vindsvolla appeared in the mirror again, and Amanda looked over to the vindsvolla egg sitting in the cradle Cassie made for it. "Cassie, what did the Prelate tell you about the vindsvolla eggs?"

Cassie cocked her head. "Loads. Why?"

Amanda held out her hand for the egg. It was always lighter than she expected it to be. "Didn't you tell me she said they had just been blessed by Heimdall before he was taken?"

Cassie opened her mouth, and then paused. She thought for a moment, and then began to nod her head. "Well, yes. Do you think that means...?"

Amanda held the egg up to the group. The light from the stars above was fading, but it still turned the feathers a deep reddish-gold color where it touched the egg. "That means the egg is blessed to go wherever it wants in all of the Nine Realms. If we use the egg, we might be able to have it help take us find the Green Askr."

"Wait." Sean stood up and joined Amanda and Cassie. "It's just an egg. How could it take you anywhere? Also, if that were true, wouldn't any of the vindsvolla be able to take anyone to Sigyn?"

Amanda held the mirror and egg up to one another and the egg shook. "I am betting that there are other ways people have tried, and they found traps similar to the one we just found at the banners. Plus, how often do you think people have a vindsvolla egg, or found this mirror?"

"Are you sure, Amanda? You could hurt the baby vindsvolla or worse." Cassie came up and put a protective hand on the egg. She stroked a couple its feathers and they stood up at her touch.

"I don't think we have to do much, or anything that will actually hurt the egg. The mirrors in Fensalir are a test, right? All we have to do is take the test with the egg instead of our magick. The egg will act like a beacon and show us where to go." Amanda held the egg up to the mirror again and spoke softly. "Show us where Sigyn is."

They all braced for a similar response to the one they just received from the tapestries, but nothing happened. For a minute they all stared at the mirror. A soft trickle of magick flowed from the edges of the frame. The egg began to glow as well, and a soft white light illuminated the surface of the mirror. A whistling sound emanated from the mirror as green magick shot forth into Amanda's cloak.

"By the Eye of the Allfather!" They all spun as Keeper Fulla came bustling up to them, her hands clutching two satchels. "Thank goodness I found you."

"Keeper Fulla." Sean put on the biggest smile he could and intercepted her. "How can we help the Keeper of Asgard?"

"I've just come from the Hall of Tapestries. An alarm was tripped, but I cannot find anything amiss. Did you happen to see anything?"

They all looked to each other with false expressions of confusion. "I don't think so, Keeper Fulla. Sean and I are running late to go take care of Draupnir. We were just updating the others on our trip to Mount Valhalla. We should be off though, Sean. Perhaps Keeper Fulla should accompany us to make sure we don't get stopped by anyone on our way." Connor was trying to guide the Keeper out of the room.

"Unhand me, boy. I must still investigate the alarm, but we have also had a disconcerting yet promising development with the alfblot. The Prelate and Lady Freyja were investigating a lake of alfblot by the Norn's Forest when they found a syirce. They were attempting various spells to close the portal when a hoard of Jotun giants charged through the syirce and attacked them."

Cassie sensed the Keeper's concern. "Are they alright? Did they... were they infected like Heimdall?"

The Keeper waved away her question. "Nay. They were able to fight off the beasts and send them back through the portal. However, as they were doing so the Prelate somehow managed to stop the flow of the alfblot into the syirce. When she did so, the portal vanished. It seems that if we can find the alfblot connected to the syirce and destroy the connection, the portal can be closed. With this discovery, we have been able to banish more of the fell portals without needing the Favoured of Forseti, but are still unable to locate the main source of the alfblot. We believe whoever is summoning the alfblot remains within our walls, and we have devised a plan to find the fiend and put a stop to this attack. We must hurry, though. With the amount of new syirces we are finding, we will soon run out of resources to guard them. If we cannot find the one summoning the portals, the Queen will be forced seal our realm, leaving us isolated until Lord Odin returns. It is the only way to be sure our attacker cannot escape, and it will also ensure that no more murderous creatures can come against us through the syirces. Sean and Amanda are to report to Valaskjalf within the hour to help to scour the city for the source of the alfblot and syirces with these." The Keeper thrust the bags into Sean's hands. "These frost lilies shall help us. I have placed a spell on them that will make them search for and trap anyone using fell magick.

We will scatter them about the entire realm to ensure no one can use fell magick and not be found. The rest of you are to report to guard Draupnir in their place and continue throughout the night." Nobody moved. Keeper Fulla had been expecting some protests, but when no one spoke she gave them look. "Right then, be about your business quickly."

Amanda had tucked the mirror into her cloak, while Sean had distracted Keeper Fulla. After the woman left to go back and inspect the Hall of Tapestries once more, she felt something rustling in the pocket inside her cloak where she placed the mirror. Lifting the side of her cloak, she pulled the piece of parchment she had found back when she had been searching from Heimdall. The list had vanished. The air in the room thickened as words began to appear on the blank parchment.

"I apologize for the intrusion, but it is the only way I can get you this message. The silly rules of this place, honestly. You must come to me tonight to my tower. You shall find me on the Plains of Idavoll, but you must be careful. There is a traitor amongst you that seeks to use the alfblot to destroy the realm. I do not know who cast the spell to summon it, but I know it searches for me, and I fear they will try to find my location through your journey. You must be on guard. Tell no one, not even the Prelate. Especially not the Prelate, as the Valkyrie has never liked me, and would no doubt forbid you to come. If you can find a way to come alone this parchment will show you the true way to my tower and I will reveal how you can find the one who has turned against us.

Yours,

Sigyn

CHAPTER 13:
THE GREEN ASKR

When the three Great Stars that shine warmth and light down upon Asgard travel to the far side of the realm, and night comes to the city, the streets empty as the denizens of the Golden Realm tuck into their homes. Even with the shields, wards, and runes to protect them, most still prefer to remain indoors because night is when the most fell moments in Asgard's history have occurred. As such, there were only the Einherjar and a few Dwarves still wandering about as Amanda and Sean made their way through the city. Amanda hid her face in her hood as they paused to let a triad of Einherjar pass.

Sean pulled open the leather bag the Keeper had given him and scattered what looked like white stars onto the road. The Einherjar nodded and did the same as they kept onward down the street. "The city will be covered in frost lilies soon. Let's hope Keeper Fulla is right about this helping us find the person summoning the alfblot. If Heimdall weren't already at the Manor, this would send him there for sure."

Amanda stepped out from the stoop they were on. Above them hung a sign with elegant runes that indicated the store inside sold herbs and other sundries. "She discussed it with the Prelate. I am sure it is safe."

Sean sped up slightly to take the lead as they headed toward the center of the city. "I know the Keeper said she put a spell on these so they wouldn't affect Heimdall, but others might have sensitivities to them. The Gatekeeper's allergy is well known because he is a god. There are far more Aesir, and it would not be as well known if they have an allergy to the lilies' pollen."

"What choice do we have? Plus, it gives us a chance to get to Sigyn." Amanda's response was hard as she focused on the road under her feet. She dipped her hand into a bag similar to the one Sean held, and mimicked his movements, scattering flowers as they walked.

Sean looked back to Amanda. "Sorry, Amanda, I know this can't be easy on you. You doing OK?"

"I don't know. I know this is the right thing to do, but now all I can think about is what if I am wrong? I mean, what if Sigyn is causing all of this to happen? This might all be her trying to break free from the Green Askr. The alfblot, the syirces, Heimdall. I thought the mirror was showing us where to go, but it allowed Sigyn to send me a note that says not to trust the Prelate. It makes it sound like she thinks the Prelate is the one summoning the alfblot. Beyond that, how does she know the alfblot is looking for her, and why?"

They stopped for a second outside a stone building deeper than it was wide. Inside, jovial songs were being sung in gravelly voices. A Dwarf covered in gray and black fur stumbled out, tried to give them a salute, and promptly fell into a bale of hay. Sean continued as the Dwarf began to snore. "I know. It has me as nervous as a long-tailed cat in a room full of rocking chairs, but you said it yourself, she is the only one who can help you."

Sean and Amanda turned a corner and came to a stop again behind a triad of Einherjar who were inspecting one of the road's underpasses. Amanda pulled the folded piece of parchment from her cloak. Back in the Stave they had all passed it around while arguing what it could mean. Even though she had been the one to insist on finding Sigyn, the goddess's words made her question whether that was still the right decision.

Amanda tucked the scroll back in her cloak. "I know," she moderated her voice lower as she spotted Keeper Fulla looking at them. The Keeper had caught up with them as they left for Valaskjalf. "I guess we will find out once I get to her."

Sean's eyebrows arched inwards. "Idavoll is not a place you want to be by yourself, especially at night. If you don't know where you are going it's easy to get lost. There have been Aesir who have lived hundreds of years on Asgard that have gone out to search the plains and never come back. Not to mention it's where the Fire Jotuns attacked us first when Ragnarok began – and you have to pass through the realm's shields. How will you get through without the Einherjar sensing you?"

"The scroll said it would guide me. Sigyn has something she wants to tell me. I am sure she will make it so I can get to her – hopefully in one piece. We just need to figure out a way to get away from Keeper Fulla."

As if on cue, Keeper Fulla made an irritated noise. Waving the Einherjar along in front of her, she beckoned to the two Favoured. "Do not dawdle, Amanda, Sean. This is not a time to stop for chatter."

"Sorry, Keeper Fulla." Amanda and Sean said, throwing clumps of frost lilies as they sped up until they were only a few paces behind. They passed through a few tufts of clouds that swirled around their feet and the lilies disappeared into the haze.

"Don't apologize to me, just do your job. The sooner we can finish our work, the sooner we can all rest secure in knowing we are one step closer to putting an end to this assault on our home. Maybe it will bring some measure of peace to the Prelate. Her Ladyship returned very disturbed from her trip with Lady Freyja."

"Do you think the Prelate will be OK? Fighting around the alfblot must have meant they got some on them." Amanda's sidestepped a puddle that gleamed from the light of the shields above them.

Fulla shuddered. "Our Prelate is strong. She is protected by wards that Lord Odin himself placed upon her. There is also her training as a Valkyrie that no doubt protects her."

Sean threw some frost lilies onto a row of chariots and into a pen of goats. "What kind of training?"

"The private kind meant only for those initiated into the sisterhood."

One of the petals of the flowers had curled up and was twitching on the ground. Amanda picked it up to examine the delicate bloom. "What do these do, Keeper Fulla? Prelate Tess said they weren't from Niflheim, so why are they called frost lilies?"

Fulla plucked the flower from Amanda's hand, glared at her, and tossed it back to the ground. The Keeper looked back longingly at the city proper as they walked. "These blossoms are from Alfheim, but they get their name from their color. They are a wonderful ingredient for potions and tonics because they accept any kind of spell and can be changed to suit almost any need you may have. Sigyn used them all the time. She showed me a spell once of how to bring them to life and control them like little poppets on a string. That was before she and Loki tried to destroy us all, of course."

They walked on for a bit in silence until they came to a spot where the paved streets met the tall grasses of the plains, and the distant stars were the only light that overlooked the sloping hills. The power of the magick of Asgard's defensive shields sent vibrations through Amanda as they approached. Fulla waved and straightened a post that had begun to lean to one side. The ground had softened with the brief rain that had blown through that afternoon.

Sean nudged Amanda, "Uh, Keeper Fulla. Don't you think we should take the frost lilies out into the Plains of Idavoll too?"

"At night? Never! Only the most foolish of enemies would try to gain entrance to our lands through those fields. It still amazes me the Jotuns managed it. Do you see those stones there? They are the only way to traverse the plains, and even so, without the right guide one would be lost in the wilderness to be certain. They would also have to pass through our shields to do so, and only those blessed by Heimdall or Lord Odin could do so. Even if Bergelmir himself came against us, I highly doubt he could manage it." Fulla sniffled and then squinted. Several of the Einherjar accompanying them were gathered around one of their brethren who was lying on the ground. "Agnarr. What is going on?"

The Aesir warrior saluted the Keeper. "Keeper Fulla, Colborn found a satchel lying on the ground. When he opened it, something inside attacked him with magick." Agnarr pointed to the leather bag still clutched in

Colborn's hands.

"By the Allfather! What trickery can this be?" Fulla bustled over and bent to inspect the bag. She frowned and snapped her fingers. The satchel flew from Colborn's grip and dropped its contents. Golden apples rolled along the street.

Amanda could feel the torrent of wild magick in the apples even from a few feet away. "What are they?"

Fulla gasped and with another motion gathered the apples into the air and back into the satchel. "Those are apples from Idunn's orchard. Who would have dared to enter the sacred grove to take these? And why were they left here?"

"If those are Idunn's apples, then we must get Colborn to the healing beds quickly. Their magick would be toxic to an Aesir." Agnarr nodded to two other Einherjar who picked up the prone form of their comrade. "What should we do with the apples?"

"They must be returned to the orchard at once, or else they will lose their power. Only the gods and the Favoured can touch the apples, and I am not about to turn them over to..." Fulla clamped her lips shut and looked Amanda up and down. "But we have other duties to fulfill tonight as well. I trust you can finish your task without my supervision, now that I must also return these apples to where they belong?"

Amanda chewed the side of her cheek as she forced herself to ignore Keeper Fulla's unsaid remark. "Not a problem at all, Keeper Fulla. It shouldn't take us much longer. We are almost out of frost lilies anyway. Once we are done, we will head back to the Stave for some rest."

Sean coughed, and then faked a yawn. "I could sure use a snooze."

"Wait a minute." Keeper Fulla pulled out another bag of lilies from her apron. "I want every inch covered from here to the Bifrost and back."

Sean and Amanda waited, watching Fulla head toward the city and the Einherjar head toward the Manor. "Well, the Norn have to be on your side tonight, Amanda. The Fates of Asgard made it easier for you to get to Sigyn than I would have thought."

"Do you think it was the Norn... or Sigyn?" Amanda turned to face the dark green hills.

"I don't think Sigyn could conjure those apples. Regardless, we can now get you out to the Green Askr."

Amanda turned to face the golden wall of magick. "Like you said, first we have to get through that."

Sean came up behind her. "Maybe the note can help."

Amanda pulled the parchment from her cloak. A soft breeze stirred the grass and their cloaks, but nothing else happened. "It's not working. Maybe it senses you here with me." Amanda looked over to Sean as she shifted her feet. "The note did say to come alone."

"I really don't like that part. There's got to be another way that doesn't involve you being alone out there with her." Sean grumbled. "Maybe you could lead the way and I could follow behind you."

"I can do this on my own, Sean." Amanda tried to sound brave even though her body was shaking. "I'll be alright, I promise. I'll meet you here when I am done."

Sean took a deep breath and squeezed Amanda's arm. She looked into his eyes and felt her nerves dance in her stomach – from his touch and what she was about to do. "Keep your eyes peeled. If Sigyn starts to do something wackadoo, get out of there. I know you need answers for a lot of things but be careful. I don't want to see you hurt."

Amanda could only nod her head. Her insides were a tornado of mixed emotions. She registered Sean's words and it made her feel guilty because it made her think of Jack, and how sweet he had been to her the night he was captured. Then there was her worry, even though she was trying to be brave for Cassie, of what tonight could mean for herself, her parents, and for Asgard. Understanding her silence, Sean left. The only sound Amanda heard from him was the sound of his boots as they slowly trudged down the road. When she couldn't hear his footsteps anymore, Amanda held the scroll out toward the plains. As if frustrated by waiting, the small piece of parchment flew into the air and began to flap in a circle until a portal appeared. Amanda could see the other end of the portal just beyond the shields. She took a deep breath and stepped through the opening and into the Plains of Idavoll. The gateway vanished and the parchment flapped its way across the dark green hills. The flying sheet paused several yards away, waiting for Amanda to follow. Hesitating for only a moment, and wondering one last time if letting a scroll bespelled by Sigyn guide her was the best idea, Amanda set her jaw and moved out into the night.

The scroll set a steady pace as it flew along, but after exercising with Lady Freyja during their afternoon training sessions Amanda found she could keep up. The sky took on a purplish hue as Amanda travelled deeper and deeper into the plains and the city faded to a distant haze behind her. The only sounds she could hear were the insects buzzing in the bushes and the crunch of the grass as she walked. The farther she went, the taller and denser the grasses grew until her boots became bogged down as if she were wading through a lake of reeds. After some time, Amanda looked back and could only make out the outline of Yggdrasil rising from the horizon. Turning back around as the clouds above hid the light from the distant stars, Amanda's breath caught in her chest. The scroll had disappeared.

Fighting panic, Amanda scanned the tall grasses, but the darkness of the open plains hid anything that wasn't a few inches in front of her. Fear settled in her stomach and she froze. The darkness was playing tricks on her mind. She thought she saw something darting about in front of her and then off to her right. A hushed cackle slithered from the hill behind her.

"Sigyn?"

Just as she was about to turn and run blindly back the way she came, the clouds parted and starlight crept up from the carpet of green grass to reveal a tower that seemed to grow out of the landscape. A glittering mass of emerald rose up like a gnarled finger, with illuminated arches at the top. As another cloud passed in front of the moon, the parts of the tower enshadowed vanished into a misty cloud, and then solidified once more as the light hit its surface. Amanda's eyes widened as she realized this was what the mentions of magickal ash had meant. The tower was only part of this realm under moonlight; otherwise it was completely invisible in a haze of ash. Amanda looked up to see several stars above that aligned as if pointing the way as well. They were identical to the ones the tapestry had shown her.

Squinting her eyes, Amanda could just make out her missing scroll flapping at an opening in the base of the tower. From somewhere high in the tower, a voice called down to Amanda. "Hello, dear, come on in!"

As Amanda approached the entryway, the grasses parted to reveal worn steps of emerald that led up and into a dimly lit circular room. Inside were stacks of old pots and urns, mostly broken or cracked, each bearing a singular rune. Amanda raised her hand and made a quick gesture. Her spell of detection flared and drifted from her hand, but nothing else happened. Holding her breath and biting the inside of her cheek, Amanda stepped up onto the first step. A flash of light flowed from the center of the room toward her, and Amanda leapt backward as something shattered far above. When nothing more happened, she swallowed and gingerly placed the tip of her boot on the dull stone ledge. Like lightning under a lake of ice, the light jaggedly shot to the point where her foot connected with the emerald. Taking her foot away, Amanda stepped back and looked up to the top of the tower once more. The lights that had shone forth from the windows had dimmed, and there was no sound except for the crickets and grasses again.

Slowly breathing in through her nose, Amanda tensed as she stepped back up and walked straight to the heart of the circular room. With each step forward the light under the floor followed her into the chamber, constantly shifting and arching in a kind of a dance. Pausing for a moment, Amanda bent down and put her hand against the floor, watching as spirals of light pooled under her palm. A rustling noise drew Amanda's attention and she saw her scroll hovering by an ornate spiral staircase. Following a small path that wound through the piles of debris, Amanda made her way toward the stairs. She brushed the top of a rust-colored urn and the dust made her sneeze. A booming noise echoed down from somewhere unseen, and Amanda tensed. A shower of pebbles and smoke bounced down the steps, but nothing else.

"Hello? Sigyn?" Amanda called up the stairs.

119

With a loud pop, and a sprinkle of notes that floated from above, the ghostly form of a woman appeared and beckoned Amanda upward before disappearing. Seeing ghosts would have once frightened Amanda enough to have her running for her room, but she had seen worse in the Einherjarium. So, Amanda grabbed her runaway scroll from the air, stuffed it into her cloak and began to climb up the jeweled staircase. As she circled upward, the light from underneath her feet and hands grew, until it ricocheted off every surface, becoming a dazzling show of light as she stepped through an arched opening and stopped.

CHAPTER 14:
AN ENCHANTRESS UNBOUND

"Welcome, my dear. I have been waiting for you for such a long time. Although I must say, I was expecting you to be a bit taller."

Amanda couldn't help but gawk. The woman who stood before her looked less like a goddess and more like the crazy lady with too many cats who lived at the end of Rivers End Road. She had bushy tufts of hair haphazardly gathered into a knot on the top of her head, kind green eyes that twitched behind a pair of motorcycle goggles, and her robes were singed black at the sleeves and hem. But that was all strangely normal when compared with the fact that she was also completely translucent. Just like the elves from Alfheim, Amanda could literally see through the goddess's form to the room behind her.

Amanda blinked and brushed back her bangs as she found her voice, "Taller?"

"We can fix that I am sure, but no worries for now. I am glad to see you made it on your own. Next time it probably won't take you as long to make it here since you know where you are heading." A frog croaked as it leapt from a pair of sad looking wingback chairs. The old fabric was half faded from one too many years sitting beside the windows that lined the room. Sigyn turned and began addressing the slimy creature as it hopped along the floor, "Not now, Garth. We have our first guest in two thousand years. Let us not be rude and bring up how late she is."

Amanda felt bolted to the floor. She wasn't sure if the icy feeling rushing through her was embarrassment for herself at being afraid of Sigyn, or at what the others would think when she told them her hopes had been pinned on someone who looked like they had spent too much time in some kind of bike-shop laboratory. She had expected some kind of dark figure that would ooze fell magick and wear billowing, black robes, or someone who would wield magick so pure that it would banish her fears for her parents and give her all the answers she and her friends were seeking. Instead, Sigyn appeared to be almost... human.

Amanda wondered for a moment if it was an act. The goddess, who had nearly destroyed the Nine Realms, was bustling about several tables laden with boiling beakers, and several lumps of shiny metal that seemed to shrink away as Sigyn approached. Every few steps, Sigyn would pause to scold or laugh at the frog as if they were carrying on a conversation. Sigyn turned suddenly. She sniffed and stared at Amanda as if trying to remember why she was there. Laughing as if Amanda told her a joke, Sigyn began to work her way back around the room.

"Yeah, OK. I am sorry I am late or whatever. I would have been here sooner, but I had to get away from Keeper Fulla…"

The goddess jumped. "Is she here? Were you followed?"

Putting her hands up, Amanda backed away a bit. "What? No, no, no. I came alone."

"Good." Sigyn cast a wary glance down the stairs. "Please, let us have a seat as we have much to discuss." Sigyn motioned towards the two chairs, which were covered with books and scrolls. With a quick swipe of her hand the books zoomed off the threadbare seats and crashed into the shelves across the room. Several glass orbs fell to the floor and rolled about, and the pages of a large book that lay on a stand shuffled and then stilled.

Amanda walked behind the transparent goddess, trying not to trip on the thick, overlapping wool rugs that covered most of the floor and several windows. Taking in the room as she walked, Amanda could see that between the windows that ringed the room were stacked cubbies made of chipped stone and mossy wood. They held random clusters of objects, which all seemed well-worn or shabby. In fact, most everything in the room seemed old. One shelf held broken figurines, and another displayed what looked like rusted musical instruments. It felt like the older portion of the city where she had found Heimdall. The wall behind the chairs they were heading toward held a rough frame for an open tapestry of string with hundreds of black beads that moved at random around an unrefined ruby. Amada watched as Sigyn sat, half-expecting her to float or fall through, but the chair seemed to somehow be able to accommodate her insubstantial form. As Amanda sat, her chair sagged and gave off a faint smell of mildew.

For a moment they studied one another, and then Amanda looked out through the window to her right while Sigyn arranged and then rearranged her robes. Apparently neither knew where to start, so Amanda blurted out the first question that came to her. "Why are you see-through?"

"Because of the tower of course. It drains my magick, which is essentially my being. I am a mere ghost of the enchantress I used to be. Would you care for some mead?" Sigyn spoke quickly, her words almost running together at times as a tankard and two steins floated over to the marble table between them.

"Yes, thank you." Amanda picked up one of the mugs and busied herself by taking two big gulps of the thick liquid.

"It is quite inconvenient only having as much magick as a rune stone. I can't step a foot out of the tower, but I can manage a message like the one I sent you… but not two." Sigyn's face clouded, and she beckoned for Amanda to come closer. "I tried two at once, but couldn't do that. Nope. Not anymore. It's all gone, all gone."

Amanda cleared her throat. "How did you do it then? Did you sense me looking for you?"

Sigyn giggled. "Of course not. Garth told me it was time, so I sent the message."

"Right." Amanda nodded because she didn't know what else to say. She had so many questions to ask, but she wasn't sure what kind of answers she would get. Sigyn seemed barely coherent, so Amanda decided to start with the most pressing questions rather than asking about Ragnarok and why Sigyn was in the tower to begin with. "So how do you know about the alfblot?"

Sigyn made a face. "Because it is fell magick. I can feel it like a rash on the realm. Can't you? It would be uncomfortable to be around, and the one summoning would be worse. They would feel unpleasant to be around."

"I don't think I've noticed anyone like that, although most of Asgard is still pretty new to me. Is there anything else you can tell me? Like a spell to use or something?"

The expression on Sigyn's face softened as the room glowed brighter. Flashes of emerald lightning danced around the room, and then the walls dulled. "Sorry. What was that?"

Amanda looked around the room. "What was that?"

"What was what, was what?" Sigyn cackled like a child learning to play with blocks. "What, what, was, was… who… you! Oh, it is such a delight to speak to someone other than Garth." The frog croaked. "Now then, I bet you want to know what I know, about what I know."

"Um… I think so. The alfblot?" Amanda prompted.

Sigyn clapped and her expression brightened. "Yes! *The traitor and the alfblot!*"

Amanda waited, but Sigyn just kept nodding to herself. "Well?"

"Hm?"

"The traitor and the alfblot. What do you know?"

"The two are linked not only to each other, but to the syirces!" Sigyn looked as if she had just revealed where all the gold in the world had been hidden. "They hurt too, the syirces I mean, and alfblot is the nasty concoction that makes it all grow. Part water and part life. Alfblot can steal part of your life if it is controlled by one who bears the mark. Did you know that? That's what the Fell Elves feed on." Sigyn took a sip and choked on her mead. Tapping her stein twice, the liquid inside began to swirl. "Mead's gone a bit sour, same as the traitor. I can't see them, but I can sense them. I am sure you can as well. It should hurt to be around them, and they will smell like ash. That's how I knew you were still safe. You have none of those qualities, but you could use your senses to find the traitor creating the alfblot. That is why they want me. That and that." Sigyn pointed to the large book on the stand before reclining into the chair and propping her chin up with a finger.

It took Amanda a second to process what Sigyn had said. "So… the person summoning the alfblot and the syirces wants you and that book, and you think I can find them by… smelling them?"

"Of course not, but yes. That grimoire there contains every spell ever written, and by whom, and when it was last used. Now that I have shared with you the information you need, I thought we could do some magick!" Hopping up from the chair, Sigyn shuffled toward the stand. Carefully she hefted the large tome into her arms. Bringing the book back she let it slide onto the table, spilling the steins and tankard. With a nod of her head the mess vanished, along with Garth. The frog and the metal mugs appeared a moment later on a table under three tapestries woven with murky creatures that glared at them. The pages of the book rustled and the table quivered with the movement.

"Let us see now. Let us see." Sigyn licked her fingers and began thumbing through the pages. "Ah, here we go! Try this one. It is one of my favorites from my first grimoire." Sigyn tapped a page and then turned it to Amanda so she could see.

Intrigued, Amanda forgot her questions for a moment and examined the page. Tiny, neat runes were written above a drawing of a hand making a rotating gesture. After the picture there was one word in bold and underlined. "What does the spell do?"

"It makes light! I am sure you do not need to start with something so rudimentary after being on Asgard for so long, but I do so love this spell. I made it while investigating the tunnels under Yggdrasil that lead to the Norn's Forest. I thought it would be a good one for us to share together, and it's probably about as big a spell as I can manage in here."

Amanda continued to study the spell. She was a bit hesitant to use her magick around Sigyn, particularly in the tower. "Do you think it is safe? Will Lord Odin be able to sense us doing magick?"

"What is he going to do? Lock you in here too?"

That didn't sit well with Amanda, so she fidgeted for a moment more. This was not going as she had hoped. She wasn't sure what she could learn to help her parents, or anyone else, with the state Sigyn was in. The idea of going back to her friends and telling them that all Sigyn told her that could be helpful was to smell people made her sigh and shake her head.

"Oh, come on. Don't be such a willywhimple."

Amanda looked. "What's a willywhimple?"

"Aesir children scared of their dreams. Now then, the spellword is simple and the gesture is a simple roll of the wrist." Sigyn demonstrated.

Sighing again, Amanda read the page once more. She lifted her hand and rolled it, leaving her palm facing upward. "*Illumina.*" A pile of feathers under a nearby table instantly evaporated. Amanda grimaced. "Sorry about that. That happens sometimes. It's kind of normal for what happens when I try simple magick."

Sigyn looked taken aback, but then a curious wonder filled her eyes. With a shaking hand Sigyn reached out and took Amanda's wrist. Immediately, Amanda felt something flow from her to the goddess, like water returning to a dry streambed. The tower shook, but the goddess feverishly tightened her grip as if she would drown if she let go. Sigyn's form began to turn opaque, and she stretched her other arm as magick cascade in waves from her fingers. Closing her eyes, Sigyn exhaled and smiled. Amanda watched with her mouth open as Sigyn began to transform from the haggard woman she was to a tall, regal beauty. The tower shook violently and Sigyn dropped Amanda's arm. Slowly she shrank back to her transparent form. Sigyn's eyes, though, seemed more focused and she stared at Amanda.

"What was that?" A cold chill ran up Amanda's spine, sending goose bumps up and down her body.

"You have it all." Sigyn whispered. Her words were slow, but almost completely coherent and unjumbled. She pinched her lips and began to wander around the room.

"All of what?" Amanda stood on tiptoe as she tried to see where Sigyn was heading.

"My magick. You possess not a favouring; you have *all* of my powers." Sigyn rubbed her forehead, and then rushed back to her chair where she quickly began flipping through the grimoire. She stopped when she got to a few pages that were trimmed with pearlescent scrollwork. Reading a few lines, she put a hand to her mouth and sat back. "All of it... you have all of it."

"What? That... no. I mean, how is that possible? I can do some things sure, but wouldn't I be able to do... more?"

"Not without the proper teaching... and not with a binding." Sigyn waved and a pile of rugs shifted to reveal a large circle of runes etched into the floor. Pushing herself up from the chair, Sigyn led Amanda to stand in the center of the circle and drew a rune in front and behind where she stood. The symbols flickered in the air, but held. "The Allfather is a cunning god. My grimoire contains every spell ever wrought, and according to the spell I *think* he used, the Allfather bound you until such time as we were to meet. He must have known this would happen, that miserable old goat. Now then, quiet, and listen to the magick."

Amanda felt like she was in a play and had forgotten her lines. She was about to tell Sigyn she should just leave, but stopped when she heard a rustling outside the window. Several notes, in sad harmony to the notes Sigyn was now humming, flitted around them and sent the air pulsing. Unbidden, Amanda felt her arms slowly rise, and then watched as green magick motes flew from her fingertips.

SNAP!

Sigyn fell back into a pile of cushions, knocking a table off kilter and sending Garth flying through the window. "By the Eye of that goat!"

"OW!" Amanda yelped as she felt a shock run up to her arms. Her fingertips had gone numb as if she had hit the funny bone in her elbows, and she tasted something sour in the back of her throat. "What was that?"

"That," Sigyn crowed as she fought her way back up from the floor, "is one powerful binding spell, and well hidden to boot! No doubt no one else has even sensed its presence. It snapped me like the taut bands of the Elfin bows, but now I know what to look for. The other Favoured are limited in power only because of the Spell of Favouring. You are limited because of the spell placed on you by Lord Odin. If you will trust me, Amanda, I will show you what an enchantress you truly are. I may be a shadow of my former self, but never underestimate one who can create runes!"

Sigyn repositioned Amanda, this time tracing symbols in the air that left gossamer threads behind her fingers, and again began to hum her sad tune. This time the notes rang high and clear as Amanda's arms rose. The force of the spell began to flow over them both, igniting a light in the jeweled floor. Uttering a string of strange syllables, Sigyn thrust her palm toward the ceiling.

Time seemed to halt as the magick hung in the air. Amanda could see the particles of the spell whirl upward, starting at her feet and rising in a circle around her body, which sent her hair and cloak flying. At its apex the column of light shot outward through the crystal walls, and the tower glowed like a green beacon on the plains. The large book on the table beside them shuffled furiously until the spell was complete.

"Ha! That was better than the time I ensorcelled Lord Thor's gauntlets to whistle every time he swung that hammer of his. When I see the Allfather next, I will have to thank him for using a spell that even in my diminished state I could undo. Miserable... bird.... thing." Sigyn tottered over to the table and picked up the grimoire.

"I don't feel any different." Amanda shook her head to try and get the ringing out of her ears.

"I suspect not, child. A good binding acts upon its intended in subtle ways. I would surmise that Lord Odin has plans for you that we all have not yet guessed." Sigyn handed Amanda the leather-bound book. "Here, I'll go first and then you." Sigyn flicked her wrist and spoke quickly, "*Illumina.*"

A little green light blinked into existence in the cradle of her hand. Sigyn let go of the light and it floated in front of them. Amanda reached out a finger toward the green ball that was dancing about like a lightning bug.

Amanda was afraid to be hopeful that Sigyn might have just helped her with her magickal problems. There was more to how the spell worked at gathering light, but if she could cast this spell she might be able to finally help her parents and Jack. Nervously, she shifted the weight of the book to one arm and raised her right hand. Amanda made the gentle roll with her hand and spoke, *"Illumina."*

A river of freed magick flowed from inside Amanda and coalesced into her hand. It felt like her body was coming alive from having been asleep. A tiny light formed on her skin and then drifted upward, followed by a note, like the sound of a Christmas bell. Amanda stared in wonder as the light grew brighter and brighter until everything in the room gleamed with green light, the musical sounds matching the growth in volume until it began to hurt her ears. Amanda dropped her hand and the light and sound vanished. For a moment she felt slightly dizzy from a sudden head rush, and her skin tingled. Her magick felt different than it had when she used it before. It felt like it was alive and eagerly waiting for her call.

Sigyn clapped and danced with glee. "Well done, well done!"

Amanda felt pride at Sigyn's encouragement. "That was fantastic. It never felt like that before, like I was in control, but what was that noise?"

"Ah, that was the sound of the spell. It is part of your gift. We are connected to magick in a way that lets us hear it, see it, and even feel it in a way few can." Sigyn conjured the light and the note Amanda heard before sounded again. When Sigyn closed her hand the bell chime faded.

"Will it always be so loud?" Amanda shook her head to get the ringing out of her ears.

"You will become accustomed to it with time." Sigyn smiled sadly. "I am glad to see my magick in full again. Your powers should now be unfettered, ready to explore the realms to your heart's desire. It is a thing of pride to see another enchantress again. We are a rare breed."

Amanda thought excitedly for a moment at the possibilities. "But why do you think Lord Odin bound me in the first place? And why do I have all of your magick, and why did the Spell of Favouring find me later?"

"No idea, no idea, and no idea, but now you can begin practicing your magick in earnest. Learn the spells and other enchantments in my grimoire. Just… keep it safe. I have them all memorized, but it could be harmful if it fell into the wrong hands and I had to destroy it. The one searching for it must know it could lead me to them. Here, this will make it easier to hide." Sigyn placed her hands on the open pages and the book shrank until it was half its original size. "That spell is on page two hundred and three and can be quite fun if someone annoys you."

"That's fantastic!" The grimoire snapped shut. The book's covering was tooled with intricate markings that centered around the clasp, which lay on the left-hand side. Like curling smoke the clasp wound around itself, forming an eye with an emerald at its center. Feeling emboldened, Amanda took a deep breath for her next question. "Are there transformation spells too?"

Walking over to the wall of string, Sigyn tapped a few of the broken yarns until they looped back together. "Of course. I once made a spell to turn a certain war goddess into a butterfly. Why do you ask?"

"Seriously? What is with you Asgardians being turned into animals? Anyway... I kind of need to turn some people back into... well... people."

Sigyn smiled slightly. "I thought I saw the book register the use of that spell. Mice, wasn't it? Very interesting way to protect someone."

Amanda's good feeling about her recent accomplishment dimmed slightly. "So, you know? I didn't know that's what I was doing at the time. Is there any way to help them?"

Humming, Sigyn spun a finger in the air, her focus was quickly returning to what it was before they connected. "It depends on the spell. Yes, most spells have a way of undoing. Some spells of transformation are made so that they can only be broken when the time is right. If it exists, then it is in those pages. If it doesn't, you will have to make it yourself or wait. Just flip through the grimoire, I am sure you will find what you seek or clues as what to do. As I said, any spell cast, whether fell or good, rests within that tome."

Amanda crossed the room to sit back down. She had hoped the answer to her parents' return would have been easier, maybe even make it OK for not telling the Prelate or Keeper Fulla about coming to the Green Askr, but nothing on Asgard had been easy so far. "How could it lead you to the one summoning the alfblot and syirces?"

Sigyn took several moments to respond. The beads on the string wall were centering around one strand, and Sigyn watched it with interest. "It contains spells that could stop whoever is behind the summoning and use of fell magick. There are even spells that could return a Disir to their original state, although that requires the help of ones who are no longer in this realm. It has spells that many covet, that could also tear realms asunder and return us to the brink of annihilation. But only I can see them, and now you can too. Given the right spells from my grimoire, I am sure we could find a way to follow the trail of alfblot back to the Disir. Alfblot is not made in just one way. It requires something to be given, and what that is can vary by the person who summons it. It is the same with the Disir. They are always changed in different ways, and gifted with different things. Alfblot is certainly easier to banish or destroy, but if even a drop remains it will continue to work toward its intended purpose until that reason is fulfilled. The spells in the grimoire could stop them though, no matter how it is made. Syirces however, are almost impossible to banish unless their link to the alfblot is severed. Like the snip of a string. Look for the fell section toward the back of the grimoire; you'll see."

Amanda flipped through the book and found a section of pages that were darker and heavier. The ink ran together in places, and the instructions overlapped several pages with various scribbled words and sketches of ingredients, but Amanda found the runes for alfblot and began to read what she could make out. The spell to create alfblot seemed too simple. There were a few spellwords and then the ingredients. All it required was someone to give a portion of their life and mix it into water – it just didn't say how your life was to be given.

The spell for the syirce, though, was much more complex, covering ten pages, and most of it didn't make sense. The spellwords seemed incomplete, and there was no mention of how to make them go away once summoned. Amanda scanned the list of ingredients and her heart began to beat a bit harder as she realized it looked like the list she had found by Mimir's well that also happened to be the parchment paper that guided her here. "It says here a syirce is made using alfblot, Elf hair, the apples of Idunn, the bark of Yggdrasil, and a sacrifice."

"A sacrifice of life, the same as with the alfblot. Whoever is using this fell magick had to learn it from one of the dark ones. You will find that with some magick, even though you have the words, you would not be able to cast the spell yourself. Fell magick requires you to have been claimed by a Fell Elf. You have to become a Disir to use. True Disir go willingly to the dark ones. Such an encounter would leave a mark. Disir... what a name..."

"Have you sensed anything that would make someone want to be claimed by a Fell Elf? Lord Mimir thought it might be one of the Einherjar."

"Doubtful. Aesir are long-lived, but not immortal. From what I have sensed, the person has sacrificed enough of their life that were they an Aesir, they would have died. Although... they could have stolen the life from others. Hmm... stolen it and taken it, then given it back as their own. That would explain the large quantities, and perhaps why the alfblot has been easier to banish than in previous encounters."

Amanda closed her eyes and rubbed her forehead. She was having trouble keeping up with all the new information, and with Sigyn's speech pattern. "So, it could be anyone. Why doesn't Lord Odin or Mimir know this, and why hasn't he or anyone else sensed them?"

"Because magick is not simple, and no one is truly all-powerful or all-knowing. Knowledge, even when constantly renewed, is never fully current." The smoke from the pile of feathers Amanda had vaporized curled up into Sigyn's face and she whirled around. "I think it is time for you to be off, dear. We are no longer alone. I look forward to seeing what spells you can master between this time and our next meeting. Remember to keep the grimoire safe, and it might be best to not let on too much about your full favouring until we know more about the reason for your binding. There could be repercussions should you utter a word."

Before Amanda could respond, Sigyn waved and Amanda found herself on the edges of the Plains of Idavoll. The grimoire vanished and Amanda felt it settle in her cloak next to the scroll and mirror. Sean had been sitting on one of the stone markers and jumped as Amanda appeared.

"By the Eye, Amanda! Are you alright?" Sean was holding his hammer and had raised it in defense.

Amanda hadn't seen it before but there were runes carved into the handle. Feeling disoriented from the sudden jump she could only make out a rune that meant 'blizzard'. "I'm fine. Sigyn sent me. She must have known you were here."

Sean looked out to the plains behind Amanda as if he expected to see some giant eye spying on them. "What was she like? Was she... evil? Did she help you find anything out about your magick or the alfblot?"

"She was not quite what any of us was expecting. As Jack would say, 'she's gone 'round the bend and then off the mountain.' She's definitely not the one summoning the alfblot. She did tell me some things though that might help us." Amanda suddenly felt a wave of dizziness that had nothing to do with how tired she was. Her stomach churned when she wondered if that was the sensation Sigyn said she would feel around the person using fell magick. "What are you doing here?"

Sean must have heard something different in her voice because he gave her an odd look. "I told you I would meet you here, remember?" A low trumpet sounded. "Come on, there's no time to chat. Queen Frigga went ahead and put the city on lockdown."

"Why? What happened? Did the frost lilies sense something?" Amanda put her arms under her cloak as Sean began to lead them back to the Stave through back alleys.

Sean shook his head. "Worse. Messenger Aesir were just sent out to all the realms. Thankfully one of them gave me a heads up. Heimdall attacked Keeper Fulla. They think that somehow the alfblot in his system made him go mad again, even after all the cures they tried on him. He stole the apples from her and made it all the way to Draupnir. Lena and Lev were there. He did a number on them as well before the Prelate showed up and put a stop to him. He's in a knocked out again – this time for good until they can be certain he is back to his old self. The Queen has decided to seal the realm and hope the lilies can still help us find the one we are looking for. With Asgard sealed, the plan is to use Lord Odin's throne and Draupnir to keep watch and keep us safe until the other gods get back."

"But if Queen Frigga is sealing off the city, why do we need to hurry? The city itself extends all the way to Yggdrasil."

"But not Idavoll, remember? The messenger told me the Queen was tagging something else onto the spell, a tracker for anyone not of Asgardian blood. That means you and me and pretty much anyone else except gods and Aesir. Keeper Fulla will no doubt tell the Prelate and the Queen she left us to go to the Bifrost and back, which we should have been done with a while ago. If they see us not back in our beds they are going to know something was up. I hope Sigyn told you something *really* good to help us because we sure could use it."

***

On the outskirts of Asgard, where the shadow of Yggdrasil covers the land, a cloaked figure waited impatiently under an overpass as the triads of Einherjar, returning from their posts guarding the syirces, traveled above. One of the guards paused to look down into the shadows. The other two with him halted as he inspected the bridge. "Did you hear Ratatosk scurrying around below, Agnarr?"

Shaking his head, Agnarr removed his helmet. His long blond hair fell down to his shoulders. "Nay, but we were charged to inspect all roads and bridges between here and the Gruneling before we secure the city. I obey my orders, unlike you, Vargnir."

Vargnir bared his teeth and moved to draw his sword as the low bellow of a horn reverberated throughout the realm. "Careful of what you say. Just because you are the favorite of Lady Freyja does not mean you cannot be cut."

Seizing upon the conversation above as a distraction, the figure below silently climbed up a tendril of one of Yggdrasil's roots, and then catapulted into the road leading to the rocky lands past the city's edge. It wasn't that the dark figure feared the triad, but to be discovered now would be more of a nuisance than a hindrance.

Winding through and around the base of Yggdrasil's back side, the lone figure slowly made its way to a rocky outcropping that faced the middle of the mountains that ring Asgard from the east, up to the north, and to the west. Only Lord Odin, the Einherjar, and the Favoured were allowed to come to this desolate place, which the Allfather himself kept lifeless as a reminder of the treachery of the past. This was the Gruneling, the place where those that even Hel herself wouldn't want are banished. A slow rolling vibration came from the lifeless ground, and a voice from beneath the shadowed person's feet spoke into the night.

"Welcome, warrior." The rasping voice brought with it a dark haze of magick in the air like smoke from a pool of burning oil. "I was surprised to hear of your alliance from my Jotun friend. Is it the hatred in your heart that I sense for the newest of the cursed breed that spurs you on this path?"

The hooded figure didn't answer, but stood unmoving until a second traveler joined them. The newest member spoke in a reverential whisper. "We are almost ready to begin, Myrkr."

"Your news is good, Disir, and your reward will be worth the effort I sense you have done. Our plan is coming close to its end, and the Asgardians still suspect nothing."

The first figure stood a bit taller than the second, and spoke without the same deference to the voice below. "They suspect nothing because I covered this one's clumsiness. When I discovered the ruse being used to conceal this one's work, I was told my centuries of waiting for freedom were at an end. Are we sure your plan will work? We still need to find a way to take the protection of Odin from the realm. The syirces, perhaps?"

"Our plan is better than that." The second figure spoke angrily to the other, and lifted a bag from the folds of their cloak. Dropping it to the ground, black liquid began to dribble

131

out of the sides and into the chains around the door.

There was a slow groan and the chains began to hiss as alfblot flowed from the bag into the cracks of the wooden door. The voice sounded stronger as it spoke next. "We do indeed have a better way. Objects of Asgardian magick of that potency could corrupt the syirces, and our prize could be lost. We will use the forest as we planned, and we must hurry. Should the wretched Odin return before we seize this opportunity, all would be lost."

"The forest is unpredictable, especially if the Norn become involved." The one the voice called warrior kneeled to the ground. "We will also need a distraction, as all travelers around the realm are being watched closely. Perhaps I should reveal myself. I would enjoy seeing their life ebb as I strike their self-righteousness from their lips."

"The Norn know as well as I that this must come to pass. Our Jotun friend will provide cover for our work. Send word to Bergelmir to prepare the imps." Dry winds blew across the door, and the voice began to diminish, along with the fell magick it brought with it.

"I will send my master your message. My pets are ready to aid us in taking the ring. However, I worry the alfblot we possess will not be enough to bring an attack." The Disir held out their hands, and fell runes gleamed around their wrist.

"The lifeblood of a god would be a potent sacrifice to add to your spells. If you use the waters from the one whose mind uses the rivers to find his knowledge, we will take yet another protection from the realm, and be able to strike. Are you prepared to end one of your own?"

"I am not afraid to make sacrifices for the greater good of our kind. We must rid ourselves of the useless rabble in order for our future to be preserved." The first figure sounded excited by the challenge.

The second traveler drew in a short breath. "We will do what must be done." Silence followed and the two cloaked figures disappeared into the desolate plains.

CHAPTER 15:
THE GODS' FAILURE

"I still can't believe that Lord Odin put a binding spell on you. Hey! Stop that!" Cassie swatted at the small ball of green light dancing around her head.

Amanda laughed as she sent the small speck of light spiraling out into the night. "I still have a lot to learn, but it finally feels like I have control of my magick. I was practicing on my parents the other day with some spells I found, and I swear I thought I saw them start to change back. Once I find the right spell, I can finally turn them back into humans, and it's all thanks to Sigyn. She definitely wasn't the monster everyone made her out to be. When Lord Odin gets back, I am going to find out why he put that binding spell on me and see if we can get her out of the Green Askr."

Cassie was shivering, so her teeth chattered as she spoke next. "I'll be curious to hear that explanation. It's too bad she didn't give you more to go on about the Disir. Basically she told you the ingredients, which we mostly knew, and that you can sense them. That's not as much to go on as her note made it sound. Are you sure she didn't say anything else about your favouring, or something that can help us?"

Cassie, Amanda and Mykola stood around a large golden stand that floated above the door to the Gruneling. The night winds from Mount Valhalla were sending cold gusts of air down into the city, and the trio was trying to huddle as close to one another as possible to keep warm. Connor and Sean were now stationed back at Idunn's orchard to prevent anyone else from stealing more of the enchanted apples.

Amanda dropped her hand, and her stomach clenched. "Uh... my favouring... no. But don't forget I can use the grimoire she gave me to find the Disir... somehow."

Cassie bumped Amanda's shoulder in an encouraging way. "That's true. Well at least you won't be having any more magickal explosions! Just try not to tire yourself out. Now that you are unbound, the spells may be easier but they could still hurt you if you try too much."

"Right... I guess I will just have to keep seeing what works and what doesn't until I get my full favouring." Amanda chided herself again mentally. She had been showing off with her spells, but she had to be careful how much magick she used in front of the others. All the other Favoured could only use their magick sparingly before they wore themselves out, where as she felt like she could use her magick for hours without tiring.

Mykola looked over at Amanda, his forehead creasing as he concentrated on her. She had been keeping the secret of her favouring from them for the last week. Every time she spoke, he seemed to sense something wasn't complete with her words. She had stuck to her story of half-truths and so far it had fooled her friend, which made her feel terrible. Cassie's emotional magick had started picking up something odd between Amanda and Mykola as well. Amanda could tell she wanted to ask them what was going on, but so far her friend hadn't said a word.

Sigyn's words about repercussions lingered in Amanda's ear whenever she opened her mouth to try to tell them about how she had all of Sigyn's magick. There had been no time to talk with Sean, or process, as they raced back to the Stave. Horns were blowing all over the city, and Amanda could see, feel, and hear the spells wrapping the city closing in on them. The magick blowing through the streets nipped at their heels and slammed the doors behind them as they crossed the threshold into their rooms. Cassie was so excited Amanda was OK that she had been satisfied with Amanda's story. Amanda told her and the others about Sigyn's erratic behavior, the grimoire, and what she learned about the alfblot and Disir– but left the part of her having all of Sigyn's magick out.

Cassie narrowed her eyes suddenly, and pursed her lips. "And Keeper Fulla still believes you found the grimoire in the Halls of Learning?"

"Thankfully, yes. She is a bit preoccupied to care at the moment. Girnka was the only one who seemed suspicious of a grimoire that had so many spells that I could perform easily until he recognized Sigyn's rune near the clasp. He assumed that made it hers, which meant my favouring would be more attuned to the spells."

"Maybe if you told them you were using it to help your parents and stop the Disir, they wouldn't care. There could be a lot in the grimoire that could help. They were happy when you showed them the spells for alfblot, syirces, and their ingredients." Cassie translated for Mykola.

"True. They said it would help with Heimdall, but it's not that easy to use this grimoire. That's why I am not sure how Sigyn thinks it can help me find the Disir. It's different than the others I've used in Fensalir. It's like it's showing me things in the order it wants to, or knows what I can handle. Also, I think the pages shuffle around each time a spell is used. Yesterday I was reading a spell about bewitching a pair of knitting needles to knit on their own at the front of the book, and today it was all the way at the back."

Cassie laughed. "The grimoire wanted you to know how to knit?"

Amanda tensed as a groan of magick seeped from the doors to the Gruneling. "No. I just thought it was interesting to read why someone would make a spell like that up. Turns out Jotunheim has some pretty cold winters every hundred years, and a Rock Jotun warlock wanted something to keep his head warm. Anyway, even with my magick unbound not all the spells work. Some can only be done certain times of the year, or won't work if I don't have the right ingredients. I am just hoping I will be able to find a fix for my parents. Then I can focus on the syirces, alfblot, and Disir, and maybe think about telling the Prelate."

"Well don't forget, you can always sniff them out!" Cassie laughed, trying to lighten Amanda's sudden downward mood swing, and pressed her nose to one side.

"Ugh, stop it or I will sniff you. Besides, I think that part may work differently for me. I mean, it has something to do with smell. When we were looking for Heimdall, I remember feeling like I had to sneeze when I was looking for the one summoning the alfblot. That and it felt like I was about to crawl out of my skin. So I am just trying to be aware of what I feel when I am around people. And yes, I am... sniffing some of them too. I am pretty sure Keeper Fulla thought I was having an allergy attack when she caught me trying to sniff her. It would help if I could narrow down my search. So far the frost lilies haven't been of any help, but Keeper Fulla keeps insisting on putting them out. Have either of you found anything else out that could help us look for the Disir? We know they usually take the Fell Elf magick to help them do something, but so far all they have done is summon alfblot and syirces. Well, and try to kidnap Heimdall too. So they have done something, but not what others have done in the past. Right?"

Mykola's dark eyes lingered on Amanda and didn't waver as he shook his head. He made a few motions and then leaned on his staff. Cassie gave Mykola a look before translating. Amanda wasn't sure what Mykola had been thinking, but she guessed it had to do with her. "He says the other info he learned is sketchy at best. The stories are all fragmented and different. What Sigyn told you about spells turning them back is good news, but I don't think anyone would believe us if we told them – or want to try. Everyone is so freaked out right now that I am sure once they find the Disir they will be destroyed without waiting to ask them why they decided to go to the dark side. It is strange that they haven't caused more of a stir, though. If we do find those spells Sigyn told you about, we might be able to save the poor fool."

"I'll keep looking, but either it is hidden or it isn't here." Amanda pulled the leather-bound grimoire from her cloak and flipped through to a spot where several tattered edges remained from where pages had been torn out.

"Who knows, maybe she thought they were in there but they weren't. I know she said it contains every spell ever written, but really? Let's consider our source. You did say Sigyn was a tad off. If the Einherjar weren't stationed around the realm's shields, we'd sneak you off to her again. But until the gods return or we find something in that book, I doubt we will get lucky to get you out there twice unnoticed." Cassie peeked her head over the page Amanda was studying.

"This is so frustrating! It feels like we are so close! Why couldn't Lord Odin have come back sooner?" Amanda sighed and shook her head. "Have you all heard anything on how long it will take the gods to get back now that the city is cut off from the other realms?"

Cassie rubbed her hands together. "It could take days or weeks for the gods to get through, depending on where they are coming from. The roots of Yggdrasil are supposed to link the Nine Realms, but I don't know if anyone has ever used them to travel like this before. Queen Frigga said it was the only way into the city she could leave open that could be securely monitored. At least Mykola can banish the syirces if they crop up. We'll just keep doing our part until they get back or you figure it out."

Mykola held up a hand to be quiet as he scanned the large mass of roots behind them. He began gesturing as they collectively shuddered at a burst of magick from the door. Amanda recognized the Zukov twins' names. Picking up the gist of what he was saying she answered him. "I haven't seen Lena and Lev since we arrived. You would think spending all their time out here would make them want to talk to other people, but they left as soon as the Einherjar dropped us off. I think they are trying to prove they can still defend the realm even without their magick."

Draupnir sparkled in the night between them, its blood-red glow illuminating the terraced stand it rested upon. Amanda let her eyes glaze over as she studied the two circling ravens that embraced the stone with the tips of their wings. The sound of the magick coming from the prison was still shrill, and made Amanda feel slightly queasy.

"Good riddance if you ask me. When Queen Frigga said the ring stays here until the gods return, and they volunteered to guard it as long as it was needed, I could have done cartwheels. See you later! I agree with you though, Amanda. I am sure they were just trying to look good." Cassie pretended to gag, and then coughed. "But this place is made for them. It's dry, lacks any sense of happiness or life, and is for people who need to learn a lesson." Cassie picked up a frost lily that had been smashed into the dirt and began picking at the petals. Something out in the veil of darkness around them moved and the group paused to peer out into the night.

When nothing happened, they all turned back to Draupnir. Tucking the grimoire back into her cloak, Amanda winced as another burst of magick came from below their feet. "I feel bad for them, but it has been kind of nice not to have them around."

"It is probably for the best for them anyway. Without their favouring, they can only use rune stones, so if we do get attacked, they wouldn't be much help. Here they have some built in space to watch for attackers. I wish we could just find the traitor and go back to the way things were. Although, maybe Lena and Lev could stay out here. Sure, the missions were dangerous, but it never felt like this. All the fun has been sucked up." Mykola began to sign to Cassie, so she continued to speak. "Mykola says we could open up the Gruneling and ask the Fell Elves trapped below if they know anything."

Amanda snapped her head to look at Mykola. She grinned at the sparkle in his normally stoic eyes. "Somehow I don't think that would go over well."

Cassie shook her shoulders. "See, this is what I mean. Why is it that all we have to talk about are the crazy people and Fell-Elf-serving people? Hey... maybe Freyja's been infected with alfblot! That would explain the change in her behavior lately. Ever since she got back from battling those Jotuns with the Prelate she has been like my Aunt Fergy after one too many nightcaps on Christmas Eve – sickenly nice. Although she is starting to come around to her old self, she did have only three ogres jump me during our last training session."

"That's almost nice of her. It could have been six like the last time, but I don't think that means she has been taken over by a Fell Elf." Amanda trailed off and brushed her hair out of her face. "You don't think Lena and Lev would resort to using fell magick to get their favouring back, do you?"

"They definitely don't like not being at the frontlines. People do strange things when they have a secret to keep or something to prove. Secrets can hurt you." Cassie's eyes darted up at Amanda and then back to the ring as she seemed to sense Amanda's turmoil.

Amanda looked away. She suddenly worried if her friends would forgive her for not being completely honest with them after all they had done for her. "They do."

Cassie rubbed her hands together. "Well, as Sean has been known to say, it'll all become as plain as a cat in a pack of dogs one of these days soon. How about we play a game where we don't talk about alfblot, syirces, or anything else that is wrong for the next five minutes? I, for one, would like to see a new spell. How about you, Mykola?" Without waiting for his reply, Cassie raised her chin up and looked at Amanda expectantly. "Mykola's in. You're up."

Amanda purposefully let her feelings about her secrets go and pulled the grimoire back out again. She flipped back and forth through the pages, "Let's see, this one makes you sound like a bird from Vanaheim that can put you to sleep. Oh! This one should be good!" Holding the grimoire up, Amanda situated her herself and conjured her little light to hover above the group. With a second motion she brought the tips of her fingers together. Slowly pulling them apart and then pinching them back together as she pulled her hand back like she was pulling a thread, she whispered so that her words were almost lost in the wind. "*Dilyagg.*"

Cassie and Mykola watched, their eyes widening, as the green light began to grow to the size of a tennis ball, and then to the size of a large shimmering watermelon. A high-pitched whinny echoed from outside the light's perimeter, and a small black animal came bounding from the shadows. Leaping into the air, a vindmare soared through Amanda's lightshow, snapping at the air with its teeth.

"Nimbus! Watch it!" Cassie took a step to the side and bumped into Draupnir's stand.

Mykola caught the foal and the vindmare snorted with amusement as Amanda's spell vanished. Amanda tucked the grimoire away as Mykola set the vindmare down and began chiding it in sign language. For a minute the boy looked stern, but then flashed the winged horse a wink.

"I don't think telling him to behave and then winking at him will make the little bugger believe you are serious." Even though Cassie looked annoyed at the vindmare, she still patted it on the head and then ran her fingers through the foal's dark mane.

Earlier that week the vindmare egg had begun to shake violently while they were all taking a break in the common area of the Stave. Cassie had followed every instruction the Prelate had given her, but she was still slightly afraid the egg had been contaminated by an imp's touch. She nervously waited to see what would emerge. The girls had squealed with delight as the tiny vindmare struggled free from its shell and tottered towards Mykola and Connor with little neighing sounds. The four of them had crowded around the small creature and gently begun to pet its head or scratch it behind the ears, which the foal had happily accepted. Mykola had held back, but the vindmare had put its head in his hand and shocked them all when nothing happened. Stretching its soft black wings for the first time, the newly hatched vindmare had leapt off from the lounge chair and floated for a minute before falling to the soft cushions.

Amanda could now appreciate why her parents had never let her have a pet. Watching the baby vindmare was another full-time job on top of everything else they had to do. The vindsvolla, the adult version of Nimbus, were always so well behaved. Nimbus was wily and anxious to get into mischief.

"To be fair, Nimbus is probably just as bored as we are. At least he should sleep well from all the walking to and from the Gruneling."

"That's what we said after his first battle practice with Freyja, and he still kept us up half the night running and dive-bombing us in our beds. Besides, he should know better than to sneak up on us like that. He blends in with the night, and he nearly scared the stuffing out of me."

Cassie took a stern tone with Nimbus, whom they had named for his resemblance to thunderclouds. The vindmare gave Cassie a snort as he trotted along merrily around Mykola. The boy and the vindmare had formed a silent bond from the moment they met, and now Nimbus wouldn't go anywhere without his companion.

"I am just surprised it did not turn into a dulhda." Lev emerged from behind a signpost, the runes carved into it pointing the way back to Asgard.

"Who knows, brother, that filthy beast may yet be one." Lena followed her twin. Both were covered in dirt, and had dark circles under their eyes. Lev's face had a slight bruise still from their encounter with Heimdall.

"Aw, is it time for us to go already? Huh, too bad for you two. We'll just take our healthy vindmare with us and go. I think Amanda has some spells she wants to work on. You should see the way she has gotten control of her magick these days." Cassie crossed her arms and smirked at the twins.

Lena gave Cassie a look that would have turned her to stone if she had the power, and then crouched over the door to the Gruneling. The chains rattled as a howling burst of energy flooded through the enchanted wood. "Whatever. I am glad we don't have one of those beasts following us everywhere we go. The only good thing he could do is carry us, and he is too small to do even that. We have more important things to be concerned with. Since we stopped Heimdall, it is imperative we be on guard and ready to defend Draupnir and this realm. Keeper Fulla was here earlier, giving us the report on what the Queen's latest plans are."

"Oh really? Keeper Fulla was giving *you* a report? I am betting she was just here to put more frost lilies out to keep Draupnir safe. And the way we heard it, is that you stopped Heimdall with your faces." Cassie was in no mood to put up with the twins.

Lena hissed, but neither she nor her brother responded. Nimbus had stopped behind Mykola when the twins appeared, but now he was cautiously sniffing the air and walking toward them. Lev stomped on a frost lily, sending the petals into the vindmare's face. Nimbus flapped his wings and reared away as if he was being attacked. Mykola came to Nimbus's defense and slammed his staff to the ground, sending a wave of air and petals back towards Lev.

"Leave him be." Amanda warned.

"Or what? You cannot do anything worse to us than what you have already done." Lev's face pulled together in a sour expression as he walked around Amanda to the other side of the stand. "Our favouring still hasn't recovered, and the gods care not for our fate so long as we can be here to guard Lord Odin's ring."

"Be silent, Lev. We agreed." Lena gave her brother a look.

Mykola tapped the ground and shook his head. He began to sign. When he finished, Cassie nodded her head in agreement. "Of course they care, but they are just a little preoccupied."

"Preoccupied? They have become lazy." Lena tried to interrupt her brother, but he brushed her away. "They depend on us, working us until we are of no more use to them. How they reacted to what Heimdall did to us is of no surprise to me. They were all apologies, but no action. We have saved Aesir, Light Elves, and the gods on numerous occasions, but when we need help they are *preoccupied*. It seems to me if they truly had the power they claim to possess, then they would be able to ensure any threat or harm to the realms was prevented. Instead, they have us do the brunt of the work like slaves. Perhaps we should relieve them of their duty, and take control of the Nine Realms."

"What does that mean?" Amanda saw her unease at the way Lev was speaking was also reflected in Cassie and Mykola's expressions.

Lev held his hand over Draupnir, sending flickering light over his fingers. "Isn't it amazing how much power is contained within such a small vessel? My sister and I were just debating what we could accomplish if someone were to put it on, even for just a moment."

Mykola stepped up beside the twins and put the crook of his staff between them and the ring. He needed no words to say hands off. There was a surge of magick, and a ghostly echo resounded in Amanda's ears. Nimbus whinnied and put his nose into the air, smelling for whatever had caused the disturbance. Apparently, he could hear magick too.

Lena begrudgingly nodded her assent. She may not like her brother's rationale, but Amanda could tell she agreed with him on this topic. Lena wiped a clomp of dirt from her shoulder. "Do not be too rash, Mykola. We could each take a turn wearing the ring. Perhaps it could help us with our problems. I am sure Lord Odin would not object to us using some of his power to stop the syirces. Wouldn't that be helpful to you as well, Mykola? You get so tired after closing one of the portals. This way we could close them all for good."

"Are you guys stupid or just idiots? Don't you remember what happened to the last Favoured who accidentally touched Draupnir?" Amanda had read about it in one of her long study sessions. The poor kid had spent a month in Eir's Manor healing.

Lena sucked in a quick breath through her teeth. "Never call us stupid. We are the only ones who are using our brains to come up with a solution to our problems. The others are content to wait to be rescued, but we are not. The gods are not as benevolent as they would have us believe. Have you ever wondered why the old parts of the city lie vacant and crumbling? It is a cursed place – cursed by mortals that the gods were supposed to reward and protect. Back before Ragnarok, there was a time where mortals were allowed to come to Asgard if they were deemed worthy through combat. They were housed in the lower levels that now lie in ruin. There were celebrations and parades for the mortals unlike any other in all of the Nina Realms. Jealous of mortals gaining access to the Golden Realm, and not being rewarded themselves, there was a conspiracy by some of the gods, Valkyrie, and Aesir. They unleased a beast upon the mortals while they slept that devoured them all.

Do you want to know what happened to those responsible – nothing. Lord Odin declared that if the mortals were truly worthy, they would have been able to defend themselves. When the mortals were supposed to return to their homes, what was sent back to them were their funeral biers. When they found out what happened, they gathered anyone with magick on earth, runes stones, and talismans, and cursed the place where their heroes fell. That was deemed intolerable by the gods, and so the Great Winter known as the Ice Age covered Midgard."

"Now wait a minute. That can't be true. There was no mention of any of that in the history scrolls." Amanda looked to Cassie and Mykola. Mykola had his head bowed. "Mykola?" Mykola's eyes slowly lifted as he pushed his hood back. He nodded.

Lena smiled like a hungry wolf that found its next meal. "It is the truth, and that is not the only story of such horror. We all know Mykola cannot lie and can sense when truth is being spoken. We could take the power before us so that we will not have to wait to help those that suffer while the gods sit idly by. Show them, brother."

Lev pulled a rune stone from his cloak and brushed it with a finger. The rune began to shimmer. A gossamer thread of magick drifted from Draupnir to the stone. "We found out about this rune to help us restore what was taken. We need but a fraction of Draupnir's magick to restore our own and then to rid ourselves of the alfblot and syirces. From there we will find a way to protect the realms from any that would do it harm – including the gods."

Cassie bristled and shook her shoulders. "No! You don't get to act all superior because you think you are doling out justice. That is exactly what the gods did in the story you just told us. Mykola can sense the truth, but *I* can sense there is something else there you are holding back. What happens to Draupnir and the realm's defenses when you steal magick to help yourself? Tell us the whole truth!" Cassie magick sang through the air toward the twins.

Lev held up the rune stone and Cassie's magick vanished into it. "Idiot. All magick can be absorbed by this stone and used as we see fit. We had planned to use it when we were alone, but now you can witness the beginning of a time where we no longer depend on the gods' favouring."

Amanda and Mykola moved, but it was too late. The rune stone siphoned the magick from the ring it needed. The defensive shields around the realm dimmed slightly, but then brightened. Lena put her hand on the stone, and there was a pulse of magick. The twins were engulfed in a red aura as the rune stone disintegrated. Lev raised his hand and black clouds gathered around it. Lena took his hand and a flare of magick engulfed them both.

Lena pointed to the signpost by the road behind them and it suddenly erupted into flames. Lev closed his eyes and extended his arms, and a dozen mirror images of him appeared around the group. One surprised Amanda when it reached out and clamped a hand on her shoulder. The twins were laughing hysterically as their magick was fully restored, but then their eyes went wide and they became silent as they stared into Draupnir's ruby.

"S-sister." Lev's voice was a whisper.

Lena nodded. "I see it too, brother."

The twins were so preoccupied that they hadn't noticed Mykola unlace his gloves and come up behind them. Faster than a striking snake, he touched Lena and Lev simultaneously on the back of their necks. The twins screamed in unison as their magick departed once more.

Lena recovered first. She was shaking but managed to take a step toward Mykola. She swung a fist, but he dodged it easily. She stumbled back to her brother. "You..."

Cassie rolled her eyes. "We know. We will pay. Just be glad we aren't going to report you to the Prelate."

"We aren't?" Amanda was surprised at Cassie's placid reaction. "Didn't you see what happened when that rune stone took magick from Draupnir? It almost brought the realm's defenses down."

"Granted, but it didn't. Look, do I think they are foul gits that deserve to be sent to the putrid dung fields in Vanaheim? Sure. But what's the point? There's enough going on. They got their magick back, although now they have to wait a bit longer to use it again. Hopefully it will make them rethink their choices. Draupnir and the realm are safe. That's my takeaway for tonight. We can deal with them later once this mess is sorted, and hopefully never have to deal with them until we get our full favouring." Cassie tensed as something passed between Lena and Lev's thoughts. "You wouldn't dare."

"What?" Amanda held up a hand, ready again to cast a spell should the twins try anything again.

Lev tossed something to his sister, and a gust of wind brought a fine mist curling up from the ground. "We will not be so easily defeated. Sacrifices must be made. If what we saw is true, we must go find answers. We must know more!" The twins held up rune stones, and a portal opened behind each of them. In an instant, they vanished.

Cassie scrambled to where the twins had stood a moment before. "We have to find them and stop them! They want to end the Spell of Favouring. What they want to do could kill everyone if it goes badly."

A mismatched sound of notes floated in the air, and Amanda noticed the mist had turned into a dense fog that was obscuring everything except for what was right around them. "Do you think this is Lev's doing?"

"No idea, but we need to find a way to alert the Prelate about Lena and Lev." Cassie's voice became muffled as she spoke.

Nimbus started squealing and rearing up, his hooves striking at something every time he landed. Mykola tried to calm him down, but the vindmare only became more and more agitated.

Something sharp dug into the toe of Amanda's boot. "Ouch, what was that?" The fog was now so thick it hid everything from the waist down. Amanda couldn't see what had hit her.

Another roll of dense clouds washed over them. "Amanda, are you still there?" Cassie called from Amanda's right.

"Yeah, I am still here." Amanda conjured her light, but it only reflected back on her from the mist. An unnatural stillness had descended over the area that made the hair on Amanda's arms stand on end.

"Are you still by Draupnir? We should get it and take it back to the city. There is something fell about this, and I can't sense anyone but Mykola and Nimbus. Hey, stop that!" Cassie suddenly sounded horrified.

"What is it?" Amanda shouted.

Taking a few steps in the last direction she remembered seeing Draupnir, her foot brushed limp chains on the door to the Gruneling. Amanda suddenly realized why the quiet had unsettled her nerves. She couldn't hear the magick coming from the Gruneling into Draupnir anymore. The stand was empty. Spinning around as a scraggly pitch of musical notes wafted from behind her, Amanda could just make out the glint of Draupnir's ruby as it disappeared into the fog.

"They're stealing Draupnir!" Amanda yelled as she sprinted off after the ring.

CHAPTER 16:
ASGARDIAN FALL

Running as fast as she could, Amanda sent her full power into her light spell and the brightness turned the foggy night into a green-lit day. Amanda saw a sparkle in the distance and nearly tripped as she hit the first pavers of the stone road leading back into the city. Yggdrasil groaned like a moaning ghost above her and Amanda looked up to try and get her bearings, but the dense cloud still blocked anything that was not within ten feet of her.

A strange scratching sound started to echo all around Amanda. She swiveled her head about to try to determine where the sound was coming from, and see where she was. Her boots slipped again and she nearly fell into a trough filled with three beehives. The bees buzzing about stopped and looked up at her. There was a loud crash to Amanda's left, and another flash from Draupnir. This time Amanda heard the keening wail of its magick.

"Sorry," Amanda called to the bees as she took off after the ring. The fog was coating everything in a fine sheen of water droplets, which made Amanda stumble several more times as she began following the zigzag of sights and sounds of Draupnir.

Amanda's breath was coming in ragged gasps as the sound of water began to echo faintly through the fluffy cloudbank in front of her. With a jolt of surprise, Amanda suddenly realized how far she had come into the city. She was in the plaza next to Mimir's well. Amanda made her way toward the sound as the clouds parted to reveal the cascading water falling into the stone circle.

"Mimir, are you there?" Amanda shivered. The scratching noises were louder now, and whatever was causing it sounded like it was coming from all sides. The water continued to fall but there was no response. Something golden bobbed to the surface and then was washed away in the current. "Mimir, do you know where Lena and Lev are? They have taken Draupnir and we need to get it back before they do something that could hurt the realm's defenses and the gods!"

Amanda felt something crunch under her boot as she stepped toward the well. She looked down and saw a shimmering branch that looked like a dousing rod beneath her foot. Bending down she picked up the piece of wood and heard a whisper through the fog behind her. Amanda screamed as black fire exploded from the branch she held. The black flames flew through the air and leapt to other pieces of wood, which Amanda now saw had been strewn around the well.

"What are you doing?" Lena stepped from the mist that had begun to rise into the sky.

The dark flames were hot, but where they embraced Amanda's hand she felt only ice instead of heat. "I don't know. I just touched the branch and it burst into flames. Where is Draupnir? How are you using it to do this?"

"Put it out now! That is fellfire!" Lev came up behind his sister, his eyes wide and frightened. He was holding the front of his cloak away from him like a shield.

"What?" The burning branch she held began to sway back and forth in her hand, and then yanked her downwards into Mimir's waters. There was a terrible wail as Mimir's face appeared in agony and then vanished.

"Are you crazy? Fellfire can destroy magick! It steals it from anything it touches." Lena's voice had grown shrill.

"I'm not doing this!" Amanda yelled and tried to pull her hand free, but found it glued to the branch that was now waving wildly underwater. "Give me Draupnir or use it to help me stop this!"

"Sister, we should go. If we are touched by the fellfire, we could lose our magick permanently. Mykola may have stolen it for a moment, but it will return. Now is not the time to be without power." Lev looked panicked, as the fire had begun to inch toward them. Several vines from floating baskets of flowers and wild plants were catching fire as they passed over the ring of black conflagration that circled the well except for where Amanda stood.

"No. You heard what she said. She is not in control of the fellfire. We came to ask Mimir a question from what we saw when we touched Draupnir's power, but we now have a chance at something better. Someone has stolen Lord Odin's ring, which means if we find it, we can use its power again. But first, she must be eliminated. Draupnir's vision was clear. She and the others are a danger to this realm. I told you, you would pay for what you did to us." Lena's smile chilled Amanda as she slipped a rune stone from her cloak and raised it toward her. The rune gathered the heat from the air and sent a spear of scalding wind toward Amanda.

Just as the spell was about to hit her, Amanda raised her free hand and twisted it, *"Transityr!"*

Her intent had been to transfer the force of the attack to the stick she held to destroy it, but the transference spell leeched the heat from the attack and exchanged it for the dirt beneath her feet. Amanda fell, as the ground she was standing on erupted in a stinging spray of molten rock and dirt. The smoke from the burning baskets and the superheated dirt caused Amanda to cough as she fell. Yggdrasil groaned above them again, this time louder.

"Hit her again, sister!" Lev encouraged. Lena extended her hand with the rune, and a dark red outline of magick formed around her body.

"Wait!" Amanda screamed as the earth rumbled, sending the twins to their knees.

The branch that had taken Amanda's hand hostage evaporated. She pulled her arm from the well, frantically turning her hand over to inspect it. Lena's scream brought Amanda's head up, and she saw the girl scrambling backward. Amanda turned as Mimir's well began to bubble with dark, viscous alfblot, which began frothing about and over the rim of the well onto the ground and surrounding benches. Once again, Mimir's face appeared, this time he was writhing about trying to fling the alfblot from his waters. Something golden flew into the alfblot. With a giant sucking sound, the ring of fellfire was sucked into the alfblot that remained in the well, and the water inside was transformed into a giant syirce. The scratching noises returned, sounding more and more agitated.

"What have you done?" Lev cried from behind his sister. He summoned a portal, and pulled at his sister's shoulder. "We must go!"

Lena's eyes met Amanda's. "Once Draupnir is ours again, we shall finish what was started tonight. Anyone that endangers the Nine Realms will answer to us." With that, they were gone.

Amanda pulled herself up. The explosion had scorched her cheeks, and her hands and knees ached from the fall, but otherwise she was unscathed. "Mimir! Can you hear me? Anyone? Help!" Amanda raced around the well's small stone wall, but there was no sign of Mimir. She brushed her hair from her face and tried to think of what she could do.

Pulling the grimoire from her cloak Amanda desperately tried to turn the pages to see if she could find a spell to help, but the pages kept fluttering back and forth. The scratching sounds had grown so loud Amanda thought it sounded like someone was trying to chew a hole through the ground.

Amanda shouted at the book, "Help me, please! We need to save Mimir!" An icy chill froze Amanda as she suddenly knew where she had heard those scratching sounds before. "Imps!"

Amanda spun to face the well as a horde of frost-blue imps erupted from the syirce like a swarm of angry bees. The imps reached her before she could defend herself, and they used her cloak to pull her downward. The imps covered her hands and quickly clamped her lips shut, keeping her from being able to cast any of her spells. The grimoire fell beside her, opening to the spell of fire she had used numerous times in her trainings. Her mind raced as the imps began to pull her toward the syirce. She had never cast a spell without speaking or using her hands. She began to try to shout the spellword through her lips, but nothing happened. Just as the imps readied to toss her into the maw of the syirce, Amanda suddenly remembered she was unbound, and reached within. Her magick ignited with her desperate need and burned in her veins. The raw power burst forth and incinerated the imps holding her and freeing her to speak. She opened her mouth to take a deep breath, and cried out, *"FIERYR!"*

A shockwave of green fire blazed to life around Amanda, and then shot through the mound of imps still surrounding her. Droplets of melted imps rained down on Amanda's face. The spell continued to burn around her, but once again she felt no heat from the fire. Amanda let the power of her magick flow from her core, and without speaking or gesturing, she hurled three more bouts of flame, sending the imps into retreat. Those that remained scattered, running off in all different directions. Amanda couldn't help but let a small smile form as she enjoyed the use of her power. The last bits of green flame around her form vanished when the last imp rounded a corner.

"Amanda!" Amanda turned and saw Cassie, Mykola, and Sean running toward her. Cassie was waving at her excitedly! "Thank the Allfather you are OK! Look who we found!"

Sean had his hammer in his hand and was swinging it to knock the vines from the floating baskets out of his way. "What in all of the Nine Realms is going on here? Cassie filled me in on the way here what she could, but when we saw the smoke all the way from Yggdrasil we feared the worst. What happened to Mimir's well, is he alive? It looks like an oil rig exploded."

"I don't know." Amanda turned to survey the well. The syirce swirled in angry waves and begun to emit blasts of fell magick. One of the blasts knocked the hoops from above to the ground where they began to sizzle and melt. Amanda threw out her hand and a shield formed around the well. "That should contain it, but I don't know how to help Lord Mimir."

"It'll have to do for now." Sean was anxiously trying to analyze their next move in his head. "Amanda, tell us what happened."

Amanda quickly recounted her marathon through the city, her encounter with the branches and fellfire, and with Lena and Lev. Cassie made a noise when Amanda told them the twins didn't have Draupnir. "I don't think any of this was their doing."

Cassie looked about the plaza. Normally the area was framed by hundreds of various types of trees. There were pine trees with bushy green branches, maple trees with yellow and red leaves, and then more exotic ones from Alfheim and Vanaheim. Now there was only red flames and smoke. Even though the fellfire was gone, its spark had ignited a true inferno that was sweeping from tree to tree. The flames were working their way toward the glass dome of Valaskjalf that curved up at the far edge of the cloister. "Are you sure? This seems right up their alley of work after what they pulled tonight."

Amanda bent to retrieve the grimoire. "Yes. The way they spoke, it sounded like they were just as surprised by the fellfire and the syirce. Lena also used a rune to attack me. She would have just blasted me with Draupnir if she had it. What happened to you two at the Gruneling?"

"It was some kind of built in safety if the ring was stolen that no one bothered to mention. Queen Frigga sensed the disturbance and was about to send the Prelate to investigate when someone attacked the Bifrost, so she conjured a portal and summoned Sean to help us. We were bloody lucky she did because the Gruneling's defenses had trapped Mykola and Nimbus when the ring was taken. I tried to yell for you to wait, but I don't think you could hear me through the fog." Cassie and the others crouched defensively as the ring of metal against metal, followed by a crashing sound resounded from beside Lord Odin's palace.

"There are also imps loose. They came through the syirce right after Lena and Lev ran away. I stopped some of them, but the others headed off toward Valaskjalf." Amanda coughed as ash began to cloud the air. "Are the Prelate and everyone else coming too?

"They are dealing with an attack by the Bifrost. It must have been a distraction so they could destroy Lord Mimir's well and steal Draupnir." Mykola signed while Cassie spoke. "But why destroy Lord Mimir?"

Sean was rubbing his neck trying to think. "No idea right now, we can sort that out later. Amanda, didn't you say you were touched by fellfire?"

"Yes. Why? Can that help us?"

"No. Maybe; but how can you still do magick if you touched fellfire? Your powers should be gone. Only the gods can survive it, and even then, they would be severely weakened." Cassie raised a hand to her mouth as Sean spoke.

Cassie pushed Amanda. "You have all of Sigyn's magick?!"

"Ow! Yes! Sorry! She told me not to tell anyone. She said there could be repercussions." Amanda bit the side of her cheek.

Cassie shoved her again. "I knew you were hiding something! And Mykola was tracking it too. I just didn't know what it was. I thought something bad had happened with Sigyn, but it turns out not so much!"

Sean looked at her like he couldn't believe what he was hearing. "Why did you keep this from all of us? I helped you get to Sigyn, and you didn't say anything about this afterward."

"I know. I am sorry. I was worried my magick might go away if I said anything. Sigyn discovered I had all of her magick when I tried to do a spell for her. She tried to help me focus so I could use it, and that is when she found I was bound by Lord Odin." There was a small explosion from inside the well. Amanda shuddered along with her shield. "Look, I will apologize later. We have to start trying to help save Lord Mimir and stop the imps. Can you sense Lord Mimir, Cassie?"

Cassie reluctantly held up a hand and closed her eyes. "It's hard to tell. The fell magick in the syirce is blocking my magick. I think he is there, but barely. We will have to do something now if we want to save him."

"What can we do? I can probably find a spell, but that will take time."

Cassie stared at her, her jaw clenched. "Right. You and I are going to have a good chat about this later, but first we have some other business to fix. Ack!" The smell of burnt wood was everywhere, and Cassie was trying not to gag from the overpowering stench.

"Do you think we could separate Lord Mimir from the magick in the syirce?" Amanda turned to Mykola. "Do you think you could use your favouring to disrupt only the fell magick?"

Mykola looked to the syirce and then back to Amanda. He gave her a shrug and then a thumbs up. He made a few quick motions, and Cassie translated. "He can disrupt both the fell magick and Lord Mimir's magick, with his staff acting as a bit of a buffer. The syirce should go away, leaving Lord Mimir. He says it might hurt Mimir, but won't kill him. Can't be worse than what he is going through right now." A building next to them cracked and crumbled under a swarm of imps.

Sean blocked a flying chunk of stone with his hammer, turning it to powder with a burst of lightning. "That will have to be our plan for now. Mykola, you are on the syirce and saving Lord Mimir, but you have to keep the syirce open long enough for us to handle the imps. We are going to send them back through the portal and then you can seal it tight."

Mykola nodded and bounded off, swinging his staff above his head like a helicopter to clear the air. When he came to the well, Amanda banished her shield. Mykola tossed his gloves aside and gripped the wooden staff tightly as he pushed it into the swirling vortex. For a minute Amanda was terrified he would be sucked in, but then the syirce seemed to shrink ever so slightly as a trickle of clear water ran through the cracks in the well's base made by the imps. Just like when air is sucked from a fire, the syirce was beginning to suffocate as Mykola sucked the magick from it.

"All right you two, we have to rustle up those imps and send them back through the syirce or destroy them. If even one escapes, it will multiply and continue to cause chaos." Sean pointed to a trail of remaining imps. "Amanda, I want you to stand between those two columns while Cassie and I herd them toward the syirce. Fry as many as you can to keep them moving, OK?"

Sean gave her a look and Amanda nodded, but Cassie raised her hand. "What can I do? I can melt them or make a few attack each other, but not that many."

"You've just got to get them to follow you back here. They enjoy mischief. Use that to get them to follow you like when a bear smells honey." Sean held up his hammer, charging it with electricity. "Happy hunting!"

Sean took off in one direction and, with a worried look, Cassie the other. Trees smoldering from the heat of the fires around them flanked where Sean pointed for Amanda to go. She tossed her cloak aside as sweat began to pour down her face. For a heartbeat Amanda waited, watching intently. Cassie and Sean looped behind the crumbling building, leaving Amanda alone in the plaza.

A high-pitched holler came from the ruined road, and Amanda saw Sean chasing after a large patch of imps. He was sending jolts of lighting at the group, vaporizing a couple at a time. "Here they come, Amanda! Get ready!"

Planting her feet, Amanda began throwing large balls of fire at the imps, leaving circles of charred stone and evaporated imps in their wake. A couple clusters of the imps tried to break off and head away from the syirce, but Amanda stopped them with more fire. "Go back to where you came from!"

The few that remained leapt over Mykola and into the syirce as Sean chased them, disappearing into the portal. "Way to go! Whew! I feel like I just ran through a pool of mud and you look as fresh as a daisy. Here comes Cassie with her crew." Sean yelled.

Cassie was running full steam from the opposite direction Sean had come. Her group of imps twice as large, but less rambunctious. They followed the girl with the same expression Lena wore when she had talked about using Draupnir.

"Help me!" Cassie squealed as she zoomed by Amanda. "I might have got them a little bit too excited! It's too much for me to control!"

"You've got this, Cassie, just lead them right up to the edge and then pull a U-turn!" Sean called through his gloves.

The syirce was starting to flicker, and a river of clear water was collecting around Mykola. Amanda wasn't sure how Cassie would be able to get the imps into the portal and not get trapped herself. "Be careful, Cassie!"

At the last minute, right as her next step would have taken her into the maw of the syirce, Cassie dove into the air and then crashed into Mykola. The boy had gone to his knees to press the syirce into the ground. The imps stampeded right into the portal as the dark vortex vanished.

Sean and Amanda ran over to their friends and helped them up. Amanda hugged Cassie. "Next time Lady Freyja tells you that you can't do something, just remind her about the time you took out a load of imps."

Cassie laughed a bit but stepped away from Amanda. "Yeah, I'll make her call me the imp-inator."

Mykola was collecting the water from the ground into his cloak. He made a few quick gestures and then took off toward Eir's Manor. The others watched him until he turned a corner. Sean held up his hammer and with a giant grunt, a sudden swell of clouds released rain down upon the charred trees, extinguishing the fire. For a minute the group laughed and washed the soot from their faces.

"Y'all, that was crazy. Who could be doing all of this? This took major coordination and planning." Sean was breathing heavily.

Before anyone could respond, there was a sharp flash of light and the

Prelate appeared. "Bye the Eye! Are you all unharmed?"

"Just slightly overcooked your Prelateshipness." Cassie tried to joke, but no one laughed as they surveyed the plaza.

"You would be proud of these guys, Prelate Tess. They defeated an army of imps and put out a syirce." Sean spoke softly.

As quickly as she could, Cassie began telling the Prelate about the events that transpired after she sent Sean to the Gruneling. The Prelate's face, which Amanda had always thought looked youthful despite her age, became drawn as she heard more of the story. Finding her voice, Amanda filled in the rest of the details and the part of how the syirce was formed.

"Lena and Lev appeared right as the fellfire did. The branch in my hand was burning with it, but it didn't hurt me. That's when they attacked me. They were acting weird, saying they saw something when they used Draupnir's magick, and then they vanished to go look for it. After that, imps came through the portal. We had Mykola use his favouring to help save Mimir while Sean, Cassie, and I used some magick to get the imps back into the portal."

The Prelate looked at Amanda sharply. "This news is most troubling. I pray Lord Mimir will recover from this attack. I would not have thought the Zukovs could feel the way they do after all we have done for them." The Prelate paused, but didn't elaborate. "What they told you is true. Our history is not all valiant. However, we strive to be better today than yesterday. Pride was a harsh trait that had to be purged throughout the years. Amanda, you mentioned the fellfire touched you. How could you use magick after touching fellfire?"

Amanda grimaced. The Prelate had picked up that point just as the others had, and her expression had gone from worried to calculated suspicion. "I haven't been completely honest with you." Amanda took out the grimoire and held it out to Prelate Tess. "I went to go see Sigyn. She taught me how to use my magick and gave me this. Not only that, she unbound me from a spell Lord Odin had put on me and now I have my full favouring. I have all of Sigyn's magick." Amanda tensed as she finished, but nothing extraordinary happened from her confession.

If the Prelate was surprised by Amanda's revelation, she didn't show it. Instead she took the grimoire and studied it for a moment, and then turned her green eyes on Amanda. Her gauntlets glowed and Amanda found herself frozen and unable to move as they inspected Amanda with their magick. The Prelate's brow furrowed as she concentrated. "You speak the truth of your favouring. I would not have sensed it before if you were bound, but I sense the full might of Sigyn within you. This is most troubling. Such magick would be a prime source to summon the alfblot and syirces. Perhaps you carry the Disir within you, but do not know it just as you were unaware of your own power." The Prelate signaled to a nearby triad of Einherjar. "We must know more to ensure our safety after such an attack as was carried out today. Take this to the Queen at once." The Prelate handed one of the guards the grimoire.

Sean spoke up as the Prelate turned to face them. "Prelate, surely Amanda cannot be the Disir. It seems to me that this all seems like part of a plan Lord Odin had all along. He bound Amanda until she met Sigyn, who could free her."

The Prelate took a breath, and her face resumed its normal calmness. "Perhaps, but even that is a tenuous connection. Perhaps Amanda was fooled by Sigyn. She has a tongue like her husband's that can create belief in the lies. And if we are to believe that Lord Odin did mean this to occur, why would he do such a thing?" The Prelate waved and Amanda found she could speak, but still was held in place.

"Sigyn didn't say or know. All I know is that I have it all." Amanda was fighting back tears. She felt the guilt for breaking the Prelate's trust just as sharply as she did for not confiding in her friends. "I am so sorry. I told you all what I thought I could, but Sigyn said there could be repercussions if I told anyone about my favouring."

The Prelate frowned at Amanda; her stance looked fearsome for a moment in the curling smoke of the destroyed plaza. "You could have trusted us. That's what allies do. Perhaps we could have figured out a way to use your favouring to help Queen Frigga, or to have kept Mimir safe. Telling half-truths was a way of forming dissension that Sigyn and Loki used centuries ago, and it seems she has passed it on to you. You also deliberately disobeyed a command from Lord Odin. That is enough to put all of you in the Gruneling and await a royal trial."

"I…" Amanda blanched and stumbled to try to respond.

"That will be up to the Queen, though. My utmost task now is to find any clue we can to rescue our lord's ring, and discover who the Disir truly is." The Prelate crossed her arms and began to pace back and forth as she processed the situation. She paused and with a nod, Amanda was free to move again. "As the last to see the ring, have you any inkling as to what direction it was taken? It is unfathomable as to why the thief would not use the ring right away once they had it, unless they were unable to. You say Lena and Lev went in search of it, which means they did not take it. Surely if they did, they would not have wasted an opportunity to use the ring." Boots striking the pavement could be heard as more triads of Einherjar began to filter in and secure the plaza.

"I don't know. There was too much fog to see. I ran through the city until I got here, and then I didn't see it again. Maybe the Disir took it and used Lena and Lev as a distraction. Maybe Lena and Lev made a deal with the Disir once they used the ring to restore their power to help them steal it. I didn't sense any fell magick on Lena and Lev though, but…" Amanda began, but the Prelate held up a hand.

"I would withhold your accusations, and give us only the facts as you know them to be. If there is nothing more you can tell us, then I must have you taken back to your rooms and watched. The fact that you have the full magick of a goddess is most distressing. That means you are more than capable of the magick being performed in our realm that has brought these attacks and the kidnapping of Heimdall. If you are being controlled, you also had opportunity and means to create the alfblot and a grimoire that could have helped you. I do not sense Draupnir on your person and you bear no mark of the Disir, so there is that, but until we discover more, we must take all precautions to prevent another attack – or worse. You will be given the Test of the Disir. It has never been performed on a mortal before, but we must know for certain." Amanda's chest constricted and she lowered her head.

The Prelate turned to the others. "Sean, report back to Queen Frigga and Keeper Fulla immediately. Tell them about Mimir and have Fulla check in on the god of knowledge. The Queen will no doubt sense Draupnir has been taken, so she will probably already be scouring the realms for it, and that will be your focus to assist her. When the Queen does not need you, as punishment for disobeying Lord Odin's decree regarding Sigyn, you will clean this plaza and work with the Aesir to restore all the damage. You will also begin the search for Lena and Lev. Regardless of their behavior, they are still Favoured. Cassie and Mykola, while I am disappointed you did not reveal what you knew about the grimoire and Amanda's trip, you have an opportunity to regain a measure of my trust. You will escort Amanda back to her quarters and ensure she does not try to flee. I want to believe she had nothing to do with the attack on Lord Mimir and stealing of Draupnir, but we need proof to ensure the safety of all. Trust is not easy to mend with the Disir about. Take this rune stone and place it…"

The Prelate's words were drowned out as Yggdrasil groaned, even louder than it had before. The giant tree shook violently, which in turn shook the entire city, and the sounds it made sounded like a strangled cry for help. They all looked up to see Nimbus flying amongst the branches of the Tree of Life, as the once green leaves began to shift and turn to a faded brown.

CHAPTER 17:
MUCK RAKING

"This sucks." Amanda stood at the window in her and Cassie's room, her forehead pressed to the glass as she watched Mykola and Cassie in the courtyard training Nimbus to hover in midair while putting his bridle on.

"Hm? Did you say something, Favoured of Sigyn?" Fulla sat in a chair just outside the door to Amanda's room.

"Never mind," Amanda sulked. It had been ten miserable days of being restricted to her room, and Amanda was about to lose her mind from boredom, and from being under Keeper Fulla's supervision – again.

Pulling herself away from the window, Amanda went to her bed, where her parents sat nestled in the covers. Keeper Fulla had brought them to Amanda the other day begrudgingly. Amanda had requested to have them with her while she was being kept in her room. Having her parents around was somewhat comforting, even though all they did was eat and squeak. But they gave her the attention she needed now in a way they had not done so in ages. Amanda patted them on the head and then flopped down on her bed.

"You might wish to enjoy this time of freedom. Once Queen Frigga passes her sentence for your crimes, this most assuredly will seem much more desirable than where you could end up." Fulla beckoned with a finger, and a book flew to from Cassie and Amanda's bedside table. "Try that one. It holds the correct pronunciation for all the Dwarf vowels. It could come in useful if we send you to the Nidavellir mining prisons."

"Please, no more Dwarf vowels Keeper Fulla," Amanda groaned and dropped her head into the palms of her hands.

"Suit yourself."

Amanda clenched her jaw. "I could be helping, you know. I could be looking for Draupnir or Lena and Lev. I can sense the Disir. Sigyn said there were spells in the grimoire that could help us find the real traitor and stop them. I just need the grimoire and to be able to use my magick." It was bad enough that she still didn't have the grimoire to try and find out who the Disir was, but upon the Prelate's orders, Cassie and Mykola had been ordered to place several wards and rune stones that would bind Amanda from doing any magick within her room.

"We do not need your kind of help. If we were to let you out, you would no doubt scurry off to hide the evidence of your crimes. The Prelate is still examining the grimoire given to you by the traitor, Sigyn. It alone is enough evidence to convict you of a royal crime. The others were only spared because they did not actually go to Sigyn's prison. I will admit it is a bit strange that the Favoured of Mani and Sol have not returned. Favoured have disappeared before but they always come back in some form or another. No doubt they are in hiding. Perhaps they fear to return because of what they saw when you attacked Lord Mimir. If it were up to me, I would keep you locked up at least until the Spell of Favouring returns the magick to the gods in five years – if not longer."

Amanda shuddered at the thought, and bit back the resentment she felt at Keeper Fulla's accusation. She got up and went to look out the window again. Cassie must have sensed Amanda because she immediately turned and gave her an encouraging wave. Amanda was glad their friendship had survived her bad decision to conceal her magick.

After sealing Amanda into their room, Cassie had turned on Amanda. She had readied herself to tell Amanda off for not confiding in her about her favouring, but when she saw how defeated Amanda was already, she forgave her. When the Einherjar had come for Amanda the next morning, Cassie had held her hand and walked beside her as they took her to the Prelate's tower where Keeper Fulla had administered the Test of the Disir.

The test had been relatively simple, but quite painful. Magickal objects and runes were set around Amanda, all of which scoured her body and soul for traces of alfblot, fell magicks, and other spells that would have meant she was under the control of a Fell Elf. Afterwards, when Amanda had described it to Cassie, she said that it felt like a scalpel had peeled back every layer of her being. The Prelate had stood by watching and monitoring Amanda to make sure she was not in mortal danger from the host of spells Keeper Fulla unleashed, and to make sure she did not attack the Keeper or try to escape. Ultimately, they had cleared Amanda of being a Disir or using fell magicks, much to the Keeper's consternation. The Prelate made a point to tell Amanda, that even though they believe she had nothing to do with Mimir's attack or Bergelmir's imps, she was still under suspicion of stealing Draupnir, and in trouble for disobeying a direct order from Lord Odin. Since then, the Keeper had smugly sat at her door every day, waiting for Amanda to receive her punishment for her other crimes.

The little news Amanda had heard from Cassie about what was happening outside of the Stave was discouraging. All of Asgard was ablaze with talk of Amanda. There had been several gatherings and announcements, and even a few petitioners that called for Amanda's banishment. Keeper Fulla was part of the group that wanted Amanda to be as far from their realm as possible, or confined in their strongest prison. The search parties sent to scour the realm for Lena, Lev and Draupnir, brought nothing new back that could help corroborate Amanda, nor give any evidence to condemn her either. The current assumption was that Draupnir was still on Asgard, as the realm's defenses were still in place, but even that reasoning did not help the fear that was spreading throughout the realm.

The mob of accusers and the Keeper's attitude toward Amanda made her think of the story Lena and Lev told them. Amanda didn't want to admit it, but she could see how the twins might feel the way they do. Keeper Fulla had cared for Asgard and its inhabitants for thousands of years, but she only cared for those she trusted – those who, like herself, were from Asgard. She barely treated any of the other Favoured with the slightest amount of respect, even though they were here risking their lives to help all of the Nine Realms.

Keeper Fulla continued to speak, even with Amanda's back to her. "It seems to me that if Sigyn had that grimoire all along, or any spells as such that could be of use, she has selfishly kept it to herself. Even if it did reveal any secrets, I doubt they would be of any help healing Mimir or Yggdrasil." Fulla's words were followed by a low groaning sound from outside.

Amanda looked to see more of the large leaves falling from Yggdrasil. "How is Mimir? Has he been able to tell you anything?"

Fulla patted her pocket, and glass tinkled. "Not as of yet. Thankfully, there was enough of his water to revive him. Of course, it will take some time for him to be whole again, and we cannot allow him to return to his well until we imprison those responsible for his attack. They could try and use him to create another large syirce, and he would not survive another such onslaught. For the time being Mimir, and his knowledge, will remain quiet but safe in my care."

"Don't you think we could put him back in the well for just long enough to get some answers? If he could talk, he could tell you it wasn't me who attacked him. He could tell us where Lena and Lev are, and probably tell us what is going on with Yggdrasil." The destruction of the well set off some kind of chain reaction of spells that was causing the World Tree to slowly go into a state of dormancy.

"And take the risk of him being destroyed once and for all? By the Eye, child, I can see why you were chosen for your benefactor. 'Tis best to wait until Lord Odin returns so he can set this all to right. He will know what to do. I just hope he hurries." The chair Fulla sat in creaked as she adjusted her position.

"Cassie told me this happened right before Ragnarok, too. Yggdrasil went dormant then, right?" The giant tree swayed and made several more mournful sounds as it shifted. The once luminous bark now looked decaying and was falling off.

"Aye. 'Tis another reason why the realm is in such a state of panic and people are demanding immediate action. The Prelate has assured them they are doing all they can. They are most desperate to try and locate Eir, for her healing magick might be able to slow the World Tree's change. I shudder to think what would happen should Yggdrasil slip into its slumber while the gods are in her roots."

"Could that really happen?"

Fulla straightened her apron and cleared her throat nervously. "It is... possible. Our only hope is for the gods to return – soon."

"It seems the Norn are on our side then. I have just received word that the first of the gods should return any day now." Prelate Tess appeared in the doorway beside Fulla. The afterimage of her portal made Amanda blink.

The Prelate had come to Amanda's room only once since the Test of the Disir. She had asked Amanda questions about Sigyn and how they found the Green Askr. Amanda had told the warrior woman about the clues they found, the banners, the trap by Lord Odin, and then the journey through Idavoll. She had even gone into more detail about how Sigyn had unbound her magick, and how Amanda was supposed to be able to sense the Disir. The Prelate watched Amanda very carefully as she spoke. When Amanda finished, the Prelate had only nodded and left. That was the last Amanda has seen of the Prelate, which unnerved her even more than she realized until just now. Amanda felt abandoned by the Prelate in a way reminiscent of how she felt hurt by her parents when they didn't believe her about Ms. Biggs' unfair detentions.

Pushing her feelings aside, Amanda brought her fist to her chest and saluted the Prelate. "Hello, Prelate Tess. Have you found something?"

Keeper Fulla stood and gave Amanda a look. "Or has the Queen made her decision, and pronounced her sentencing?"

"The latter." Keeper Fulla looked excited. The Prelate spoke carefully. "The Queen has decreed that we do not believe you had any culpability in the events that transpired the night Lord Mimir was attacked. She feels she would have been able to detect Draupnir's power on you by now, or sensed where it was hidden, once your magick was blocked from you. You have already been cleared of the other charges, which leaves your disobedience to Lord Odin's decrees. On this matter, you shall receive punishment – cleaning the Rimstock Stables." The Prelate rarely shed her armor but had done so today. She wore the same tunic and pants as Amanda and the other Favoured, which made her seem only a few years older than Amanda.

"Really? That's it?" Amanda was surprised, but felt vindicated and relieved as well.

Keeper Fulla took in a sharp breath. "Is this wise, Prelate? That petty punishment is meant to instill discipline in the Favoured. How could it possibly rise to the level of repercussion needed for her actions?" Her voice shook with anger as she spoke, but she maintained her composure in front of the Prelate.

"That is something you will have to address with the Queen. Amanda, if you choose to accompany me, I will warn you 'tis not for the faint of heart. Do you accept your punishment?" Folding her arms behind her, the Prelate waited for Amanda's response.

Without hesitating, or caring what it was they would be doing, Amanda shouted with glee. "Are you kidding me? Yes!"

"Very well then. Please meet me at the stables in half an hour's time." With that the Prelate opened a portal and stepped through it.

Amanda felt elated. She rushed to grab her cloak but was stopped by Fulla at the door. The woman held up a rune stone and passed it over the opening, which was followed by a sound of someone snapping harp strings. "Whatever you have done to garner the Norn's favor and fool the others will not work on me. You are to stay by my side at all times as we head to the stables. Any use of your magick, or attempt to escape, will earn you passage to the Gruneling no matter what the Prelate may say. Understood?"

"Got it. Can we go now?" Amanda felt even antsier with her freedom so close.

The Keeper's voice was grave when she spoke next. "You may not be so jubilant once you see what task is before you."

Thirty minutes later Amanda and the Prelate stood atop a platform that led down to the stables, and even though she would never say it aloud, when she saw what was before them Amanda did almost wish she had stayed in her room. Fulla left them as quickly as she could, after depositing Amanda into the Prelate's care.

The Rimstock Stables were situated beside the gate leading from the Bifrost, so that anyone travelling by vindsvolla would first need to pass Heimdall's normally ever-present gaze. It was open on all four sides, with an open lattice for a roof that was held aloft by giant wooden columns. The stalls were solid gold and bore a rune with a name for each of the vindsvolla, who were usually around unless they were away with the Einherjar. Today, however, the stable stood empty. Well, almost empty.

"I just never thought there could be anything so horrible." Amanda's voice was muffled as it came through her hand clamped firmly over her nose and mouth. The sight below was making it difficult for her to not lose her lunch.

"I did warn you." Prelate Tess's voice carried over the sounds of screeching and hay being tossed about. "The task before you will be most unpleasant."

A tiny cry drew Amanda's attention. The entire wooden floor of the stables was covered in wriggling wyrms. The grubby creatures had long bodies with overlapping layers of slimy, green plates that formed a shell of sorts. Their flat heads looked like a hammerhead shark's, complete with pointy teeth, but they flew on translucent wings that were small and could only hold them aloft for a moment or two as they jumped around the stable floor. Where frost imps were small wrecking balls of destruction, these wyrms were just plain disgusting. They munched on anything they could find, and were sweeping stinking piles of manure everywhere with their barbed tails.

"So my punishment is to clean this all up?" Amanda gagged as the she watched the wyrms play tennis with the rotten core of an apple. The usual sweet smell of hay had been replaced by a repugnant stench.

"It is. Wyrms can be smaller than a snail one day and grow to the size of a sea serpent the next if they are given proper nourishment." Prelate Tess's demeanor towards Amanda was aloof. "The Nidhogg serpent was a wyrm that dwelled in the realm of Hel and ate the roots of Yggdrasil. It grew to be so large that even Thor gave second thought to battling it."

"Where did they come from?" One of the buggers squeaked with glee as it jumped into a pile of vindsvolla droppings.

"If you are asking about these wyrms specifically, on the tail of an unsuspecting courier to be sure. In terms of the universe, the wyrms first appeared during the time of the first gods." Prelate Tess led them down a set of stone steps to the main floor of the stable where the fresh hay and food for the animals was usually kept. The wyrms had strewn everything about and upturned all the troughs. "Some have long thought the wyrms to be part of the balance of the universe."

"I would have thought they would have been wiped out after Ragnarok." Amanda shifted her foot to avoid stepping through a hole in the floor. "It looks like they've eaten everything in sight. This is going to take hours to clean."

"This is your chance to make up for your disregard for Lord Odin's decree. Of course, if you would prefer, you are free to return to your room."

"No!" One of the wyrms jumped at Amanda, causing her to duck quickly to avoid its snapping teeth. "How do I get rid of them?"

The Prelate turned to the bag at her hip. "Normally, they are little more than pests, but these have feasted on magick of some kind and are growing stronger. They will need to be caught and sent to one of the nether regions." Tess held up a handful of finely spun nets of gold that looked like they belonged to a very debonair fisherman. "These were enchanted to trap wyrms for a time and should suffice for your task today. You are to use no magick, but instead catch them and then I will send them from our realm."

Tess thrust a pair of gloves with black fingertips at Amanda. "Wyrms can cause havoc with our magick with just one bite, it would be best to be most careful. These gloves are made for the Valkyrie to wear during battle to protect them from fell attacks."

"Thanks, and thanks again for giving me this chance to redeem myself." Amanda said, trying to meet the Prelate's eyes.

The Prelate nodded, keeping her eyes fixed forward. "Begin."

For the next two sweaty hours, Amanda grabbed as many of the wriggling wyrms as she could and tossed them into the glittering nets. When the wyrms realized they were being rounded up, they began to launch themselves at Amanda. The wyrms would slither up or jump into the air, trying to take bites out of her boots, arms, and hands.

"Gah!" Amanda screamed as she caught a manure patty in the back of the neck. The little culprits emitted cries that she swore sounded like laughter. "Stop it!"

Prelate Tess calmly regarded Amanda. "Are you giving up?"

Amanda's chest heaved a great sighed. "No. I'm just so… I don't know, angry, frustrated, confused, and fed up with everything going on right now. I've tried to not complain. I've tried to follow your orders the best I can, even when I think there is something else I could be doing to help. Since my favouring found me, I have been attacked by Jotuns, told I was the Favoured to one of the biggest traitors Asgard has ever known, had to catch up on four years' worth of training, been accused of trying to destroy the realm and Lord Mimir, and now I am digging around in vindsvolla droppings and wyrms."

"Is there regret in you for your decision to join us?"

Amanda let out another sigh as she considered her response. "Not really. It's just not what I was expecting. I thought having magick would be more fun, and that we would be able to help my parents and Jack a lot sooner. Instead, it just feels like everything keeps getting stacked against me. I wanted to be a part of something good and help, but every time I get ahead something else smacks me back down." Amanda hung her head. "I am sure you probably wish I hadn't been chosen."

"Most assuredly, that is not the case. There may be some unexpected sojourns on your journey so far, but I still see in you someone of good moral fiber. It is why I argued on your behalf to the Queen to lessen her original sentence from time in the Gruneling to this. I know you think your journey has been arduous, but know this – Lena and Lev's tale of hardship far surpasses your own. This punishment may seem harsh, and an act of condemnation, but we have rules to abide by in order to ensure that all my charges and the realms are safe. I cannot play favorites, and I cannot take chances when our enemies have such insidious methods at their disposal that any friend can become a foe with the right spell." Prelate Tess lifted Amanda's chin. "Hear me, Amanda. You are more than the sum of a few strange entanglements. You are one of us, for better or worse. And yes, you have completed your punishment."

"Thank you." Amanda sighed. She felt a thrill of relief at the Prelate's words.

Prelate Tess nodded and produced the grimoire. Handing it to Amanda, "We could find no spell that we could ascertain that could be of help. Perhaps it is something only you can find. We hope you can do so with haste."

As Amanda held the grimoire once more her guilt returned. "I will find it. I know I still have a lot to learn, and I am sorry for not telling you sooner. There is so much about magick that I don't know, and I assumed as a goddess of magick Sigyn would know best."

"'Tis something only time can teach. You would do well to learn that trust in your comrades is important. And while I believe Sigyn meant no ill will when she told you to not confide in us it was still the wrong thing to do. Now, then, shall I help you finish with the wyrms?" The Prelate joined Amanda, and they began to gather the final few wyrms. "I would like to be rid of them, as there are very few things in all of the Nine Realms that I consider to be more disgusting to be around. A Disir perhaps might rival them, however.

"What do you think the Disir really wants? I mean, they have to be the one who took Draupnir, but they haven't done anything with it. The stories we found on them all seem to point that they immediately attack. Granted, there was an attack, but it came much later. Why go to all this trouble, and then do nothing?"

"The dark ones have cunning and wit that rival Lord Mimir's – but only for things most foul. They created the infernal pits where they captured and enslaved many of our brethren throughout the Nine Realms. Anything they create is made to bring about utter chaos. War to a Fell Elf is peace, and so they battled until their own kingdom was destroyed in the nether realms of Svartalfheim. This was when they first used the Disir to try to regain a portion of what they lost. A Fell Elf who has a Disir cannot die. This is why the Disir are coveted by the dark ones, and why they are compared to the Valkyrie who could both give and take life. The motives of the current brood of Disir are a mystery, and their actions are indeed strange. The Norn, the Fates of Asgard, would be the only ones to be able to truly tell us. Perhaps they were created to steal the ring of Lord Odin so it could be used to free the Fell Elves locked in the Gruneling."

"Couldn't I could go back to Sigyn to ask her what spells she was talking about?" Amanda trailed off, leaving the question of when she would be allowed to see her benefactor again hanging in the air.

The Prelate did not answer for a moment. "Not all things can be solved by magick."

The wyrms were crying out in their pile, and a gathering of hungry eagles and ravens had begun to circle overheard. Amanda shielded her eyes with the gloves as she looked up at them. The Prelate seemed unwilling to discuss Amanda's question further. "Prelate Tess, what will happen to Mimir and Heimdall's Favoured if they are not healed by the time the Spell of Favouring is complete?

"None know. We assume their magick will be lost, but in truth only the

Norn can say. We are hopeful their magick will transfer to the Favoured as it has in times past. There has never been a god who has not passed on his or her magick to their Favoured save for the first time the spell took effect. During the first incarnation of the spell's use of the gods' magick, they laid their powers to rest in what objects they could. 'Tis how some of our more enchanted weapons and items were created."

"What about the other gods, like Sigyn? They have never had a Favoured before."

Prelate Tess turned towards Amanda. "We assume Hel has returned to her realm of the dead, but none can enter to ascertain if that is true or whether she has ever had a Favoured of her own. Loki has never been heard from, so we assume he is lost to the void, and until you, we assumed Sigyn would never have a Favoured or need one. In truth, I must confess that I am baffled as to why your favouring only found you now." Tess's bare arms flexed beneath the gauntlets that glinted in the light. Their dark marks seemed sinister in the light of the day. "Thank the Norn they have not seen fit to send us the Favoured of Loki or his daughter, Hel. Our realm could not stand two more of you." Prelate Tess was trying to make Amanda feel better, but it didn't quite have the desired effect.

"I honestly am sorry for what I did."

Prelate Tess caught the last wyrm and threw it into the bag, quickly tying it shut. "I know. Your favouring is unknown to us and, whatever the Norn have planned, Sigyn has a history you should be wary of. For now, though, since you have passed our tests and completed your punishment, I also think it time I release you from your seclusion. You are free to return to your lessons, and free to use your magick. If Sigyn should contact you, I would ask that you consult with me about seeing her *before* you do so this time."

"Thank you Prelate Tess, I will." Amanda cried with relief and went to leave, but hesitated. "Was this punishment a test too?"

Prelate Tess raised her arm and golden magick encased each bag of wyrms. She raised them in the air and began heading back towards the Bifrost. "I am a Valkyrie, child, my sight still sees good and ill in all. I chose you when I saw good in you back on Midgard and I still see good in you now. I just had to make certain. My eyes are not as sharp as they once were."

Amanda smiled this time with the Prelate's joke, and then hurried back to tell the others.

CHAPTER 18:
A DULHDA BRINGS A TWIN STONE

The light from the stars above had almost faded to black by the time Amanda made her way back to the Stave, where she found Sean and Cassie playing a game of rune wars in the common area. They were so engrossed in the game they didn't hear Amanda arrive.

"Of course, it doesn't mean she is in the Gruneling. She's probably with Keeper Fulla doing another one of her tests." Cassie was facing a table that held nine glowing circles.

"But she is supposed to be with us now. When we get back from training, we are supposed to take over her supervision so Keeper Fulla can do her work." Sean was studying the table.

"Well, we will wait here until Keeper Fulla comes back. Take that!" Cassie skipped her rune stone into the goal and threw her fists up in celebration.

Sean flopped back. "DANG IT! I was sure I had you on that one." His fingers were crackling, singeing the sofa.

"Take a chill pill next time, Sean-Sean. Amanda will be fine. Your worrying about her is next level. Like, you showered in bad cologne level." Cassie tapped the table and the field disappeared.

"It's nice to know he is at least somewhat concerned for me." Amanda pulled the gloves off, splattering the floor with clumps of straw as she stepped into the room.

"Amanda!" Sean jumped up from his seat. "Are you ok? Cassie and I were wondering where you were when we got back and you weren't in your room. Does this mean they let you off the hook?" Sean wrinkled his nose at the smell coming from her clothes.

"Free as a bird, but not before I had to wrestle some wyrms. The Prelate said it was my punishment for disobeying Lord Odin. They finally believe that I don't have Draupnir too."

"That's fantastic! And for the record, I was worried too. I just was keeping a level head." Cassie smiled. She stood to give Amanda a hug but stopped as she caught a whiff of the smells from Amanda's wyrm battle.

Amanda chewed the side of her cheek. "Sorry. Let me get cleaned up and I will tell you all about it."

Amanda moved to head to their room, but Cassie threw up her hands. "Wait!" She ran to a bowl and grabbed two rune stones. She came back to Amanda and dropped them into Amanda's hand. "You smell like you swam in a sewer and then took a bath in Muspelheim tar. You take one step into our room and we will be smelling like that for a month. These should clean you up."

"Thanks." Amanda held the rune stones up and let her magick activate the spell in the stones.

Scents of lavender and jasmine blossomed in the room, and the air began to foam around Amanda's clothing. The spell scrubbed her clothes clean, gently brushing the grit and grime away, and then deposited a twig of white flowers in her hair before flying out through an open window. Amanda smiled.

"I…" Amanda turned her head suddenly as a rising claxon of bells reverberated in her ears.

She had grown to ignore most of the sounds of magick that were pervasive in Asgard, but whatever was happening sounded angry and completely overwhelmed her. She clamped her hands to her ears. As if someone flicked a switch, the ever-pervasive lights from the shields vanished. Even the flames suspended above the basin, and the torches in the hallway were extinguished. Sean grabbed his hammer and held it at the ready. The sudden darkness made Amanda blink as her eyes adjusted, and she shook her head to try to make the ringing in her ears stop. Several of the other Favoured joined them and they all stared up through the glass ceiling.

For several silent minutes, flashes of magick illuminated the dark sky, making the rolling clouds seem like swirling monsters. A rumble of thunder shook the Stave, but there were no other sounds that Amanda could hear. Cassie was holding her breath as Connor and Mykola arrived.

"You OK, sis?" Connor put a hand on his sister's shoulder. Cassie could only nod with wide eyes as she tried not to hyperventilate.

Cassie was afraid of only of two things, the dark and bats. She had told Amanda about her first mission on Asgard in Svartalfheim. She and some of the other Favoured had gotten lost and were attacked by bats that lived in the deep caverns. Two of the Einherjar that were sent to rescue them were turned to stone, and Cassie had almost shared their fate. She never could bear to be in complete darkness ever again. Amanda put a hand on her shoulder to soothe her as well.

"Look!" Someone down the way called out, and Amanda and the others were relieved to see three triads of Einherjar sprinting down the hill. The Einherjar came marching through the arched doorway into the common area and surveyed the Favoured.

"Agnarr!" Sean waved to the lead guardsman. "What's happening?"

"That is what we were sent to determine. Our guess is that something has finally severed the power from Draupnir to the realm. The Prelate sent messenger rams for us as soon as the realm's defenses failed. She has commanded us to take you all to safety." The warrior's spear emanated light from the tip and the staff, showing every line in his golden armor.

Sean turned to the other Favoured. "Connor and Mykola, could you guys take a group and go make sure everyone is here? This would be no time for someone to be missing if they are just taking a nap. Everyone else, come with me, Amanda and Cassie, and we will head to the Prelate. Everyone try to remain calm, but be on guard!"

Before anyone could answer, something fell outside and landed in the grass. Amanda thought it looked like a cross between a black frog and a komodo dragon. The creature made a noise somewhere between a croak and a hiss and then bound away into the darkness.

"No!" Cassie looked like she had seen a ghost and started screaming. Her magick channeled her fear and sent several of the other Favoured running to their rooms. "That was a dulhda! Where is Nimbus?'" Cassie looked wildly around them.

Connor tried to reassure his sister, but his hands were shaking as her magick was overwhelming his senses with fear. He managed to bring his fists together, and his skin turned to hard stone, blocking his sister's magick. "Relax, Cassie. He went back to Mykola's room a while ago. I am sure he is fine. Why don't you go check on him, and meet us back here once we've checked the rest of the Stave? Sean can take the first wave and help the Prelate."

"I… I shouldn't. Should I?" Cassie looked to Amanda.

Amanda was trying not to let the icy sensations flooding her system make her scream. "Go. We'll be fine." Amanda tried to smile reassuringly as Sean pulled her out of the Stave and into the valley.

Once they hit the top of the hill, Amanda summoned her green light and the last remnants of Cassie's spell faded. She momentarily enjoyed the fact that it was the second time she had cast a spell without speaking. Her magick seemed to be finally within her control. Her smile faded when she noticed the streets were completely empty and dark except for a few wards that circled the homes of the Aesir residents. It was like there had been one large magickal blackout. Even though Amanda had travelled at night around the city, there had always been the shields and streetlights to go by. Now, not even the lamps atop the poles were illuminated. More footsteps came from behind them. Several more triads of the Einherjar appeared and the group divided to accompany them to various other parts of the city. The clouds above had suddenly dropped, and a dense fog obscured their vision – just as it had the night Draupnir was stolen. Her clothes were damp with sweat, and the lack of light made them chill and cling to her skin.

Amanda followed Sean and Agnarr toward Lord Odin's hall. "Do you think Agnarr was right?" Her words sounded loud as she whispered them to Sean.

Sean's mouth was a hard line as he gave a small nod. "It's the most likely explanation I can come up with." Sean seemed even more jittery than normal.

"But how?" Amanda pushed the light ahead of them as they walked. Several faces peered at them through magickally sealed windows as they carefully headed toward Valaskjalf.

"The Disir had to have a found a hole in the defenses somewhere, and smuggled Draupnir out. As much as we like to think the gods are all-powerful, even they can overlook some things." They reached one of the larger crossovers, where the road dipped below another street. Sean was charging his hammer, trying to channel his nervous energy. The crackling electricity snapped like a bug zapper. "One thing has been bothering me, though, since the attack on Mimir."

"Just one thing?"

"The Disir. They have been all around us. They have to be someone in charge to have gotten that close to Mimir's well. Whoever they are, they are close to us, and we haven't known it. I just can't wrap my head around that. Someone we know is working for Bergelmir and using fell magick."

"You heard what Lena and Lev said, and the Prelate confirmed it. Not everyone on Asgard has a clean history. But there is something else. They probably knew about Bergelmir and what he was doing on Midgard the night I was claimed. They must also know where Jack is." The idea made Amanda's skin tingle with anger and dread. "Hey!" Amanda hadn't been paying attention as she and Sean rounded a bend in the road, colliding with Agnarr, who had stopped to inspect something in the middle of the road.

"Apologies, Favoured. I thought I saw something in the shadows." Agnarr thrust his spear forward, and a dazzling light lit the dark street. Dark runes were carved into the stone walls that supported the road above them.

Amanda and Sean took a step back. Two syirces blazed with fell magick on either side under the runes. Amanda looked to Sean, and he gave her a grim nod. The runes written were for Mani and Sol with the rune for Favoured just below. But there was something else that made Amanda's vision constrict and her breathing become shallow. A slimy trail of alfblot lead from the runes into the Syirces. In the ground beside the syirces, the runes for Sigyn and Favoured were burned into the ground with an "X" through them. Amanda threw two tiny columns of flames toward the alfblot, and the fell portal and liquid evaporated instantly.

"They had to have seen us coming and left that for us. They left that for me." Amanda felt her hands shake slightly as she spoke.

"They've become Disir." Sean whispered.

"RIBBIT!"

"What was that?" Amanda squinted hard into the darkness at the sound that had come from behind them. They were standing just down the street from the plaza they had been heading toward. *"Dilyagg."*

Amanda tried to increase the size of her light, but the enlargement charm seemed to slip from her fingers before she could finish the spell. She tried it again with no results, but on the third try the light grew and she almost dropped the spell. As the light continued to illuminate the buildings around them a dulhda hopped onto a stone bench, smashing it to bits. The nefarious creature had grown to be the size of an elephant. The dulhda's skin glistened like asphalt after a heavy rain, and was tinged green in the light. Leaning forward, a barbed tongue shot out at Sean and Amanda.

"Watch out!" Sean pushed Amanda out of the way, and she barely missed being hit. Sean was not so fortunate. He lay on the ground shaking.

"Sean! No!" Amanda cradled his head in her lap.

"J-just a-a p-paral-lyzing t-toxin. W-will b-be o-ok. F-fry it." Sean stammered and then seized up, his body becoming rigid and unmoving.

Agnarr was holding the dulhda at bay with his spear. The bright light at the tip left searing blisters across its face. "To Hel with you! Your master shall not use its pet to harm another!"

The grotesque frog sprouted several boils across its skin that leaked putrid fluids onto the street. Each of its webbed feet was the size of a cart and ended in curved talons. With a swipe of its foot, it knocked Agnarr back into a cluster of statues that ringed a tree with blue leaves. Leaning forward, the dulhda opened its mouth towards Sean. "RIBBIT!"

Amanda jumped to her feet and summoned a ball of fire. *"Fieryr!* Over here, you big ugly toad! Leave him alone!"

The dulhda's bulbous eyes swiveled toward the light from Amanda's green fire and opened its mouth again. Its tongue waggled back and forth like an attacking snake. With a slurping noise like a drain being unclogged, the dulhda inhaled and sucked the fire right out of Amanda's hands.

"Whoa!" Amanda felt unsteady and wobbled on her feet. The dulhda hadn't just eaten the fire, it had eaten her magick too. That meant it must have absorbed her enlargement charms as well, which made it grow.

The dulhda, sensing Amanda's disorientation, lashed out with its tongue again. Amanda barely had time to dive out of the way as the tongue took out a chunk of the building behind where she had been standing. She tried to conjure more fire, but her magick felt erratic and sluggish. What she could summon hit the dulhda, but the spell was absorbed through the frog's skin.

"Sean, help me! I don't know how to beat it!" Amanda crawled to her knees, but there was no response from Sean. She tried a few more spells that she could remember from her training, but they all seemed to only feed the dulhda. The dulhda leered at her and opened its mouth again.

"You should know better than to play with dulhdas, dear."

Appearing beside Amanda was the ghostly form of her benefactor Sigyn.

"Sigyn? Help me. I don't know how to stop the dulhda!"

The dulhda, sensing new magick, sent its tongue through Sigyn's spectyr as she thrust her hands on her hips. "You should know it for it is in the grimoire I gave you. I put it in there after the time I sent one after Queen Frigga."

"You what?" Amanda dove again, as the barbed wrecking ball came her way.

"She deserved it."

"Can you get rid of it? We have to stop it before it hurts someone else." Sean was still not moving and the dulhda was trying to take them out like flies. Agnarr was just now starting to try to get to his feet.

"I doubt I could take care of it from here, and that is quite inconvenient. Open page one hundred and eleven." Sigyn's form smiled and then vanished, replaced by the grimoire, which blazed with green light.

The tiny book bounced twice in the air and then dove into Amanda's hands, where it began shuffling through its pages. Amanda was surprised to find the spell was a simple chant and not a spellword, but the dulhda was coming her way again, so she ignored her curiosity.

Raising an outstretched palm she spoke as loud as she could, "Take you now from this place and return to the nether space. The realm beyond and below and burned be the place you are to go! Return from whence you came, and let all else remain the same."

Bubbling energy flowed through Amanda and shot toward the frog. For a moment the dulhda was swinging its tongue back and forth as it lowered its head to charge, but then, with a sound like a giant zipper opening, a green cage slammed shut around the dulhda. Prelate Tess and Keeper Fulla came speeding toward Amanda just as the dulhda vanished, leaving only a foul-smelling puff of smoke.

"Well done, Favoured!" Sigyn's spectyr had returned and was clapping her slender hands together.

Prelate Tess and Keeper Fulla stared open mouthed at Sigyn. Sean sat up suddenly, and Amanda ran over to him. Her friend was coughing and spitting.

"Are you OK?" Amanda helped the boy to stand, receiving an unexpected shock of electricity.

"Whoops. Sorry about that. Having trouble focusing. The dulhda venom is vanishing now that it's gone, but it makes your mouth taste like you gargled with rancid sea water and my head feels like it's made of pudding. I'll bounce back, though. You were amazing, Amanda."

Amanda felt her cheeks redden. Sean was looking up at her with his bright eyes and she found herself smiling back at him. The Prelate cleared her throat.

"I feel like I have repeated this one too many times recently, but perhaps one of you would like to explain what transpired here?" The Prelate stared at Sigyn's silhouetted outline.

Keeper Fulla was circling the charred runes, and then saw the writing above. "What is the meaning of this?"

"We found them on our way to you, Prelate." Agnarr righted his helmet as he limped toward them.

"Agnarr! You're OK." Amanda cried out in relief.

"I have taken harder hits from a baby troll." Agnarr stumbled, but caught himself. "Perhaps it was a bit harder than I thought."

The Prelate took Agnarr's forearm. "We will see you to the healing beds, but first we need your report."

"We found those runes, along with two syirces and alfblot. We believe it to be from the Favoured of Mani and Sol. Prince Thor's Favoured believes, and I agree, that this is a sign they have become Disir." Agnarr held his arm across his stomach. "That is when the dulhda appeared, and attacked us."

"I stopped the alfblot to the syirces and they vanished, and then Sean and Agnarr were hit when the dulhda found us. I tried to use my magick against it, but it just absorbed the spells. Sigyn appeared and showed me the right spell to use to send it to a nether realm."

Sigyn hiccupped. "No need to thank me or anything. Although, I would take some mulberry wine if you have it lying around."

The Prelate ignored the goddess. "Clearly the dulhda was sent to distract us to give the thief more time to escape. But this would mean we now deal with three Disir, two of which were Favoured. This has never happened before. Worse, by now we have lost the trail to find Draupnir."

Keeper Fulla cast a few frost lilies to the ground. "The lilies cannot trace the fell magick since it was destroyed by Amanda." The Keeper gave Amanda an annoyed look. "Perhaps that was your plan all along?"

"There are no grounds for such an accusation, Keeper Fulla. Be silent unless you can fathom another way to search for the traitors." The Prelate was studying Sigyn, who was taking in several large breaths as if she were enjoying a stroll around the city.

Fulla's voice was low. "I am tired of you ignoring what is right in front of us. We are under attack by a cunning foe who has stolen Lord Odin's ring from your protection! The Disir are loose in our land once again, and we must stop them. You must act, and stop sheltering these mortals over the fate of our realm. There are other ways they can tell us who took Draupnir and how we can get it back. If you will not act, then I shall!" The Keeper pointed a finger and Amanda jerked backward as magick invaded her mind.

"I think not!" Sigyn raised a finger and the Keeper suddenly coughed as frost lilies spewed forth from her mouth. The magick crawling through her memories vanished, and Amanda opened her mouth to yell at Keeper Fulla. Sigyn waved a finger to her, and then addressed the Prelate and Keeper Fulla. "I may not be able to do more than use a charm used on Light Elf younglings, but I will not let you do such a thing to my Favoured. Such a spell would leave her unable to assist you in the future, and she has much she can help you with."

"And how can we trust you with your history?" Prelate Tess frowned at Sigyn.

"Because she can help you find Draupnir with this." Sigyn winked at Amanda and the grimoire flapped open. When it stopped moving, magick welled on top of its pages. Red filaments of a spell began to weave into a stone the size of Amanda's fist. "That is Draupnir's twin stone. Or, more accurately, the twin stone of the ruby that sits within the ring Draupnir. It holds not the magick that Draupnir is imbued with from Lord Odin, but it should be able to help you sense Draupnir and perhaps gain insight to its whereabouts and who now wields it."

Keeper Fulla made a noise of surprise. "And how do you come to possess this stone, and know our lord's ring is gone?"

"I can tell the power of Lord Odin has left this land because how else would I be here? The tower that holds me was built by the Allfather. His magick still holds, but it is weakened without his presence or the ring's. The stone was a gift. Now then, to use that stone you will need Amanda. Since she has my full might, she can perform the necessary spell to connect the twin stone with Draupnir. Amanda, you must place the stone on Draupnir's stand and use these four spells - *revlyia percetod gregorie deobscurant.*"

Amanda looked to the stone on the grimoire she held and then Sigyn. "But I have never done four spells at once before."

Sigyn smiled. "But you have all my magick to do so." With that, Sigyn went rigid and vanished.

CHAPTER 19:
THE SECOND FAVOURED

Bergelmir roared with triumph as he twisted Draupnir around his finger. The ocean of magick it contained was even vaster than he had suspected, and as he wielded its energies the magick lit up the cavernous throne room in Utgard with a blaze of light. His servants had delivered the ring into his care moments ago – and with it the realm of Asgard's most powerful defenses. With a flick of the wrist, Bergelmir tested the power of the ring and watched the polished mirrors of ice that showed the city of Asgard in chaos. Queen Frigga's barriers may keep them out, but Bergelmir's spies allowed him to see in other ways, and as he watched the power of Draupnir slowly raised the realm's shields. Then with another gesture he brought them down once more.

Oh, how the Jotun lord wished he was heading to the realm of the gods to crush them with his armies. The inhabitants of Asgard were running around like scared mice trying to figure out what was happening. Bergelmir howled in victory again, "Never again shall you see your golden realm safe! You are now but pawns for me to play with."

"I see you are wasting no time in making use of your new asset." Without being summoned, the dark pool of air materialized beside the Frost Jotun lord's head.

"And I see you have grown stronger as well." Bergelmir swept through the room toward the mirrors, and away from the voice. "Now that I possess the ring, your prison is but a hole. With it I command enough power to level any realm I choose, including Asgard. They shall all kneel before my feet and rue the day they dared consider the Jotuns to be defeated."

A low, grim laugh, like the precursor of an earthquake, shook the room. Several shards of ice fell from the ceiling. "Let us not forget our bargain. The ring shall be used to break the last of my bonds, and then I shall deliver unto you the power not only to rule the Nine Realms, but to remake them as you see fit."

Bergelmir glared at the vortex in his throne room. "I tire of waiting for your plans to come to fruition. An avalanche does not stop to consider the trees in its path. It devours those that stand in its way. Why must we wait? We have the power we need now."

The room darkened as the mass of fell magick sent tendrils toward Bergelmir, pressing him against a mirror that showed the Prelate shouting orders. "We wait till both of our might is fully restored. You will need more than a wave of force to defeat that withered fool, Odin. Think for but a moment and consider Draupnir more than the blunt force of a fist. With it we can be fortified for when Odin returns, ready to catch him at his weakest. Once the Spell of Favouring has robbed the Allfather of his might, we shall use his power against him and strike with precision. We will strike while Asgard is low, force the god to show himself, and then he shall fall. There shall be no rebirth for the gods this time."

Bergelmir held up his fist and Draupnir glowed. The fell magick retreated. "Do not threaten me again. With my acquisition of the ring, I am now more than your or Odin's equal even before the spell is complete. I have built an army that none suspect. With each new minion my power grows. Perhaps the one with the power should lead us, not a prisoner that must steal to regain his might."

"Have a care, Bergelmir. Your servants in the Golden Realm are bound to me. Their minds may obey you, but their souls are mine. The power they took links them to me in ways your kind has never been able to do with those you have possessed. Should you betray me, you will never know which of your servants is truly yours, and then we shall see if you can withstand the full might of Odin without mine aide. Let us have a bit more patience. We shall wait until the moment we can use the syirces and alfblot to their fullest advantage. Even now their presence in the Golden Realm strengthens me. Just as Sigyn's Favoured's presence moves the realm further into chaos."

A shuffling sound echoed from the hallways and Jack was escorted into the chamber by a gaggle of imps, followed by a Jotun giant. Jack's expression was blank, and his eyes stared at the floor. His clothes were tattered and he had several cuts along his forearms. Bergelmir snorted and snapped his fingers. An imp appeared with a vial of golden liquid and ran toward his master as fast as he could. The darkness seemed to cringe at the sight of the container. Grabbing Jack by the back of his tattered jacket, Bergelmir pulled him up so that Jack was at eye level, making him stare into the Jotun's cold blue eyes.

"Your words may be true for now. But let us see if you are so confident once I show you how useful this one has been to our cause." Bergelmir snapped again and Jack's eyes fluttered.

"Wha-what. What did you do to me Bergy?"

"I took control of your Jotun side." Bergelmir took the vial, popped the cork from its top and held it above Jack's mouth. "And with this, I take control of your Asgardian side." Bergelmir snapped Jack's head back and poured the liquid down his throat.

Jack coughed after he swallowed. "Tastes like green Jell-O." Jack felt his insides convulse, and it was all he could do not to vomit.

Warmth flooded in Jack's feet, as if they had been dunked in a tub of hot water. Jack looked down to his hands as the warmth passed upward and through his body, bringing with it bright pink skin. Flexing his fingers, Jack felt a rush of emotions, and for the first time in weeks he felt as if he were himself again.

"Well, that's one heckuva a dye job, Bergy." Jack grinned fiercely. "You should take that act on the road. Not sure what you mean by Asgardian side. Is that like Luke's dark side? Man, it feels good to be normal."

Bergelmir didn't respond. Instead he held up the hand that bore Draupnir. Jack tensed, unsure of what would happen. With a roar, Bergelmir thrust his hand into the vortex and drew forth a drop of alfblot. Quickly, the Jotun lord drew a symbol on Jack's forehead. Jack began to scream as his skin rippled and turned back to the same shade as the Jotun lord, then back to normal, only this time it was also tinged with grey and purple.

"You will never be normal again, boy. In fact, you are now more unique than all who have called Midgard home. I am curious though, Favoured, will your benefactor show himself from whatever shadows he has been hiding in once we reveal who you truly are to your friends and what you have done for us? You are now my Disir, and through your blood I can control mortal and Asgardian alike."

Jack's eyes blazed with blue fire. "Yes, Master."

***

Amanda and Sean stood in front of two giant doors shaped like golden half-moons and stared up at the glass dome of Valaskjalf. Amanda shifted her weight and brushed her bangs out of her face while chewing on the insides of her cheeks. The sky was lightening as the stars rose into the sky. It would have been a pleasant sight if it didn't remind them all it had been several hours since the last time the shields provided from Draupnir were seen.

Cassie glanced nervously over at her friend and motioned for her to be patient. Cassie, Connor, and Mykola had met them with Nimbus and the rest of the Favoured while they were on their way to Lord Odin's palace with the twin stone. The Prelate commanded them to fall in line with the others and now the entire group of Favoured stood outside the glass dome, waiting for further instructions. The other Favoured whispered back and forth about the rumors they heard regarding Amanda and the dulhda while Amanda filled in her friends. The Einherjar and even the Aesir were dispatched on vindsvolla to watch for any sign of invasion. Nimbus nipped at Mykola's fingers, and the boy rustled its head. The young vindmare was dancing around, sensing the nerves of the group.

Growling a bit in the back of her throat, Amanda glared at the door, willing it to open. "It's been over an hour!"

"I know, but I am sure they will be out any second. They are probably just sorting out how to proceed with the new information we got from Sigyn and about Lena and Lev."

Amanda blew her breath out through pursed lips, and Cassie cringed again. "If that is the case, then why aren't we a part of the conversation? Sigyn gave me the twin stone."

Cassie held up her hands. "I am not the one you need to preach to, but you might not want to let them see how irritated you are. I am pretty sure that even though we can't see them, they can see us. So, maybe settle down a bit? Tensions are higher than Mount Valhalla. Take a breath." Even though the dome was made of glass, the interior was shielded by magick to prevent anyone from seeing into the palatial throne room. Concentric golden walls overlapped one another at the base, and the glass above was covered in thousands upon thousands of runes, all of which read some form of protection.

Amanda inhaled through her nose and then let it out slowly. She suddenly felt more relaxed. "You're right, I… Hey! Are you trying to coax me down with a bit of magick?" Amanda could just barely pick up a few notes of magick coming from Cassie's direction.

"I'm just trying to help, Amanda. You don't want to get in front of the Queen half-cocked. At least try to remember that we are not the ones in trouble for once – yet. You go in there like an angry cocker spaniel, and you might end up like the dulhda."

"Let her try. I am tired of being the ones who find out the information, and then are told to wait while they decide what we should be doing. Also, is no one going to say anything about the fact that Keeper Fulla attacked me?" Amanda yanked one of her gloves up her forearm.

"Keeper Fulla should be put out to pasture in my opinion, but she does have the ear of the Queen. My bet is it's Keeper Fulla in there who is trying to convince them to send us all and Sigyn to the Gruneling so they can see what else she is hiding in Sigyn's tower, and to keep us out of their way until Lord Odin gets back." Cassie bit back a yawn and her stomach gurgled. "Connor, can you hurry up!"

Connor had been to the Mead Hall and was passing out mead and stew. He ignored his sister as he offered Amanda a bowl, but she refused it. "Come on, you have to eat."

"I will not eat until they tell us what they are doing. Let's not forget that I am the only one besides Lord Odin who knows where the tower is, and I am certainly not telling the Keeper so she can go raid it. If it is the twin stone that has then upset, then that is their own fault. How could they not have known about the twin stone before? I mean, Sigyn had it when Lord Odin locked her up. I saw it when I went to visit her, so it's not like she was hiding it. Did he not take inventory of what she had in the tower? If it never came up before, then why would they be mad about it now?"

I don't think they were mad – well the Keeper was – probably just a bit surprised is all. Keeper Fulla doesn't like surprises. She would do anything to keep this realm safe, which actually sounds a lot like Lena and Lev now." Connor took a sip from his stein. "I can't believe they have become Disir. Sure they were always a tad on the snotty side, but this…? Say, you don't think Fulla is…"

Cassie was nosily slurping her stew after she grabbed a bowl from her brother. "Ha! No way. She gets nervous when she has to carry frost lilies around the city, or hears Bergelmir's name." She turned to Amanda, "Also, you know you are shouting right?"

Amanda turned to see the Favoured eying her. "Sorry."

"So, Amanda," Sean turned Amanda back so their conversation couldn't be overheard, "Is that what Sigyn was like when you met with her?"

Amanda nodded. "Like I told you, the tower drains her magick, and after being by herself for so long she has lost touch a bit. Although, she seemed much more coherent than when I was with her. Maybe having me here and around is helping her."

"Maybe. I mean she did give you those spells to use to find Draupnir. Do you know what they do?" Connor dumped Amanda's stew into his bowl and took two large bites.

Amanda pulled the grimoire from her cloak. It felt heavier than before and there were new creases on the spine. "No. I looked them up on our way here. Surprise, surprise they were right in front waiting for me. They each are a form of banishing concealment spells or revealing things that are stolen. I tried to see if there were any spells about Draupnir specifically, but there are so many spells in here it could take days to find anything. I still can't find anything on finding a Disir." Amanda snapped open the claps and began flipping through the pages. "Next time I see Sigyn I am going to see if she can add a spell to find a spell."

One of the Favoured passed the group and they all paused. Cassie locked eyes with the girl. "Well shove off already. Nothing to see here." When they were alone again, Cassie turned. "The others heard about your favouring Amanda."

"Ugh. Great. Well, it was going to come out sooner or later. At least now I have no more secrets from anyone. Not that it does us much good right now." Amanda continued to flip through the pages of the grimoire. "All the magick of Sigyn isn't going to help if we can't stop the alfblot, syirces, find Draupnir, help my parents, and save Jack. Some of these spells don't even seem like they would ever have any use. When would I need to transform a mouse into a cup or make myself blind to help find my way through a maze?"

"Cups are better than mice any day." Connor laughed at his own joke, but the others just stared at him. "Sheesh."

One of the doors slid open and the entire group snapped to attention. Everyone fidgeted for a moment and there was a small gasp as the Queen of Asgard calmly walked out of the palace. "Hello, Favoured."

"Majesty." Some of the Favoured murmured, but they all brought their fist to their chests and bowed their head.

Queen Frigga looked at each of the Favoured as she began to speak, "I know many of you have concerns surrounding tonight's events. Be assured, we are quite safe. The Einherjar and Aesir have reported there are no foes in or around the barriers I have erected. The syirces that were still open have all vanished. While our foe might toy with the might of our lord, they clearly still fear us as they have not launched a salvo to attack us with their new weapon. The earlier attack at the Bifrost was a group of wayward ogres that have been dispatched. You must know these things to know that while we have suffered an attack and a loss, we are still Asgardians, even you, and we fear nothing. We are warriors. This is what we have been training for. Ready yourselves and defend our realm!" Raising a hand, the Queen summoned scrolls that flew to every Favoured. "These are your orders. Those of you with earthen and healing magicks will report to Yggdrasil to help the gods and our lord return as well as to help keep the World Tree from completely going dormant. Those of you who have strength will be stationed at our gates. The rest of you will work with the Einherjar to scour our realm for the Disir. While their betrayal saddens me, with the Favoured of Mani and Sol becoming our enemy they may have unwittingly given us ways to find them through our connection to their magick. Be on guard, and be safe. On the Wings of Asgard."

There was a rippled rustling as the Favoured murmured their reply and began to open their scrolls. Amanda unfurled hers to see there was one word: 'Stay.' Amanda glanced to the others and saw looks from her friends that told her they had received the same message. The other Favoured quickly began to splinter off to their various tasks. Soon, the Queen stood before only the five of them.

She surveyed them for a moment before speaking, "Now that we are alone, I have words you should hear before we proceed. There is a story you must know about Lena and Lev." Amanda and the others again looked to each other, uncertain of what was happening. The Queen let them take a moment before continuing again. "Lena and Lev Zukov were not the original Favoured destined to be claimed for Mani and Sol by the Spell of Favouring during this time of the spell's incarnation. The original Favoured were killed before the Prelate could get to them. They were killed by Fell Elves; the last loose Fell Elves that now reside in the Gruneling. The spell then moved on to Lena and Lev. We believe the dark ones somehow knew the list of potential Favoured and planned to use the Zukovs as their agents within the realm."

Amanda felt her stomach drop as the Queen spoke. She began to breathe faster. "But how? Why?"

Queen Frigga's head pivoted slowly to Amanda and she took a few steps toward the girl. "We believe the same traitor, the Disir, working with the Fell Elves and the Frost Jotuns helped. They must have been turned before the Spell of Favouring began. How they knew who the spell would select though is a complete mystery as only the Norn possess that knowledge. Clearly this was the start of a long-term plan that is now coming to fruition."

Cassie raised her hand. "Queen Frigga. Why are you telling us this?"

The Queen smiled a sad smile. "Because we want you to know that the time for any secrets have passed. We withheld this knowledge from you, thinking it would keep you safe and help Lena and Lev to not be treated any less than the rest of the Favoured. To be fully truthful, we are not certain if they are now or were ever in control of themselves, or just fell slaves. Unknowingly they could have been the ones to bring the alfblot to Asgard." Queen Frigga paused, and collected her thoughts. "I do not know what will happen to them, but, should we be able to capture them, they shall be cared for instead of being destroyed. If there are spells in your grimoire that can help Amanda, then we are in dire need of them. We are moving forward together with this knowledge that we must all be careful. We need to trust each other. You need to know that we are not perfect. We learn from our mistakes, just as you do."

Amanda's anger softened as the Queen spoke. She was still irritated at Keeper Fulla, but she could now understand why they needed a moment before addressing them. This night brought up things with much more far-reaching consequences. Still, she fully expected an apology from Keeper Fulla.

"Thank you, Queen Frigga." Sean bowed his head. "Can we... is there a way to help the Zukovs?"

"We must find the first Disir and destroy them. We must end this assault once and for all. Come, let us enter Valaskjalf and see if we can use the gift given to us by Sigyn."

CHAPTER 20:
THE TWIN STONE

As the door shut behind them, Amanda stopped suddenly. The light that had spilled in through the opened door vanished, replaced by a slow-rising illumination from the runes etched into the surface of the dome. Cassie nearly collided into Amanda as they both rubbed their eyes to adjust, while Queen Frigga walked calmly past them. Like little flashlights, the runes projected light into the palace with a soft glow that created wavy patterns on the floors. The throne room was completely open except for the columns that arched upward to support the dome above, and were draped with chains of shimmering stones that shifted as they started to follow the Queen.

Hlidskjalf rose like a bird taking flight in the center of the hall. It sparkled with a mixture of gold, glass, and rubies. Unlike Draupnir, whose magick always felt like a tidal wave, the throne held its power in a peaceful way that commanded attention. Tilting her head as they approached, Amanda could hear the lively tune of magick it radiated. Two giant wings ensconced the padded throne's seat, below which stood Keeper Fulla and Prelate Tess.

Queen Frigga settled herself onto the throne. Amanda and Cassie stopped at the bottom of three steps that led up to where the others stood, and beyond that another three to the throne. Connor, Mykola, and Sean stood on either side of the girls. Nimbus trotted about the room, enjoying the swirls of light. It suddenly felt like a courthouse proceeding to Amanda with the Prelate, and Keeper Fulla as the jury and the Queen as the judge.

Queen Frigga rubbed the tips of her fingers together, and then rested a hand on an empty stand beside the throne. Amanda recognized it as the one that had held Draupnir when it was above the Gruneling, and then felt the magick in the air grow thick and loud in the back of her mind. "Now then, Amanda, what can you tell us of the twin stone and Sigyn's words?"

"I saw it when I visited her in the Green Askr. She wasn't hiding it." Amanda pursed her lips together as she spoke next, "If anyone had bothered to visit Sigyn, instead of keeping her locked away, maybe she would have shared it sooner."

"Watch your tone. I find it hard to believe that an enchantress, who might want to earn her freedom, wouldn't be more forthcoming. Is it fate or planned timing that she also was able to produce this at the exact time Draupnir was stolen?" Fulla pulled the twin stone from her apron and handed it to the Queen. "Lord Eitri should be able to verify if it is from the same mine as Draupnir's stone. However, as communications are disrupted by your shields, I have not been able to get a hold of him. All we have are the claims of the traitorous goddess."

The Queen examined the facets of the stone for a moment and then twirled a finger in a circular motion. The chains above swayed and shifted until a three-dimensional map of Asgard could be seen from where they bunched together. Queen Frigga held the ruby up to the map and focused a trickle of power through it. Immediately the map flashed angrily and zoomed toward the city, stopping in a slow rotation as it showed Valaskjalf.

Queen Frigga passed the stone to the Prelate, who examined it and tested it again, receiving the same results. "I am inclined to believe Sigyn had positive intent. Why would she have needed to tell us about it before now? Its power signature does match Draupnir's when magick is focused through it. There are slight variations, but it resonates within the same magickal spectrum."

Amanda watched as they took turns examining the stone. "She could have forgotten what it was. She has been trapped inside the Green Askr for too long. She's kind of…"

"Mental?" Cassie offered.

"No." Amanda looked at Cassie and then made an exasperated sound. "Well, maybe, but not in a bad way. She's just a bit out of touch with reality. She's been trying to help us, just in her own way. She knew there was a traitor in the realm and gave me the grimoire to help find the Disir. She said there were spells in there that could help us stop them, or even change them back. I just haven't found which ones yet. Maybe if we let her out of the Green Askr, she could help us find the right spells to use."

The Keeper had been stewing while Amanda spoke, her face completely red and her cheeks puffed out like a blowfish about to explode. "Your grace, we all know what the enchantress is capable of. We cannot allow her to be free! We all saw how she appeared outside of her confinement. Perhaps she did the same and went to Midgard to Lena and Lev, or the Jotuns, or the dark ones. As we have learned, her tower is not far from the Norn's home in the Forest of Fates. Perhaps she spied on the Norn to gather the knowledge of the upcoming claiming of the Favoured. She has swindled us in the past. This could all be an act, perpetrated to deceive us. I think our best course would be to send her to the Gruneling so she can pose no more threat to us, and send her Favoured along with her. Since she has arrived, there has been one disaster after another. Her presence has been just as disruptive as Sigyn's would be."

"So much for moving forward with trust. Don't think I have forgotten that you attacked me out there, or how you have always treated me as if I am to blame for all of this." Amanda looked to the Queen and then the Keeper.

Amanda opened her mouth to speak again, but Prelate Tess's stern voice cut her off. "Well spoken, Amanda. Keeper Fulla, you tested the girl and found nothing. I myself tested her and verified she has had nothing to do with our current conditions. Your continued accusations are unwarranted and are beginning to cross the line into slanderous malintent. You also attacked her this evening, without permission. You teeter dangerously on the precipice of letting your own prejudice condemn you and relieve you from your post. Unless that is what you desire, be silent!"

Keeper Fulla sputtered for a moment, and then moved to the Queen. "I have done only what was necessary for us all! Surely you see past this, my Queen. She was bound by Lord Odin! Clearly that means our lord thought she was a danger!"

Queen Frigga sighed. "Peace, Keeper. My husband does not always share his council with me. His need for layer upon layer of protection stems from the knowledge he gained before Ragnarok. When I shared with him news of Amanda's claiming he made no mention of danger. Our communications have been limited, but if she were true threat, he would have warned me or made some mention of the binding. As it stands, it seems his plans are playing out as he expected."

"Queen Frigga, we must regain order. Lord Odin could not fully know of the dangers we face. He would not want our realm in such turmoil. If he knew of this, then…," Fulla was shaking a thick finger at Amanda, but was silenced by the Queen as she rose suddenly.

"You know better than to question your lord! He has kept us safe for thousands upon thousands of years. We have spoken on this enough, Keeper Fulla. In this instance I wish I possessed the insight my husband purchased from Yggdrasil and Mimir, but until he returns, we shall use what we can. Amanda, can you help us find Draupnir? If it is somewhere we can reach, we will ready our forces to reclaim what was stolen from us." The Queen ignored Keeper Fulla as she shuffled angrily at her words.

Prelate Tess held out the ruby to Amanda. Taking the gem, Amanda looked into its crimson heart. "I will try. Sigyn said I needed to place this on Draupnir's stand. May I?"

The Queen motioned for Amanda to approach, and removed her hand from where it had been resting. Amanda carefully placed the twin stone on the golden platform and took a step back. She pulled the grimoire from her cloak and flipped through it to look at each of the four spells she needed to perform once more. The spells were relatively simple, and the gestures made an easy pattern she could follow. All she had to do was bring her ring and middle finger to the center of her palm and then open them toward the stone as she spoke.

Setting the grimoire aside on a nearby statue, Amanda readied herself. "I have no idea what is about to happen, so be ready. *Revlyia percetod gregorie deobscurant.*"

The sound of magick rose in an orchestra of song, and the room vanished, replaced by a vista of complete desolation and destruction. Amanda cried out and turned around, dust and heat stinging her eyes. All around her as far as she could see was nothing but parched dirt and dry grass that crumbled and floated up to a smoke-filled sky. Nothing was recognizable except for, what Amanda could only guess was, the withered form of Yggdrasil, which looked frighteningly similar to the way Amanda had seen it moments before. A hand latched onto Amanda's arm and she felt herself being pulled through some kind of void. The barren wasteland was replaced by a forest of trees with golden leaves and iridescent bark. There was a clanging sound and Amanda turned to see three interlocking triangles, each with a rune in the center lit by ruby-red fire. The triangles were held by three figures, one blue, one black, and the other golden.

The figures' forms were blurred but they began to chant, "In this time and in this place, take this life to save one of Odin's race. Through sacrifice we submit our thrall, and give her our power, one and all. To wait till the hundredth year whilst the fires of Surtur burn clear. A guardian of nothing will she be, chained until twilight's time is free. By the power of Yggdrasil's life and death the rebuilding shall be made done, and we call forth the Favoured to be spun. But all be warned by the Norn, when newly found of magicks Favoured be unbound, again the fire of Ragnarok will come round."

Fire leapt from the triangles and raced toward Amanda and into her heart. The world around her vanished, leaving only Amanda writhing as green flames burned her soul. Amanda cried out and fell back into Sean's arms as the throne room reappeared. The Prelate motioned to the Keeper, who grudgingly produced a stein and passed it to Amanda.

"Whoa there! I've got you." Sean held Amanda while she gasped for air and looked about the room.

After taking a sip and letting the mead calm her, "Wh... Did you see that?"

"We didn't see anything. Just thought you had gone a bit mental." Connor patted Amanda's shoulder. Mykola was on her other side with Cassie and Nimbus. The vindsvolla nuzzled her cheek.

"I'm OK. I'm not sure what that was, but that is not what I was expecting. All of a sudden, I was somewhere else. I think it was Asgard, but everything was broken or destroyed. The sky looked like it was bleeding, and Yggdrasil was completely black and burnt. The worst part was the smoke. It hung like low clouds that clogged the sky." Amanda felt the Prelate tense as she described the vision. "Then I was in a forest with golden leaves. There were three people holding a symbol I have never seen before, but there were runes.

One for the past, one for the present, and one for the future. I don't know who they were but they all recited the Spell of Favouring. The magick from the spell came for me, and…" Amanda looked up to Sean who was still holding her.

Sean gave her a wink, and Amanda felt dizzy again but for a completely different reason. "Sounds like you had quite the trip. Happen to get any postcards that can tell us what it all means?"

The Queen looked to the Prelate, who nodded in unspoken agreement. Tracing a line between several dull gems that dotted the map of stones hanging above them the Prelate spoke solemnly. "It is as we feared. What you saw Amanda, I believe, is about the meaning behind the Spell of Favouring's last passage. We were so focused in looking for a pattern as to why and where the syirces were found, and finding the Disir, we never considered why all of this was happening now."

"We assumed it was because Lord Odin and the other gods are away, ma'am." Sean stood slowly with Amanda.

"That may be part of the truth, but what Amanda just told us, and what her favouring is, makes me think otherwise." The Prelate began to walk to the side of the dais. Touching a rune on the floor with her foot, the dais hummed smoothly as it, and the floor Amanda and the others stood on, spun to face the back of the palace. Yggdrasil looked like it had shrunk to half its original height. "We assumed all along that the attacks were to weaken us while Lord Odin was away with the rest of the gods. We assumed that the reason for the alfblot and then the syirces was to open us up to an attack, and that if we could find out where the next one was to occur, we could capture the Disir. All along the Disir's pattern of behavior has been different. I ask again, why and why now? Lord Odin has been away many times before, as well as the gods, so what is special about our present circumstances? We have seen Yggdrasil like this before. Before Surtur attacked us and began to burn the Nine Realms. It is because Amanda is here. It has to do with your favourings."

"How do you mean?" Cassie's stomach grumbled again. "And, uh… does anyone have anything to eat?"

Sean fished an apple from his cloak and tossed it to Cassie. "How could this tie to our favouring? Do you think they are trying to prevent the gods from giving up their magick to us? Maybe that is why they went after Heimdall and Mimir: to test it out."

"No." Amanda hugged herself. "It has to do with the end of the Spell of Favouring. What I saw was the future, wasn't it?"

Prelate Tess nodded; her gaze went vacant as if sharing Amanda's vision. "Aye, I believe so. After the destruction of Ragnarok there was nothing but smoke and fire, and then silence. The Spell of Favouring acted upon me as an anchor, holding me to this realm. Everyone, everything, was gone or burned. I was alone. The magicks it spun nourished me but kept me chained to one spot with only the appearance of a new rune upon the gauntlets to mark the passage of a hundred years. I was the focus of the spell and the one mentioned. It was a price I gladly paid, but would not readily endure again. Nevertheless, it worked. What you saw was recounting that destruction and time, and then what is to come if we are reading the meaning of the spell's words correctly. With Amanda here, Ragnarok could come to the Nine Realms once more. Without my sisters, there would be no way to stop it."

Amanda looked at the Prelate. She knew the Prelate was the focus of the spell, but never gave much thought to what it must have been like for the Prelate after her sister Valkyrie died along with the rest of the Nine Realms. To be alone in that destruction even for a moment had been horrifying and made her feel such loneliness. Amanda reached out to touch the Prelate's shoulder. The hardened metal of her armor now seemed more protective than it had a moment before. For a moment the two looked at each other as they shared the memory.

Keeper Fulla gave an exclamation of validation. "I knew it! She is the reason for this entire mess! Bind her, Queen Frigga, I beg of you. She belongs in the Gruneling!"

Queen Frigga turned on the Keeper. "Keeper Fulla, your counsel is no longer welcome. Leave us until I bid you to do otherwise!"

The Keeper reeled back as if she had been slapped. Clenching her fists in her apron, she scurried down the steps, nearly knocking Cassie and Amanda over. As she passed a few of the Einherjar that stood beside the columns, she muttered something under her breath. The Prelate's keen ears must have caught the words because she frowned but did not repeat them.

After the big doors slid close, the Queen addressed the Prelate, her gown having turned jet black from her anger. "Are you saying that Amanda is the one mentioned in the last line? 'Magicks unbound?' Can it really be so?"

Amanda nodded hesitantly, but then with more assurance. "The spell I used was meant to reveal who is holding Draupnir, and where, but it also found a way to figure out why." Amanda spoke with more certainty as her mind began to connect the vision to what the Prelate said. "When I first came to Asgard, I read about the spell. I am guessing all the Favoured did. I just skipped over the last few lines, the part about magick's Favoured and Ragnarok happening again. Whoever has Draupnir thinks that is what is happening now. I am magick's Favoured because my favouring is just that – pure magick. It has no elemental or emotional or any other parts, and I am now unbound. They think that me being here means that the Spell of Favouring is going to end and Ragnarok is coming. The Disir, Bergelmir, all of them are just waiting. They are trying to make moves they think will help push it along. That is what Cassie sensed Lena and Lev wanted to do after they connected with Draupnir. Maybe that is why they became Disir – to help end the Spell of Favouring."

Cassie had been chewing noisily, trying to block out the Prelate's overwhelming sense of hurt as she thought about her sisters, but she stopped mid bite. "End? It can't end. I always thought that part was just fluff." She looked to the Queen and Prelate, but neither spoke. "Right? I mean, that spell keeps us all alive. It's why we even have our favouring to begin with. If it ends, if Ragnarok happens again, won't that be the end of... well, everything?"

The Prelate nodded. Her eyes were not sad or frightened though. She had a look of firm determination as if she were sizing up her enemy. "Perhaps. The Norn's words always have a variation of truth to them. Even if we were to study it for a century, we still could not fathom the depths that the Norn placed within the spell when they wrote it. We need to gain knowledge, knowledge that only the Norn possess."

"Well, can we ask them?" Everyone turned to look at Amanda. "Let's stop waiting around for the next syirce or Disir attack and go directly to the Norn to get some answers. Maybe what they tell us can help us figure out how to stop the Spell of Favouring from ending, or how to prevent Ragnarok. They can also tell us how the traitor knew who the first Favoured of Mani and Sol were to be."

For all her grace, Queen Frigga couldn't help hide a moment of fatigue as she pushed more magick into the air around them to feed the barriers to seal the realm. "That may be wise, but it would be most dangerous. I would go myself, or send the Prelate, as we would be the best to stand against the Norn and their tricks, but we are needed here. I cannot leave without leaving the realm completely open."

"Then let *us* go, Queen Frigga. The five of us will go to the Norn, and get the answers we need. Amanda's vision spoke of trees with golden leaves. That's the Norn's home. Maybe the twin stone was telling us that is where Draupnir was taken from Asgard. Send us to go defend the realm as you just said we need to do." Sean brought his fist to his chest.

Connor nodded and did the same. "We'll beat it out of them if we have to."

The Prelate shook her head and then smiled. "From the mouths of mortals. My sisters are no doubt beating their shields in Valhalla with battle fervor at your words." The Prelate banged her gauntlets together. "Our enemies may think us on a path that leads to nothing but destruction, and are using it to help themselves, but we shall prove them wrong."

The Queen drew herself to her full height and held out a hand. "Let it be as you say. I grant you permission to travel to the Norn's forest and see what you can discover." With a small twist of power, Lord Odin's throne caused the map to shift and show the forest Amanda recalled was beyond Sigyn's tower. The trees swayed as the map focused on the details of the trees.

Prelate Tess beckoned them to stand around the floating map. "Here," she pointed a finger to an arched portal that was inset into the tree line, "is the gate to the mysterious woods, and the beginning of your mission."

Sean shook his head. "We will have to take some extra rune stones with us to help. Magick is like a porcupine in a dress shop there. It pokes holes into things you don't want it to."

"What Sean has said is true. Our magick does not always work properly within the confines of the Forest of Fates. Even my husband skirts the forest when he can, for he knows that the home of the Norn is just as fickle and capricious as they are. The Norn are beyond the gods as the gods are beyond mortals."

"You've been inside the forest before?" Amanda asked.

"Several times." Sean's answer was short and his face twisted while he looked down. "The last time, we were tasked to find fate stones – what the runes are made of. The stones are left behind by the Norn whenever they use their magick in this realm. I'll admit it would be a good place to mask bringing anything in and out of the city if they could get by the guards and through the shields where the forest meets the city. No offense, Queen Frigga, but who knows if your bindings even affect the forest."

Cassie had been silent for some time. "I can't believe I am even going to say this, but where is Lady Freyja? Shouldn't she be here for this? She's been in the forest more than anyone except for you Prelate Tess."

"Lady Freyja was sent to Yggdrasil to try to find where the gods and Lord Odin could be travelling through." Queen Frigga checked the sky above them. "We should hurry if you are to enter the forests."

***

"I still think it would be better if they had let Connor come with us. Five Favoured are always better than four." Her voice was light, but Cassie wasn't joking.

"I would agree, but the Prelate had a good point that he could probably help Lady Freyja with his connection to her brother." Sean adjusted the hammer hanging from his belt, and then the hood of his cloak. He had been even more fidgety since they left for the forest. He held a rune that guided them along the plains.

Cassie shaded her eyes to view the rising forest that was coming into full view as they crossed the plains in the dying light of the day. Mykola strode beside her, silent as always. His mood was even more stoic without Nimbus present. Mykola had made sure Nimbus knew to stay with Connor before they left. He didn't want to take a chance the Norn's magick would hurt the vindmare.

They had spent the rest of the late morning and into the afternoon learning about how to enter and exit the forest. The group had to enter as one during the hour of twilight and leave the forest same way by dawn.

The forest changed those that stayed within its confines for too long. The last person to enter the woods had left one minute too late and was never the same again. Amanda had asked about rainbowing there and back, but was told they could only use the rainbow portal in dire cases, as it was unknown where they would end up. Before they left, the Prelate gave them each a rune stone from her bag to help them while they made their way through the forest. Everyone except Mykola; rune stones never worked with his magick.

"Mykola wants to know if every has figured out what their rune stone is for." Cassie shook her head for her response while posing the question. "The rune didn't make any sense and nothing happened when I tried mine."

"Mine either. Probably something to do with the way they were made. I wouldn't waste any time worrying about it till we are in the forest. Just remember to follow my lead, OK?" Sean held up a separate set of rune stones guiding them through Idavoll toward the forest crowned with golden leaves.

Amanda's mind was torn between focusing on the mission and what the Prelate had told her before they had left Valaskjalf – her parents were missing. She assumed they were still in her room, and had asked the Prelate to see if the Einherjar could check on them. An hour later, one of the triad had come back and whispered something to the Prelate. The Prelate had looked over at Amanda, and then given the guard a few more instructions before coming over to relay the news. At first Amanda had been terrified that her parents had escaped or been eaten by one of the creatures on Asgard. The Prelate assured her that they would search the entire Stave until they found them.

"We're here."

Amanda looked up at Sean's words. She recognized the trees from her vision. The gate they stood before looked like a weaver's spinning wheel, wrapped in wisps of an airy fabric that looked like cotton before it was carded. The fabric rose and fell as if the gate was taking deep breaths and letting them out slowly. It wasn't the air that moved the fabric around the gate though, it was magick. A magick so deep Amanda could feel it resonate through her entire body.

"No wonder the forest changes those who enter it." Amanda whispered. "Can you feel it?"

"Creepy. Maybe we could just try to talk this all out with Bergelmir and the Norn over ice cream instead." Cassie tried to lighten the mood, but no one laughed.

Sean looked back to Cassie. "Now is not the time, Cassie. Be on your guard and be on time. You go in at sundown and you come out at sunrise."

Cassie cleared her throat. "Check. No problem. All we have to do is find three scary goddesses to give us some answers, right? That should be a walk in a... forest." The group shivered collectively, but no one moved.

The tendrils beckoned invitingly, but they reminded Amanda of a spider's invitation to a fly. Sean stood with his back to the group, the last of the day's light clinging to his cloak. Before them the shadows of the forest stood proud and imposing. It felt like silent eyes watched the small party within the hauntingly beautiful forest. A deathly stillness fell over the gate as the last of the red light streamed from the sky, followed by the burst of a light that marked the time of twilight. A pair of ghostly diamonds appeared like doorknobs to an invisible door.

"There they are, just like before." Sean drew in a deep breath and held it, as he reached forward and pushed one of the knobs.

"Any last words of advice?" Amanda looked to their leader. Prelate Tess knew there would be no objection, and they were all sure Sean wouldn't have it any other way, so she had given Sean the lead.

A strange expression was playing out on Sean's face, but the boy pushed it away and brought his hammer up as he stepped through the doorway. "Don't get lost."

"Well, duh." Cassie rolled her eyes and followed.

As each one passed through, they turned to shadows just beyond the door. Amanda was the last, but before she followed, she called forth her little green light and perched it onto her shoulder. "Stay with me, little guy, I have a feeling we are going to need you."

CHAPTER 21:
THE NORN'S FOREST

Amanda gazed in awe at the forest around them. She realized she had been on Asgard long enough to think of it as normal, but walking through the portal to the Norn's realm quickly reminded her that there were stranger places beyond what she had so far experienced. A cascade of golden leaves slowly drifted down upon them. Where they landed, the leaves broke apart and became rivulets of gold before being absorbed into the soil. A flock of small glowing creatures buzzed by their heads, giggling like school children at recess. The tiny sparks of lights formed the shape of a large butterfly and then tore apart in opposite directions, leaving streams of light fading behind them. The forked leaves that swayed above the iridescent trees formed a cloud of gold, silencing all sound except for the giggling flies. When they vanished the air hung heavy around them. Amanda could feel the weight on her shoulders, like her cloak was absorbing the essence of the forest's silence. The only light came from the trees themselves, their white bark illuminating in a ripple along four paths that spread out from where the party had entered. Amanda sent her own glowing ball of light out, but it quickly faded and she was unable to call it back to life.

"Are those sprites?" Cassie was peering through the trees. "Maybe this place won't be so bad after all. If you catch one, they are supposed to bring you luck."

Mykola nodded. He unhooked his staff and looked like a seasoned explorer setting off for adventure as he tested the ground with butt end of the pole. The changeable creatures reappeared and began darting between the dense trunks, changing forms as they passed behind each tree. One minute Amanda thought she saw a bird with a long fiery tail, and the next she saw a manta ray with a small purple rider on its back. One of the white trees shook beside Mykola, and he reached out a palm to its smooth bark. Sean took in a sharp breath as Mykola made contact with the ancient tree. For a moment nothing moved, and then his gloved hand began to glow, as the iridescence of the tree was drawn into the fabric. Mykola pulled his hand back to reveal a white palm print that glowed on the bark like an afterimage. It reminded Amanda of when she had touched the sides of the Green Askr.

"Whoa!" Sean rushed up just short of grabbing a hold of Mykola's hand as he reached out again. "Probably best to not touch too much in here. Those gloves are enchanted to help keep your magick in check, but here in the forest it looks like they aren't much help. You're our back up in case the Norn turn on us or the forest does, so let's not get the forest worked up about us being here right from the get-go. I'd say now is a good time for everyone to try out their rune stones that the Prelate gave us."

Mykola made a show of his hands and then backed away from Sean while he and the others pulled their runes out and held them up together. The stones were gnarled and each bore a single rune that looked like the face of a grumpy old man. Sean's stone began glowing and suddenly his hammer began to crackle with electricity. Cassie gasped and put a hand to her head as her rune stone began to give off a faint glimmer of light. Amanda watched the others and waited as she tried to use her magick to call forth the stone's power. A moment later she could feel her own magick come pouring through the stone and slam into her body. The trees around her became brighter and she could hear and see magick weaving through her, her friends and the forest.

Sean was the first to recover. "I feel like I just chugged the biggest bottle of cough syrup and Red Bull. When I was in here before, it took hours before I felt like I had any kind of charge, but these stones must help get us hooked up to our favouring faster – like a lightning rod."

"Might have helped if the Prelate had warned us," Mykola frowned slightly and Cassie blinked at him as she fought to regain her senses. "Nothing to be jealous of, Mykola. I know you can't turn yours off, but getting your favouring turned off and on feels like someone forced us through a blender and then tried to put us back together."

There was too much going on around them for her to concentrate, so Amanda decided to pocket her rune stone, losing her connection to her favouring. It felt strange, and she felt like she had lost one of her senses, but she wanted to focus.

Sean's face was tight, and he was rattling several rune stones together. The rune the Prelate had given him was tucked into the wrappings around the hilt of his hammer. "The Prelate said these rune stones were the first ever created from the fate stones given to the Asgardian people by the Norn. They no longer work but the Prelate said they should be able to sense the Norn's presence." The stones in his hand began to move slowly, like twitching insects, inching this way and that, and then skittering to the edge of Sean's palm toward the path to the left. "Those paths wind through the forest like a maze. Take the wrong turn and we'll end up right back here, so we need to keep together and follow the stones' directions carefully. We'll need to keep an eye out for fyglja as well. They are more likely to appear as we get closer to the goddesses, and they are definitely not good luck. Remember, if they touch you, they can steal your fate. The Norn are supposed to control our fate, but a person without one will never leave this forest alive." Sean looked the group over as if guessing who would fall first.

"How will we know if we're in here too long?" Amanda was looking up through the trees and the darkness of night was barely visible.

Sean held up one final rune stone. It was blood red, but as they watched the face of the stone cracked and a flake of red dropped to reveal white stone underneath. "Once this is all white, we need to be out of here."

After the warning they all gladly let Sean take point, keeping quiet except for the swish of their cloaks. Amanda felt something brush by her cheek, and she tried to fight off the urge to check for invisible spiders. As they walked, Amanda looked around into the forest for any sign of an immortal goddess. "What do the Norn look like?"

"No one knows what they really look like. Stories say they can look like anyone past, present, or future." Sean swung his hammer, which was glowing to light their way, at a sparkling at an unruly clump of grass in his path.

Amanda watched as the blades that had come loose from Sean's swing drifted lazily to the ground and knit themselves back into the soil. "What do we know about the Norn?" In all of her reading and trying to catch up, Amanda couldn't remember much being written on the mysterious goddesses.

"They are the embodiment of time. Each goddess represents a different phase of life of the person they are talking to. Urd represents what has been, Verdandi, what is, and Skuld, what is to come. The Norn spin their magickal web, entangling all in a pattern only they know, and trap those in the fates they deem fit. It was the Norn who first prophesied Ragnarok, and it was Skuld who showed the Valkyrie the spell of preservation that saved the universe from Surtur's destructive pyre. But since the Great Rebirth, none of the goddesses have been seen." Amanda stared at Cassie as she finished. "What? I thought they were cool."

The conversation lapsed as the forest collapsed in around their path, creating tunnels where the trees bent and braided over one another. Absentmindedly Amanda began brushing her hair from her face and tapping the sides of her cheek. With each step, she began to hear whispers in her mind and feel more and more like she had been plugged into an electric outlet. The buzz made her head feel fuzzy yet alert at the same time. Amanda reached for her rune stone and summoned just enough magick to call forth her little green light, its presence giving her mind something to focus on.

"Twinkle, twinkle little fuzzy." Cassie stumbled as she swatted at a floating ball of twigs and leaves. "Pretty sprites."

None of the others seemed to notice, but Sean looked even more strained, as if he were ready to smash anything that crossed their path. Cassie and Mykola slowly halted to gaze at the trees beside them. Amanda waited for them to move, but when they didn't, Amanda spoke up.

"Cassie, are you guys feeling alright?" Amanda sputtered out the words like a racecar engine, as if she couldn't get the words out fast enough. When Cassie ignored her, Amanda grabbed her shoulder.

"Yowza!" Cassie jumped like she had been shocked and danced around for a moment rubbing her arm. "What in the name of the Crown Jewels of London did you do that for?"

"I didn't do anything. You were ignoring me." Amanda fidgeted with her collar.

"Pipe down you two, I think I hear something." Sean stalked over to a pair of trees and began snooping around like a basset hound looking for game.

"But Amanda bloody well electrocuted me." Cassie pouted.

Amanda shook her head to try and rid it of the excess noise coming from the trees. "Guys, something is wrong. Can't you feel it?" Mykola gave a dismissive wave, and then stopped to wiggle his fingers like he was conducting a symphony. Amanda slapped his hand and Mykola jumped just as Cassie had. "See? It has to be the magick in the forest."

Sean thought for a moment and then slowly shook his head. "Maybe it's a defense mechanism of some kind. But why would it go off now?"

"What if we get stuck in here? We have to get out of here now!" Cassie was starting to panic and, now that her head had been cleared, her magick was sending out emotional waves that were washing away the forest's magick.

Amanda connected with her rune stone and sent her transference spell to suck the magick from the air around them. "*Transityr.*" A gong sounded in Amanda's head and the air rebounded back on her, sending her to her knees.

"Careful, Amanda, nothing works like you think it should, even with the runes." Sean slurred the last few words and then froze.

Amanda tried to get up, but her cloak felt like it was nailed into the dirt. "Cassie. Help!"

Cassie nodded several times and held out shaky hands with her rune stone cupped in between them. "Alright, Mister or Missus forest, whatever you are, stop this at once!" Nothing happened. "It isn't working!"

"You're too anxious. It has to be getting in the way." Amanda had dropped her rune stone, severing her from her favouring, but she still felt like her body was a live wire for magick. She swung her head toward Mykola as a thought hit her. She reached out and grabbed onto the dark-haired boy's foot.

Mykola's eyes widened and he tried to jump back, but Amanda tightened her grip onto his boot. The magickal build up in Amanda's veins flowed through to Mykola, shocking him awake from whatever spell they were under. As his head began to clear Amanda could see him process what was happening.

"Mykola… we need to fix this… neutralize it. Can you do that?"

Mykola nodded once to Amanda and she let go. The boy stood tall and began to twirl his staff over his head, his hair swinging with the movement of the air. Each pass of the white wood sent a wave of magick around the group. After a minute, Mykola paused and placed a palm to the ground, sending a ripple through the underbrush that turned the ground white.

Instantly Amanda's felt her body lighten. Cassie and Sean began to blink rapidly as they woke up from the forest's spell. "Well done, Mykola. I think the trees were trying to distract us, but without my favouring my body just took the magick it sent our way in until it could find a way out. That must have been the shock you felt, Cassie. The forest must be trying to keep us from getting close to the Norn."

"Quick thinking, Amanda." Sean touched his fist to his chest. Amanda felt a small swell of pride. She had impressed herself too. "I'll admit it makes sense. That must be why whenever I was in here before, I felt like I wanted to be anywhere but here."

"A forest can't want anything. Can it?" Cassie stepped back from a branch that hung by her head.

"You tell us. Do you feel anything?" Sean was holding the rune stones out in front of him, making sure they hadn't gone off course.

A slowly rising roar poured through the trees, sending a cloud of murky air up to the line of Mykola's circle. Mykola shuddered and pointed in the opposite direction. The trees had parted to reveal another path.

"I don't need any magick to feel that. I think we made the forest mad. I believe the expression is 'follow the yellow brick road' right?" Cassie and the others ran quickly from the dying noise. As they moved, the white outline of Mykola's magick followed them.

After an hour they paused on a hill. Below them, spread out like grounded stars, were thousands of glowing portals just like the ones they conjured when they traveled by rainbow. These portals were of all various sizes, some just big enough for one to pass through and the largest looked like the entire group of Favoured could have entered side by side. The path they had been following splintered apart into a tangled maze that looked like a board game as it twisted toward an unknown ending.

"Is that beacon of yours doing any dancing?" Cassie peered towards Sean's palm, but the stones weren't moving.

"It stopped when I got to the top of this hill. I think it has something to do with that." Sean pointed to the ground beneath them. A large rune was etched into the forest floor.

"Choose?" Amanda looked up to make sure her translation was correct.

"Choose what?" Mykola answered, as Cassie spoke to the group.

"Maybe if we choose the right portal it will take us to the Norn." Amanda tried to see beyond the edge of the valley. "Let's go see if we can find anything that will tell us which one is the right one to choose."

Amanda paired up with Sean, and Cassie with Mykola, and they made their way down to where the path split into its tendrils of choices. Stopping at a portal that looked just about her size, Amanda peered around the edges, which were ringed in light. Stepping beside the portal, Amanda looked at it from different angles, even inspecting the forest floor for markings, but there was nothing to differentiate it from any of the others.

"How much power do you think has gone into creating each of these portals?" Amanda spoke more to herself than the others. Sean could only shrug his shoulders. After investigating several more portals, they turned back to regather on the hill.

"One of them has to be different, or else how will we know which one to choose? The only one that felt different was that large one on the other side." Cassie put her hands on her hips in frustration. Mykola nodded in agreement.

Amanda looked over to the portal Cassie was pointing to. It was a bit larger than your average size portal, but other than that it was identical to the others. "I didn't sense anything different about it, did you Sean?"

Sean remained silent. He was kneeling beside a tree, trying to think. A welcome breeze rustled through its leaves. It had been muggy inside the forest until now, so the temperature change was welcome until Amanda spotted what it had brought with it. A group of white figures were now clustered on the opposite side of the valley and were starting to move quickly toward them.

Quietly Amanda asked, "Are those fyglja?"

Sean leapt back from the tree he had crouched under. The ghostly forms slithered like a nest of snakes around the portals, getting closer and closer. Mykola unhooked his staff from his back and drove it into the ground before taking off his gloves.

Sean brought his hammer forward, "Everyone get ready!"

"What do we do?" Amanda backed away as the fyglja surrounded them and began slowly circling just beyond the protective border Mykola had placed around the four of them.

"Mykola, do you think your defenses will hold if they attack?" Sean watched as the fyglja circled, his eyes watching for signs of aggression. Mykola shook his head. Sean held up his hammer and began charging it. He sent a small jolt of lightning through Mykola's protection, but it passed harmlessly through the revolving spirits. "Amanda, I want you to try to cast your fire spell, like you did with the imps. See if it will take them out or at least get them away from us."

Amanda reached into her cloak. "Oh no! I left my rune stone back when I grabbed Mykola!"

Sean bit his lip. "We can't risk Mykola dropping his protection of us just yet. Cassie. Can you sense anything? Think they will obey you?"

Cassie held out her hands and sent a wave of magick toward the fyglja.

"Leave us be!"

When nothing happened, Sean shook his head. "Alright, then. I'll distract them while you all try to get as far away from here as possible."

"We need to stick together, Sean. We aren't going to leave you behind to fight something you can't touch." Amanda felt the grimoire in her cloak and tried to recall anything that could help them, but without her magick the spells were useless. "If we run, we run together. We can take the portal on the far end and hope we get it right. Hopefully they won't be able to follow us."

One of the fyglja opened its mouth wide and roared. The same murky air from earlier flew from its open maw and curled around the edges of the circle. Sean looked to each of them and nodded. "Looks like we don't have a choice. We go through the gap on their next pass. Now!"

Leaping forward, Amanda slid halfway down the hill and then sprinted as fast as she could towards the closest portal. The fyglja screamed like a pack of hungry jackals and took off after them. Running was never Amanda's strong suit, but her time training on Asgard had definitely improved her athletic abilities and coordination. She kept pace with Sean, her hair flying behind her with their cloaks, the portals leaving dancing spots in her vision as they passed by. Cassie and Mykola managed to make it ahead of them and lead the way.

"Almost there, keep going!" Sean sped up and jumped over a pile of branches.

They had almost made it when Amanda made the mistake of looking back to see how close the fyglja were. She crashed into a pile of stones that formed the perfect tripping hazard. Before anyone could react, Amanda stumbled through a smaller portal to her side. The swirling colors blinded Amanda as she screamed and fell through the tunnel. When the lights vanished, Amanda found herself in a dark cavern with a glowing honeycomb of facets on the walls like an electrified beehive. Scenes flashed on each pane, and Amanda was surprised to see Wreathen's town square, which was now starting to see some patches of dry grass through the snow. Another pane blinked as it showed a dark dungeon where a lone, dark figure sat. Amanda panted to catch her breath and swallowed hard. Light shone down on her from an opening in the ceiling.

"Cassie, Mykola... Sean?" The sound of her voice echoed around her on the translucent walls.

A voice like the sound of a spring rain floated from behind Amanda. "Hello, Amanda Elizabeth West. We have been expecting you."

CHAPTER 22:
THE FATES OF AMANDA

Sweat began to gather on her brow as Amanda turned slowly. Hot wind blew in her face, causing her to squint as her eyes watered. When she opened them they were filled with the sight of three goddesses, each wearing her face. The smallest of the goddesses, who Amanda assumed to be Urd, looked like Amanda did when her family first moved to Wreathen. She had worn the polka-dot dress on her fourth birthday, and Jack had told her she looked like a red and white leopard. The middle figure looked to be only a little bit older than Amanda was now, but she was terrifying. Cassie had said Verdandi represents what is, but this version of her looked like pure evil. Wreathed in green flames, the goddess's eyes glittered like silver moons. Skuld was the final goddess and stood tall and proud, but was dressed plainly in the robes of an Aesir. The goddess of what is to come had lines around her eyes that made her look like Amanda's mother after a stressful day at the store. She held the golden disc of flames that the gods and Favoured wore, but it was crumpled as if it had been crushed.

Of the three goddesses, Urd was the only one who seemed familiar. The other two goddesses frightened her because she felt something menacing in how they presented her future self. Each goddess radiated magick that, as it touched Amanda, made it so she could almost see what they were thinking – and they were not pleased.

"Can you not recognize yourself?" Verdandi rose from the platform where they stood. It was carved from solid gold into the form of a crashing wave. Floating toward her, the goddess of the present spoke again, "What you cannot see, we can see for you. 'Tis time you come face to face with your destiny."

"We know what you have come for, Amanda, Favoured of the goddess Sigyn, and what it is you unknowingly need. You seek to ask us of a spell wrought by the Valkyries, and to know who is behind the actions that are unfolding within the Nine Realms that lead to destruction. There is more to be found if you have eyes to see." Urd stood with her hands clasped, an unseen wind sending her pigtails flying. The goddess of what was pointed to a cluster of the hexagonal panels, which shifted to show Amanda and Jack on the bus to the museum, the attack by Bergelmir and Jack's capture, and then a frozen prison where a boy lay amongst a pile of frozen rugs.

Amanda felt her heart skip several beats. "Jack?" His clothes were tattered but she knew it was him instantly from his denim wardrobe. He appeared to be unharmed and his skin had turned pink again. "He's alive?"

"Aye, your friend is mostly unharmed, and will soon be returned to your realm. However, be warned. It will cost you to bring him back. He currently belongs body and soul to the Jotuns." Skuld stood still, like a living statue, with eyes that held no emotion except regret.

"What do you mean? How can I help him?" Amanda felt a wave of despair and then anger come from the goddesses as they looked to one another at Amanda's question.

"To truly help him and the Nine Realms, you should leave this place and hide from any who want you to use your magicks. The boy's bonds can be broken by that which made them. Shall we tell her the rest, sisters?" Urd giggled.

"Why save her the grief that is to come? It shall mold her to be what our prophecy started centuries ago – a destroyer. The one to turn all the realms over to the fires within." The cackle that Verdandi issued sounded like Ms. Biggs after giving them a pop quiz.

"She does not believe us. I say we let our minions have her and wait for it to be done with." Urd had begun to skip down steps that were sculpted in the side of the platform.

"No. She must be told. Your destiny is to be the one who will break the realms, in order for the shadow of the past to be forever cleansed. In your path lies destruction, ruin, and death. The Spell of Favouring will end by your hand. You will bring about Ragnarok and end all mortal lives." Skuld lifted her chin and gray hair swept down to one side.

"So it's true." Amanda felt like she had been punched in the stomach. "But there has to be a reason why. I would never deliberately hurt anyone." Amanda looked to each of the goddesses, but their eyes only glowed with a dark intensity.

"Maybe not now, but soon you will find a reason. The Jotuns are but the first in a dark wave that shall sweep through the realms, bringing back the chaos and misery from before your time began, and you will bear the responsibility for it. Do you think that what transpires about the World Tree is not of your fault?"

"That was someone else! Please, you have to tell me how to keep the Spell of Favouring safe, stop Ragnarok from happening again, and save Jack and everyone else. Or at least tell us who the Disir is that took Draupnir so we can stop the alfblot and syirces and keep the realm safe." Amanda was fighting with the range of emotions that were coming from the goddesses as they buffeted her with their magick.

As one the goddesses all stilled. "There is no saving the spell. You will bring about Ragnarok."

"Never! Tell me something! If the Spell of Favouring is destroyed, won't that mean the end of the Nine Realms? Is that what you want?"

"You seek a splinter when it is the door you should look for. There are more than the traitors that lie in your midst, more than those from Niflheim that now conspire on Midgard and Asgard to invade this realm, and more than a ring that now resides in the mortal realm to be concerned for. They are but pawns in the great weaving of this spell, and the least of what is to come." Verdandi laughed and pointed to the panels behind Amanda.

Horrific images of wars flickered to life at her command. Dark figures swarmed around the edges of each panel; one in particular that even the light seemed to hide from. Bergelmir and his army of Jotuns roared and beat their chests as they advanced on Asgard and then Midgard. Yggdrasil stood empty of its leaves and was burning with green flames. Finally all of the panels showed Amanda as Verdandi depicted her. The flames that surrounded her engulfed the Nine Realms as she raised her arms.

"Accept your fate. All this must come to pass. You will bring more death than your benefactor ever did." Skuld looked down like a disapproving judge.

"There has to be another way." Amanda pleaded desperately.

As one the Norn began to speak, "*In this time and in this place, take this life to save one of Odin's race. Through sacrifice we submit our thrall, and give her our power, one and all. To wait till the hundredth year whilst the fires of Surtur burn clear. A guardian of nothing will she be, chained until twilight's time is free. By the power of Yggdrasil's life and death the rebuilding shall be made done and we call forth the Favoured to be spun. But all be warned by the Norn, when newly found of magicks Favoured be unbound, again the fire of Ragnarok will come round.*"

"I know the spell, but how does that help?"

Again the goddesses spoke, "*Then will the dark mark awaken, and the dark Favoured be forsaken. For life to be restored, death will meet death, mortal and god will be joined, and Surtur's joy will give way to mourn. Find the hate within to win this tale for all mortals' hearts to be quelled, and the required favouring be at end.*"

"You know all you shall need." Verdandi smiled with black lips and a wave of fyglja swept into the room. They coalesced into a dark gray portal in front of Amanda. "Best be on your way; your friends are in need of you."

"Remember our words." Urd waved to Amanda.

"All our fates hang upon it. Tell your mistress we bear her no ill will and soon her prison shall be her heart's desire. Her sacrifice has not been in vain." Skuld turned away from Amanda as another gust of hot wind picked her up and sent her headfirst into the void.

Unlike rainbow travel this journey was instantaneous, and Amanda found herself screaming as she stared at a startled Cassie, Sean, and Mykola. Sean grabbed Amanda and pulled her down hard. "Watch out!"

Just as Sean had pulled her to safety, a swarm of flying shapes raced above their heads. At first Amanda thought they were fyglja, but the squealing chirp made her stomach clench as she realized they were wyrms. After they passed, the group stood and Amanda got up to examine their surroundings.

"Where are we?" She brushed brown dust from her hair and reached up to touch a dirt ceiling that was interlaced with roots. She was reeling from her brief encounter with the goddesses, and very glad to be away from them.

"Where are we? Where were you? You look like you were sucked through a vacuum cleaner." Cassie examined Amanda. "You fell through that one portal, so we followed. It brought us here, but you weren't here. We've been looking for you for hours."

"Hours? I was with the Norn for just a few minutes. The portal I fell through took me to them." Amanda sniffed as the tang of earth reached her nose. Her voice felt unsteady.

Sean grabbed Amanda by the arm. "You found the Norn? Are you OK? Did they tell you anything?" His mood had gone from anxious to almost completely unglued.

Amanda hesitated. "They said dark things are coming, the Jotuns and something else. They didn't have much to say about Draupnir, but I think it's somewhere on Midgard. They spoke in so many riddles it was hard to tell what they were saying." Amanda felt lightheaded and held up a hand. "I'll tell you the rest later, but we were right – Ragnarok is coming and the Spell of Favouring is going to end. And there is no way to stop it." No one spoke for a minute. "They did show me Jack. He's still alive, but under Bergelmir's control."

"I guess that is good news. Although not sure how much it helps if we are all meant to die." Cassie translated for Mykola.

"Down!" Sean hauled both girls to the floor while Mykola pressed into the side of the tunnel. Another pack of wyrms flew by. "Let's get out of here and we can talk about the rest of it. We've only got an hour before sunrise." Sean looked down. The rune stone he showed them held only a small section of red. "And we also have to be on guard. One of us managed to let out a group of trapped wyrms that have been following us to try and eat us." Sean frowned at Cassie.

"I said I was sorry. I tried to make them go back in, but my magick wasn't strong enough to handle them all." Cassie huffed, and looked to Mykola for sympathy. Mykola cocked his head to the side and motioned for them to follow.

Sean helped the girls up. "Next time, don't push anything unless you know what it does."

No one spoke as the collective pace moved them along as quickly as the low-ceilinged tunnel would allow for. They passed several stony outcroppings that looked similar to the gnomes in the Isens' yard; Sean marked each of them with a rune, glaring at Cassie if she accidentally touched one. The tunnel shrunk a bit, and for a while they walked hunched over, each grabbing their own cloak so the person behind them wouldn't step on it. Finally, the tunnel opened up to what looked like a more civilized cave.

Wood paneling on the floors and walls bore large white metal spikes that were hammered through the boards into the stone underneath. The walls sloped outward from the floor and then up to the ceiling, which drew their attention. From an unseen source above a river of water rushed down toward them. The water would have drenched them completely, but a crystalline trough redirected it toward the end of the tunnel where it turned again and fell into a large ring of stones that resembled Mimir's well. Mykola pointed toward the well and then at small alcoves along the walls. Basins covered in gold leaf held smaller founts of water from offshoots from the raging river above. A golden raven in flight was perched on each basin, looking as if it would carry the water it caught behind it into the air.

"Look!" Cassie pointed through the spraying water to a light that looked like it came from the forest trees. It was barely visible, but they could see it where the floor beyond the well swept up toward the ceiling and an opening.

"An exit at last." Mykola signed with relief, and Cassie nodded as she spoke and drew her hood over her head. A cold mist was falling on them steadily, mixing with the dirt and soil they had just trudged through.

"Just in time." Sean sighed.

"What's that?" Amanda pointed not in the direction of the end of the tunnel, but at one of the basins on the left side of the larger pool. An emerald hung from the beak of the raven. It looked like a large cat's eye setting on a golden band.

"It's a ring! It's Draupnir!" Cassie clapped excitedly.

"Draupnir is on Midgard and not an emerald," Amanda said trying not to get caught up in the excitement from her friend. Amanda began walking toward the shimmering stone. "It does have power, though. I can hear it. Maybe we could use it to help us find our way out of the forest in time."

"Stop!" Sean's commanding voice made Amanda pause. "The rune above it says, 'Do not remove'." Sean pointed his hammer toward an etching above the basin.

Amanda moved to turn away, but the ring's gleam drew her back, pushing Sean's voice from her head. Something within the emerald spoke to her, promising to aide her. She fought with herself, reeling from the revelations the Norn had shown her, and the desperate need she felt to find any hope to cling to. Amanda's fingers hovered an inch from the ring as she fought to hold her hand back, but the ring was pulling her like a magnet. Unable to resist, she rested her hand on the ring. Upon making contact she could feel the power inside the ring react to her touch. Pulling it free from the bird's beak Amanda backed away slowly and then turned back to the group.

The emerald was small, but so full of power. Even through her glove, the power of the jewel's magick tingled down to the palm of her hand. Amanda smiled and looked up to the group to see them looking extremely alarmed. Mykola was unlacing his gloves and pointing at something behind her, Cassie was yelling at her, and Sean was spinning his hammer furiously. The ring beckoned to her again and she stared down at it. Whispering words entered her mind again, and she felt the ring's power soften as if it realized who held it. The gold band fell apart into a long thin chain. Something tapped Amanda's shoulder and she brushed it aside, scratching the back of her hand on something sharp. Amanda froze as a reflection solidified in the facets of the stone she held. With a scream, Amanda leapt toward her friends. A wyrm the size of an elephant hovered where Amanda had stood a second before.

"I told you not to touch the ring! When will you all start listening to me? It appeared as soon as you took it." Sean was pushing them toward the exit behind them, keeping himself between them and the wyrm. The giant wyrm unhinged its jaw and began snapping at them furiously, only kept at bay by Sean's hammer and electrical jolts as he blocked each attack. The wyrm hissed after it was blocked again and launched itself into the air to begin dive-bombing them as they ran toward the opening.

Circling around them, the wyrm cut them off from their escape. It dove once at Amanda and Cassie, and Mykola reached out a hand to stop its descent. The wyrm shrieked and backed away. The necklace pulsed and Amanda could feel its magick connect to something inside of her.

She held up the necklace and cried out, "*Fieryr!*" Fire shot forth from the necklace as it dangled from her hand, and the wyrm beat backward into the ceiling, trying to retreat.

Recovering quickly, the wyrm started to push back against Amanda's attack. Just as it opened its mouth to bite down on Amanda's outstretched hand, Sean jumped from an outcropping of rock he had climbed and brought his hammer down in an arc. The wyrm tried to dodge, but it misjudged its spacing and collided with the water flowing from the river above and was washed down into the large well. Not wanting to waste an unexpected reprieve, they ran up and out through the opening in the ceiling. As the forest's muggy air washed over the group, they collapsed, panting and holding their sides. Amanda held up the necklace to make sure it had survived unscathed and then laid her hand down on top of it.

"Way to go, Amanda!" Cassie yelled in between gasps. "How about you listen to Sean next time?"

"Sorry. Whatever this is called to me. It said it could help."

Sean rolled over. "It better! That was one macdaddy wyrm it released. So, it is either really helpful or really bad."

Mykola was the first to get up and motioned for them to look around. Sean's jaw dropped and he slowly came up to one knee. Around them stood twelve statues of warrior women with winged gauntlets around their wrists. Each held a spear that was buried into a stone podium and stood at an angle away from their armored bodies. Beside them stood winged horses rearing up, like they were about to take flight.

"These are statues of the twelve Valkyrie that sacrificed themselves at the end of Ragnarok. They gave their power along with the Favouring Spell to bring the universe back to life." Sean reached up and touched one of the shafts of the spears reverently.

Amanda studied the closest face beside her. Its bearer had a long braid down her back and a studded shield that was slung over her shoulder. The words from the Norn whispered in Amanda's ear, '...and give to her our power one and all'.

"Brunhilda is the one in front of you, Amanda. She was a mortal like us that found a way to Asgard disguised as an Aesir. Once she was there she trained to become an apprentice to the Valkyrie Birghid. Birghid knew what she was, but she saw how valiantly she fought and convinced Lady Freyja to make her immortal and a true Valkyrie." Sean brought his fist to his chest.

"Guys, look!" Cassie was still pointing to the statues, but she had walked over to the center dais, which was empty save for a pile of small glittering moons. "Fate stones! We can use this to help get out of here. If we have enough of them we can use it to focus the rainbow portal." Cassie smiled and picked up one of the stones from the pile and tossed it in the air.

As the stone hit Cassie's hand she was yanked backward by her cloak. Three wyrms had grabbed the hem and were hauling her toward a rustling bush. Two more wyrms dove from above the statue of Brunhilda and knocked Amanda backward with their tails. Sean dodged an attack as a wyrm screeched by his head. Recovering quickly, he threw his hammer to smash the wyrms holding Cassie's cloak into the stone podium. Mykola arrived just as one of the wyrms moved to take a bite out of Amanda's foot. Taking the crook of his staff, he hooked the wyrm's neck and spun to throw it toward Cassie, who had jumped to her feet.

Knocking a few twigs from her hair she glared angrily at the wyrms and drew a deep breath. "Make mincemeat of yourselves, you buggering snakes!" The wyrms turned and began to snap at one another.

Amanda held up the necklace, but before she could cast her spell a pair of wyrms barreled into her. Cassie drew up beside her and commanded the wyrms to fight the others. "We got this, Amanda. Go grab as much fate stone as you can so we can get out of here!"

Amanda raced to the dais and started to scoop up as many of the stones as she could, which looked like glittering lumps of coal, and put them into her cloak. Around her she could hear the others begin to taunt their attackers as the battle fervor began to reach each of them. A small wyrm jumped out from the stones and Amanda stepped back.

Amanda held up the necklace again and cried out, "*Fieryn!*"

Green flames danced from the necklace and made the small wyrm vanish under its heat. Amanda ended the spell, but the flames didn't stop. Her spell took on a life of its own, spreading to the other wyrms battling her friends. When the flames ignited from within, the wyrm would explode in a burst of green ooze. Sean's hammer and the green fire met together, catching the last enemy beneath the brunt force and ferocious heat.

"I didn't see that coming!" Sean crowed, but his face froze as he looked down at the rune keeping track of their time. "We need to leave *now!*"

"Everyone think of where we first came through to the forest. I doubt we can make it through to the plains, but I will get us as close as I can." Cassie placed a hand on the stones and drew the portal with the other.

Clutching her cloak, they all ran through the portal. The doors to the Plains of Idavoll stood before them. Its outline and the handles were barely visible. "Come on!" Amanda called, and they ran toward the doors.

As the last edges of night turned to rosy pink, they fell through the gate and onto the green grass of Idavoll. The light of the morning crested overhead and dawn broke over a pile of Favoured gasping for air for the second time that night. "So," Cassie wheezed, "can we go to sleep now?"

They all laughed and picked themselves up off the dirt.

"You know," Amanda started and then stopped. She looked down at her hand, which had begun to burn. She took a step forward, and then her world turned upside down.

CHAPTER 23:
A HEALTHY HEARTH AND AN INNOCENT GODDESS

Amanda was running in a shapeless land filled with clouds that smelled like ash and death. Yggdrasil loomed like a hangman's tree in front of her, charred and broken with its large branches reaching out to her as if asking for help. A figure stood at the base of the tree holding something that glittered with blood-red light. Amanda tried to call out, but no sound came forth. The figure turned and Amanda's chest constricted as she recognized Jack, but he no longer looked like the friend she knew.

Jack no longer wore denim, nor looked at her with a mischievous twinkle in his eyes. This Jack looked malevolent and wore black armor. He held out a hand that looked like a bloody claw from the red light that it was bathed in. Amanda reached out to take the tiny object he held from him, trying to understand what had changed him, but the land solidified around them and she found herself suddenly standing in the plaza facing Mimir's well. Around her was nothing but debris and rubble, and the glass dome of Odin's palace was cracked open like an egg.

Darkness and cold overwhelmed her, and she shivered uncontrollably as a piercing finger of ice began to travel from her hand and into her body. The scene before Amanda changed again as it began replaying the image of Yggdrasil, Jack, and then the ruined city like a broken record. Amanda was rooted to the spot as she turned into a statue of ice. And then, like a spring thaw, a slow heat began to spread through her body, causing her skin to tingle. Amanda's eyelids fluttered and a hazy orange and black mixture replaced the dark vision.

"Hello?" Amanda's voice sounded scratchy, and her mouth felt like it was full of cotton balls.

"Welcome back, my poppet. Your journey to the nether realms is finally over." A face came into view above Amanda, topped by a large basket of brown hair that was threaded with gray, and tied back by white band. "I am Mette, and I welcome you back from Hel's gate."

The room came into focus, and Amanda found herself lying in a bed in a small, green room. A fire burned in a corner hearth, with specks of light and fire swarming from the heart of the flames towards Mette. The tiny orbs playfully made their way over the floor and up to the woman's palms, where she was holding a rune stone. The stone absorbed the little lights like a vacuum, glowing brighter with each orb it swallowed.

"Where am I?" Amanda's voice cracked. Mette produced a stein and poured some mead into Amanda's open mouth. "Thank you."

"My pleasure, child. You are tucked in safely at my lady Eir's Manor. You've had us quite worried. It took three of us to keep you from taking a trip to the afterlife." Mette looked like she was probably in her late forties, but Amanda knew she had to be thousands of years older and definitely an Aesir by the white robes trimmed in runes that she wore.

"I'm in the Manor?" Amanda swallowed another mouthful of the syrupy liquid.

"Yes, child. That nice boy, the Favoured of Prince Thor, and the others brought you here after that nonsense in the Norn's forest. It was a good thing, too. You were quite delirious, and the wyrm's venom was spreading quickly. I am surprised I have not met you sooner, what with you being the newest Favoured." Mette gave a soft laugh as if she had told a joke or shared a secret with Amanda.

Feeling some strength return, Amanda lifted her head to see more of the room she was in. The green coloring on the walls came from twisting vines that were dotted with small pink and red flowers. The bed was situated in the middle of the room under an oval window in the ceiling that glowed with warm light, and a rug that looked like it had been woven from fluffy cotton balls covered the wood floor.

"Now hold still dear, I am going to do one tiny adjustment." Watching Mette as she used the rune stone like a physician's flashlight, Amanda saw she had thick forearms and hands that looked worn smooth from constant use. Drawing a symbol with the rune stone in the air above the bed, the rune stone left tiny flames hanging above her like a constellation. Mette smiled and with a wave of her hands, sent a shower of tiny filaments down on Amanda. "How does that feel?"

Amanda felt her extremities being given life again and she groaned as the last bit of coldness left her. "Much better, thank you."

"Let's get you upright and see if you still want to thank me." Mette chuckled and hefted Amanda into a sitting position as if she weighed nothing more than a feather.

Sitting up made the room spin for a minute, and Mette caught Amanda's shoulders to help her from falling backward. With a few taps on her shoulder, neck, and forehead Amanda could sit without support. Amanda saw an ugly green star on the back of her hand between her thumb and forefinger, and held her fist up to Mette. "Is this from the wyrm?"

"It is. I am afraid it will always be there as no magick in any realm can remove it. You were lucky the wyrm's beak barely broke through your glove, and that your friends brought you here as soon as they did. Otherwise the wyrm's poison would have consumed you and your magick. The healing hearth of Eir, a couple of runes, and time were needed to draw it out and disperse it back to where it came from." The woman smiled and Amanda could smell lavender and eucalyptus wafting from her robes. "Yes, you will have a small scar, but it is better than losing the hand all together."

"I agree." Amanda stretched her fingers and shook her wrist gratefully. She felt like she had been sleeping for years, but all she wanted to do was lay back down onto the soft pillow. "Is everyone else OK?"

In answer there was an agitated knocking on the door. Mette turned and called through the paneled wood, "One moment." Turning back to Amanda, "You have had more visitors than most. Mistress Sigyn even sent her spectyr to check up on you. It gave some of the others a fright, but Sigyn and I have a history. She saved a friend of mine once. I am glad she has a Favoured."

"Really?" Amanda cradled her hand.

Mette smiled as she nodded, and opened the door to reveal several anxious faces. "Stay well until next we meet, Amanda."

Cassie flew into the room. Upon seeing Amanda, she burst into tears and she descended on Amanda with open arms. Amanda could feel her fear and worry through the hug – literally. "I'm OK, Cassie."

Mykola and Sean came in more calmly than Cassie, but both their faces held worried expressions. "Good to see you're feeling better. We've had to talk Cassie out of camping out here ever since we dropped you off."

Cassie hugged Amanda hard again and then stepped back, wiping her face. "I'm just so, so, so glad that you didn't bugger off."

"Um, yeah, me too." Amanda laughed. "Although, I do feel like someone left me in a bucket of ice and then microwaved me back to life. So, what happened? The last thing I remember was getting out of the forest."

"When we came through the gate you collapsed, so we brought you here. We didn't know about the scratch you'd gotten from that jumbo-wyrm until the healers saw you." Cassie touched Amanda's hand gingerly.

"I didn't even realize it myself. Thanks for taking care of me guys." Amanda hated that they were all staring at her, especially because she was only wearing a white robe that left her shins and feet exposed.

Mykola tapped the side of his head and pointed to the bed. Cassie sniffed and then translated. "Mykola wants to know if you had any weird dreams."

Amanda thought for a minute, "Just something about Jack and Yggdrasil." Amanda didn't know what she had seen meant, but she was sure it was tied to what the Norn had said to her. She knew she should say more to her friends about her connection to Ragnarok and the end of the Spell of Favouring, but she couldn't find the words to start.

"Getting bitten by a wyrm is supposed to give you some pretty cockamamie dreams according to the legends. If you survive, that is." Everyone turned to stare at Sean as if he'd just told them the sky was blue. Sean shifted uncomfortably on his feet as if he had stepped in vindsvolla droppings.

"Well, she's all better, right?" Cassie cocked her head and squinted at Amanda. "Hey, your eyes have changed."

"What do you mean?"

Cassie pulled a mirror from her cloak and held it up so Amanda could see. Her eyes had gone from a light shade of blue to almost metallic silver. Amanda swallowed as she felt her face flush. Her eyes looked just like Verdandi's.

Cassie moved her head from right to left examining the new look and nodded once. "I approve! Must be an aftereffect from the wyrm poison huh? Pretty original look I am guessing."

"I reckon so. Looks good on you, Amanda." Sean smiled, and then froze as everyone in the room turned to stare at him again. "I mean, for eyes and all."

Changing the subject quickly Amanda asked, "So how long was I out for?"

Cassie hiccupped, and brought a hand to her mouth. "You were in and out of it for four days."

"Four days?!" They all nodded and sat in silence for a minute letting Amanda process the news. "Did I miss anything?"

"The Prelate and the Queen weren't happy about what you told us about what the Norn said. They've been quite anxious to know what else they had to say. Queen Frigga tried using Lord Odin's throne to search for Jack and Draupnir, but no luck yet. Keeper Fulla didn't believe us, of course. She has been pouting ever since the Queen snapped at her." Cassie translated for Mykola.

"Prelate Tess had the spellmages make some new rune stones from the fate stones to help the gods travel faster through Yggdrasil's roots before it goes completely caput – and it's actually been working. Prince Thor and Lord Freyr were the first ones back, and they said Lord Odin isn't far behind them. Connor and I have had extra training sessions with Prince Thor and Lord Freyr now that they are back. That's where he is now. He's pretty ticked off that he keeps missing all the excitement but said to tell you this wouldn't let you off of your next rune war match."

Amanda laughed. Her sides ached a bit and she stretched to try and alleviate the pain. "How is it with them back?"

"Like working the farm on a hot day... by yourself... with only a rake when you need a shovel. They seem to be on edge about something, and they aren't saying what. The Prelate has been having more and more meetings inside Valaskjalf. I think they were hoping for more from our mission." Sean frowned and tapped his fingers on the hammer's handle.

Cassie scoffed. "What more could we have done? Amanda bloody well nearly died trying to get them the information we did get."

Sean held up his hands. "I know, but we still don't know who the first Disir is, and they can't find Draupnir, even though they know it's on Midgard somewhere. Not to mention they're worrying now about the Spell of Favouring." Sean folded his arms and looked to the floor as he spoke his next words carefully. "The Prelate announced we would be going through the Trials of Fenrir, which means they think there is going to be a real fight sometime soon. They are calling all the Favoured back from their assignments for it. We've been training for this, but the trials are supposed to be worse than anything we've faced before. It's like a final exam. Prince Thor told me the last time they had something like this there was a war going on in Alfheim that the Favoured had to fight in. It sounds like they are gearing up for something bad even though they say Lord Odin will be back, but I don't think he is going to make it before Queen Frigga runs out of steam. If that happens, anyone can get in, which might mean that the Disir could launch a full attack with Bergelmir or maybe even stop the Spell of Favouring."

Amanda thought back to her experience with the Norn. The three goddesses told her she would be the one to help bring Ragnarok about, but she didn't think that would help anyone to know that right now. Maybe she should leave to stop whatever was happening. But leaving meant that she wouldn't be able to save Jack, which is maybe what would turn him into what she saw in her dream. "Has anyone found my parents?"

Cassie laid a hand on Amanda's shoulder. "Not yet, but Agnarr is on the case now. He will find them soon, I am sure of it."

They all stayed silent, as Amanda closed her eyes. When she opened them again, Mykola gently motioned to Amanda to see if she were feeling up to leaving. Amanda nodded, but then looked down at her dressing gown and then to Cassie. "Can you help me with some new clothes?"

"No sweat." Cassie ran out and fetched the blue and gold tunic and pants to replace Amanda's medicinal getup. "And don't forget the necklace. The Prelate said it was yours since you found it, and almost died for it too. Let's get you back to the Stave. Nimbus has practically taken over your bed, but I am sure he will share."

***

The next day Amanda felt much better. Her hand and arm had a slight ache to it, but otherwise she was feeling well enough to make it to the Mead Hall and back. The Prelate stopped by in the morning with Keeper Fulla to check on Amanda. Keeper Fulla stood outside the door with runes to keep their conversation private, and barely sniffed in Amanda's direction until

Amanda got to the part about the Norn telling her that there was no stopping Ragnarok. That sent her into a full-on meltdown. Prelate Tess had to shut the door on the woman so Amanda could continue. Amanda tried, but she found she couldn't bring herself to tell the Prelate any more about the Norn's words and her future fate. So instead she skipped on to the part about the necklace and the wyrm. The Prelate mistook Amanda's pauses for fatigue, and so didn't press her. Afterwards they spoke briefly about the search for Draupnir and Jack.

Unfortunately, there wasn't much to tell, which left Amanda's stomach twisting as she thought of Bergelmir readying Jack to attack them. Before she left, Prelate Tess asked Amanda if she felt well enough to participate in the trials that evening. Amanda thought about it for a minute, and then nodded her head. Shortly thereafter the Prelate and Keeper Fulla left, reminding her to rest and take advantage of a day free of training.

Amanda wasn't sure if she was up for the trials, but it gave her something to occupy her mind as she wandered about the city. She played with the emerald around her neck, reliving the time with the Norn and feeling an enormous weight of guilt for once again keeping something from her friends and the Prelate. In her heart she knew the Prelate would stand by her, but should she? If she was destined to bring about Ragnarok and end the Spell of Favouring, maybe it would be better if Amanda wasn't on Asgard. The Norn said she would cause more death than Sigyn. How could she say those words to her friends and not expect them to be wary of everything she did. She wasn't going to stand by and let her friends get hurt, but if she left that meant Jack and her parents were trapped, stuck in their form, or worse. Cassie was always good for conversation, but she wasn't sure how to tell her friend that no matter what she did she might end up hurting her. Connor was with Lord Freyr, Mykola was busy training Nimbus, and Sean had been called to the Einherjarium to set it up for the trials with the Prelate, Queen Frigga, and Keeper Fulla. That left only one person, but Amanda wasn't sure if she would be allowed to see the goddess or not.

"It is about time!" A snarky voice sniffed from beside Amanda, and Amanda jumped as Sigyn's tower materialized around her. The emerald walls were vibrating and Amanda could see a couple of cracks forming from Sigyn's use of her own magick. Amanda fell into one of the worn arm chairs that were piled with scrolls again. Sigyn stood above her, arms crossed with a stern expression that looked like it could have brought the entire city down with it. "It's polite to send a note to inform others that you are well, especially after they visited you while you were sick. I sent you the twin stone, and get not even a thank you for it, and then I have to find out you were poisoned by a wyrm from Garth! He wouldn't stop croaking about it for hours! So, are you well?"

Amanda pushed her bangs out of her face and awkwardly tried to free herself from the scrolls that were jammed in around her. "Yes. Sorry. I just got out yesterday and up and about today. And thank you for the twin stone. It did tell us some things about…"

Sigyn cut Amanda off. "Never mind that! Please tell me how you managed to get bitten by a wyrm and…" Sigyn froze mid-sentence. She raised a shaky finger and pointed at Amanda. "What is that?"

Amanda felt a tiny tug at her neck and looked down to see her necklace was lazily floating in the air with the emerald sitting upright, bobbing along like a cork in the water. Sigyn's eyes sparkled with the emerald, not from light but from tears. Extending her hand, the necklace rose from Amanda's neck and floated over to the goddess. Sigyn's expression was that of someone who was reunited with a dear old friend. She laughed once and brought the jewel to her chest.

"I thought this lost, but it seems the Norn have another plan for it." Sigyn lifted her fist from her chest and unclenched it. The necklace floated back to Amanda.

"I found it in the tunnels beneath the Norn's Forest. It was just hanging from a statue by one of the wells. I didn't know what it was, but it just seemed to call to me. When I picked it up was when the wyrm appeared that scratched me." Amanda twisted the necklace's chain around her fingers. "Do you know what it is? It doesn't feel like a normal piece of jewelry, and I think it actually helped me connect to my favouring when I was in the forest."

"I have no doubt that it did. That is the stone where I first laid my powers to rest. As you know, the Favoured act as a vessel for our powers while the Spell of Favouring renders the gods powerless as a price to renew life. When the gods first came back, they needed to lay their powers down, but there were no Favoured. We each chose an item to house the magick. For example, Thor used his hammer. You've heard of Mjolnir I am sure."

"I thought the Dwarves made the hammer for Thor." Amanda regarded the necklace with new respect.

"While the Dwarves like to claim they forged the great weapon, they only helped shape it from the raw form it was in. For me, it was a necklace given to me by my son. When the time came, I settled my magick in the necklace you now hold and became just one step above mortal. When I was banished to this tower, the necklace disappeared. It seems the Norn knew they would have need of it for you. They probably forgot that they set a wyrm to it to protect it, those cantankerous old goats. I've never needed to relinquish my powers because the tower took my magick, but I have wondered from time to time where it went."

"Do you want it back?" Amanda offered Sigyn the necklace.

"No, no. That is from a time past for me. Its future is with you." For a moment Sigyn tilted her head, her hair shifting to one side. "It should be a most interesting talisman. Its magick is wild and unpredictable, just like my grimoire's. I can feel it will be of use to you in the future. You've already felt its connection to your magick, but also know that the necklace detects your fount of magick. Beware its glow, for when it shines its brightest your powers run dry and threaten to consume you."

"But I thought I had all of your magick?"

"Power is not without end. Even I need to rest up before performing certain spells. As you grow with your magick, you will find the limits you possess too."

"Speaking of limits. How are you feeling? You seem a bit more... stable than when I first visited you, and you helped us out with the dulhda."

Sigyn laughed. "That is a polite way to put it. Being immortal has its ups and downs, and my time alone was... challenging. But I am on the mend. I am not completely whole though. My mind still wanders. Being alone... sometimes wandering along your memories is the only comfort you have. That night with the dulhda took a lot out of me, and when I shared the revealing spells, it... well, it took a lot out of me in a way I had not expected."

"What do you mean?"

Sigyn just shook her head. "Not the right time. Now then... what were we talking about?" Sigyn's eyes drooped and shrugged her shoulders. Her focus was starting to waver.

Amanda wanted to tell her about everything that had happened since the twin stone and the revealing spell, but she still needed advice, so she shifted topics. "I need to ask you something about the Norn. They spoke to me... told me things."

"Did they now? Be careful then, because what they say has a way of coming true, but just not in the way you might expect." Sigyn backed away and walked over to her web of beads and began moving them around.

"So, what they say doesn't always come true?"

"They are not all knowing. They just know the current the river tends to run. They do like to pester you if you don't move when you need to, and they will put things in your path. However, it is your choice to go around, over, or through them. Take me, for example. I am in this tower because they had me write a spell for Surtur. The one that caused the first Ragnarok. I am surprised you didn't ask me about it on your first visit. I have paid my dues for it, or that's the way it seems now that the Norn have finally found a new use for me. It's why you were claimed. 'Tis about time those snotty wenches forgave me. All of this was their fault to begin with." Sigyn spoke half to Amanda and half to the wall beside her.

Amanda felt her brain swirl with its usual confusion in trying to follow Sigyn's speech pattern. "Wait, they asked you to create that spell? That spell is why everyone thinks you are... evil!"

"They were the ones who started everything with that prophecy of theirs, and by the rings of the Dwarf lords, if you do not fulfill the destiny the Norn dole out for you when they ask… well, let us just say they make sure to wreak havoc with your life. They turned me into an ape for a week when I first refused to do what they were asking. I mean, they wanted me to help Surtur and Loki, and by the Eye, that certainly made no sense. Thanks to all of that, I've been stuck in this tower as long as Garth has been a frog. No matter what they told you, remember we always have a choice. My choices were to follow that fool of a husband of mine into Muspelheim or let him and Surtur find a way to actually end all life. Not much of a choice, but there was still one."

Garth croaked and some of Sigyn's hair became unbound as she leaned forward to grab a stein from the floor. She tapped the errant curls and they wound back up into the mass on top of her head. "If it was not for me creating that spell, Surtur would have found another way and that would probably have meant total annihilation. No, the Norn told me I had a choice. I could either give the fire demon what he wanted or watch my family and the realms become nothing but chaos and ash."

Processing what the goddess said, Amanda thought for a moment. How could she know that Sigyn was telling the truth? Every account she had read or been told said that thanks to Sigyn's spell, Surtur destroyed countless lives, cities, and realms. But then Amanda remembered something the Norn said. "The Norn said to tell you your sacrifice has not been in vain, and that the tower will be soon your heart's desire." Amanda watched as Sigyn froze with the stein at her lips.

"If that is the case, there is a spell I would like to teach you. It is for the breaking of things. Well, almost anything. I just made it up, but I have a feeling it will come in handy."

The grimoire appeared at the goddess's words. During the next few hours Sigyn never once looked Amanda in the eyes again, and whenever Amanda tried to talk about the Norn or anything else, Sigyn would ask her to stop speaking in Dwarf and continue practicing the spell.

It was fun practicing magick with Sigyn, and she felt her energy returning with each spell. Even though the goddess could only perform the tiniest of spells, she did so with such finesses and ease, it made Amanda realize how clumsy she had been so far. Instead of thinking of each spell she cast as singular, she started to learn ways to have them flow together the way the spells she had used to find Draupnir did. However, she still had much to learn. By the end of their time together, Amanda had broken nearly every piece of furniture or urn in the tower. Just as before, Sigyn bade Amanda goodbye and sent her back to the border of Idavoll. Amanda wasn't sure, but she thought Sigyn was crying as she cast her spell to send Amanda away.

Amanda pondered whether or not to try to go back and talk to Sigyn, or tell the Prelate about what had happened with Sigyn and the Norn, but judging by the position of the stars above and the horns blowing around the city she only had just enough time to make it back to the Stave to change for the trials. She felt the knot in her stomach loosen as she mulled over Sigyn's words about being able to have a choice in how her fate played out. She didn't know what it would mean, but she decided that she definitely needed to talk to the Prelate as soon as the trials were over. She also vowed to get Sigyn out of that tower as soon as possible. Being imprisoned for something she was forced to do was unacceptable.

Cassie sat on her bed braiding and unbraiding her hair as Amanda pushed open the door to their room. "There you are! I was starting to think you fell through another portal."

"I was visiting with Sigyn." Amanda picked up the rune stone on their dresser and changed into a fresh uniform. Her time with Sigyn had left a few scorch marks on her boots and pants.

Cassie dropped her hands in her lap. "You what? How?"

"Sigyn has been monitoring me, waiting for me to want to come see her."

"Interesting. So? What did she have to say? Did you tell her about the Norn? Or do you want to tell me about the Norn? You barely said a word last night after we got back to the Stave."

"I don't know what to think. I still don't. What they told me wasn't good – for any of us."

Cassie gave a small laugh. "What else is new? Everything about us being here isn't good news if you think about it. We are the results of a spell that was needed to stop the end of the world. We have to give up a part of our lives with our friends and family back on Midgard in order to fight monsters that would kill us if they could. Any of that sound like good news?"

Amanda had been splashing some water on her face. She stopped and wiped her face dry. "Not really, but this is *really* bad. The Norn said I could hurt you and… everyone. They said I will bring Ragnarok back and end the Spell of Favouring. They said I would… hurt a lot of people."

Cassie pushed her chin out and scooted closer to the edge of her bed. "Well now it all makes sense. Look, you know I can feel what you are feeling. I know this is messing you up inside, and I can't say that it doesn't scare me. But I know you. You got some bad news, but we can beat it. I am not going to pretend that I know how to make what the Norn said not come true, but just know I will be right there with you. Although, if my session with Lady Freyja is any indication, none of us will survive these trials and it won't matter. She's back to her old self, yelling and all."

Amanda swallowed the lump in her throat. Cassie wasn't going to push her to talk about it anymore, but she had said enough to help give Amanda some hope. "Do you think it will be that bad?" Amanda pulled her hair into a ponytail and stretched her neck.

"Probably worse than we could ever come up with. Lady Freyja wouldn't even tell me what we would be facing, just that I probably wouldn't make it out alive."

"She's said that before."

Cassie smiled encouragingly. "So let's go make them all they eat wyrms."

CHAPTER 24:
THE TRIALS OF FENRIR

An hour later Amanda and Cassie had scarfed down two pints of mead and a bowl of stew that was enchanted to give them extra energy, and were on their way to the Einherjarium. They hugged before Cassie left to find her brother, and she made Amanda promise to avoid all wyrms at any cost. Amanda had been paired with Sean to take the trials and Cassie with her brother. Amanda found Sean checking his hammer. The other Favoured were grouped in their pairs, all of them ringed around the Prelate who stood with her hands clasped behind her back. The Prelate's white battle armor glowed with fiery light as twilight approached.

"Favoured," Prelate Tess began, and the whisper of words vanished from the assemblage. "Tonight will be a true test of your training. As you are aware, there have been several attacks against our realm, and we must rally together to defend ourselves. Our enemies have brought down our defenses and may even stand amongst us. It is time we show them how we respond to their tricks of fear and deception. The Einherjarium has been enchanted to conjure the strongest of the Frost Jotuns, along with other threats. You will face them now *en masse*. We will introduce you to the field in groups of two. You are to remain with your compatriot and work together until you defeat your enemies. I will monitor your challenge, along with Lady Freyja, and together we shall evaluate your progress. Remember, you are the Favoured of Asgard! Do not run from fear, and you will find victory's path!"

When no one spoke, the Prelate tapped her gauntlet, "I call forth the Favoured of Lord Balder and Hodur, followed by those favoured by Aegir and Lady Sif!"

Amanda saw Carlos and a small boy named Kwame walk forward, followed by a very tan boy and blond-headed girl. Sean turned toward Amanda, "How are you feeling?"

"As best I can be. I got some practice with my magick this afternoon... I think I can take on a few Frost Jotuns. Besides, this is one step closer to freeing Jack."

Sean didn't respond with his usual smile. Instead they watched their friends pass through the golden chain curtain and into the darkness of the

Einherjarium. A screeching sound lit the air with electric currents and the group remaining outside took a collective step back. The Prelate continued her roll call.

"What do you think will be inside for us?"

"Besides Frost Jotuns? Probably something in the Norn's realm." Sean frowned.

"Why does the Forest of Fates make you so upset?"

"Remember I said I had been in there before? The first time was because Prince Thor said I needed to spend a week in there. He had said his father made him do it, and so he required it of all his Favoured. He told me all the same warnings we got, but he brought in Keeper Fulla to elaborate a bit more on what could happen if you stay in too long. It happened to her once a very long time ago. She was sent in to gather fate stone and was trapped by a pack of fyglja. The Aesir she was with all barely made it out, but Keeper Fulla made it out five minutes too late. The things she told me she saw during those five minutes make Ragnarok sound like a tea party. But I still did it. I went in and out of there for seven days, and not a week doesn't go by where I wake up from a nightmare of that place. I wanted to go in to help, but it was a lot harder to be in there than I thought it was going to be," Sean and Amanda watched as another set of Favoured entered through the curtains, followed by the sound of something bellowing. "That's why Keeper Fulla acts the way she does. Nervous one minute, scared the next, and then all angry-like. The Queen and the Prelate make exceptions for her unless she gets really out of hand, like she did with you." The ground shook and Sean unhooked his hammer from his belt.

"Thanks for doing that, for going with me." Amanda gave Sean's hand a small squeeze. She suddenly felt sad for Keeper Fulla, and made a mental note to be nicer to the Keeper.

"Favoured of Prince Thor and Sigyn!" The Prelate looked to them.

Amanda and the Prelate locked eyes, and she reminded herself that as soon as the test was complete, she needed to let the Prelate know what she was told about the impending Ragnarok. Amanda and Sean slowly made their way up to the gate. The Einherjar drew back the curtain. Amanda looked to Sean, and then they stepped into darkness.

A chill immediately swept over them, and they closed ranks. The invisible floor rumbled beneath their feet, and then the night exploded in front of them in the form of two snarling Frost Jotun giants in full battle armor. They appeared to be in the pit of a crater in the middle of a frozen mountain range. The falling snow was bruised black and purple, and the air smelled of frozen trash. The giants ran toward them through the dirty snow that was rough with sand and soil.

Amanda felt her chest tighten not in fear, but in anger, which surprised her a bit. A moment ago, she had been terrified, but now she could feel her hatred of these creatures fuel her magick. It was like she was in a trance. All she could think about was her parents, Jack, and Bergelmir. She rolled her hands, summoning crackling and spitting fire made of green flames.

Sean took off and pointed at the Jotuns' feet. "Amanda, distract them with some of that fire and I will try to whittle them down."

Amanda grinned fiercely, feeling more alive and in control of her magick. With a fluid gesture, she flung the fire at the Jotuns and brought up a shield around herself and Sean. The fire blew chunks of the giant's armor off, and Sean began to attack their exposed areas. One of the giants nearly toppled over as Sean hammered its knee with a sideswipe, and then followed it up with an electric jolt to the chest that cracked the Jotun's frozen skin. Leaping clear, Amanda's fire followed Sean's attack and punched a hole through the giant. With a snarl, the giant began to disintegrate. Sean moved on to the second Jotun giant and threw his hammer straight through the Jotun's right hand. Amanda directed a column of fire large enough to take the Jotun's head off its shoulders. The rest of it began to melt into a puddle of steaming water. Amanda dropped her wards and smiled fiercely in victory.

"That was way too easy. If that's what the Jotuns are going to bring against you and me, we got this in the bag." Sean was walking toward Amanda when the giant with no head suddenly hooked Sean by his face with a jagged piece of its mangled finger. Sean was wrenched backward and thrown into a large boulder.

"Sean!" Amanda held out both hands, "*Fracatore!*"

The Jotun's arm snapped into pieces. Amanda sent Sigyn silent thanks for the new spell. With another wave the same spell hit the ground and sent a shockwave of air toward the giant. The Jotun giant's remnants were flung backward, shattering as they impacted the mountain's walls. Sean was trying to sit up when Amanda reached him. He had a nasty cut above his right eye and he was cradling his throwing arm.

"Are you OK?" Amanda asked as she dropped to her knees to help her friend up.

Sean grimaced. "I spoke to soon. Look out!" Sean threw his hammer and it collided with a Jotun imp that jumped at Amanda from the boulder above them. He grimaced again and dropped his arm.

Amanda cast a ring of fire around them and turned to Sean. "We have to get you out of here. The Prelate and Lady Freyja should be watching. Hopefully they will send someone to come get you."

"No way. I've been in worse shape than this. Just help me up." Amanda tried to argue but jumped to help Sean as he tried to stand.

The face of rock in front of them wavered and the other groups became faintly visible as if through a haze. She could see a Cassie fighting a swarm of wyrms and Mykola fighting rock trolls. The upper levels of the stadium were also visible, but she couldn't see anyone in the stands. In the minute she took to survey her surroundings a new combatant rose in front of them. It was a blue woman with a black overcoat, a string of pearls, and blue ice for eyes with a black line for a mouth.

"Hello, Ms. West. I hope you have missed me as much as I have missed you." It looked like Ms. Biggs, but the voice belonged to Bergelmir. Amanda had seen this version of the monster before, but only in her dreams. It was a nightmarish combination of Amanda's teacher without Bergelmir's armor and other harsh features. This version of the possessed Ms. Biggs raised a clawed hand and a dozen imps rose on the field. A blustery gale howled through the crater they stood in, followed by the sound of someone screaming.

It took Amanda a second to realize she was the one screaming, as she began to cast volleys of spells at Ms. Biggs' form. "What are you doing here?"

With the same air of haughtiness only Ms. Biggs' expression of disapproval could convey, he held out a hand and stopped Amanda's attacks. With another look of disdain, Bergelmir clenched a fist and fired off a blast of ice. Amanda barely had time to deflect it. "'Tis time you are claimed for your true purpose."

The imps surged forward, but Sean somersaulted through the air and dispatched a swath of them with a sweep of his hammer. "Don't let it fool you, Amanda. It's all still part of the test."

"An illusion can still kill you, Favoured." Bergelmir threw several large spikes of ice, causing Sean to tumble to the ground as they knifed through the air he had just occupied. Ms. Biggs' lipless mouth split into a maniacal grin as Sean cried out as he landed on his injured arm.

Amanda was shaking. "I don't care if you are part of this test or not! You and the real Bergelmir will pay for everything you have caused!"

Bergelmir roared and the small form of Ms. Biggs deflected one of Amanda's spells. "If this is your best, then perhaps we were wrong about you. You are not a weapon for us to use. You are a weakness to be exploited. You are a distraction that allowed us access to the realm, and now you have no further purpose." Bergelmir laughed at Amanda and sent another wave of imps toward her.

Amanda threw a ball of fire at the fiends, but it fizzled before connecting with the Jotuns. The imps swarmed over her and Amanda felt her soul contract. Her fierce confidence was extinguished as if someone had blown it out. A dark shroud fell over everything, and Amanda saw all the building nightmares she feared from the moment she first discovered the magick of Asgard – Jack lying motionless, her parents lost and trapped as mice somewhere in Asgard, her friends lying amongst the rubble of the Golden Realm, and the Norn sending a wave of fire toward her that spread throughout the Nine Realms. Amanda tried to resist, but the darkness grew stronger with her fear.

In desperation Amanda conjured her little ball of green light and held it aloft. "I will not let you beat me!"

"It is too late, child. You are part of the darkness. Part of the prophecy that will be the downfall of all you hold dear!" The words came from all around Amanda. They didn't sound like Bergelmir, but like Freyja's taunting speech and Keeper Fulla's accusing glances.

"Not if I don't want to be. I can choose." The light above Amanda grew brighter with her words. "I can have the courage to find another way!" The green light blazed and Amanda expanded it, overpowering the darkness that ensnared her. Amanda felt her rage fueling her magick. Pointing at the small sun and shouted, "*FIERYR!*"

The arrow of green flame connected with the light, and tongues of fire and light showered the arena, catching Bergelmir in the chest. The darkness began to dissolve around Amanda until she could see Bergelmir and his imps were also melting. Amanda strode over the melting Jotun and stared down at it. She wished it had been the real Bergelmir.

Sean appeared next to Amanda. Amanda grabbed his cloak as he tried to stay upright. "Well done, Amanda. You did it! Better save that trick for the next time you see old blue face."

"Trust me, I will." Amanda scanned the arena around them, which had reformed with the other Favoured's battles. "Is it over?"

"Don't know, but let's try to head out and see."

Amanda felt something warm on her chest and was surprised to see her necklace was glowing slightly. Amanda helped Sean, as much as he would let her, as they walked back toward the gate, which was much farther away from them than they had realized. A boulder the size of a house blocked their path, so they skirted round it. As they passed through its shadow, the air around them froze. There was a dip in Amanda's stomach, and her body suddenly felt agitated. Her skin stung as if she were being bitten by tiny insects. Fighting off a sneeze, she shook her arms as they kept walking until they heard their boots crunch on snow.

Stepping out from the shadow, the boulder vanished and the world was filled with far away snow-capped mountains. Sean took a tentative step back. They were suddenly on a plateau overlooking a dark precipice. The snow falling around them was clean and white, and the air smelled of fresh rich earth and frost. A trail stood before them, lit by torches that bore blue flames and purple runes.

Sean switched his hammer to his uninjured hand and swept the area around them. "Amanda... something's not right..."

Warning and realization flared into Amanda's senses like the cold creeping to her toes from the snow. "Sean? Disir..." Amanda whispered, but he motioned for her silence.

A swarm of imps erupted from the shadows around them, overwhelming the pair in seconds before they had time to react. The imps became bands of ice, constricting their arms and forming a gag over Amanda's mouth. The gag was emblazoned with a rune, and she felt her magick leave her as it flashed to life. The imps parted as three figures appeared on the edge of the chasm. One was holding a pair of mice; the other had someone mechanically following them.

"Favoured of magick. It has been too long, but we had to wait until our time was right." The dry voice greeted them, causing Amanda's throat to clench shut. A red glow spread out before the Jotun, who twirled the ruby ring Draupnir on his finger.

"I told you we could take them, Master." Fulla presented Amanda to Bergelmir, while clutching Amanda's parents to her chest. "And we have another Favoured to test your new powers on too! Let us see if it takes hold of him as it did this one." Fulla indicated the smaller boy standing beside Bergelmir.

Jack looked past Amanda. "What is your command, Master?"

Bergelmir grinned. "Welcome them back to Midgard my Disir. They have come to us at a very special place. It shall be here that the Frost Jotuns will enslave the Nine Realms."

CHAPTER 25:
ROCKY MOUNTAIN HIGH

The red exit sign mocked Amanda and Sean as they sat chained to the floor. It blinked on an off in no particular pattern above the only door into the room, which had been frozen shut after Bergelmir's imps tossed Amanda and Sean into a dilapidated office. Amanda could barely make out the wording on a faded map that hung askew beside the door that read, "Colorado Rockies."

Amanda banged her feet on the concrete floor. Her mouth was still sealed shut by a band of ice, but the rest of her shackles had been transformed from solid ice to metal chains with a snap of Bergelmir's fingers and a dose of Draupnir's magick. Sean was similarly bound, except for the gag of ice, and their chains were looped into rings fused into the floor. His hammer taunted him like the exit sign by being just out of his reach, but still close enough to not enact its returning enchantment.

Sean took a sharp breath as he tried to shift his weight. He turned toward Amanda, and she could see his eye was swollen shut. "It isn't any use. I'm sure they reinforced the chains with magick, and even if we could break free of them we would have to deal with those." Sean pointed to runes that had been carved into the floor, eerily similar to the ones in Sigyn's tower's floor.

Amanda read the runes, some to block power, two to harm any who tried to escape, and the rest to absorb magick. She tried casting another spell but nothing happened. All of Sigyn's magick at her disposal, and they were still trapped. Frustrated and in some pain from her numbed lips, she reached out and gently touched Sean's forehead and then his injured arm.

Sean winced and blinked, but he understood her unspoken question. "It looks worse than it probably is. The arm will heal, but I will probably have a scar from this cut. Just add it to the list. Nothing to be done about it now until we get back to Asgard. I've been trying to rest and let my energy recharge while I think, but I can't see a way out except to get past those runes and rainbow back."

Amanda shook her head. She held out her hands and then drew the rune for friend on the floor. Sean nodded and winced again. "There's that too. I know you won't be leaving without your parents, and I am guessing that was

Jack beside Bergelmir. So we need to break out, save your friend and parents, and then get back to Asgard from… wherever we are."

Amanda pointed to the sign. Sean glanced at it without turning his head. "Yeah, I saw that too. But where in the mountains are we? And why?"

Amanda breathed in a deep sigh through her nose and shrugged. The sound of steam hissing through the cracks around the door made them both tense. They shared a look as their prison door swung open to reveal a figure backlit by windows looking out over white-capped peaks.

"Keeper Fulla." Sean's voiced hardened and he struggled to his knees.

Fulla waddled into the room. Instead of her usual smock, she now wore a heavy fur robe that glittered with golden lining. "How are you, my meddlesome pests? Are you surprised to see me? I bet you did not expect someone like me to be part of Master Bergelmir's grand plan. No one ever did. No one ever paid any attention to poor, worried Fulla until my master told me there was a greater destiny for me than cleaning up after Midgardian brats." Something squeaked from Fulla's pocket and she pulled out Amanda's parents.

"Hmgrgfifril!" Amanda mumbled from behind her gag.

"So sorry, didn't quite catch that. Here, let me remove your binding. But be warned, any use of magick will result in severe penalties." Fulla placed emphasis on the last few words with a sly smile. With a touch, the ice melted from Amanda's mouth.

"H-how c-could you, Keeper Fulla? And wh-what are you doing with my parents?" Amanda's lips were still numb and she struggled to get her words out.

Fulla walked over to Sean and dropped the mice in his hand. "Because it was my destiny. These were just my insurance should I need them, but now that you are here they are as useless as any other mortal." Dark tendrils of magick crept along Fulla's forearms and they revealed fell runes branded into her wrists

Amanda began to shake as the fell magick filled the room. Fulla's presence suddenly felt like acid had been dumped into her stomach. "Disir," Amanda hissed through gritted teeth.

Keeper Fulla's face had grown grey and withered looking. "Indeed. Me. The foot maid to the Queen is now more powerful than any of the gods. I took more than just physical might as the other Disir before me did. I wove the fell magick I took into my being so that I am now unlike any other in the history of the Nine Realms, and you had no clue as I walked among you. My Asgardian magicks shielded me from your sight, and once I had enough alfblot it was easy enough to penetrate any ward placed by the Queen. It was I who took Heimdall and corrupted him. I who set the imps loose that stole Draupnir, which I sent to my master through the Norn's realm, and I who loosed the dulhda. Although, the dulhda was done with the aid of some new friends. And it's all thanks the Norn. That is how I know this was the fate they planned for me. When I was touched by their fyglja, it opened my eyes. I saw things – things not even Odin knew. At first it was overwhelming, and so I returned to the forest. In its depths I fell through a portal into Niflheim. My master found me and restored me. He *freed* me. He helped me sift through my new knowledge, and even gifted me with powers to command his imps. All I had to do was help him with a plan to free the dark ones by bringing the alfblot to the realm, and then finally by becoming a Disir. Then we waited until the time was right, when the Spell of Favouring would be ready to claim Odin's magick – that time is now."

Amanda was trying to block the screaming whispers that floated around her from the fell magick Keeper Fulla displayed. "You haven't been set free, Keeper Fulla. You traded serving the Queen for serving monsters that want to destroy the Nine Realms. Sigyn told me about the spells that you are using. She told me what those spells cost. You yourself even told me what it means. You are cursed."

Keeper Fulla flung her hands forward. Amanda was wrenched from the floor and thrown against the back of the office. "I am tired of hearing you speak. You presume to lecture me on the risks of magick? You are nothing but a passing vessel. The first foolish Disir lacked foresight and control. I entered into this pact with certain protections in place." Fulla released Amanda and she collapsed into Sean.

Sean managed to catch Amanda, and keep Keith and Liz safe, but the effort caused him to cry out in pain. Amanda and Sean struggled to untangle themselves. Fulla clucked her tongue and continued her diatribe. She reveled in boasting of her exploits. "Pathetic. You may have the magick of a goddess, but you have none of her resiliency. There were many times I thought that you might have caught on, but as a true mortal you were always too absorbed in your own affairs to put the pieces together. The Favoured of Mani and Sol were just as easy to manipulate to lead them to their true purpose. Their hubris made them think they could steal power from the gods, and with my nudging they thought they were doing it for the good of the realm. I even pointed them to the rune to steal Draupnir's power without them even realizing it. The twins now serve us in an even greater capacity, as I knew they would. It is why I had Master Bergelmir kill the originally intended Favoured of Mani and Sol. In fact, this place is where it happened. It acts as a foothold for Master Bergelmir to gain entrance to this realm whenever he so chooses just as the fyglja showed me it would."

"Wait, what…" Amanda's jaw snapped shut as Fulla slammed her down into the floor.

"Yes. The fyglja showed me much. You were the wild card, Amanda. I knew you would need to be watched. And what better way to do that, than with minions of mine own? Everyone thought poor Fulla lost her senses carrying the frost lilies around, you were the only one to even ask about them, Amanda. I told you that frost lilies could be transformed to suit almost any need possible."

Fulla cast the bunch of petals to the ground. Sean and Amanda watched as they bent in on themselves, like self-folding origami swans. Imps rose from the ground, screeching and raking their claws against the floor as they slowly turned blue. Amanda cried out as a sharp pain dug into her side. An imp wriggled free from her pocket.

"You finally see it? Is it not masterful? I fooled the host of Asgard, the Queen, and the Prelate. They confided in me all while my imps scurried about right in front of them. They carried the ingredients for the alfblot and the syirces all over the realm, even around Lord Mimir's well. All I had to do was cast the spell from where I was and it would call forth the fell magick, even when I was half a realm away. They also brought me the life they stole from those they touched to fuel my magicks and create the alfblot we needed. I could have crushed you all at any time, but it was sweeter to savor how blithely ignorant they were to my workings. Keeping you alive was my only real limitation, Amanda." Fulla glowered at Amanda. "Once you fulfill your purpose, you shall bother us no more!"

"But why?" Amanda tried to nudge her way over to Sean to help roll him over from his bad arm, but the imps chittered at her angrily.

"Because of Master Bergelmir's plan, of course." Fulla suddenly bent and grabbed Sean's face. "When I told him what I saw, he told me of his great plan to rid ourselves of the Spell of Favouring."

"But the Spell of Favouring saved you. It saved everyone. You don't know what you are doing by trying to mess with the spell, Keeper Fulla, or with me. The Norn showed me things that would happen. You are causing Ragnarok to happen again. It will destroy the Nine Realms." Fulla pushed Sean back to the floor and picked up one of the imps while Amanda spoke.

Scratching the imp on its head with a black fingernail, Fulla paced a slow circle around them. "That is exactly what we want. I have seen it with the glimpse the fyglja gave me. We are preparing a fortress to weather the onslaught. When the flames die as they did before, we will rebuild the Nine Realms as we see fit. We will create our own perfect paradise without mortals and gods." Fulla nuzzled the imp and sent it back to the floor.

Sean slapped an imp from his shoulder. "You can't win, Keeper Fulla. Once Lord Odin returns, he will take the entire might of Asgard and destroy you."

Fulla laughed. Her eyes were wild. The runes on her wrists burned brighter as she spoke. Her voice rose in shrill waves, making it almost incomprehensible. "As you have experienced, we can now enter and leave the Golden Realm when and where we want. All thanks to me. Even as we speak, the hordes of Niflheim pour through the fell portals into Asgard.

There will be no army for the Allfather to command."

Sean and Amanda looked shocked. Despite the pain, Sean began to thrash about toward the edge of the circle of runes in the floor. "You traitor! The Jotuns will kill everyone. But then, you don't care about that do you?" The runes in the floor glowed as he stopped just shy of them.

"At one time I would have fought for the gods' survival, but they have become antiquated. I will create something better from their deaths." Fulla clucked her tongue again.

"We will find a way out of here and stop you. You've forgotten that I have all of Sigyn's magick. I am betting you didn't account for that with these runes. *Transityr!*" Amanda tried to transfer Fulla and her imps for the snow flowing past the windows. Sean and Amanda yelped as an ice cold current coursed through their bonds and numbed their limbs.

Laughter echoed through the room. Amanda tried to catch her breath through the blinding pain. Bergelmir appeared and the office dissolved into a wooden stage that faced out into an auditorium. Bergelmir uttered a few syllables and Amanda's parents vanished from the floor beside Sean, reappearing a second later in Bergelmir's hand. Amanda's heart stopped as the Jotun trickster tapped each one on the head. The mice began to shake and grow, shedding their fur and slowly changing back into their human forms – complete with elastic-waisted pants for Keith and pens in Liz's bun.

"Amanda?" Liz blinked for a moment and then jumped when she saw Bergelmir. "What is going on? What are you?"

Keith took Liz by the shoulders and moved her behind him. "I don't know who you are, sir, but why... how did you bring us here? Wherever we are."

"Mom, dad, are you ok?" Amanda reached out to her parents, but they both vanished. "No! Where did they go?"

"I returned them to your home. I suspect the protective magicks placed around the house will envelope them and they will have no recollection of their transformation or our encounter." Bergelmir held up a hand that was framed by red magick, which thudded loudly in Amanda's ears. "Consider it a gift."

Amanda stared at the Jotun. "A gift?"

"Indeed. It is not in my nature to be kind to mortals, or those associated with Asgard, but as with Fulla, I consider you to be of use. I believe this one is also something you desire." Bergelmir pushed Jack forward. Jack's face was expressionless, and his eyes burned blue. His skin was normal again except it was crisscrossed with purple and blue marks. Bergelmir snapped his fingers and Jack came out of his stupor. "He has served his purpose. Consider this a second gift."

"Amanda?"

Amanda grabbed Jack and pulled him into a hug, but kept her eyes on

Bergelmir. "Are you OK?" Jack nodded. Amanda gave him a brief smile and then placed him behind her. "I don't know what you think these 'gifts' are going to do for you. We are still going to stop you and stop the invasion you sent to Asgard. *Fieryr!*"

Bergelmir held up a hand and Amanda's fiery assault disappeared in a puff of smoke. "I had hoped you would be pleased. Instead you seek to do me harm. It matters little. The finite power you wield would be like trying to use a candle to melt a mountain of snow. I simply thought we could come to an understanding with the gifts I have given you." With a nod, the runes from the office appeared around Amanda and her friends.

Amanda stepped back from the runes. "I will never do anything that would help you. You attacked me, kidnapped Jack, used Fulla to attack Asgard and me, and so much more. I am going to make you pay for all of that. Someone told me once that no one is truly all powerful. Let's find out. *Fracatore!*" Amanda threw her arms wide as a shockwave of magick and concussive force slammed into the floor, shattering the runes that surrounded them. Taking a step forward she sent another wave of concussive force at Fulla with one hand, knocking her back, and with the other she directed a continuous stream of fire toward Bergelmir.

Freed from the runes, Sean held out his hand and his hammer appeared. He threw it at Bergelmir, who caught it with a sneer. Fulla regained her balance and ripped a giant board from the floor. Amanda clenched her fist and the floor broke under Fulla. The shockwave knocked Bergelmir back a step, surprising the Jotun as Amanda's flames burned a hole through part of his armor. Reacting quickly, the Jotun lord dropped Sean's hammer and caught the flames in his hand. Draupnir glowed and began absorbing the fire as it continued to pour forth. The boards in between them began to smolder and creak. Bergelmir held up his other hand and Jack began to convulse. With another gesture, several cuts slashed down Sean's cheek. Amanda dropped her hands and rushed to help her friends.

Bergelmir rolled his hand as the last of Amanda's fire was sucked into Draupnir. "Pathetic. Your concern is your weakness! What I gifted you I can take away. You want to see my power? Observe." Bergelmir cupped the hand wielding Draupnir and red lightning cascaded into the room, slithering into the air until it enveloped Sean. The boy screamed as the magick pierced his body.

Amanda watched in horror as the same purple and black marks that Jack bore began to appear on Sean. Sean and Jack's eyes suddenly glowed with blue light and the boys turned and grabbed Amanda. "Stop it! What are you doing to them?"

"Showing you the future. I will control the Nine Realms just as I now control your friends. And it is all thanks to you. You will help me one way or another. Now be still. Attack me again and my next gift will send your friends to the realm of the dead." Bergelmir released his hold on Jack and Sean, and the boys looked confused as they let go of Amanda.

Sean was shaking. Amanda could tell he heard Bergelmir speak even while the Jotun was controlling him. His skin were still marked.

Fulla clucked her tongue. "Kill them, Master. Or at least bind them and let the Norn have their way. We need no mortals for our victory."

Bergelmir strode behind Fulla, who looked at him adoringly. "I can sense the spell within her. She is a key. To unlock the Spell of Favouring and completely free ourselves of its control, she must have her magick. But you are correct that she needs to only be alive – nothing more. For now, let us see if she will be more amenable to our wishes."

"I think you two have been drinking too much of your own alfblot. Amanda would never help you." Sean slumped backward, panting with pain. He held his injured arm as his body convulsed slightly.

"Insolent mortal!" Bergelmir flew across the stage and backhanded Sean. Sean grunted and rolled into the wall. Grabbing Sean by his hair, Bergelmir began cutting a rune into his cheek. "I will suffer no more of your feckless words." Sean opened his mouth to speak, but screamed in pain instead as the rune he now bore glowed angrily.

Bergelmir dropped Sean and twisted Draupnir around his icy finger. He leaned down to the boy and a maniacal expression slowly came over the Jotun's face. "You think your fellow Favoured will not help me? She is already doing so. Or has she not told you?" Even now Yggdrasil begins to turn dark and decay. 'Tis not because of what we do, though it does aid us. Fulla told us that you saw the Norn. She said they told you that Ragnarok was inevitable. Fulla knew this as well, but she thinks they told you more than that. Perhaps they told you how *you* will bring about the end of the Nine Realms." Bergelmir smiled and the angular features of his face twisted maliciously.

Amanda's breath caught in her chest. "I choose not to believe what they say will come true. Sigyn said I have a choice."

Sean looked up defiantly at the Jotun, but then saw Amanda's expression. He tried to speak, but between his arm and the pain the rune was giving him he couldn't manage to say more than, "What?"

"Truly? You would take advice from someone who has suffered because of the Norn's words?" Fulla laughed at Amanda's startled expression. "Indeed. I know why Sigyn wrote the spell for Surtur. Would you like me to tell your friends what else I have guessed from the knowledge I gained? I think Ragnarok will start by your hands. I think it will be you that severs the Spell of Favouring. I have seen the green flames dancing across the realms when I close my eyes."

Amanda didn't answer. She didn't need to. Bergelmir and Fulla both cackled as her demeanor gave them their answers. Sean looked at her again, pleading with his expression to deny Fulla's words.

"We will fight you." Jack came to Amanda's defense.

Her friend's confidence snapped Amanda out of her own fears. She felt embarrassed for letting Fulla and Bergelmir make her feel ashamed of something that hadn't even happened. "You're right, Jack. We will fight. I will fight to make sure that none of that ever happens."

Sean grunted, but through his teeth he yelled as loudly as possible through the pain. "As my friend Cassie would say, 'go melt yourself.' Or better yet, fry!" Sean cried out in pain, and then held out his hand. There was a rumble of thunder as lightning crashed through the ceiling.

CHAPTER 26:
FROM BATTLE TO BATTLE

Unfortunately, the lightning had the same effect on Bergelmir as a fly smacking into a window. Fulla on the other hand was blasted off of her feet and into the velvet curtains.

"Die, mortal!" The Jotun summoned a wintery gale of ice and snow that spun Sean off of his feet into the air.

"Sean!" Amanda braced herself and cast a shield around Jack as large chunks of ice began to hurtle down on them. Imps rose from the floor around Amanda and began to claw and bite at her. *"Fieryr!"*

Something pulled Amanda's focus to the core of Bergelmir's blizzard, and she aimed a blast at its epicenter just as the storm reached its zenith. When the two opposing magicks collided, Amanda could feel the pressure of Bergelmir's might crash against her own magick. She felt like she was being swallowed by an avalanche, but she pressed on. Her green flames started swirling in the spiral of wind, sending fire and ice shooting through the room. A large chunk of ice hit Fulla's shoulder and she fell to the floor. Another slammed into Bergelmir, knocking him off balance. Amanda cast another wave of fire and she heard Bergelmir cry out in rage. The winds died and Sean landed in one of the auditorium chairs. Amanda grabbed Jack's hand, and they ran toward Sean.

"Foolish mortal! The frost will claim you! I had hoped that you would join us voluntarily, but I see I must employ other means!" Bergelmir drew his sharp fingers upward and red lightning erupted from his hands.

Amanda barely had time to cast a protection spell before the magick collided with her shield. She dropped to her knees with the force of power digging into her defensive spell. Fulla had managed to free herself from the curtains and was using her magick to fling the auditorium chairs at them. Jack came to Amanda's side. An imp was scratching at the shield, and he bent down to pick it up. His skin instantly turned bright blue, but still had the strange markings around his wrists and face.

Taking a deep breath, Jack's eyes glowed and he spoke with a tone Amanda had never heard before. "Fulla, Bergelmir is going to betray you. You knew you couldn't believe him. You should take him out first!"

Fulla had jumped toward them but paused with her fist in the air. She pivoted and flung her hands toward Bergelmir. "You think you can be rid of me? I am a Disir! Even you cannot undue that!" As Fulla attacked Bergelmir, Jack and Amanda helped Sean through the auditorium doors and into a dark hallway.

"Jack, what was that? How did you make Keeper Fulla turn on Bergelmir?" Amanda quickly looked around the corridor. Something slammed into the wall behind them and several of the ceiling tiles fell.

"No idea. It started happening when I was back with Bergelmir in his ice palace. Happy to tell you about it later. Can you get us out of here?"

Fulla's unconscious body smashed through the wall and flew through the glass window. "No time for a rainbow portal. Run," Amanda screamed as they heard Bergelmir bellow.

The floor was slightly slick with ice sludge, causing them to slip as they scrambled down the corridor. After a few turns they were tearing toward a door with a blinking exit sign above it. Amanda felt her chest burn slightly around her necklace but ignored it as the burgeoning sense of hope flooded her with a bit of strength. Sean was breathing heavily and held a hand to his face when they made it to the door. Amanda grabbed the handle and pushed as hard as she could. The sound of magick screamed in her ears, and ice engulfed the door, trapping her hand. A roar echoed from the way they had come. Amanda heard angry magick snap around them and the walls were encased with a neon-red light.

Frantically Amanda pulled at her hand, as the sound of scratching steps echoed toward them. "I'm stuck!"

"Jotun... trap." Sean hissed through clenched teeth. He held out his hand and his hammer appeared in a blinding flash of light. With it he began hammering around Amanda's hand without trying to hit her.

Jack stopped Sean and broke the ice with the heel of his hand. Amanda stumbled backward as she pulled herself free. The light from the moon shifted and Amanda saw what she thought was a shadow was actually a tunnel carved into the mountain. "Look!"

Jack walked up to the opening and peered into it. "They must have dug it into the mountain for some reason. Maybe it has a way out. Anyone got a light?"

Amanda called forth her glowing green orb. Jack stared at it in wonder. Sean was doubled over and looked worse than he had before they encountered Bergelmir. Blood was streaming down his face and into his eyes.

"You... go." Sean held up his hammer and turned back to the corridor.

"Let me try something first, we aren't leaving you behind. *Fracatore transityr.*"

Sean jumped as if he had been slapped, but then let out a sigh of relief as the rune on his cheek cracked and then disintegrated into the floor. "Thanks.

How did you manage that?"

Amanda held out her hand and gave Sean some support as he stood with her help. "I've been thinking about how to layer spells since Sigyn told me the ones to use to look for Draupnir. I figured if I could break the spell and then transfer its magick out, it shouldn't be able to hurt you anymore. I am just glad it worked. Do you think you can summon a rainbow portal?"

"I doubt it. Besides, I am betting that red glow wasn't because it's Bergelmir's favorite color. Can you do anything… you know, now that you're blue?" Sean still had a hand to his face as he looked over at Jack.

"I - I don't know. I haven't really been able to test it out." Jack kept his eyes forward, looking deeper into the tunnel.

"There is no hiding from me!" Bergelmir's bellow echoed behind them. They all froze as the tunnel shook.

Amanda put a hand to the wall. "We need to move. He sent some kind of spell after us. I can hear it. I can send him and his spell chasing a couple hundred illusions of myself, but it will only work for a short while. Bergelmir probably knows thousands of spells. I've only been lucky so far."

"Lucky and brave. Do what you can and let's see where this tunnel leads us." Amanda nodded to Sean and she cast her spell.

After a few hurried minutes they broke through a frozen gate into a large cavern. It was full of glowing stalactites and stalagmites that shone with blood-red light. Sean staggered over to one of the rock formations and leaned into it. Amanda and Jack scanned the walls.

"There's got to be a way out of here." Jack jabbed at the walls.

Amanda tripped over a few loose stones. "I don't see anything."

Sean was able to speak, but his injuries were taking their toll. His voice was raw, "We've maybe got seconds before Bergelmir finds us and I don't think he will be as nice as he was before. Look for a rune or a lever. Jotuns don't like to be trapped either; they always have some kind of a backdoor."

Amanda laid her hand on the wall and yelped. An electric jolt shot through her body, throwing her head back. The magick in the stones latched onto Amanda's hand, holding her in place. "I can't move!"

"It must be another spell. It's acting as a barrier, keeping us inside and trapping us if we touch it. We've got to…" Sean was cut off as the entrance they came through exploded, sending cannonball sized chunks of stone and twisted metal into the room. Sean spun and fell to the floor as one of the pieces smashed into him. Jack was pinned to the floor by several large boulders and a metal bar that wrapped around him. Bergelmir barged into the room like a battering ram and snarled at Amanda. The light danced like demons on the wall as the ring sparkled on the Jotun's finger.

"Sean!" Amanda had been spared from most of the shrapnel, as she had quickly cast a shield around herself.

"You should worry not for your compatriot as he will be waiting for you when I am done with you!"

Amanda tried to conjure a ball of flame but the magick sputtered and died. Bergelmir was on her before she could try again and grabbed both hands in a giant fist. The chill froze her fingers and sent needles of pain into her skin. Bergelmir cast an eye about the room and then lifted Amanda from the floor by her neck.

"You... can't... win..." Amanda struggled to speak as the cold robbed her of her breath.

"Even now you do not see it. Even if you were to escape, your friends cannot survive what is to come. Their deaths are your cause. Bid them farewell." Bergelmir's eyes narrowed viciously as Draupnir began to glow like the heart of the sun.

Amanda desperately grabbed a hold of Bergelmir's hand. With her last breath, she summoned all the magick she had left. "*Fracatore.*"

Bergelmir howled as his hand broke apart. Draupnir seemed to hover for a moment as if indecisive, and then fell into Amanda's hand. The power crackled and fizzled like exploding fireworks as it flooded into Amanda's system. Amanda felt her hands begin to move in a complex pattern and a blast of pure energy sent Bergelmir crashing backward into the tunnel.

Bergelmir staggered up from the floor and leapt at her like a mountain lion. "You cannot defeat me! I still retain more than enough of the ring's power to defeat two puny Favoured!"

"Want to bet?" With little effort, Amanda raised the pointed stones to pin the Jotun to the ceiling. Using another gesture, she sent Bergelmir's magick into the stones around them, causing the Jotun to bellow in agony as his magick was ripped from his being.

"You have won nothing, younglings. The Jotuns will be your downfall before this evening is ended!" Bergelmir gave a roar and vanished with a large cracking sound, followed by the stones exploding from the sudden void of magick.

"Good riddance. Now let's get out of here." Sean pushed himself up with his hammer. The marks that had appeared on Sean's skin were fading, and he suddenly seemed much stronger. He stepped over to Jack, and with a few swipes of his hammer he had Jack free. "You've got to conjure the portal, Amanda. With Draupnir, the magick keeping us here shouldn't be a problem to bust through. Just think about where you want to go and use your magick to open the door there."

Amanda nodded and raised her arms. She thought of Asgard, of the Bifrost, of the Stave and of Cassie, Connor and Mykola. She felt the ring pulse and she breathed a sigh of relief as she saw the familiar glow appear. The three of them jumped through the portal and landed on a pile of white petals that scattered to reveal the glittering stone pad leading up to the Bifrost.

"This is probably not the first time someone has wished we didn't have to make a pit stop at the Bifrost before we get into the city. Hopefully we can make it across the bridge before..." Sean turned toward the gate behind them and sucked in a breath. "By the Eye."

Draupnir's power sang in Amanda's ears like an opera, but it faded away as she saw what Sean was staring at. It looked like someone had driven a truck through the gate to the Bifrost. The side towers were listing toward the edge of space, missing chunks of their main structures. Everything around them was covered in the petals of discarded frost lilies.

"What are those? They look like frozen trees." Amanda pointed to large blue forms that were sending off small tails of blue-white fog.

"Those aren't trees. Everyone who was on the Bifrost, and probably all of Asgard, has been frozen." Sean was scanning the area around them as he ripped a strip of cloth from his cloak to make a bandage for his head and then another for a sling for his arm.

"We're too late." Jack bent to pick up a bunch of petals and frost lily stems.

"Fulla," Amanda whispered in anger. Sean's face grew tight. "She ordered them to attack. We've got to get to the city."

"I will help. I owe Bergelmir." Jack clenched his fists and stared at the gray marks around his wrists.

"Jack, no. You should go back to Midgard," Jack gave Amanda a confused look, "I mean Earth."

"He would not be any safer there, Amanda. He will probably not make it here, but we need all the help we can get." Sean's words were short and he was trying to control his breathing.

"I'm stronger than I look."

Sean ignored Jack and picked up a spear that was lying on the ground. Sean tossed the elegant weapon to the boy.

Jack caught the spear and expertly twirled it between his fingers. He spun, placing the butt of the spear on the ground, and flipped in the air. "I just remembered. Bergelmir gave me some new moves."

Amanda gaped, and then remembered Jack's battle with the Einherjar. "Jack, I know you want to help, but you don't know what you are getting yourself into. What if Bergelmir takes away your new fighting skills in the middle of a battle? You really could get hurt."

"So could you, Amanda. I am tired of being treated like some kind of chew toy. I handled myself against Bergelmir back on... Midgard... so I am betting I can take on whatever else is here." Jack didn't wait for Amanda's reply and walked up the steps toward the Bifrost.

A damp rain began to fall, and then turned to sleet. Amanda could feel the cold through her Asgardian clothing, but Jack seemed unfazed. They all froze as a comet of yellow lightning rocketed through the sky and dropped into what remained of the gate to the Bifrost. The form of a warrior in white armor with fiery red hair struggled to rise from the tangled golden vines that she had landed in.

"Cursed wretch from the pits of Hel!" In a flare of angry light, the Prelate freed herself from the gate and stood.

"Prelate Tess!" Amanda called as the trio ran toward her.

The Prelate turned, ready for an attack, but smiled fiercely when she saw them. "Praise the Allfather you are alive! We saw you vanish, but were unable to see what happened as the realm was besieged."

"What is our status Prelate?" Sean banged his chest.

The Prelate looked concerned by Sean's appearance, but returned the gesture. "We are beset by Frost Jotun imps and giants in numbers we have not seen for millennia. Bergelmir has created an army that fuels him even now. He appeared amidst a swirling maelstrom of power that washed through the realm and froze anything it touched. Queen Frigga had just enough power to contain the spell before it consumed us all, but it trapped her as she did so. With her lost, so went our last defense. Bergelmir now wields new magicks that allow him to control Asgardians the same way he used to be able to control mortals. The Favoured that were in the midst of their trials thought it was all part of the challenge. By the time they realized the threat to be real they were nearly buried by the Jotuns' sheer numbers as they poured in through fell portals that sprung open around them. Prince Thor and Lord Freyr were carried away by battle, along with a small contingent of Einherjar. It seems Lady Freyja has joined the enemy. She attacked me to keep me from helping the Favoured, and then Bergelmir appeared and struck me from behind. We were truly betrayed and caught unaware."

"Lady Freyja is on their side? Man, who else is a traitor? Keeper Fulla is the one who helped get the Jotuns in and took us back to Midgard. She is the original Disir. Has been for a long time." Sean shook his head in disgust.

The Prelate closed her eyes and frowned. "The lure of our enemy is its claim to easy power. The Favoured have been overtaken in the Einherjarium or the Stave, and the Einherjar and Aesir battle with them to keep our foothold in the realm. Bergelmir and I battled, but his power seems to have grown."

"He was using this to amplify his own magick." Amanda held Draupnir up for the Prelate to see.

"Bless the Norn! Draupnir! We but need to return the ring to its rightful place in Valaskjalf and the Jotuns will be banished. 'Tis most likely why they have formed a protective hedge around it." The Prelate looked hopeful and then noticed Jack and frowned again.

"Prelate Tess this is Jack, my friend. Remember? He was the one we were trying to save."

"Hello." Jack nodded.

"A Jotun!" The Prelate raised her arms, but her gauntlet's glow stopped her. A curious expression came over the Prelate's face, and she nodded. "Ah, I see it now."

"See what Prelate?" Sean raised his hammer, expecting an attack.

"The Norn have seen fit for another choosing." Prelate Tess's gauntlets flashed at her words.

Amanda's eyes widened. "You mean Jack is a…"

"A Favoured of Asgard. It was hidden from me before as he was taken before we could encounter one another on Midgard, but there is no doubt."

Sean looked dumbfounded. "But that means his benefactor is… Loki. He is the only god left, right?"

"Low key who?" Jack whispered to Amanda.

"Jack, you're a Favoured like me. You're one of us!"

Trying to process the information Jack slowly shook his head. "I guess it makes sense. Bergelmir said I wasn't a mortal. He said I had a Jotun and an Asgardian side. I had no idea what that meant, but if I am one of you it helps answer some questions. I might have some answers to some of your questions too. I saw Bergelmir change Billy into an imp. That is probably what he was doing the night he found you, Amanda. But the part about controlling others might have come from me. He was working with some swirling dark cloud and they made me drink something that gave me these marks. He said he was taking control of my Asgardian side."

"It would make sense. The Jotun trickster has never before been able to control Asgardians. Loki is part Frost Jotun and part Asgardian. Your current form is that of a Frost Jotun, and must be part of your favouring. This gives you a link to both races that he could exploit. However, he has never been able to transform mortals. That was the magick of the Fell Elves, and clearly they are at play here as well. There is much to sort out, but there is no doubt you are a Favoured, and we will need all the Favoured to defeat our foe if what you say is true. If we survive tonight, we will have to delve into what meaning the Norn might have for all of this. Jack, are you here to aid us in our dire times?"

"I'm ready to try."

A slow rolling rumble of thunder began to build as the Prelate spoke. "It seems Bergelmir was incorrect, Amanda. You were not the last Favoured to be claimed. Welcome then, Jack, Favoured of Loki. I claim you for Odin and for Asgard. Now, shall we see to saving our realm?"

CHAPTER 27:
WHEN GODDESSES COLLIDE AND A TRICKY RETURN

Amanda's insides twisted with a gut-wrenching lurch as they passed from the Bifrost into the city. The sight of the city in ruins made her think of pictures they saw in one of their history books of a European town after World War II, but with more ice and snow. The frozen Aesir, Einherjar and other creatures stared at them lifelessly as they ran through the streets. The saddest sight was Yggdrasil. It now stood barren, devoid of any foliage, and Amanda was reminded of her visions from the wyrm's venom.

It may have been hours since they were here last, but the entire realm seemed to have gotten a bad case of frostbite. A dark, creeping sludge was slung about the streets and bottom of buildings, and it clung to their clothes as they ran. Amanda had given Jack her cloak to help keep him warm, even though he kept insisting he didn't feel the cold. Amanda had asked if they had seen Cassie, Mykola, or Connor, but the Prelate had only shaken her head.

Pulling them into a small building that held a bar and several stacks of dirty dishes, the Prelate held out a hand for silence as a pair of Jotun giants barreled down the street. Once they passed, the Prelate turned to Amanda and Jack. "You two will need to make your way to the palace. Since Amanda has her full powers, she should be able to defend against any attackers you meet. Jack, you will need to be wary, as we do not know how your favouring fully works, so follow Amanda's lead. Sean and I need to find Prince Thor and Lord Freyr to free the Favoured and try to take the focus from Amanda and Jack's mission." The sound of a thousand Frost Jotuns could be heard all over the city. It seemed to energize the Prelate. "Do not stop for anyone or anything. Even if you do find your friends, you must continue on."

"We won't fail you." Jack held the spear up Sean had given him and nodded with determination. "We'll get Draupnir back to where it belongs and send the invaders packing."

The Prelate looked to Amanda as she held Draupnir in her hand. Its power still flowed through her, but its initial strength seemed to have diminished. "You must make it to Valaskjalf. The Jotuns have undoubtedly surrounded it to prevent the return of Draupnir, and to try to gain access to the power of the throne Hlidskjalf. The magickal protections surrounding the palace can only hold out for so long without Draupnir to power them. If they break into the palace or prevent you from placing Draupnir on the stand beside Lord Odin's throne, we are all lost."

"I won't fail. I can do this." Amanda echoed Jack.

The Prelate brought her fist to her chest, "Let your fervor deliver righteous retribution on our enemies. Now go and use your favourings to save this realm. On the Wings of Asgard." The group returned the salute and then splintered.

Snow was beginning to pile up on the roofs of the buildings they passed, and they dodged their frozen allies as they ran. Amanda wished they could stop to free them, but there was no time and too much at stake to slow down even for a moment. Amanda passed Queen Frigga with several Aesir, who were frozen in glass-like ice and collecting snow on their shoulders. The Queen had her hands up to the sky as if she were trying to break free. The Aesir were frozen mid-run. It looked like they were hurrying to their Queen to aid her. Amanda shuddered at the sight, and also at the thought of what kind of power it would take to keep the goddess trapped. The ring pulsed as it passed by the Lady of Asgard, but Amanda kept running.

A crash sounded somewhere off in the distance and Jack adjusted his spear slightly, "How did we not know places like this existed?"

"They have to hide it from most mortals. Not everyone could handle knowing there were other realms and creatures. Even after everything that happened the night of the Winter Festival, it was an adjustment for me."

"But you did it, and now you look like you belong here. You'll have to tell me the full story sometime when we aren't trying to save the world. Or is it worlds?" Jack ducked as they passed under one of the overlapping bridges.

"Realms," Amanda answered and smiled briefly. She felt good to have Jack beside her, even if his voice didn't hold its usual excitement. "And you'll have to tell me what happened with you and Bergelmir. I tried to find you, but…"

Jack stared ahead as if he were weighing what to say. "It's OK. I know you would have gotten to me eventually. Whatever happened to Ms. Biggs? I think… watch out!" Jack grabbed Amanda, and they slid on a sheet of ice as a boulder smashed into the street where she would have been a moment later.

A large Jotun laughed above them, sounding like a bear with a cold, and the streets in front of them exploded like a bubble bursting in boiling water. The force that shattered the street threw Amanda from her path and into the side of one of the stone homes that lined the main thoroughfare. The impact sent a spider web of cracks into the building's foundations, and made

Amanda drop Draupnir as her hands went numb. Amanda was dazed for a moment, but then frantically began to crawl around, searching for the ring.

"Jack!?" Amanda called.

"Is this what you are looking for?" Standing in front of Amanda, looking fresh and unfrozen was the goddess of battle. Lady Freyja bared her teeth as she wielded both her sword and Draupnir.

"Freyja." Amanda spat.

The goddess's blade sent sparks across the street, carving a deep groove that ended at Amanda's knees. "Lady Freyja to you, mortal." The goddess's sword moved so fast that it cut through the stones of the street like they were warm butter. "And I will be Queen when the Frost Jotuns complete their invasion. Bergelmir has promised me this realm when the others are conquered, and I intend to be rid of you disrespectful fleas once and for all."

"So, you betrayed us for power too? You are willing to go through Ragnarok again to be a Disir?" Amanda still felt dizzy from being blown across the road. She tried to raise her hands to cast a spell but couldn't get her focus.

"I am no Disir," Freyja hissed. "That is the path for the weak. I am doing what I must. I am no longer content to let a spell dictate my fate. The night of your trip to Sigyn, I found Keeper Fulla casting a spell on the lilies she had strewn about. Imagine my surprise when the imps came to life and I saw the Disir's mark she bore. At first, I thought to take her head for treason, but as I listened to her speak I began to understand her actions. She believes herself to be a part of some grand design, but all I wish is freedom – no matter the cost. I am caged by a spell, and that it is a cage I intend to be free of. What good is it to be a god if one must be stricken with mortality every century?"

"And not even you can get out of the spell on your own can you? So, you had to take the help of a Frost Jotun. Some goddess you are." Amanda was goading Freyja to stall for time to come up with a plan. There was no way she could take the goddess in a fair fight, but maybe she could think of the right way to use the spells she knew to give her an advantage.

Freyja's gauntlet ground on the hilt of her sword, twisting it into the ground, "Take care mortal. Bergelmir has ordered you brought to him alive. That is the only reason I do not remove the traitor Sigyn's first and last Favoured. Now come." Freyja grabbed Amanda roughly and herded her back the way she had come from.

"What will you do when Lord Odin returns? You will be no match for him and the rest of the gods. Bergelmir may claim he has enough power, but how can you trust him?" Amanda tried to pull her arm free, but Freyja sunk the sharp tips of her gloves into her arm to hold on. Jack appeared from nowhere, jabbing the butt end of the spear in Freyja's back, knocking her forward.

"You dare?" Freyja screeched, and with a sweep of her blade knocked them both back. "Do you think that we have not thought of the Allfather? Even gods can be laid low. All we need to do is hold Odin until the Spell of Favouring takes him and the others. Bergelmir has promised me protection so that I shall be spared from the spell's consummation. Once the Favoured hold their benefactor's magick we dispatch them and will speed the spell to its ending through you. Mortals can be killed a fair bit easier than the gods."

A cloud materialized in front of Amanda, Queen Frigga's royal bearing evident even before the clouds dispersed at her feet. "The Favoured will not be harmed while I still draw breath." Frigga's hand rose like a claw and a column of power masked in fog punched Freyja squarely in the chest, sending her back several feet. The Queen wore long robes that billowed out, but her ageless face remained calm and still.

Amanda's teeth chattered with the resounding energy that charged the air. Freyja recovered from the blast and leaned forward. Touching a claw-tipped hand to the ground she bared her teeth, like a lion ready to pounce. "I've waited centuries to do this, Frigga. Are you ready to go toe to toe with a war goddess?"

"Child, have you forgotten that war will always bow to the elements?" With a casual gesture like waving hello, the Queen of Asgard summoned a gale force tunnel of power against Freyja. The devastating attack leveled the buildings behind Freyja, but the goddess only took a step backward. Amanda and Jack stood wide-eyed, plastered against the side of the street, awed at the amount of raw magick in the air.

"Is that the best you can do? Your power wanes as the Frost Jotuns enter this realm, while mine grows with each footfall." Freyja moved with an overhanded attack, followed up by multiple attacks from other fronts as she spun like a hurricane.

Looking almost bored, Queen Frigga deflected the blows with watery shields of mist. "Not at all, my dear, it has just been so long since I have been allowed to unshackle my powers. I am simply enjoying the moment."

"And while you delay, I sense our forces gaining advantage and cornering your beloved Prelate. She may have slowed our assault, but I can sense she tires beside the other mortal." Freyja swung her fist and caught the Queen. Spinning, she tossed the Lady of Asgard into the air and through the doors of the Mead Hall.

Amanda used the moment to summon a ball of fire and launch it toward Freyja. The goddess dismissed it with a growl and spun to parry an attack from Jack. Amanda cast several shockwaves of magick and fire, causing Freyja to jump around like an acrobat at the circus. Amanda thought she might actually be able to win if she could keep the goddess from being able to attack, when Freyja picked up a broken beam and threw it at Jack. Amanda desperately hurled a spell to break the beam but was too late. Jack raised his arms to try and defend himself, but the wooden pillar passed harmlessly through him.

Queen Frigga flew above and landed between Jack and Lady Freyja. Holding up a hand she turned Jack solid again and then erected a barrier of magick around the two Favoured. "While I appreciate the effort, children, this battle is not for you." Draupnir vanished in a puff of smoke from Freyja's hand, and reappeared in the air in front of Amanda. "Thank you for bringing my lord's ring back to the realm. Even its presence here on Asgard was enough to help me break free from Bergelmir's spell. Take it and help us end this night's attack." Freyja moved like an attacking snake against the Queen before she could say anything else. Amanda grabbed the ring and Jack and ran. They barely made it down the street and out of site as buildings began to collapse from the aftershocks of the battle they left behind.

The sounds of the battle from the city could now also be heard all around. The invaders were taking root in the city and several Jotuns tried to intercept them, but they were no match as Amanda sent a volley of fire at them and Jack used the spear like he was born to it. Amanda only paused once to get her bearings and because her necklace had begun to glow slightly. The dome of Valaskjalf was creeping up from the tops of the buildings, and Draupnir burned in her hand as if anticipating its return to its rightful place. The stepped levels of the city they could make out were lit, but not by a golden glow. Instead, an ill purplish color was gathering in the sky. Amanda cast her green light to give her something familiar and to ignore the destruction of what was happening around her.

Rounding a corner, Amanda and Jack stopped as two cloaked figures blocked their path. As their cowls came down, the two blond twins raised their heads. Jack pushed Amanda out of the way as, in unison, the twins pointed a finger and a fiery tendril of fellfire shot toward them.

The spell should have slammed into Jack with enough force to send him flying, but instead he just sneezed. "Pardon me." The Zukovs hissed and Lena raised a finger again. A bolt of searing sun fire screamed toward Jack. The magickal lance made Amanda's cloak smolder, but otherwise Jack stood looking perplexed. "You know, I am new to this magick thing, but I think you might be doing it wrong."

Amanda laughed, the sound making her heart soar as her friend turned and smiled at her for the first time since they were reunited. Seizing upon the distraction, Amanda came up behind Jack and they began to circle around the twins. "Keep doing… whatever it is you are doing," Amanda whispered and then took a good look at the Zukovs. Her stomach churned when she saw the marks around their wrists. "You've become Disir."

Snorting, Lev switched from his new fell magick and tried to conjure a vision from Jack's worst nightmares, but nothing happened. "We have been set free, and we now have the power to save this realm. We will save it first from you, and then anyone else who tries to stop us from ensuring the realm will never face such dangers again. We have seen what becomes of this realm if you are not stopped. The future inhabitants of Asgard will thank us."

"Look, that's insane – even for you. You don't want whatever it is they are promising you. It will kill everyone you have ever known on Midgard. What did they tell you about being a Disir? Did they tell you what it costs? Help us get Draupnir back to Valaskjalf to stop the Jotuns, and we will find a way to save you. I am sure once we have freed the realm, we can break the binding on you."

Lena laughed. "You have no idea of what you are talking about. We are now more alive than we ever were. We took the power to take Draupnir, but we will keep it for ourselves. Keeper Fulla was the one to give us this power, and we promised her our help, but the realm's safety must come above our promises." Once more the twins attacked using fellfire, but again their magick failed as it collided with Jack.

"Are they doing something?" Jack spoke out of the side of his mouth to Amanda.

"How are you doing this?" Lev demanded. "How did you block our combined magicks? We were promised our powers would become that of the full might of the gods by becoming Disir!"

The air around them began to shimmer with heat, Lena with her sun fire and Lev with fellfire, causing the snow that was falling around them to evaporate before it touched the ground. Amanda felt just as confused as the twins, but she tried to hide it from showing. "It's because of Draupnir. Now that we have it, your powers can't hurt us."

The twins glanced nervously to each other. "You are lying!" Lev waved and Amanda bit her cheek to not scream as she saw a giant wyrm rise up in front of her. Lev's illusions were becoming more and more solid as he began to combine his magicks. Amanda was sure given time, he would be able to make them wholly real to those who could see them.

Jack clearly didn't see anything and just shook his head. "Why don't you two just head on back, take two Tylenol and call me in the morning?"

Lena and Lev began cursing and firing wave after wave of fire, fellfire, and visions at Jack, but he just stood there and yawned. Amanda, on the other hand, could see every nightmare Lev conjured, and her hair was even singed by one of Lena's beams. If Jack wasn't there to shield her she was sure she would be dead, but she kept up the pretense and tried to look unconcerned as they continued to circle toward the road to Valaskjalf.

"Let's go, Jack. There isn't anything these two can do to us now. We've already won."

"Wait!" Lev called out as they moved to walk past them. Something was churning inside his brain, although the way his eyes darted about it looked like he couldn't hold a thought for more than a second.

Amanda turned to look at the boy, only to find he had disappeared, along with his sister. A sound like nails on a chalkboard reverberated in the air around them. Amanda looked to Jack, "Where did they go?"

Jack's forehead creased and he pointed to a sign that hung crookedly from the building. "They are standing right there. Can't you see them?"

Lev's laughter came from the spot Jack indicated, and Amanda could see the wording was mirrored. "She is still susceptible to our powers, sister, but he is not!" The twins laughed as Amanda realized too late she had been tricked.

Jack shifted suddenly and Amanda saw him fall to the ground, wrestling with an invisible attacker. "Amanda, run!"

A noise behind her made Amanda spin, just as Lena appeared, her finger pointed at Amanda's chest. "*Fieryr!*"

Amanda's fire collided with Lena's heated attack, sending a shower of green flames into the air. Again, Lena fired at Amanda, but this time Amanda didn't have time to react. The heat seared through her clothing and burned a hole through her shoulder. Amanda cried out and held a hand over the wound. Lev's concentration must have been broken because he appeared on top of Jack, pushing the shaft of Jack's spear towards his throat.

"Finally, we will be rid of you, pest. Draupnir will be ours, and with it we will keep the realm safe!" Lena stood sideways and pointed like she was firing a gun, this time in line with Amanda's forehead.

As the magick built in the Russian girl, time seemed to slow. Amanda looked to Jack and Lev, and then back to Lena. The keening note from Lena's spell was an ugly sound that she remembered hearing when Lev had cast his illusion. They sounded almost identical but not quite. Amanda held up her hands and yelled, "*Transityr!*"

Lev started screaming as his hands began to radiate an intense heat. Jack took advantage of the distraction and slammed the staff into the side of Lev's head. The boy crumpled to the ground.

"Ah, no! Go away! Mama! Papa!" Lena was swatting at something in the air in front of her.

Stepping up from the pavement Amanda held up her hand as a green ball of flames appeared. "Here's a taste of real fire."

"Ahh!" Lena fell to the ground. The spell missed her, but hit the overhang of an adjacent building and a dump-truck-size load of snow fell on top of the girl.

Jack pulled himself up using the spear. "What did you do to them?"

"They may know how to use their own magick, but not how to use each other's."

Jack whistled, "Smart thinking! Your shoulder going to be ok?"

"It will have to be. How did you avoid their spells and the fellfire?" Amanda looked around to try to get her bearings. The battle with Lena and Lev had taken them off course, but thankfully she still had a hold of Draupnir and it gave a tug towards its home.

"No idea. It must be the favouring right? Part of my magick?"

"That makes as much sense as we need for right now. Loki was a god of illusion and fire. Maybe you are immune to their magick. If you could tap into that, maybe we could blast the Jotuns out of our way together."

"I don't know if it works that way. When I am blue the only thing that seems to happen is that people tend to do believe whatever I say. But I also don't feel like me."

Amanda thought for a minute. "Do you think you can stand being blue for a bit longer? I have a feeling we might need your other talents."

"I will do what I need to."

CHAPTER 28:
THE RULERS OF THE RING

They made it through the streets and to the plaza before they encountered anything else. Hiding behind the trees that ringed the palace, they counted what amounted to a small army of Frost Jotun giants that were lined up around the base of Valaskjalf. The towering behemoths were larger than any Amanda had seen before. They easily rose above the first level of the city. Lord Odin's palace may have only been a few hundred yards away, but it might as well have been across an entire ocean because there was no way they could make it through.

"What do we do now?" Jack tucked himself into the green needles of one of the trees that ringed the plaza as a swarm of imps passed them.

Amanda was hiding in a cypress tree. "I don't know. I was hoping we would be able to sneak in somehow. I know the Prelate said I could blast away, but I don't think I can take them all at once." Amanda held up her necklace, which thankfully was dark. For some reason it seemed that since her time on Midgard, her power had diminished.

"Do you think you could use Draupnir to help?"

Amanda looked down at the ring. The once brilliant stone was now dark as well, and the sound of its magick was barely a whisper. "I don't think it has much left. Bergelmir must have pretty much drained it dry. Do you think you could make them fight each other?"

Jack shrugged. "Sure, but that might make it even harder to get through."

The Jotuns were beginning to lumber about restlessly, and Amanda could hear imps skittering all around them. There was no way through or around them, but they had to get inside the palace for the plan to work. Without Draupnir in place they had no chance to banish the Jotuns from the realm. What was worse if Odin returned now, he would have to fight all of the Jotuns, and from the way Freyja had spoken it didn't seem like he had much time before the Spell of Favouring would leave him powerless.

There were Aesir and Einherjar in their way too. They stood in an unmoving ring around the Jotun giants, lifelessly staring at nothing. Amanda felt sick as she realized they were acting as a shield to the giants should there be an attack. A noise, like the sound of a stampeding herd of buffalo in the distance began to make the streets vibrate. Amanda looked about to see what was causing the disturbance, and then she saw a flash of electricity.

"ON THE WINGS OF ASGARD!" Sean's call preceded him and a cohort of others, including the Prelate and Cassie.

From the other side of the plaza came another war cry, this one shouted by Connor with Mykola charging alongside. Nimbus soared above them, knocking the heads of any Jotun giant he could. A corps of Einherjar followed the younger vindsvolla, flying on their own steeds, hurling spears and axes down on the Jotuns, taking care to avoid their brethren below.

The horde were momentarily caught off guard, but began to swing into action. Like a moving carpet of insects, the imps rose up and descended on Connor and his contingent. The giants smashed craters into the streets as they tried to flatten Sean, but he danced out of the way and hammered chunks from their legs and arms. Imps were melting around Cassie at her command, and she was even able to free several Einherjar from the spell Bergelmir had placed on them. Mykola was dodging about, twirling his staff. His touch could only harm magick, not creatures, but his touch freed the enslaved as well. Soon, half of the Jotuns were fighting those below and the other half were trying to swat the Einherjar from the sky. Amanda wanted to join in the fight to help her friends, and take a chunk or two out of the Jotuns, but Draupnir was almost silent.

"Looks like we got a diversion." Amanda looked once at Jack, who nodded in agreement, and they darted out from behind their hiding spots.

It should have been easy sailing to Valaskjalf, for the attack from two sides and above left large gaps in the blockade around the palace, but Draupnir began to glow brighter and brighter as they closed the distanced between the ring of trees and the palace. The giants noticed the light, and several peeled away from the battle to charge toward Amanda and Jack. Jack threw the spear with surprising accuracy, but it only glanced off of the giant's head. Amanda shattered one of the giant's weapons, and then burned it with fire so hot that it melted into a puddle. The Jotun's compatriots slipped in the water, giving them enough time to slide past.

Amanda nearly toppled over as a handful of imps threatened to trip them. The imps were rolling bowling balls of ice toward their feet, but Jack caught her just in time. She hurled a few volleys of fire toward the small creatures, sending them packing. A pack of Jotun giants that looked like a cross between a boulder and a polar bear broke off and blocked their path.

Jack stopped and Amanda nearly dropped Draupnir as she halted. Her necklace began to glow in warning. She was panting from the sprint. "We can't make it."

"You've got to. I'll distract them and you make a break for it." Jack pulled Amanda's cloak from his shoulders and handed it to her.

"Jack, you can't, they will kill you." Amanda pleaded, but Jack just ran toward the Jotuns.

Waving his hands, the growling giants focused on him. "Hey! You need to go that way! Bergelmir told me he would be looking for you over there. You better get going or he is going to be mad at you. You know what happens when he gets mad."

For a moment the sound of Jack's words hung in the air, as they formed their spell, and then the Jotuns began to turn and stumble away. Jack kept speaking to them until they were attacked and taken down by Nimbus and the flying Einherjar. Jack walked ahead of Amanda, sending any enemy in their path in the opposite direction. When they made it to the palace, Amanda slowly crept past her friend as he kept talking to lead the Jotuns away.

Suddenly a wave of Jotuns came toward them. Jack gave Amanda a long look before he was overwhelmed. Jotun imps began to tear at her as she tried to grab the hooped door-pulls that were slick with sleet. Amanda turned in a circle, casting fire at anything that moved until she was clear. Pulling with all her might, the doors slowly slid open. Another round of imps tried to fight their way past her and into the palace, but she vaporized them before they could gain entrance. Slipping through the small opening between the door panels, she used her good shoulder to close the door behind her. Amanda tried to calm her racing heart as her eyes adjusted. No outside light illuminated the glass dome, so the throne room remained dark. The colonnades of golden columns, carved of various figures and creatures in battle garb, looked menacing in the shadows. Amanda panted for a minute and called forth her little light. The green ball of magick cast enough light for Amanda to make her way toward Hlidskjalf.

BOOM!

The glass walls on all sides shuddered with the monumental impact of a thousand angry Frost Jotuns attacking along the perimeter. Amanda screamed and backed away from the walls. Several giants were crawling over each other toward the top of the dome to see if they could find a way in. The Jotun imps were frantically clawing at the doors to try and follow her, and several possessed Einherjar were trying to pull the doors open. With a flash Bergelmir appeared, riding a giant creature that eerily resembled the snowman spider Amanda and Jack made, but ten times the size and with a lot more teeth. It leered down at her as it jabbed the sharp points of its legs at the golden doors Amanda had passed through a moment before.

BOOM!

The force of the spider's blow radiated outward in waves across the dome. Amanda wasn't sure how the glass could withstand the impact, but it held. Bergelmir sent a volley of frozen magick that made several hundred of the runes etched into the glass vanish. The ground was shaking from the force of the combined attacks, and Amanda saw one of the columns dislodge the head of a golden Dwarf. Draupnir glowed even brighter and a beam of light blossomed from the ring and connected the ring to the triangular stand that stood upon the dais. Valaskjalf reacted to the presence of Draupnir as if it had been waiting for just this moment. A crown of golden points rose up from the perimeter of the dome, encasing the palace in an outer shell. The sounds from outside were now muffled, but no less persistent. Amanda felt Bergelmir begin to pour his full power into the assault and the doors shuddered with another tremendous impact.

Amanda used the brief respite and dashed toward Hlidskjalf. Draupnir sang a chorus of joy as Amanda reached the top of the steps. She placed the ring gently onto the stand. For a moment Amanda held her breath, and then was thrown back onto the soft cushions of the throne by a pulse of pure magick. Golden power flowed from the throne through channels in the floor, illuminating runes along its path. The air bloomed with life and the scent of a summer storm blew through the room, washing away the tang of snow that had permeated everything that night.

"It's over. I did it." Amanda sighed with relief.

In response, the area that the doors occupied began to creak and buckle. The golden light began to change to the color of a dark purple, and the walls around her began to fold inward as if being crushed by a giant hand from outside. The entire dome of Valaskjalf splintered and shattered, and Amanda screamed as she held up her hands to cast a spell to protect herself from the large slivers of glass as they rained down.

"Ha ha ha." The deep laugh boomed around her. Bergelmir strode in calmly, surrounded by an aura of magick so vile it made Amanda's stomach churn.

Fell and Frost Jotun magick flew about the plaza, and wrapped around the warriors that still fought, rendering them unconscious. Cassie and Connor were fighting back to back as the attack knocked them to the ground. Amanda's heart felt as if it were tearing in half as she saw Nimbus and the Einherjar riding the vindsvolla fall out of the sky. Bergelmir stopped and raised his hands toward the sky, and a hole opened up as if he was tearing apart the very fabric of space. Amanda looked up to see a castle covered in ice and buried in the sides of two mountains above her. The power flowing from Draupnir to the floor now flowed upward through Bergelmir as more imps and other Jotuns began to rain down on Asgard from Niflheim

"Thank you, Amanda." Bergelmir's voice echoed and shook every building in Asgard. "Only you could have helped me finally absorb not only the full might of Draupnir, but all the rest of the power that flows through Asgard, and soon Yggdrasil itself.

Amanda looked to the World Tree and saw it turn slightly transparent. "What do you mean? I placed the ring on the throne. You should be gone."

"The spells around Asgard are old and complex, and given time I assure you they could be broken. But as in all things, timing is all that matters. The power of the wretched Gray Beard allows for certain privileges in all realms, but especially in this realm. The connection of Yggdrasil to Asgard and Asgard to Odin is so interwoven, that access to one allows access to the other. I can now use the power of the World Tree to attack any realm I choose." The floor Bergelmir stood on began to turn black and crack.

"But the ring controls Odin's power when he is away, and his power keeps you away."

"And now I control that power. You are to thank for so many things. Just as I turned Fulla, I turned the ring to my will. When the ring's powers were activated on the pedestal they were transferred to its new owner – me. I can now take hold of the Spell of Favouring and hold it until you are ready to sever it. And now, not even Odin can stop me." Bergelmir cast a hand to his side and the ground began grow and form a rocky outcropping that was covered in black ice.

"I will stop you!" Amanda attacked with all of her might, but the magick felt slow and the Jotun lord banished it as if she was hurling balls of tissue at him.

"Take a look around, foolish mortal girl. Your Prelate, the Favoured, the cursed gods, and all the others are now under my control." Bergelmir snapped and Amanda felt something inside her break. "And now so are you."

"What have you done to me?" Amanda felt hollow, and Sigyn's necklace glowed so bright it hurt her eyes.

"Temporarily suspended your powers. You shall watch as I conquer each realm and you shall know it to be because of your existence. And when you ripen to fulfill your destiny, you will unleash Ragnarok and end the Spell of Favouring. For now, watch as we finish the Golden Realm once and for all." Raising his hands again, the full might of Asgard poured forth, forming a column that rose into the sky like a black needle.

The giant snowman spider lowered its head into Valaskjalf, grabbed Amanda in its mandibles, and lifted her high so she could see the death of Asgard. Amanda beat her hands against the spider's grip, and then the world shook with a blinding light.

A storm of thunder and wind poured forth from Yggdrasil and surrounded Bergelmir. The Jotun roared in anger and then in pain as the armored form of the Lord of Asgard descended, grabbing his power from the air and wrenching it back to its rightful purpose.

CHAPTER 29:
A BLINDING SUN

Amanda remembered one winter when a blizzard had blown in overnight, and the entire town of Wreathen was blanketed by two feet of snow in an hour. The roads were closed, the grocery store was raided of all common supplies, and the people on the streets hurried as fast as they could to get back inside. For two weeks the town seemed to be a deserted frozen wasteland. Nothing moved outside except phantoms in the drifting snow. On Christmas morning, the weather finally broke. Like all good kids, Amanda was up early to see what Santa brought her. That morning, Amanda was playing with her new Candyland board game that had been stuffed in her stocking. She had chosen to be the green gingerbread man because it was her favorite color, and was busy skipping her figurine across the land's bright candy squares. When she had dashed out of bed the sky had been dark and gray, as it had been for the past few weeks, so when a pink glow rose in the window, Amanda had been momentarily blinded by the glare. The beautiful rose-colored light of the sunrise was making its way across the floor to where she lay. Amanda recalled watching through the window as light flooded the landscape, turning the mounds of snow into a blinding mirror that danced with sparkling diamonds.

Seeing Lord Odin enter his palace to assume full command of his power was like watching that light play on the millions of snowflakes that were gathered into hills around her house. Amanda watched in awe as the ruler of Asgard slowly descended from the air. With his power supply cut off, Bergelmir had dropped like a stone to the floor. There was no doubt in the Lord of Asgard's countenance that he was the supreme power in his own realm. As he strode over to the Jotun, Amanda felt like an ant watching a hawk approach its prey.

The Allfather folded his arms and watched Bergelmir struggle to rise to his feet. The golden eagles' wings that wrapped his helmet covered one of his eyes, but the other flashed with anger. "Bergelmir, you have gone too far this time." The sound of Lord Odin's voice was like a sonic shockwave, silencing everything in its wake. The Jotun monsters both in and around Valaskjalf froze to see what happened next.

"Graybeard," Bergelmir rose and twisted his neck as he spoke. "You are too late. Asgard is ours. The Jotuns have defeated your defenders."

"Have they now?" Wavy black hair, tipped with gray, curled around the bottom of Lord Odin's helmet. His breastplate, gauntlets, and boots were layered with golden chevrons that lay over black chainmail. Lord Odin pointed to Amanda. "I still see a Favoured who has resisted your machinations."

"She is the one who started your downfall. She has been our pawn all along." Bergelmir laughed and waited for Odin to turn on Amanda.

Lord Odin banged a fist to his chest in challenge. "I do not see it that way, trickster, and if that is your victory then it is hollow. You should have stayed in Niflheim. Take your army and depart or else suffer the consequences."

"Nay, Odin. Your time is at an end. Look around. You cannot defeat us all, and she is now powerless. You may have stopped my acquisition of all of Asgard's powers for a moment, but I still retain what I took, and with it I will crush you beneath my heel. Once you are broken you will watch as I consume all you have fought to protect and remake it as I see fit. It is time for the twilight to finally claim you once and for all. Say hello to Hel when you arrive in her realm." Bergelmir threw his head back and roared, "Take him."

The hordes of giants and imps leapt into action. The giant spider tried to skewer Odin as he rose from the ground, a hundred spears flew into the air, and wintery blasts of cold magick were hurled with the promise of death. Odin's black velvety cape billowed out as he raised his armored fists and unleashed a band of magick that heated the air. The air's temperature rose so sharply Amanda could feel her extremities begin to tingle again, for they had gone numb from the cold touch of the spider's hold on her. The attacking pack of Frost Jotuns and their various attacks hissed with steam and cried out in anguish as they melted.

Amanda found herself falling through the air, only to be buffeted by an undercurrent of air, slowing her fall. The air current set Amanda on the floor, and then whirled back toward Bergelmir. The spiraling air gathered debris and shards of glass. The Frost Jotun raised a protective hand against the assault. Amanda expected Bergelmir to be torn to shreds, but instead the ancient foe of Asgard started laughing.

"My apologies, Lord Odin, but you will have to do better than that." The hand the Jotun held up displayed the ruby ring Draupnir. The ring was glowing as it began to absorb the energy of Odin's attack into its facets. Bergelmir snapped and the shrapnel heading his way vaporized. "You may not currently channel your power through the ring, but it still remembers what to do when it encounters your magick. Combined with mine own power, and that from the realm I now possess, it makes me infinitely stronger than you have ever been." Bergelmir whipped his hands together and unleashed a hailstorm upon the Lord of Asgard, followed with several spells that rippled the air as they flew.

Odin flew upward and evaded the attack with the majesty and speed of the bird on his helmet but was still pummeled by golf ball-sized hail. The Allfather recovered and blasted Bergelmir with a lance of lightning. "Enough of this! I will endure you no longer!"

"It is I who shall suffer you no more. Ragnarok approaches again thanks to your newest Favoured. Your time has come to an end. Journey to the void between realms or to Hel's embrace. I care not." Bergelmir used the power of Draupnir and his own magick to begin absorbing Odin's power from the air and hurl it like a relentless tidal wave against Asgard's ruler.

The assault of magick and power washed over Lord Odin, sending him flying through Hlidskjalf. Odin's fall severed one of the wings from the throne. For all his might, Odin's own power was proving to be his undoing, as it couldn't touch Bergelmir. Bergelmir flew to Odin's side and raised a fist to deliver a killing blow. Desperate, Amanda grabbed her necklace, hoping to reconnect with her favouring as she had in the Norn's forest. Green flames curled up her arms and surrounded her body. Eyes flashing with magick, Amanda launched her own attack. Bergelmir had ignored Amanda after he'd severed her powers, so her attack caught him by surprise. The green flames charred through the giant's outer garment and left a steaming hole in his back.

Bergelmir roared with anger and pain, his howl shattering what little glass was left of Valaskjalf's dome. Bergelmir turned slowly to face Amanda, hatred burning in his eyes. Slowly he took a step toward her. "You think you can play amongst the gods of the realms, mortal? Prophecy or not, I am finished with you! I shall consume your power and use it to end the spell that brought you here!"

Bergelmir turned his power inward. With each step he began to morph and grow. Fueled by Draupnir's fantastic might, Bergelmir grew until he stood half as tall as Yggdrasil, and unfurled taloned wings that leveled even more of the city around the palace as they swept open. The Aesir and other inhabitants of Asgard remained still or encased in their prisons. Amanda's magick had gone dormant again, and the necklace glowed once more as Bergelmir leered over her with teeth as long as she was.

Lord Odin appeared at Amanda's side "Miss West! I have need of you!"

Amanda hunched for safety as Bergelmir grew a tail that crushed the last of Valaskjalf's columns, and then swept the roof off the Mead Hall. "What can I do?"

Odin studied Amanda for a moment, and she could feel his magick overpower the air like an overdose of adrenaline. The Allfather held out his right hand and a large spear appeared. The shaft was a braid of gold and white metals, and the fearsome head shone forth with an inner fire.

"Amanda West, are you a true servant of the realm?"

"Yes, of course."

"Then take hold of mine spear, Gungnir, and let us defeat the enemy of that realm. Bergelmir may be able to wield the power that flows through Draupnir, and from this realm, but there is much more about my magick that he has yet to learn. You have the magick of a goddess, and more than he even suspects. Join your magick with mine, and we shall send the Jotun back to the wastelands of Niflheim."

Odin turned the spear toward Bergelmir as the Jotun lord lowered his head and roared. Amanda grabbed ahold of Odin's spear, and watched as her magick engulfed her entire body again. She felt connected to the power more deeply than ever before, and she reveled in the feeling as it washed away her fear and doubt. The Lord of Asgard let his power flow into the spear and guided Amanda's to do the same. Together, they rose like a green and white star that bathed everything with its light.

"A foolish effort. I command the darkness, the frozen, and the might of the heavens. Welcome your defeat and embrace death." Bergelmir dove toward them, the dark heart of his being hungry to absorb Amanda and Odin. The Jotun belched forth a tidal wave of fell magick that flooded the land with darkness and collided with the shield Lord Odin cast about them. The impact of Bergelmir's magick made every bone in Amanda's body ache as it flooded into the core of her being.

"Hold Miss West, hold!" Lord Odin tore something deep from within and uttered a few words that were lost to the raging magick around them. Amanda closed her eyes as the shadow of Bergelmir's open maw descended upon them. She felt her magick leave her as Odin released their power in a final blast.

With a thunderous crash, the entire realm shook. The pressure against them felt like they were slowly being squeezed into nothingness. Amanda poured all the feelings of frustration, determination, rage, fear, worry, hope, and joy she had experienced since the night of her claiming into her magick until she felt completely spent. And then all lay silent. Amanda stood tense with her arm extended, not daring to move, until she felt something land on her head. Slowly opening her eyes, Amanda found herself standing alone in the center of a crater with chunks of ice raining down all around her. With a shaking hand, Amanda brushed a piece of ice the size of a baseball glove from her hair.

"Lord Odin?" Amanda turned to see the Allfather kneeling before a mountain of ice rubble.

The Allfather turned toward Amanda as a halo of golden energy encased him. Magick emanated forth, growing in size as it gathered in power. The realm's shields ignited once more as Odin fueled them. The Allfather turned and lifted his hands. The Great Stars that gave the city light rose in the east. With another gesture, plants and rubble flew through the air, finding their way back to their homes. A large piece of stone that once formed the base for one of the columns of Valaskjalf shook as the magick washed over it, lifting it into the air. A slow rolling cheer sounded in the distance, and then finally built to a chorus of praise as the Aesir, Einherjar, and the Favoured were freed from their icy prisons and awakened. Amanda saw a fallen Jotun turn back into Billy and then vanish. Amanda guessed that all the other mortals Bergelmir kidnapped were being returned to their homes.

"Miss West." Odin drew Amanda's focus back to him. His voice before had been vibrant and robust, but now it was quiet and almost sad.

"Lord Odin, we did it! We defeated Bergelmir!"

"Aye. Today was a great victory for the realm. I sense the Jotuns and other traitors retreating, and those ensorcelled are coming free. With the last of mine might, Asgard has begun to mend herself." Lord Odin smiled again, but something was wrong. He seemed to be shrinking. "Miss West, there is much to be said in the days to come, but for now listen to me closely."

"What's wrong? Is it Bergelmir or the syirces?" Amanda moved to walk toward Lord Odin, but he held up a hand and instead beckoned her to follow him toward Hlidskjalf.

"Nay. The Jotun has been destroyed, and Hel has found herself another inhabitant to torture. Draupnir, however, has gone missing once more." The dark hair under his helmet was turning a frosty white, and wrinkles appeared around his deep brown eyes.

"But how? Bergelmir was wearing it when he transformed. It's got to be in that pile somewhere."

"I know not how nor where it has gone, but I can no longer sense my ring's power." Slowly making his way across his ruined throne room, Odin struggled up the steps to his throne. "Our comrades will be here soon, and my magick will fuel the defenses from now until the Spell of Favouring has completed its cycle, so the ring is not of dire importance. I tell you because you must know that there is more to this than Bergelmir's simple plan for conquest."

"You mean about the Spell of Favouring ending? I don't know how to stop it or what to do. The Norn said there was nothing to be done. They also said I was going to be the one to end it and bring about Ragnarok." Amanda waited for Lord Odin to respond to her confession. The dome was slowly piecing itself back together and the glittering diamond map of Asgard was forming over Amanda's head.

The Allfather nodded as if her words confirmed his thoughts. "That would make sense. The spell was always meant to end. I have known this ever since I sent my ravens to find you. For now, you must hold true to your course. I sense that you are to be of great importance to us in the future. Until we know where the ring went, and how fell magick was used on Asgard and by Bergelmir, we shall have to stay vigilant – and together."

Amanda watched Lord Odin as he sat down slowly onto his throne. He seemed so weak suddenly, and then it occurred to her that it wasn't fatigue she was seeing. The Spell of Favouring was beginning to close its loop, and Lord Odin's power was waning. She could tell his pride was slightly wounded by having someone watch his transformation, so she just nodded. "Tell me what I can do."

"Trust yourself. Magick can be deceiving. Spells are not set in stone. They themselves are flexible. Fight." Odin conjured his spear again and for a moment looked every bit the fearsome warrior that Amanda saw come to her rescue, and then his armor faded as his garb was replaced with brown linens. His mighty spear became a shepherd's crook, almost like Mykola's, and his helmet a wide-brimmed hat. The Lord of Asgard had become in all appearances a wandering peasant.

Amanda opened her mouth to speak, but a battalion of Einherjar jogged through the mending streets toward the palace, and upon entering formed a kneeling circle around their ruler. Lord Odin kept his gaze outward, and then looked up more and more of the inhabitants of the city began to pour through the streets toward Valaskjalf. Amanda's heart leapt as she saw Mykola and Cassie helping Sean hobble toward the palace. She looked to Lord Odin, who gave her a slight nod, and she knew they would speak again soon, so she ran toward her friends.

A golden portal opened in the middle of the courtyard in front of Valaskjalf, and the Prelate walked through, smiling proudly with Queen Frigga and Jack following behind her. Jack now wore the same blue and gold outfit as the other Favoured did, but his looked fresh where Amanda's was ripped and torn from battle. Amanda smiled as she realized the blue suit kind of looked like Jack's old denim clothing. He looked around and gave her a simple wave when he saw her running towards him.

Amanda threw herself onto Jack and wrapped her arms around him. His skin was still blue and quite cold, but she didn't care. "Are you OK?"

"I'm fine." Jack gave Amanda a small hug and then pushed her away. "Prelate Tess was just filling us in on her battle with Freyja."

"While leading the Favoured to the Stave I found Queen Frigga, who had all but dispatched the traitorous goddess, and joined the fray. We would have had her imprisoned, but a portal appeared to spirit her away. She leapt through and we were then overwhelmed by Jotuns, and could not give chase."

Queen Frigga touched the Prelate on the shoulder. "Pardon us, children. I do not mean to be rude, but we must see to our Lord."

The Prelate nodded. "The Queen is right. We will have plenty of time for tales later. I look forward to hearing yours, Amanda, as I am sure it is most thrilling."

Amanda watched them as they walked through the crowd, and then was engulfed by Cassie and the others. Cassie immediately began peppering her with questions. After hearing about returning to Midgard, and then more details on battling Freyja, Lena, and Lev, Cassie was beside herself with excitement and disbelief. Freyja being a traitor meant no more practice sessions with the goddess, which sent her powers into overload so that they all were now nearly drunk on happiness.

Jack was the only one who remained aloof, until Cassie's magick permeated the air. His skin began to turn normal, and his smile brought laughter and tears to Amanda's eyes. Amanda hoped they could find a way to remove the marks he still bore, but for now she was happy he was safe. Mykola and Connor had taken over the story, telling how they paired up with Prince Thor and Lord Freyr to help take down the Jotuns around the Einherjarium and free the Favoured. Amanda noticed Jack and Mykola kept looking at each other, and Jack even gave him a small smile. She was about to lean over and ask Cassie what was going on between the two boys when Nimbus sneezed on her. The group laughed, and Mykola picked up the vindsvolla to get him away from the frost lilies that were still scattered about. Cassie took advantage of the interruption and pointed out that it was she who brought reinforcements in the form of imps and Jotun giants that she had enthralled to attack each other, and that by the time Prince Thor and Lord Freyr got to them, it only took one huge lightning strike to vaporize half the Jotuns who attacked them. Amanda made a mental note to ask Jack about what she saw later.

Sean was mostly silent, only adding in brief additions to the tale. He seemed reluctant to talk about the battle, even though Connor and Mykola both swore he had taken out over a hundred Jotun giants with just his hammer. His arm was in a sling, and he winced when Amanda bumped it when she gave him a hug. When they got to the part about the battle around Valaskjalf, it had only been sheer coincidence that they arrived at the exact same time to give Amanda a way through the Jotuns. The cacophony coming from the streets that were now filled with groups joyously celebrating was becoming overwhelming. Amanda filled her friends in on what she could about the final battle with Bergelmir and Lord Odin, leaving out the part about Draupnir. As the crowd around her quieted and then knelt, she fell silent too.

Odin stood with light from the stars above streaming down on him, and even without his armor he still looked impressive. "Asgardians! Tonight we faced a cunning foe that preyed on what they thought was a weaknesses, and we showed them how wrong they were. Tonight, we defeated Bergelmir. Not through the might of the gods alone, but with the combined might of the gods and their Favoured. Tonight, we have shown that we can survive any coming darkness together and that we will restore peace wherever evil lives. Tonight, war was declared throughout the realms, and tonight we answered the call with victory!"

The crowd erupted with cheers and shouts, and then someone pointed to the sky. For a minute Amanda thought the Frost Jotuns were attacking again as dozens of figures fell from the sky toward them. She and the others braced themselves.

"The gods have returned!" One of the Favoured shouted.

Amanda realized that what she had thought was blue skin was the glint of magick radiating from their golden armor. The joy of the crowd poured through Cassie and the others, and Amanda yelled in excitement with the rest. With Lord Odin's return, Asgard was safe again. Although, Amanda noted no one seemed to notice his change. Lord Odin bade them all to return to their homes, rest, and verify that all those who attacked the realm had been dispatched. Amanda and the others walked back to the Stave, watching bits of brick and glass fly from the streets to rebuild the homes they passed.

CHAPTER 30:
THE MISSING GODDESS

The Stave was fairly well put back in order by the time the group made it to their common area. They collapsed into the leather furniture, and for a moment no one spoke as they let the night's events sink in. Cassie of course couldn't stand the silence and began to pester Sean about his arm. Without Fulla, and since the Mead Hall was still fixing itself, they had to fend for themselves for food. They foraged around and found only leftover stew and stale mead before some Aesir came to bring fresh mead and food for them. Jack decided to take over Lena and Lev's room after they ate, and left to take the hottest shower he could stand. When he got back, they were in the middle of the third round of Amanda defeating Connor at rune wars. Jack sat down next to Mykola just as they were interrupted by someone clearing their throat.

"By the Eye!" Sean stood straight and banged his fist to his chest, wincing as he hit his bad shoulder.

Prelate Tess, Lord Odin, and Queen Frigga entered the common area. "Good evening, Favoured. May we join you?" Lord Odin asked, but did not wait for permission.

Queen Frigga extended a hand and the room rearranged itself to include more seating. The gods sat on a long bench with a high back while Sean, Cassie, Jack, Mykola, Connor, and Amanda all crowded into the other chairs.

"Now," Lord Odin began, "Let us start at the beginning. Miss West, I should very much like to hear of your claiming and your time with us so far, and then I would like to hear of your time with Bergelmir, Master Jack."

Amanda began telling the story and this time she made a point to leave nothing out. When she talked about Sigyn she realized she should make time to go make sure she the goddess was OK. She paused only when others jumped in to add their parts. When she reached the part with the Norn, the others became still as they listened intently. She shared how the Norn told her of the wars and Ragnarok to come. Cassie took her hand, sensing her friend's unease as she spoke of how they told her that she would be the one to start the Ragnarok that would destroy everything and end the Spell of Favouring. Taking another moment, Amanda brushed her bangs from her face and waited to see if anyone jumped up to tell her to leave when they heard of the Norn's words. When they didn't, she felt her face flush and tears sting her eyes as she let out the breath she had been holding. She swallowed to regain her composure before continuing gratefully. The others spoke up again as they talked through their race through the Norn's forest, the trials, and the events back on Midgard. As she spoke of Fulla's revelations on how they spirited away Draupnir, combining fell and Asgardian magicks, all three of the Asgardians leaned in to hear more.

At last Prelate Tess spoke, breaking her side's silence. "It seems we were blind to the idea of mixing fell and Asgardian magick to enter our realm. Just as we were to Fulla's deceit. We will work with the Light Elves to rectify that. With Fulla gone, the syirces and alfblot should dissipate as well. They also found where Fulla was sending the alfblot not used for the syirces – the Gruneling."

"Perhaps it is as we feared." Queen Frigga began but fell silent at her husband's touch.

"Please continue." The Allfather gestured to Amanda.

Amanda looked to Sean and began to tell the story of their battle with Bergelmir in the mountain range on Midgard. Jack piped up at this point and told them of his time in Utgard, the spells Bergelmir used on him, what happened to Billy, and what he could remember after Bergelmir took control of him. Amanda tried to put on a brave face as her friend spoke, but she couldn't help but shed a tear or two. She had had nightmares of what was happening to Jack while he was captured, but what he had endured was far worse than she could have imagined. Jack finished with fully waking up on Midgard with Amanda.

Amanda reached over and gave his hand a squeeze, and then began to describe how they escaped Bergelmir with Draupnir. Lord Odin tapped the side of his staff as he pondered Amanda's words when she spoke of his ring, and her use of it on Midgard. Amanda continued telling her side of the tale through defeating Bergelmir. She stopped after she told the others how Lord Odin began to rebuild the city with his spells to let the Allfather tell more if he so desired.

"It is most interesting to hear that Bergelmir was not responsible for Yggdrasil, even though he used it to his advantage. We will have to study this, and revisit our protection of Midgard. Keeper Fulla created an entrance into the realm with the death of the original Favoured that must be sealed. We must also ensure there are no more like Lena and Lev." The Prelate looked to Queen Frigga, whose dress had remained dark as night for the past fifteen minutes. The Queen nodded her assent.

"What about Lena and Lev?" Sean asked.

"We have found no evidence of Lena or Lev's whereabouts. We believe that they spirited themselves from this realm just as Lady Freyja has." The Prelate looked at them sadly for a moment. "Their fates are their own now."

"On a more positive note, Heimdall shall be himself again soon. As soon as Lord Odin returned, those poisoned by the alfblot began to awaken with no discernable repercussions." Queen Frigga looked to Cassie. "Miss Pritchett, the Prelate and I have discussed your training. I would like to continue it."

"Done! I mean, of course, Queen Frigga, that would be brilliant. Cheers!" Cassie smiled and everyone leaned away to avoid getting infected by a bout of giddiness.

Lord Odin spun his staff and leaned it toward Amanda. "You should be proud, Miss West. Not many mortals could have faced Bergelmir thrice and lived to tell the tale as you just did. I myself do not favor the thoughts of battles from before, nor relish the idea of battles to come."

"You mean we didn't defeat him?" Connor gripped the arms of his chairs.

"The Jotun now dwells in Hel, but just as evil can lurk in the corner of a mortal's heart, so can does Bergelmir still be found or restored. An evil of his might cannot be completely returned to the void, only relegated to a prison for a time. And Amanda's words and what we heard from Jack indicate even he has fellow conspirators that may seek to release him. I fear the Jotun may be in league with an even greater evil. That is our true enemy we must watch for and find."

"Will there be more attacks?" Sean had been sitting still for too long and was getting fidgety.

"We have given ourselves a respite, I believe, for a time. I sense there is more afoot that we shall have to prepare for. It seems that the words of the Spell of Favouring are at a time where they shall become reality. We have kept parts of it silent until now. However, events have changed our need." For a moment no one spoke. Lord Odin looked to the Prelate. "Granddaughter, 'tis time to share your tale."

"Granddaughter?!" Cassie sputtered, looking back and forth from Lord Odin to Prelate Tess, but the others shushed her.

Prelate Tess stood and held her gauntlets in front of her. "After Ragnarok, we had no idea what to expect. The spell left so many mysteries that we were not sure what it would truly do. I remember the light of my sisters, and their chant, and then I awoke on the Plains of Idavoll. I was alone, save for the gauntlets that were chained to the earth. Just as Amanda shared from her vision."

"For a hundred years." Mykola motioned, and Cassie spoke, not in a question but just a statement of what they were taught.

"Aye, but what I have shared only twice before is that in that time I learned from the runes on these gauntlets the words that the Norn spoke to Amanda – the second part of the Spell of Favouring." The Prelate indicated for Amanda to speak.

Clearing her throat, Amanda spoke quietly. "In this time and in this place, take this life to save one of Odin's race. Through sacrifice we submit our thrall, and give her our power, one and all. To wait till the hundredth year whilst the fires of Surtur burn clear. A guardian of nothing will she be, chained until twilight's time is free. By the power of Yggdrasil's life and death the rebuilding shall be made done, and we call forth the Favoured to be spun. But all be warned by the Norn, when newly found of magicks Favoured be unbound, again the fire of Ragnarok will come round." Amanda took a breath, "Then will the dark mark awaken, and the dark Favoured be forsaken. For life to be restored, death will meet death, mortal and god will be joined, and Surtur's joy will give way to mourn. Find the hate within to win this tale for all mortals' hearts to be quelled, and the required favouring be at end."

The Prelate nodded. "Until Amanda shared them with me again, I did not understand their meaning, but I believe I do know a part of what is to come. I believe those words are part of a lesser spell that was enacted upon Amanda's claiming. Not as a part of something destructive, but as a warning. I believe Lena and Lev are the dark Favoured mentioned, but beyond that I do not know what it means."

Everyone furtively stole glances at each other. Amanda kept her eyes down as slowly all turned to see her reaction. "Well, I say bring it. We don't know what it means, but Sigyn and even you, Lord Odin, said that there are choices that I can make to make sure that the Norn's words don't come true. So, that's what I plan to do. Not let anyone else control me or use me. I may not have had the same claiming as you all, but I am a Favoured."

Lord Odin laughed. It was a deep belly laugh that broke the heaviness of their conversation. "Well said, Amanda! You were born to be a Favoured, so do not let their words make you run away from that. We stand together or not at all."

Cassie's hand touched Amanda's, followed by Connor, Sean, and Mykola, although his hand was gloved. "We are in it together. I know you would never intentionally hurt me, Amanda. We will keep each other safe."

The others in the room all nodded, and Amanda heard the lilting music of magick rise at the unspoken vow that formed between them. Lord Odin, Queen Frigga, and Prelate Tess spent the rest of their visit discussing what was to be done in the upcoming days. Prelate Tess told them she would continue to lead the lessons of the Favoured, and they would all focus on helping Jack catch up on his training. Amanda had to bite the side of her cheek from laughing in sympathy for what he was about to endure. Queen Frigga also decided that she would not only be training Cassie, but Amanda and Jack as well, especially focusing on helping Amanda learn more about the true nature of her spells and magick. Amanda thanked the Queen, but also requested that Sigyn be released from her tower. The Allfather said he would consider it once he talked with the goddess. It felt for the first time like there was a plan in place that really made the future seem bright with possibility.

The Aesir brought them more food and they ate together, retelling more of the battle and any nuances they could think to add. Afterward, Lord Odin suggested the group turn in and get some rest as their activities would resume in a few days, but surprised Amanda by asking if they could go take the trip to Sigyn then and there. Amanda grabbed a new cloak and uniform, and decided to check in on Jack, before heading out with the Allfather. Amanda knocked on his door. There was a moment, and then the door opened.

Jack stood in the doorway still wearing his new uniform. "Hey. What's up? Don't you have to be somewhere with Lord Odin?"

"Yes. I just wanted to make sure you were ok."

Jack smiled, and Amanda saw the spark of her old friend in his eyes. "I'm making do."

"I just... I am sorry." Amanda felt tears in her eyes again.

Jack opened the door fully and gave her a hug. "Hey. No tears. What do you have to be sorry about?"

Amanda gave him a squeeze and then stepped back. "I feel like you got dragged into all of this because of me. You should have been the one to go when Ms. Biggs showed up while we were making that snowman spider. Maybe you wouldn't have been taken then."

"You can't think like that Amanda. The way I see it is that we were meant to go through what we did. I am just glad we can go through this together." Jack smiled a real smile again. "You and me against anything else these... Jotuns or whatever plan to throw at us. Now go. I don't want the king of this place mad at me for holding you up."

Amanda gave Jack another hug again and promised to come find him for a longer talk later, but she felt another huge wave of relief to know she and Jack were going to be ok. She found Lord Odin waiting for her in the common area and they set off. They were silent until they reached the Plains of Idavoll. Amanda was relieved for a bit of silence, as she started to process everything from their earlier conversation.

Lord Odin, as it turned out, did not need any guides to lead him to the tower. Halfway through the plains, the Allfather broke the silence and his question surprised Amanda. "I am sure you have noticed my appearance, Miss West. Is there nothing you would like to ask?"

"I thought it might have bothered you, and I didn't know if it was proper." Amanda blushed.

"While I have to admit it is not my most favored of aspects, it is one I bear with pride. I still possess a remnant of magick that allows me to appear in my armor and full power, but that will fade soon. None of the others can see through my guise for a time though, 'tis best to not scare everyone all at once. A small lie to help keep the peace for a bit longer."

"I guess that makes sense. But why can I see it?"

"When I asked you if you were loyal to the realm and to Asgard, by saying yes and laying a hand on my spear I did share a bit of my power with you."

Amanda felt touched. She knew in the heat of the battle there hadn't been much choice, but he had chosen to trust her regardless. "Thank you, Milord, that means a lot to me."

"I believe it well deserved."

"There is something you said when you asked for my help. You said I had more magick than I suspected. What did you mean by that?"

Odin stroked his beard and stopped them in a dense patch of grass. The wind shifted the brim of his hat slightly. "Truthfully, I am not certain. There is precious little I know of this time after Ragnarok. What I do know only comes in glimpses. Perhaps in the way Fulla was given glimpses by the fyglja. What I have been told of your favouring, your connection to Sigyn and her full might, does not fully explain your full command of some spells so easily. Couple that with the fact that you are the only mortal I know to have handled Draupnir and survived unharmed, makes you more unique than most."

Amanda chewed the side of her cheek. "Is that why you did it? Why you bound me? Did you see something about my future that made you think I shouldn't have my magick?"

"A little. However, let me say that while I may be fearless in battle, the fear I had for you and your power was for your own safety more than ours. I knew that when you were chosen by the spell there could be repercussions with Sigyn being denied her magick. I thought this the best way I could come up with to quickly keep you safe from yourself. My apologies if it caused you doubt. I had expected to be present at your arrival."

Amanda felt a chill run down her skin thinking about the forethought Lord Odin had given her without him even knowing who she was. "You are probably right. I did manage to dump snow on my teacher by accident." Amanda laughed at the thought. "There is something you should probably know, though. I don't think I have Sigyn's full powers anymore. Before, I felt full, like a cup of water that had to be careful not to tilt to the side or risk spilling. Now, I just feel... normal."

Lord Odin murmured and something rustled in the night. Hugin and Munin flew from a cloudbank above and settled on their master's shoulders. First Hugin leaned in and chirped into Lord Odin's ear and then Munin. Afterwards they took off, one racing toward the city behind them and the other toward the heart of the plains. "I have asked our friends to investigate the matter a bit more. I would not worry though. You are linked to Sigyn, and she still has need of you. It might prove to be a blessing as you can now learn of your powers without fear of their full might."

Amanda pondered that for a moment. "Lord Odin, I know you bound my magick because you worried about me having the full magick of Sigyn, but that doesn't explain why Jack and I were chosen. After all this time of

Loki or Sigyn not having a Favoured, why us and why now?"

"That is a very good question. In answer, is the phrase on Midgard still, "Be careful to know your history, or you are doomed to repeat it?"

"More or less."

"Then let us hope we remember our lessons well. Why does anything happen when it does? The answer is because it was needed. For now, let us enjoy this evening stroll, rather than weigh ourselves down with thoughts of future darkness and questions. Maybe you would like to hear a tale from an old man?"

For the rest of the walk the Allfather played storyteller. As the city's current reigning oldest resident, he had plenty of tales to tell, so that the journey through the plains was filled with lessons from history. Amanda felt honored to be trusted and laughed as the Allfather told stories of times where Prince Thor and Lord Freyr had to pretend to be dancers, dressed in what she could only assume looked like unitards that were covered in flowers, to gain entrance to the throne room of a warring Dwarf lord.

The light was setting on the Plains of Idavoll as the Lord of Asgard and Amanda came toward Sigyn's tower. Odin let Amanda lead the way up the steps as they decided the climb would be more respectful than just appearing in front of Sigyn in her quarters. Amanda stepped through the threshold and stopped. The room was dark and quiet. There was no bustle of paper, no smell of smoke, or even the sound of beads moving. Nothing stirred.

"Sigyn?" Amanda felt cold. She rushed into the room and cast her spell for light.

Odin stepped through the arched doorway. Taking stock of the room and Amanda's reaction he raised his staff and knocked it on the walls three times. A small wind, with barely more than the strength of a breath, moved scattered paper on the floor under the three tapestries to the left of Amanda. Hugin and Munin appeared in the windows and squawked. Lord Odin nodded to the tapestries, and Amanda pushed the first one aside that bore a woven image of Yggdrasil. The other two had images of Odin and a dark figure with burning eyes. With a tug, the wool rugs fell to the ground, revealing a dark chamber empty except for dark runes that were etched into the walls. A syirce spun fell sparks of magick onto the emerald floor.

Lord Odin entered the room beside Amanda. "It seems we have found at least one answer this evening. Your magick is no longer full because Sigyn once more roams the Nine Realms."

The End

A GUIDE TO THE PRONUNCIATION OF NAMES

<u>Names</u>

Andhrimnir – ond-hrim-meer – The Chef of Asgard.

Balder – bawl-der – God of Light.

Bergelmir – bair-ghel-meer – Ruler of the Frost Jotuns.

Eir – ai-r – Goddess of Healing.

Forseti – for-se-ti – God of Justice.

Freyja – frei-ja – Sister to Freyr. Goddess of Love, Beauty and War.

Freyr – frei-r – Brother to Freyja. God of Fertility, Farming and Soil.

Frigga – fr-ih-ga – Queen of Asgard. Goddess of Prophecy and Clouds.

Fulla – full-ah – Servant of Queen Frigga. Keeper of Asgard. Magick to see and correct mistakes.

Heimdall – heym-dahl – Gatekeeper of Asgard. Possesses far-reaching sight.

Hel – hel – Daughter of Loki. Goddess of Death.

Idunn – ee-dune – Keeper of Apples of the Gods. Goddess of Youth.

Loki – loh-kee – Adopted son of Odin. Husband to Sigyn. God of Tricks and Fire.

Mimir – mihm-eer – God of Knowledge.

The Norn – no-rn – Goddesses of Fate.

Odin – oh-din – Ruler of Asgard. God of Wisdom, War and Runic Language.

Sif - Goddess of the Fields.

Sigyn – seg-in or see-gin – Wife of Loki. Goddess of Magick.

Skadi – skah-dee – Goddess of Winter.

Skuld – skoo-ld – Norn. Goddess of What Will Be.

Surtur – ser-ter – Ruler of the Flame Jotuns.

Tess – Thrud. Prelate of Asgard and the last Valkyrie. Grandaughter of Odin. Daughter of Thor.

Thor – th-oh-r – Son of Odin. God of Thunder and Battle.

Thram – th-ram – A Dwarf Warrior.

Urd – oo-rd – Norn. Goddess of What Was.

Verdandi – ver-dahn-dee – Norn. Goddess of What Is.

Places & Creatures

Aesir – ey-zir – Inhabitants of Asgard.

Alfheim – alv-heym – The Realm of Light Elves, the fair ones.

Asgard- ahs-gahrd – The Realm of the Gods.

Bifrost – biv-rost – The Rainbow Bridge that connects all realms to Asgard.

Dwarves – Inhabitants of Nidavellir.

Einherjar – in-hear-ir-ahr – Warriors of Asgard.

Einherjarium – in-hear-ir-ahr-ee-um – Training Grounds of Asgard.

Fell Elves – Enemies of Asgard.

Fensalir – fence-ah-leer – The hall of Queen Frigga where the Favoured train their magick.

Fyglja – feeg-leh-ja – Creatures from the Norn's Forest.

Gimle – ghim-leh – The Stave of the Favoured.

Ginnungagap – ghin-nung-ah-gap – The great chasm at the beginning of time where all creatures came from.

Gruneling – grune-ling – Prison of Asgard.

Hel – hel – The Realm of the Dead.

Hlidskjalf – hlith-skee-yalf – Throne of Odin. Grants Lord Odin and Queen Frigga the ability to see anywhere in the realms.

Idavoll – ee-da-vull – Plains bordering Asgard.

Jotunheim – yaw-toon-heym – The Realm of Rock Jotuns.

Jotuns – yaw-toons – Enemies of Asgard.

Knud –knew-deh – A butterfly from Alfheim.

Light Elves – Inhabitants of Alfheim.

Midgard – mid-gahrd – The Realm of Mortals.

Mimir's Well – Well containing Mimir's head near Lord Odin's Palace.

Muspelheim – moo-spell-heym – The Realm of Flame Jotuns, the fiery ones.

Nidavellir – knee-dah-vell-ea – The Home of the Dwarves.

Niflheim – niv-ul-heym – The Realm of Frost Jotuns, the cold ones.

Norn's Forest – Home of the Norn. Forest of Fates.

Svartalfheim – szvar-talv-heym – The Realm of Fell Elves, the dark ones, and Dwarves.

Utgard – ooht-gard – Castle of Bergelmir in Niflheim.

Valaskjalf – vahl-la-skee-yalf – Palace of Odin.

Vanir – vah-nir – Inhabitants of Vanaheim.

Wyrms – whir-ums – Annoying creatures that can feed on magick.

Yggdrasil – ig-druh-sil – The World Tree and Tree of Life.

ABOUT THE AUTHOR

Futurist by title and interior designer by trade, Mark E. Bryan is a nationally recognized, award-winning creative.

Already a published author in a variety of disciplines, Mark's passion for reading and writing brought him to create this book as his first novel. With a love of storytelling, and a deep curiosity for exploration, his literary adventure transcends boundaries, pushing limits, leaving readers wanting more.

In his personal life, Mark resides with his husband and three fur children in Columbus, Ohio.

ACKNOWLEDGMENTS

This book's journey has been a lengthy labor of love. Starting with a singular chapter of smoke and debris, it grew with me in life and love. I give thanks to God for the abilities He has given me.

Along the way I have been given advice, encouragement, and words of hope by numerous friends and advisers (Shannon, Michele, Sarah, Keith, Micheal, and Sara,) who read my words and told me I could keep going. To you I send you a forever-grateful hug.

To my editor, Tom Jacobs, thank you for your expertise and guidance. You gave insights to the world I was creating that were unexpected, right, and collaborative.

Tony, your art brought what was in my head to colorful life. Thank you for sharing your talent to make my dream have faces.

Doug, thank you for giving the book its first step toward professionalism.

To my family, thank you for pushing me to be a creative person with a love of reading.

To Sam, who is the most wonderful cheerleader and marketing strategist, thank you for the energy you give to us all.

Shaun, for every rewrite, tear, frustratingly-prolonged delay, and car ride where you allowed me to work while you ferried us to our destination - your love was shown through your actions, hugs, calming words, and firm pushes. This book is here because of you.

PREVIEW: THE TOUCH OF THE VALKYRIE

LEFTOVERS

Ms. Madge Biggs fidgeted with her necklace as she seethed quietly on her front porch. Her eyes were permanent slits as she stared at the neighbors. They were carousing about, making a noisy, messy ruckus in the center of her cul-de-sac. The children were playing tag, chasing each other and screaming at decibel levels that made her ears want to explode. The parents were just as annoying. They mingled about, complimenting each other on whatever disgusting pasta salad or fruit dish they brought to the block party that took over the cul-de-sac.

Most of the families she knew, but her eyes narrowed in on the two newest ones that had taken residence in the house directly beside and across from her own. Her fingers twisted her necklace, almost breaking the string of pearls, as she squinted even harder to study them and their brats. The boy couldn't be more than ten and the girl was probably only a year older, which meant they would be starting at Wreathen Middle School in the fall. Her school. Or, it was.

Closing her eyes, Madge pursed her lips together as she sifted through her memories of the night when everything changed. She remembered the Festival, and the way her car bounced about on the way home, no thanks to the hatchet job the auto repairman had done. Then there was the insufferable boy who always wore too much denim, the girl who was the *real* cause of her consternation, and then something blue and wriggly. But her memories vanished until she woke in the snow. Then there was the blinding sickness that followed for weeks afterward. Even now her fingers still twitched and cramped every time she touched anything cold.

She had been forced to take a leave of absence, and then Principal Carmack had suggested to the School Board that it was time for her retirement. There was nothing she could do to fight them off, enfeebled as she had been. The embarrassment of it all almost made her wish she hadn't recovered. The entire school board had sided with those who rose up against her. After all she had done for them and this district, they had cast her out.

"I will make them rue the day," Madge whispered so harshly that a passing bird screeched and wheeled away.

But again, they were not her main point of consternation, nor were her neighbors' frivolities. It had all started with Amanda and Jack. They were the ones who had put her in this position. That girl had been a nuisance all year long. She was constantly late, never prepared, and always disrupting her class. And then the day for the trip came, and Amanda had shown her true colors, and attacked her. Stalling the buss and causing the snow to fall on her after making her fall into the snow. How she managed it, Ms. Biggs still hadn't figured out, but she knew that was just the first salvo after what came later. She and her irritating friend, Jack, had been lying in wait for her. The boy had distracted her while Amanda had probably set some kind of feral rat loose to attack her. She had planned to prove it once she was well enough, but then they had vanished, no doubt knowing the retribution she would bring down on them. Or perhaps their families had come to their senses and sent them off to military school. The day she came home from the hospital, she made plans to confront the Wests and Isens the next day. That night lightning shook their entire neighborhood. The next morning the Wests and the Isens had packed up their cars and left. The sale signs appeared in their yards soon after. Madge had felt as if her vindication had been stolen from her. Now she had no way to prove it was Amanda and Jack who had started the sickness that cost her so dearly. But she knew it with every fiber of her being – and she would make them pay one day.

Madge jumped as something crashed inside her house. Her eyes darted back to the block party. The new boy and girl were nowhere to be seen. "Those hooligans! I will not let another pair get the best of me!"

Throwing open her screen door, Madge barreled into her taupe entryway. She scanned her pristine black and white sofa in her living room. The pillows were still neatly stacked, and her china set was untouched on the credenza. Madge leaned into the dining room that held her portraits from grade school into college on the walls. The picture frames were askew as if something had blown through the room and into the kitchen. She slowly stepped into the room. Without warning, something slithered around her ankle and hauled her into the air.

"What in the world? A booby trap? When I get down from here, you will be sorry!" Madge clutched her pearls while trying to wiggle in the air to free her feet from whatever contraption had ensnared her. She spun for a few seconds, her face turning red as she became even more irate.

"She will do."

Madge's stomach lurched. The voice coming from behind her was too old to belong to any child. It was dry and crisp, and somehow familiar. A trickle of sweat slid across her forehead as she spun once more to find a woman in golden armor, and another unseen intruder standing in the shadow of the hallway to her bedroom.

"Are you certain? She cannot even defend herself against an entrapment rune." The woman in armor spoke, her harsh voice lilting at the vowels.

Madge began to struggle even harder. "Who are you? What are you doing in my home?"

"Her soul has been touched, her heart bleeds with hatred, and she is a descendant. She will be our messenger." The dark figure moved toward Madge, and the shadows clung to him as if he were pulling them forward. Two tendrils shot forward and wrapped around Madge's wrists. Another covered her mouth, and the enshadowed figure's voice reverberated throughout the house as he uttered a series of scratchy syllables.

***

Amanda breathed in deeply and opened her eyes. The smell of grass and dew mixed with fragrant berries made her wish she could lie down and enjoy the mid-morning warmth coming from the star above. Short, curling trees ringed the plateau where she sat. She looked past the trees and down into the blue mist of nothingness that swirled below the floating mass of land that she alone occupied. Looking up, she counted over two dozen other floating plateaus within sight, which were all about the size of two football fields put together, leading up to Ljos – the crown city of Alfheim.

The realm of the Light Elves was comprised of not one large land mass like Asgard. It was filled with islands of land that drifted in the air throughout the entire realm. The largest of these islands was Ljos, which was about half the size of the city of Asgard. One of the scrolls Amanda read about Alfheim said that if you fell off of one of the floating islands, you would continue to fall until you hit Svartalfheim. Amanda pulled away from the edge as she felt a sense of vertigo, returning to her quiet meadow. The weather on Alfheim always felt like a continuous spring. The air was always fresh and carried the smell of sweet flowers, and the plants and trees were forever their brightest green hue. Each day on Alfheim was filled with dappled light from the great star, Aurvandil, which continuously shone above the realm. It never diminished or dimmed, so there was never any darkness or night. The only way to tell the passing of time was to mark Aurvandil's position as it revolved around the sky. All creatures who lived on or visited Alfheim drew sustenance from the star's light. Amanda's first time on Alfheim, she had been so consumed with the energy and radiant nature of the realm that she didn't realize she hadn't slept in two days until they prepared to leave.

Closing her eyes again, Amanda stilled her breathing and turned her palms upward. She bent her thoughts to the breeze around her, feeling it sweep her bangs across her face. Reaching out with her magick, Amanda tried to connect with the current of air. For one breath, the wind stilled and then blasted her face with a sharp gust.

Amanda rubbed her forehead. Her studies of Asgardian magick were progressing. Queen Frigga had begun to show her the other arcane tomes of eldritch magick that only the most accomplished mages were privy to, and Amanda had begun to master some of the new spells. However, some of the spells proved to be too great for her to complete now that she no longer had Sigyn's full fount of magick.

The Queen and the Prelate wanted Amanda to explore the magick of the other realms as well. Prelate Tess had sent her to Alfheim several times before to relay messages, and to even help the Light Elves with one small battle against a mercenary band of trolls. This time, though, she was visiting Alfheim to see if she could harness more of their magick. Some of the other Favoured had begun to master the elements on the other realms just as easily as they did on Asgard. For Amanda, so far, each attempt had only succeeded in giving her severe headaches. She had found that without Sigyn's full powers, she was more successful in using her magick when she was able to use spellwords or incantations. Light Elven magick used none of those.

Amanda looked down to the grimoire Sigyn had given her. She had been reading about the magick of the Light Elves while waiting for them to join her. Unlike the Fell Elves' fell magick, most of the spells and incantations of the Light Elves of Alfheim were all silently conjured. Their spells required neither gestures nor spellwords, and no sacrifice of soul. The grimoire could only describe the theory of how to use Light Elven magick versus giving her the precise methodology to practice. Dwarven magick had been the only other race's magick she had been willing to try, and she had had some moderate success. The only issue was the guttural dialect made it was hard for her to pronounce every syllable. With Asgardian magick, her spells so far had all been singularly intentional, even if unspoken, but the Elven magick went beyond that as well.

"Favoured."

Amanda turned. "Is it time, Davyn?" A small boy with pointy ears and two stars on his cheek stood a few inches from her. He was bent toward her so he could whisper.

The Elf nodded as a butterfly the size of a small hawk flew past them. Even though he looked young, Amanda knew by the stars on his cheek he was over two hundred years old. Light Elves earned a mark in the shape of Aurvandil, which twinkled like a captured portion of the star's light on their skin, for each hundred years they lived on Alfheim. The marks started on their faces, but could be placed anywhere they chose. Davyn pointed to the creature. "The knud are being drawn to the nest. We will begin our conclave to transform the Hel bees shortly. As requested by the Prelate, you are to join us."

Amanda nodded and brushed her hair back as she rose. "Did Queen Os find out where the Hel bees came from?"

Davyn motioned for Amanda to lower her voice. Turning, he inspected several lumps on the far edge of the plateau they stood on that looked like radioactive blueberries. The pockmarked orbs shuddered, releasing a green mist into the air. The giant butterfly that passed them a moment before flew over the cluster and into the cloud. The beautiful creature froze, turned gray, and fell into the Hel bee hive, where it began to slowly dissolve.

Davyn made a sign with two fingers as if waving good-bye. Quietly he spoke, "May the light of the Lady and the wisdom of the Lord guide you." Turning to Amanda, Davyn leaned close. "Our good Queen has no knowledge of any travelers passing near Hel that would have picked up the fell creatures. This is the tenth cluster we have found in our realm in seven days. For now, we will deal with the infestation one hive at a time until we can tell if there is another reason for their appearance. I caution you to remain as silent as possible while we work our magick. Any noise and the hive could send forth its swarm. All Hel bees possess the power to kill any one creature they touch, and the nest is just as dangerous. Should they spawn, they would fly straight to our sacred flower, the Hvonn. Its nectar is the only thing the fell creatures crave, and their touch will prevent the flower for blooming for three millennia. If that were to happen, we would not be able to renew our magick and our realm would begin to fade. Come. The others have taken their position."

Amanda followed Davyn silently, feeling a twinge of regret for having caused the knud to meet its demise. From her experience with the Elves, and her studies, she knew Davyn would only think of it as part of the natural order, but to Amanda it was a mistake. Her first time on Alfheim, she had accidentally knocked a pot of Vanaheim oil onto the Queen. Amanda had been mortified, but the Queen simply smiled and with a wave, the stain fell away from her dress. The Elves only showed concern when the natural order was interrupted, or when the other realms were threatened. Beyond those conditions, Amanda didn't think the Elves could be upset by anything. Their calm nature felt soothing after Amanda's encounter with the Disir and fell magick on Asgard half a year ago.

As Amanda and Davyn walked, a dozen Elves rose in a circle around the Hel bee hive. A moment before, the plateau had been empty, save for Amanda and the hive, but now the Elves appeared as if stepping off the rays of light from Aurvandil. Amanda nodded to each of the Elves and mouthed the words of greeting she had been taught.

Davyn pointed to a spot beside an Elf that had ten times as many stars as he did. The Elf's eyes flashed with golden light as he studied the hive and then Amanda. Words floated into Amanda's mind, "*Child of Midgard. We welcome your presence.*"

Amanda let her thoughts respond. "*Thank you, Leif. I am here to help in any way I can."* Amanda still felt unsettled by the way some of the Elves communicated. Those who gave up their voices to strengthen their magick were able to communicate directly into the minds of anyone they chose. Amanda was glad it was just for speaking and not for actually reading her mind.

Leif's mind speech was soft and he took great care to send his words slowly into her mind. *"Your strength will help quicken the transmutation, to be sure. Elven and Asgardian magicks combine to form some of the most potent spells in the Nine Realms."*

Amanda again focused her thoughts. *"I have been practicing, but I am still unable to cast as you do. Without spellwords or incantations my magick doesn't do what I want it to."*

"Worry not. The light of the Lady and the wisdom of the Lord will guide you." The Elf turned and held his hands, palms up, to the hive. The rest of the Elves joined him, as did Amanda.

Amanda looked around the circle. They Light Elves ranged in height, from no larger than a toddler to taller than a small tree. All Light Elves had translucent blond hair, and their skin was equally see-through. Their garments varied, from the finery of a silk robe to embroidered leather trousers with a loose tunic. Noticing that some had their eyes closed, while others had their faces turned upward to the star above, Amanda decided to close her eyes. She felt and heard the magick begin to hum around them. Elven magick sounded like a symphony of instruments, each part adding to the melody, but still individually distinguishable. It felt like the spring breezes Amanda had been enjoying just a few moments ago – warm and natural. Leif's mind touched hers, and she tried to summon her magick. She focused on the swirl of power from the Elves, and their intent to transform the Hel bees. As she thought about transformation, she felt her magick fly free to join the Elven spell. Her magick had changed of late, growing deeper, and it added a baritone undertone to the song of magick from the other Elves.

"Focus on the Hel bee hive, Favoured. Feel the death magick that inhabits it. Concentrate on it. Death and life are not too far from one another. They can be substituted. That is what we are here for today, to change the magick's course and intention by bending it. Our magick follows the natural order." Leif's words seemed easy, but Amanda had no idea where to begin. *"Just listen, mortal. Let your desire guide your magick."*

Amanda pressed her eyes closed even harder. She could hear the magick swirling around them and could feel it wash over the hive. Each time a pass of magick touched the hive, and the Hel bees inside, it stirred and became more agitated.

Suddenly Amanda could see clearly in her mind's eye. A vast and shadowed realm took shape. Dark, swirling forms moved past her, their touch powerful and inviting. There was a flash, and suddenly Sigyn appeared. The goddess was wielding her full magicks, casting spells that Amanda could feel deep in her core.

"You must yield to the magick," Sigyn whispered. Her eyes flared with light, and Amanda felt her body shake. Amanda opened her mouth to speak, and the vision faded.

"Favoured, we have to hurry." An Elf farther down the circle spoke into her mind.

Amanda shook her head, trying to see Sigyn once more, but the goddess was gone. *"What was that?"*

"I sense nothing, but I agree with Flaitia, we must hurry. We may be too late to prevent the Hel bees from hatching." Leif's magick changed direction and a cocoon formed around the gathering. *"I will protect the realm while we continue our work. You must add your strength to the spell and focus it."*

"I still don't know how!" Amanda opened her eyes. The hive began to writhe, fully wakening with the Light Elves' presence and magick. A section of the lumpy mass peeled back to reveal the deadly swarm. The Hel bees were wet with green mucous, so they fluttered their wings to dry them.

"You must act now. Our magick is consumed with feeding into the spell. You must direct it!"

Amanda closed her eyes again. This was too much. Why had the Prelate and Queen Frigga insisted she be a part of something so important when she had no idea how to help? They told her this would help her to evolve the magick of her favouring. Casting spells without words was one thing, but bending your magick to your will without the need of a spell was something that would make her more adept at magick than even the most powerful of spellcasters. It would make her one of the most powerful Favoured ever too. The possibility both excited and unnerved her. The past few months she had finally felt like she had been one of the Favoured all along. They had all accepted her. Without Lena and Lev, she had felt like she had moved past being the Favoured that might bring about Ragnarok and end the Spell of Favouring to just a Favoured.

Amanda wished for the thousandth time she still had the full favouring of Sigyn. The sheer power she had once wielded would surely have helped more than what she now possessed would. Pushing that thought from her mind, Amanda focused. Maybe her vision had been a message from Sigyn. There had been no sign of her in months, but maybe the goddess could sense she needed help. Her magick still flew about with the other magick of the rest of the Elves, but she could tell it was still separate – like runners running on a parallel track.

Leif had said their spell was meant to transform the Hel bees' natural form into something else, but he had never said what. The other Elves were reaching their peak. Their magick was meant only to aid Leif as he guided the magick to Amanda. Why had he not let her take charge of protecting them so he could complete their task?

"Yield to the magick. Follow the natural order. Bend; do not break or destroy. That has to be the key. The spellwords and incantations force my magick to my will. I can't force the Hel bees to change – it has to be natural," Amanda whispered to herself. "What would be the natural opposite of something that can kill so easily?"

Amanda thought of the bees, the Elves, and what it is they were trying to protect. An idea blazed into Amanda's mind. Reaching with one hand to the ground and the other to the sky, Amanda gathered the power being directed toward her into each hand. With each breath, Amanda's arms slowly moved in a counterpoint semicircle on either side of her. As her arms moved, Amanda took the magick and spun it forth until it was no longer swirling about them, but creating a funnel that spiraled upward. She let her magick flow freely and it merged with that of the Elves'.

"Hurry child," Leif's voice echoed in Amanda's mind. The Elf's mind-spoken words sounded softer and more distant as a buzzing sound began to emanate from the hive.

Stars blossomed from underneath Amanda's eyelids, as if she could see the spell coalescing. The various sounds of magick crashed around her, and Amanda focused her intent on the magick to permeate the Hel bee hive and swarm. The magick exploded and all became silent. Amanda slumped over and took several gulping breaths before opening her eyes.

The Elves around the circle stared in wonder at the tiny grouping of flowers that stood where the hive had been seconds before. Soft, white petals began to bloom, revealing a pink center. The flowers grew upward and wove around each other. The topmost flower opened and a tiny filament of light gleamed brighter than the light from above, rendering the Elves even more transparent than before.

Amanda smiled and then looked to Davyn, who was staring wide-eyed at Amanda. A gasping sound wrenched Amanda's attention to Leif. "Leif!"

The older Elf was gripping the side of his neck as what looked like amber liquid spilled through his fingers. *"Be... still. You... have wrought... something... quite... marvelous."*

Davyn and the others gathered around Leif. One of the Elves turned to the light above and vanished. The others formed a circle around Leif, and their magick sputtered forth toward him. Amanda kneeled next to the injured Elf and slowly pulled his hand away. A dark mark pulsed on his neck as red and black lines grew across his skin. When one of the lines touched a star on his face, Leif shuddered and his skin became completely transparent.

Amanda held his hand. "Leif. Tell me what happened. What I can do?"

Leif's lips quivered into a small smile. *"There is... nothing to be done. My time has come... as I always knew it would. I could sense at least one of the Hel bees would... escape before we brought about the hive's transformation. I knew... that it would attack any who prevented it from reaching our... Hvonn."*

"That's why you cast the protection around us?"

Leif nodded.

"And now, I shall return to the Light… having witnessed… a true miracle. You have created a new Hvonn. It will… strengthen our realm. May the… light of the Lady and the… wisdom of the Lord guide you."

Leif convulsed once more as the angry veins of Hel bee venom traveling his body collided with the rest of the remaining stars that shone on his cheeks and forearms. Amanda looked to the Elves around her as their voices united into a single, clear syllable. Leif's body began to break apart into tiny flares of light that flowed up to Aurvandil. A great flash of light blinded Amanda, and Leif was gone.

End of Preview | The Touch of the Valkyrie

Made in the USA
Monee, IL
23 February 2020